The Devil on May Street

Also by Steve Harris

ADVENTURELAND

WULF

THE HOODOO MAN

ANGELS

BLACK ROCK

The Devil on May Street

STEVE HARRIS

VICTOR GOLLANCZ
LONDON

First published in Great Britain 1997
by Victor Gollancz
An imprint of the Cassell Group
Wellington House, 125 Strand, London WC2R OBB

A catalogue record for this book is available from the British Library.

ISBN 0 575 06426 9

Typeset by SetSystems Ltd, Saffron Walden, Essex
Printed in Great Britain by St Edmundsbury Press Ltd, Bury St Edmunds, Suffolk

97 98 99 5 4 3 2 1

The Devil on May Street is dedicated
to the memory of

Barbara Joan Harris
(the best mother I ever had)

Reginald Roy Challacombe
(who amazed me with magic)

Stephen 'Mil' Martin
(Mr Opposite Effect)

Emmie Challacombe
(it had to have been that blood!)

Richard 'actually I was just leaving' Evans
(who gave me a break or two)

and all the dogs:
Lucy, Jenny, Jenny, Cindy, Jekyll

Acknowledgements

As usual, many people helped along the way. And a few dogs, too. Special thanks are due to Dookie Combes-Donovan (he's not *my* dog, mister!); Cindy # 2 (all bark and lick); Jason and Debbie, Phil, Geoff (the desert of all knowledge), Sarah and Barb; Elizabeth Sites (a fine romanticist!); Raffles (a howling hound); Laney 'CRS' Cummings (for a few wonderful expressions and lots of support); Florence (for more support than I deserve!); Steve and Lynn Andrews (for reminding me); Jo '700 pages? What *were* you thinking of?' Fletcher (for publishing this); Hazel Orme (for excellent edit); Elsie Rotenberg (for eagle-eyed error-spotting and more); Steve Crisp (whose illustrations get better and better); Debbie Harris; Simon 'Motormouth' Wady (Chapbook? What chapbook?); Chris Long; Poppy, Polly and Roger (dogs); all my friends from the *blurred* part of my past, and last, but certainly not least, my readers, whoever and wherever you are. I'm thinking of you all!

Any inaccuracies in time, place, continuity, procedures, geographical locations or the calibre of Dirty Harry's Magnum are almost certainly mine. Everything that's right is either by luck or the efforts of someone listed above. Today is Kool Day! Enjoy!

Chapter One

A Boy and His Dog

Whomp!

If a scaled-down Cruise missile had flown up the hall, hit the front door and detonated, Stevie thought, it would have sounded like this. The impact shook the entire house.

Of course, if it *had* been a missile there would have been smoke and rubble and there wouldn't have been the growling, or the sound of claws trying to dig through wood. And the following sound – of whatever had just been posted through the door being torn to shreds by oversized white fangs – wouldn't have occurred.

Even though he knew he was wasting his breath, Stevie yelled, 'Pack it up, Dookie!'

He pushed his chair away from his desk and stood up to peer out of his bedroom window for trails of blood on the front path. More than one stand-in postman had carelessly let his fingers protrude through the letter-box as he delivered the mail. And as far as Duke – now officially listed *Dangerous Dog* – was concerned, this was an open invitation to *taste.*

There was no one on the path and no blood on the flagstones. Dookie was safe: he wasn't going directly to jail – and from there to his doom. He was going to live to fight another day.

The mystery delivery person had been in a hurry. Stevie could see no sign of them on the street.

'Probably the paper,' Stevie decided, glancing at the heaps of his homework. In the light of all that work-yet-to-be-done, rescuing the Monday edition of the *Gazette* seemed an interesting proposition. Stevie glanced at the scratched face of his Casio G-Shock – the one that Johnny never tired of calling a G-Spot – and learned that he'd wasted three hours and eight minutes of his precious young life writing an essay on D. H. Lawrence's *Sons and Lovers*. Some books took you by the lapels and dragged you in; this one attained the attitude of a man trying to push-start a diesel train and seemingly put all its force into keeping you out.

It had gone ominously quiet downstairs. Stevie left his room and took the stairs two at a time.

The Dukester might have been a 'devil-dog' on his last warning and the authorities might have demanded he wear a muzzle when outside, but you wouldn't believe it to look at him now. He lay on the floor, ears pressed back, tail curled under, and looked up at Stevie with a doleful expression that read: 'I dunno what got into me, boss.' As his master approached, Dookie pressed his head to the ground, among the scraps of white paper he'd torn up, and averted his eyes.

'I'm not going to beat you, you silly animal,' Stevie said kindly, squatting beside the dog and stroking his head.

Dookie looked up uncertainly and then rolled on his back, exposing his belly. Stevie tickled his chest and wondered how many times the dog had done this in front of its previous owner, the mystery man whom Stevie, Johnny, Becky and, probably, Duke himself were dying to meet down a dark alley one night. That bastard had laid a curse on his new puppy, from which the grown animal would never escape.

At least everyone *else* said he'd never escape it. Deep in his heart, Stevie didn't believe this was true. Dookie had responded well to love and attention over the past eighteen months, and barring those three slips – and the letter-box attacking, of course – he could be classed as a *good* dog.

He began to pick up the scraps of paper, remembering how he'd chosen Duke at the dog-rescue centre. He'd fallen for him on sight. 'That one,' he'd said to his dad as his eyes met those of the black Labrador cross.

'Looks like he's got some collie in him,' Andy Warner had observed. 'Perhaps some bull-terrier, too, in his distant ancestry. You sure, kiddo? This isn't a well-looking animal, y'know.'

But Stevie *had* been sure.

At that time no one knew Duke's history, not even the rescue centre. All they knew was that the RSPCA had found him tied up in the back garden of an empty house, starved almost to death. He was just another abandoned dog, left to die when his owners moved out.

Stevie looked at the soggy scraps he'd rescued. Until they'd been put through the letter-box they had evidently been a single sheet of photocopier paper. Some had writing on them in ball-point but it was going to be a while before he could reassemble enough to make out what the message had been.

The two days after bringing the dog home were enough to reveal that he hadn't led a pampered life. He stole food – from seemingly inaccessible places – and drank from the toilet bowl, and Stevie had watched as Duke climbed into the bath, applied his nose to the plug-hole, snorted water back from the U trap and lapped it up. This was a dog who had been left alone for long periods.

He sat down at the big round dining table, pushed back the cloth and began to straighten out the tiny bits of paper. Those with no writing on, he left on one side. He laid out the marked ones before him.

When he looked up, Duke was standing in the doorway, wearing a hurt expression.

'C'mon, Dookie!' he encouraged, patting his thigh. 'It's OK, boy. I know you didn't mean it. Come over here with Stevie.'

The dog thought about it, then trotted over and sat beside him, leaning against his leg.

This dog is going to need a lot of TLC. His dad's voice echoed in Stevie's ears.

'You've come to the right place,' Stevie said, ruffling the thick fur at the back of the dog's neck.

When Duke settled down, his head on Stevie's shoes, Stevie turned his attention back to his paper puzzle.

On the third day after he'd brought his new friend home, Stevie had taken him for his shots.

The first hint of trouble came when Duke apparently recognized the building. He went rigid and stood stock still. Stevie tried to cajole him along, then to drag him, but Duke wouldn't budge. When Stevie bent down, intending to pick him up and carry him inside, he found himself staring at a mouthful of exposed teeth. And that big white grin was a very scary thing indeed. Stevie showed no fear. He sat down beside his dog and put a comforting arm around his neck. He ignored the Harley-Davidson growl to which Dookie treated him and told him softly that this was for his own good.

Abruptly, the fight went out of the dog. He thrust his head up under Stevie's chin. A few moments later Stevie realized that Duke was shivering with fear.

Stevie already knew that the message he was reassembling had been delivered by Johnny. He would have recognized the almost illegible handwriting anywhere. What he didn't know was what the message said. He now had the word DOGBOY, which was Johnny's favourite way of addressing him these days, and a few other snippets, *swing, believe, found* and *vanishing*. It had been a long message for Johnny, who normally simply posted notes saying things like: *down field. B there or b* □. The reason he'd recently taken to posting notes rather than knocking at the door or phoning was unknown.

'Probably because I'm s'posed to be busy preparing for my exams,' Stevie muttered darkly. He glanced at his G-Shock again and was not pleased. It was almost three thirty already. Once you started to do all the stuff your parents and the sodding school wanted you to do, the day vanished, and the holidays began to evaporate the moment you took your eye off them. Two weeks had already passed in a blur of what Stevie called 'doing other people's stuff.' All he'd wanted to do this holiday was make the motorbike run, take it down the field and ride it over the rough ground. And all he'd done so far was tidy his room and try to stay awake while he read *Sons and Lovers*.

That was the trouble with being 'clever': people made *plans* for you. A levels. University. A profession. For some unfathomable reason, his mother wanted him to be a doctor.

Stevie didn't know *what* he wanted to be when he grew up but he knew what he *didn't* want to be. And doctor was high on his list of careers-to-avoid. It ranked alongside politician, bank manager and tax inspector.

Another thing Stevie knew was that although he was thought to be 'clever' he wasn't *clever*. Johnny was *clever*. *Clever* enough to know what would result if he was seen to be 'clever', so no one expected him to amount to anything or to stay at home and do schoolwork during the holidays.

Same went for Becky, too. Except it was more complicated where *she* was concerned. Nothing much was expected of Becky because she had Social Problems.

But dumb old Stevie hadn't had the nous to play it dumb.

The message now read:

DOGBOY

you wont believe this bu

'What won't I believe?' Stevie asked, searching for the next piece of the jigsaw. At his feet, the dog gave a deep sigh.

'Oh, this is Duke,' the vet had said, as Stevie led him into the examination room. 'We've met.'

Stevie wasn't surprised that Mr Meegan recognized him: the dog had certainly recognized the surgery. And although Duke had allowed himself to be led in, he'd disgraced himself in the waiting room.

Mr Meegan smiled thinly, turned away and took a black nylon thing down from a peg on the wall. He handed this to Stevie, who looked at it in puzzlement. Finally Mr Meegan said, 'Perhaps you'd put that muzzle on him before we begin.'

'They can drink while wearing this kind of muzzle,' Mr Meegan said, 'they can vomit safely and they might manage to eat a chocolate button or a thin biscuit, but they can't open their mouths wide enough to bite anyone.' He grinned. 'And I happen to know that this dog will defend himself if he thinks it's necessary. Where did you get him?'

'The Anstey Close Dog Rescue,' Stevie replied.

The vet nodded. 'And what do you know about him?'

'He's called Duke, after John Wayne, and won't answer to anything except "dook". He's around two years old and he'd been abandoned.'

Mr Meegan grimaced, then sighed wearily and did one of those little told-you-so shakes of the head that were all the rage among Stevie's teachers. 'Doesn't surprise me,' he said. 'In fact, it's amazing he's still alive. Put him on the table for me, would you?'

Stevie picked up Duke – who was shuddering deeply – and placed him on the table, standing. Duke sank down and made like a jelly.

'It'll be OK,' the vet said, and began to check the dog, handling him carefully. Duke looked as if he was trying to pretend that none of this was happening. 'He's still a little underweight. Otherwise he doesn't seem too bad.' The vet looked up at Stevie and added, 'Considering . . .'

'Considering?' Stevie asked.

'See this little knob on his right foreleg?' Mr Meegan asked, indicating what Stevie called the dog's elbow.

Stevie nodded. He'd wondered about it.

'Accident damage,' the vet said, with irony in his voice.

'How do you mean?' Stevie asked.

Mr Meegan ignored his question. 'There's more, but it isn't evident. You'll only see it when he walks. Does he limp?'

Stevie nodded. Duke's legs were stiff: sometimes he had to struggle to get up and his back right leg was a slow starter. Stevie'd thought it was due to his having been tethered for so long and said so.

'I'm afraid it's a little worse than that. He "ran into a wall". At least that's what his owner told me when he was brought in as a pup. His injuries would seem to suggest that he had been *thrown* at one. I've seen similar damage before. It isn't uncommon. People take a puppy home, it pees or craps on the floor and they get mad at it. Most try the standard house-training techniques. Some resort to violence.'

'He came in with a broken leg?' Stevie asked.

'When he turned up here, three legs were badly shattered. If you ever take him through an airport metal detector, he'll set it off. I've put pins into two of those legs. It's pretty likely that he'll end up crippled, unless you keep him in excellent condition and as fit as a flea.'

'Why did you give him back to his owner?' Stevie asked.

Mr Meegan shook his head. 'I didn't want to, believe me,' he said. 'The RSPCA prosecuted but in spite of my evidence we lost the case. The owner claimed in court that the dog had been hit by a car. It was ruled that there was sufficient doubt as to what had caused the injuries and the owner took him home.'

Duke gave a small growling moan as Mr Meegan probed the bones he had pinned.

'The other problem,' the vet continued, 'will be aggression. This dog is going to be frightened for a long time. And he'll bite through fear. He's nipped me before now. It'll take a long time for him to feel safe again.'

Apparently satisfied with Duke's condition, Mr Meegan went to the other end of the room and searched through various drawers. He came back holding a hypodermic and grinned at Stevie. 'This won't hurt a bit,' he said. 'But you hold him and I'll jab him.'

DOGBOY
You wont believe this but Ive found something weird
You know the house in Southend Road,
the one by the alley that leads to the playing field???
You know if you walk down the alley
you can see through the fence
into the back garden???
Do that. Come down and look. Quick!!!!
Theres a kid in there on a swing.
And he's vanishing.
Hurry up, for gods sake Dogboy!!!!
Going back now
Johnny

Stevie frowned. *A vanishing kid*? he thought, picturing a child sitting on a swing, slowly becoming transparent until all that was left of him was a Cheshire-Cat-style grin. *Johnny's finally cracked.*

It had to be a ploy to get him out of the house, but he was surprised that Johnny hadn't come up with something a little more convincing.

'Dad?' Stevie shouted. As he waited for a reply, he realized that however unconvincing Johnny's little note had been, it'd worked. He was hooked. If he hadn't been, he wouldn't have been calling his dad hoping his dad wasn't at home, because if he wasn't, Stevie was going to put Dookie's muzzle and lead on him and walk him down the street to Southend Road – a distance of fifty yards or so – and go down the alley and peer through the fence. He was going to do this not because he believed Johnny's story but because he wanted to know what lay behind the note.

The reason Stevie had been a good boy so far and attacked the mountain of homework before getting on with the things he wanted to do was that he'd made a deal: his dad would let him have Duke but Stevie had to work his bollocks off for his exams. Even in the holidays. His father's presence in the house had kept him at it: Stevie's dad, good old Andy Warner, worked from home. This didn't mean Stevie *saw* any more of him than he would have if Andy had caught the 07.34 to Waterloo each morning since his dad spent hours locked away in what he called his workroom, writing articles for computer magazines. What it *did* mean was that Stevie couldn't bunk off without his dad finding out. And if his dad discovered he'd gone out when he was supposed to be working there might well be big trouble. Dad had been living on a knife edge for a couple of months now and once or twice had reminded him that if the exams went badly, the dog simply went.

'Dad?' he yelled again. 'Andy? You home?'

Duke looked up at Stevie, cocking an ear.

Andy was either up to his elbows in computer guts or not in the house at all. Stevie was banking on it being the latter.

He glanced at Johnny's message again, then grinned nervously at the dog. 'Let's go see,' he whispered.

As far as parents went, Stevie supposed, his were OK. They had their weird ways but Andy didn't beat him to a pulp like Heater Heatley's dad.

But even if your parents weren't the murderous kind there were still things that sent them ballistic. You could push his mother's Big Red Button by mentioning drugs or mental illness or by letting Duke lick your plate after you'd finished with it, and his father turned into a ravening monster if you disturbed him while he was working. No one but Andy ever went into his workroom. This wasn't a written rule, or even one that had been discussed: it was just how it was. Knock on his workroom door while he was busy and if you'd forgotten to put on the Kevlar vest, riot helmet and asbestos gloves you were well and truly up shit creek sans paddle.

But Stevie was pretty sure that Andy was out.

Over the past few days he had begun to notice something weird about his father. Andy apparently had an exceedingly small bladder: when he was working, he chain-smoked and drank gallons of tea or Coke. On a normal day, he'd visit the kitchen perhaps ten times to collect fresh supplies and go to the toilet twice for each drink he consumed. But on at least three days during the last week he'd neither got himself drinks nor peed them out again. Today was another of those days.

Either he was in there with a sixteen-pack of Coke and a bucket to piss in, or he was out. But Stevie had seen him enter his workroom that morning and hadn't heard him come out again.

He stood outside the door and sniffed. At his feet, Duke was doing the same thing, except he had his nose right up against the gap at the bottom of the door and was sucking in air like a vacuum cleaner. There was no smell of smoke. Stevie rapped on the door. 'I'm making tea. Want a cup?' he asked the smooth, magnolia-painted panels. If Andy was inside, the offer of tea would dispel his anger at being distracted. Hopefully.

There was no reply.

'Whaddya think, El Doggo?' Stevie whispered.

Duke snorted.

'Me too. He's out, isn't he?' He took hold of the door handle, moved it down and pushed. The door opened and Stevie looked in at an Aladdin's Cave of computer pieces. Andy wasn't home.

He entered the room and picked his way through the minefield of computer parts, cables, plugs, power cords and magazines to his dad's desk on which his computer stood, showing a screen of text. Andy's computer – assembled mainly from bits he'd got for nothing for review purposes and had somehow never given back – was one of the variety known in the trade as a 'great-big fuck-off' machine. This meant it was stupidly powerful and capable of running any kind of software Andy needed to test. It also meant that Stevie wasn't allowed anywhere near it.

The tower that stood beside the desk housed the computer's guts. The case was off it, showing cables as tangled as spaghetti; daisy-chained drives, add-on boards of all shapes and sizes. Stevie avoided this like the plague. All he was interested in was (a) what was on the screen and (b) the window behind Andy's desk.

Dookie followed Stevie into the room, sniffed and homed in on a torn wrapper from a long-gone bar of chocolate, trapped beneath the case of a 386 computer. Stevie watched as he delicately removed it, then whispered, 'Take it outside, Dookie, or he'll know we've been in here.'

After the dog had gone, Stevie turned his attention to the

screen. He would have liked to see a confession that Andy was the Winklebury Rapist and that he'd just gone out to perpetrate his fifth attack. Or that he was Goldilocks, the other oddball the paper kept on about just now. Or the first chapter of the book Andy often claimed would make him rich and famous. What it actually was, Stevie learned to his disappointment, was part of his father's work-in-progress, a manual for a new IBM database.

He fought off an almost overwhelming urge to search Andy's files for documents containing the words 'fuck, erection and sex' and turned his attention to the window behind the desk.

It was open a crack. Given that it was mid-summer, that Andy chain-smoked and that it felt like an oven in here, this wasn't surprising. But it *was* surprising in the light of his dad's recent purchase of an expensive portable air-conditioner, 'so I don't have to have the bloody window open and listen to them drilling the road every other day'.

The air-conditioner wasn't even turned on.

The other surprising thing was the clear space on Andy's desk, which was always strewn with print-outs, mail and bits of computer. The clear space, strangely enough, was directly under the window-sill. And although Andy had cleared the junk off his desk, a thin layer of Silk Cut 100s ash remained. In it was an almost perfect print of the left foot of Andy's size nine Nike trainer.

Stevie wondered where his old man had gone and why he'd found it necessary to leave through the window. But what he *really* needed to know was if he was likely to meet Andy coming back the moment he himself got outside.

It didn't matter, he realized suddenly. If Andy had gone to such lengths to prevent his son knowing he'd gone out and then saw Stevie, he was going to act like a truant spotting a teacher and bugger off in the other direction.

Duke had done a similar job on the chocolate wrapper to the one he'd executed on Johnny's note. He lay on his back in the hall, surrounded by bits of blue and silver foil and looking pleased with himself.

When he saw Stevie he rolled over and got up, ears back, tail swishing gently. He looked a little concerned – as if he wasn't sure whether he'd been a good dog or a bad dog.

Stevie ruffled his fur. 'Messy git.' He smiled and picked up the bits so that Andy wouldn't see them if he got back first. It wasn't likely he would connect the wrapper with an invasion of his room, but you couldn't be too careful. It was like borrowing the copies of *Playboy* that lived under Andy's side of the bed: for safety you had to memorize their position and order before you took them out. That way you could put them back *exactly* as you'd found them and no one would know the difference.

Stevie binned the evidence and looked down at his dog. 'Shall we go and look for Johnny?' he asked.

Duke was one of the quickest learners Stevie had met and had an amazing propensity for language. In three short months he'd got to grips with every way you could suggest a walk – even down to knowing what it meant when you spelled out the letters: r-o-u-n-d t-h-e b-l-o-c-k.

Stevie's mum had claimed that dogs merely responded to the rise and fall of your voice and that when you said, 'Walkies,' you always said it in a certain way. She had had to rethink this when she had asked Duke, in the flattest, most depressed voice she could muster, 'How do you fancy being dragged down the field for ten minutes?' and had then been forced to make good her offer when the dog wouldn't stop jumping up at her and barking in excitement.

Duke evidently thought that searching for Johnny was the best offer he'd had all day. He bounded up the hall, swerved into the lounge, did his usual wall-of-death run across the back of the sofa, hammered back down the hall, skidded across the shiny kitchen floor, jumped up at Stevie and head-butted him in the lower abdomen. He might be intelligent, but he wasn't the world's most graceful mover or the most gentle. If you'd wanted to trash a china shop and you didn't have a bull handy, Duke would be the next best thing.

Stevie tottered back a step, hit the back door and slid down to his haunches, moaning through gritted teeth while his dog tried to get him to his feet again by using his snout as a kind of crowbar.

'Stop it!' Stevie hissed, and the dog obeyed instantly. He slunk away, tail curled under, and sat down in the hall facing Stevie, eyes averted. When Stevie got up, he saw that his dog was trembling.

He took the extendable lead down from the top of the freezer and waved it around. Duke didn't look up. 'Dookster?' he said. 'Walkies?'

Stevie had no idea how dogs managed to display such a range of expressions on faces that seemed designed primarily to house teeth, but Duke's face was now a blend of terror and hopelessness. Stevie didn't believe any animal should have to feel that way. 'It's OK, Dookie, I'm not hurt,' he said gently. 'Let's go find Johnny!' he encouraged.

Duke risked a quick wag.

'Good boy!' Stevie said. 'He's a good boy! Stevie's favourite devil-dog! C'mon!'

Duke got up and trotted across to him. Stevie patted him, slipped on the muzzle and fastened it. Duke snorted – half complaint at the muzzle, Stevie guessed, and half happy because he knew it meant walkies. He clipped the lead to the dog's collar, opened the back door and they went out into the blazing sunshine.

'It's love, I think,' Stevie had overheard his mother say, shortly after Duke's arrival. He'd just left the lounge with his dog at his heels and paused, waiting to see what else was said. He didn't normally eavesdrop on his parents but he'd picked up a few interesting pieces of information this way. He knew, for example, that Jacqui was worried about Andy flying off to America because she kept dreaming of falling and thought it meant that he'd be involved in a problem with an aeroplane.

'It's mutual,' Stevie had heard Andy reply. 'The dog loves him, too. That's a one-man dog, and the man is Stevie.'

'God forbid anything should happen to him,' Jacqui replied.

'Stevie or the dog?'

Jacqui laughed. She had a pleasant laugh and, as far as Stevie was concerned, she hadn't been making the best use of it lately. 'Both,' she said, 'but I meant the dog. If anything goes wrong, Stevie will be heartbroken.'

'The dog's got road sense, sweetheart,' Andy replied. 'He'll be OK.'

'I just wouldn't like anything to happen, that's all,' Jacqui said. 'Wouldn't like to see them parted.'

At that point, Stevie had wandered off, not terribly interested in how the conversation continued. His mother worried, just like mothers the world over.

But this had been before the biting offences and Duke's subsequent narrow escape. These days, Stevie sometimes *wondered* what life would be like if something happened to Dookie. And he sometimes entertained the idea that he was receiving a weird psychic wave from somewhere, that he was plucking snippets of knowledge about stuff from out of the ether. One of these incoming waves brought him a mixed-up feeling that something *was* going to happen to Dookie.

Something terrible.

He knew this didn't make him crazy. One afternoon, just before the holidays, he'd waited for Becky at the school gates and had walked her home – not because he 'fancied her something rotten', as Johnny maintained, but because she was the only person he could think of who would listen to what he had to say and not fall about laughing.

Becky *had* listened and had set his mind at ease. 'I think everyone has those feelings from time to time,' she'd said, holding his gaze with those clear grey-green eyes, which were undoubtedly her best feature. 'I've been having them ever since the middle of last year. Not often, but once in a while I start thinking, Oh, fuck, here we go; this is where the shit hits the fan, for no apparent reason.' She smiled and shrugged. 'Hormonal, I guess. Either that or I'm as cracked as the Liberty Bell. So that makes two of us. And Johnny makes three.'

'Johnny?' Stevie asked, amazed. Owning up to having odd feelings wasn't Johnny's style.

Becky grinned. 'I've got what they call listening skills,' she said. 'I may be an ugly mug, but people feel safe with me.' She made a face like a puzzled gargoyle and revised the statement. '*Some* people feel safe with me . . . well, half a dozen or so of 'em, anyway. Nope. Wait. Scratch that.' She grinned again. '*No one* feels safe with me, but people *always* want to tell me stuff about themselves. Fuck knows why.'

Stevie chuckled. For all her cares and woes – and she had plenty – Becky was one of that rare breed who made you feel sunny no matter how dark the skies were.

'Anyway,' Becky continued, 'I know several other people who think they have premonitions, forebodings, presages and any other seeing-into-the-future words you can think of. Sad fact is, none of them are right. Like I said, it's one of those weird growing-up and getting-pubes type things.'

'You don't think it's important, then?' Stevie had asked.

Becky beamed. 'Nah, course not! Unless it *is* important, of course. How would I know?' Then she'd pecked him on the cheek and gone through her gate, leaving him more or less where he'd started from but feeling a lot happier.

A ginger tom lived in the house three doors down from Stevie's. It was one of those big-shouldered, muscular cats that strutted tail up, displaying balls that looked two sizes too large to be comfortable. It was the kind of cat that made you think of a lion; the kind that gave off an aura that said, '*I'm the boss around here, and if you wanna know why, just come fuck with me!*'

Unfortunately, Duke *did* want to fuck with the cat. Cat was cat was cat, as far as he was concerned, and cats were made to be chased.

They said dogs had lousy memories, but Duke knew where that tom – named Leonard – liked to hang out on sunny days: in the shade behind the fence of its own tiny front garden.

Ordinarily, Stevie would have kept the dog on a short lead as they passed this house, but today he was thinking about premonitions and vanishing kids and his father, who'd snuck out of the house through the window, and as Duke pulled he let the extendable lead play out.

Several of the uprights in the low picket fence that bordered Leonard's sleeping place were broken where Duke had butted them on earlier occasions. Another went west before Stevie snapped out of his day-dream and tried to pull the dog back. But it was too late: Leonard was at home and had remembered an old score he had to settle.

Hissing and spitting, he flew through the gap and launched himself at Duke's head, claws extended. What followed resembled a cartoon fight sequence in which all that can be seen is a ball of dust from which arms and legs appear and vanish.

Then it was over.

Leonard took off at speed and Duke stood snorting and foaming through his muzzle, blood dripping from his nose and above his right eye.

'You stupid git,' Stevie said, kneeling beside him. 'That's the third time in a fortnight he's done this to you. Won't you *ever* learn?' He pulled out a Kleenex and dabbed the dog's nose, which obediently stopped bleeding. The cut above his right eye, however, was another matter, but the blood flow was slowing so the best thing was probably to leave it alone.

A couple of minutes later, Stevie and his dog stood in the alley that led to the playing field, peering into the back garden where the famous vanishing kid was supposed to hang out.

Duke snorted.

'You're right there,' Stevie said, moving his head so that he could look up the garden towards the back of the house.

There was no kid.

In fact the house, from what Stevie could see, didn't even look as if anyone lived in it. A window on the lower floor looked as if it had been hit by a football when God was still in short trousers, paint was peeling from the rotting back door and the window frames were falling in. The back garden would have given Stevie's mother a blue fit: what had once been the lawn was either compacted dirt, or patches of dead stuff that looked like straw. Dandelions and nettles grew around the perimeter. Rusting junk that had once been serviceable washing machines and refrigerators was strewn about everywhere and . . . over in one corner was a dead Honda moped. Perhaps a P90 or P70. *Which might well come in handy for my rebuild, or for spares, if the owner wants shot of it*, thought Stevie.

However, although the house looked empty and the garden was overgrown, there was some evidence that the place was occupied by people with kids. In the centre of the lawn stood an A-frame swing – not one of those cheap and cheerful ones that collapsed when anyone over four sat on them but a proper tubular-steel-and-chain playground-type swing, dug deep enough in the ground to hold steady no matter how high you went.

Beside the swing, around which Johnny had based his fairy story, other toys lay scattered about: a bubble-shaped sit-in-and-use-your-feet-like-Fred-Flintstone car, an array of plastic tools, a few deflated balls and a proper leather football and many die-cast Dinky cars.

'Well, Dookster, there's definitely a kid hangs round here, and it's definitely a boy,' Stevie told the dog. 'But I think he must have finished vanishing and entered the Twilight Zone while you were still showing the cat who was boss.' He looked down at the dog. 'And who *was* the boss?' he asked.

Dookie snorted and wagged.

Stevie grinned and shook his head. 'Nope. Wrong. Maybe you'll come out on top next time. Let's go see if Johnny's around.'

The Brookvale Community Recreation Area was a smallish area of bushes, young trees and neatly manicured grass through which a stream ran – or would have if there'd recently been a downpour; the Loddon, the river that fed the stream, had been diverted deep underground when Brookvale had been torn down in the late sixties. There was a fenced-off play area and along the path that bisected the green, a few wooden benches.

Johnny was neither sitting in the shade under the slide smoking – as Stevie had expected him to be – nor anywhere on the rec. Stevie let Duke off the lead and headed towards the fence at the far side of the green.

Beyond it was the western part of the town's orbital main road, imaginatively named Ringway West. Beyond that, maybe two hundred yards away, a steep bank towered up to the railway line. Sandwiched between the far side of the road and the bank was a big overgrown field that the town developers had somehow missed. It was one of Duke's favourite places.

Stevie leaned on the chain-link fence, peering across the busy road to the field, which wasn't easy to see. Way off to the left, in the field, there was a little clump of small trees and bushes. A while ago, Johnny had found a stash of brand-new nudie magazines over there, hidden in a trunk in that thicket. Each magazine's cover claimed it contained the country's 'Hottest Material!' and boasted things like 'Girl on Girl – Fifteen Sets of Lesbian Love Pix Inside!' or 'Shaven Delights: Every Girl Totally Nude!'

'Someone,' Johnny had said, raising an eyebrow, 'has built themselves a little wanker's paradise here.'

They'd conducted a brief search for soggy tissues, found nothing, pronounced the place safe to inhabit and had browsed through the magazines. Since then, Johnny had been conducting a part-time one-man surveillance of the thicket in case the wanker returned. He was hoping that the onanist in question would turn out to be the world's most hated physics teacher, Duncan O'Brian, who lived nearby, and Johnny had taken to toting his mum's Pentax around, complete with 500mm mirror lens.

The wanker had never returned, but Johnny hadn't given up hope.

Stevie stared at the thicket and concluded that the undergrowth was too lush for him to catch a glimpse of Johnny's trademark red T-shirt. He'd have to go round there himself if he wanted to know for sure.

He checked his watch. He hadn't intended to stay out for more than fifteen minutes and twenty had slipped by. He could visualize what was happening at home. Andy had just climbed back in through the window of his workroom, leaving another Nike print in the cigarette ash – this time facing the other way. He'd mopped the sweat from his brow with the big polka-dot handkerchief he always carried and now he was lighting a cigarette and deciding he was thirsty. In another thirty seconds he was going to pass the dining room on the way to the fridge, glance in and see the reassembled note his son had stupidly left there. Then he'd study it, call for Stevie, and when he got no reply, he'd trot upstairs and barge into his son's bedroom. And when he found Stevie gone, he was going to blow a fuse.

Of course, there *was* a chance that Stevie had merely inherited his father's imagination (said by his mother to be vivid, but Stevie hadn't seen much sign of it) and his mother's we're-all-doomed pessimism. Perhaps Andy wouldn't return for hours. *Then again he might*, Stevie thought, and hated himself for it. Johnny wouldn't have given a stuff if his mother was mad at him, and Becky would subject her father to a long string of invective, probably ending with 'Fuck right off, you motherfucking motherfucker!' There was a distinct advantage in having been diagnosed as having Tourette's Syndrome.

But Stevie was neither Becky nor Johnny, just poor little mild-mannered Stevie Warner with no Superman underneath. And although he hated himself for worrying about what people thought of him, there didn't seem to be a lot he could do about it.

Stevie began to walk back across the green. Duke was inside the fenced-off playground, digging frantically. Two small children, a boy and a girl, around five or six, were huddled up at the far side of the playground, looking worried. Stevie hurried over to them. The boy had been crying and Stevie wondered where their parents were.

'What happened?' Stevie asked. 'Did Dookie jump up at you?'

The girl put her arm protectively around her brother. 'Is that *your* doggy?' she asked, nodding over at the corner where Dookie was still digging.

Stevie nodded. 'Did he hurt you?'

'He's frighted my brother. He's only four,' the girl said.

'Did he jump up at him and growl?' Stevie asked, wishing he'd stayed indoors and forgotten about the stupid note. If the parents arrived, the kid was going to bawl, and when *that* happened they would think that the dog had tried to bite if not actually succeeded. And they'd complain . . .

'He frighted Sam,' the girl repeated. 'Chasing. *I* wasn't frighted. But he might dig it up and I wouldn't like that. I *might* be afeared if he did do that.'

Stevie ignored the girl's last concern: the dog had no chance of digging up the tough surface. 'He chased your brother?' he asked worriedly.

The little girl shook her head.

'What then?'

'He chased a gobbling,' she said. 'They live all underground down in the nasty, don't they?'

'A *what*?' Stevie said, certain his ears must be playing tricks.

'A gobbling,' the little girl insisted. 'An bad *red* gobbling with all teeth and claws.'

The little boy began to sob again. His sister hooked her arm clumsily around his neck and pulled his face against her own. 'Frighted my Sam again now,' she said, and sighed theatrically. 'You mustn't let your doggy dig it up,' she added.

'My dog chased a goblin,' Stevie said, more testing the words to see how dumb they sounded than asking a question.

'It *wasn't* a gobbling at first,' the girl explained patiently. 'It was a pretty star and it comed out there,' she said, stabbing a finger at the other corner of the playground – the one closest to the dry river bed. 'All shiny, it comed up. Blue and stuff. White and twinkly and blue.'

'This star came out of the ground?' Stevie asked. The kid was spinning him a yarn. He didn't know why and didn't care and Dookie hadn't hurt either of the kids – which was brilliant. The rest, whatever it turned out to be, wasn't important.

Over in the corner, Dookie was still scrabbling furiously at the rubberized surface.

The girl nodded, heavy-handedly smoothing down her snivelling brother's tousled hair. 'And it talked,' she said. 'It said, "Hello, Melanie. Hello, Sam." And I said hello back and Sam waved. It might have been a fairy and it might have been a star. And when Sam waved, it wobbled all up and down all sparkly.'

'And then what?' Stevie asked, trying to keep the grin off his face. He glanced over at the dog and shouted, 'Pack it up, Dookie!' The dog ignored him.

'And then,' Melanie said disapprovingly, 'the doggy went and chased it, all growly and cross. It was a nice fairy until then. I was all happy. And that doggy jumped up and tried to bite it. And he *did* bite it and it felled down to the ground and went *poof!* and it fizzed across the ground and in the middle was the gobbling.'

'And Dookie chased the goblin?'

'Is your doggy called Dookie?' the girl asked. 'He's a *bad* doggy. He jumped on to the gobbling and it was black and then it was red and got up and ran round and the doggy chased it. And it came here and it tried to climb up Sam's leg with all its claws and things. It was *ugly*. And it scratched Sam's leg. Look!'

Stevie looked. Just above the boy's knee were five inch-long scratches that ended in what looked like tiny burns, perhaps caused by the hot end of an extinguished match.

'Are you sure the dog didn't do this?' Stevie said. But dog claws didn't leave burns. Goblin claws, though . . .

Melanie shook her head. 'He camed and woofed and Sam cried and the gobbling jumped down and runned over there,' she said, pointing to where Dookie was now sniffing deeply. His hackles were up and his muscles were tensed.

'And the gobbling lifted up the ground,' Melanie said, 'and went underneath, down in the nasty.'

Stevie smiled, 'Well, I don't think he'll come back up again, what with Dookie ready to bite him and everything. I think we'll all be safe.'

The expression that settled on Melanie's face suggested that she often had a hard time making her elders take her seriously: it was a cross between patience sorely tested and gloom. 'I know you don't believe me,' she sighed, 'but if your doggy digs him up again, there'll be trouble.' She emphasized the final sentence by wagging her index finger at Stevie in admonishment. *Just like her mother, presumably*, Stevie thought.

He nodded. 'OK, I'll take him away,' he said. The main thing was that Dookie hadn't done anything wrong. That was what mattered. The scratches on the kid's leg were too fine to have been put there by the dog's claws. What the tiny burns were was anyone's guess.

Dookie had begun to scrabble again and Stevie had to yank him away by his collar. He crouched in front of the area and examined it. The soft, rubberized surface was slightly scratched but there were no cracks or holes down which a rat or some other small rodent might have fled. Yet a corner of the 'carpet' *did* stand proud of the edging stones. Stevie reached for it and felt a tiny chill of fear. Maybe if he pulled it up something dreadful *would* shoot out from under it, shrieking as it went for his throat.

A moment later, Stevie took hold of a corner of the surfacing and tugged, elbowing the growling Duke out of the way.

Nothing happened. The surface wouldn't budge. He glanced up at the dog, who looked expectantly from him to the corner and back again. 'Sorry, dog, can't do it,' Stevie said, shrugging. 'Gave it my best shot. And, anyway, the gobbling's long gone by now, I should think.'

The dog gave an encouraging *woof!* and looked pointedly at the corner.

'We've gotta go home,' Stevie told him, feeling a back-arching shiver hit him. It had something to do with the word 'gobbling', he thought.

It wasn't until he had the dog on the lead and was heading back for the alley that he admitted to himself that he hadn't used all the force he could muster on the corner of the synthetic surface. He hadn't done it because part of him had believed Melanie's claims.

As they were approaching the alley, Duke stopped suddenly. Stevie walked past him, letting the twenty-five-foot lead play out behind him. Duke knew the length of the lead by heart, and always timed his sniffs or leg-cockings so that they finished a foot or so before his neck was yanked.

This time, the lead reached the end and tightened. Stevie's grasp on the handle was loose and it flew from his fingers, the spring inside it winding the cord back inside and dragging the handle back towards the dog.

For a second Stevie was scared to turn round in case what was on the other end of the cord wasn't Duke at all, but . . . *something that lives underground, down in the nasty?*

He shook his head in disbelief at himself and turned back to face the dog.

Duke was around thirty feet behind him, his legs splayed out in an upside-down V, his head lowered to the right front one.

As Stevie hurried back, he understood what had happened – it was easy to tell from the way Duke was trying to nibble at his foreleg. He'd picked up a thorn or a flea had just bitten him. The best bet was a thorn – there were plenty of rose bushes on the green and Dookie was wont to plough through them like a tank if anything attracted his interest.

Stevie crouched down beside him, pulled his head away and saw that the dog had chewed off two thin patches of fur, each about two inches long and an eighth of an inch wide. They ran alongside one another like rails. He tried to get his mouth back to his leg and Stevie had to hold him in a head-lock. The dog, he noticed, as he tried to make him stand still, had an odd odour about him. Not the usual hot-dog-that-needs-a-bath-in-the-near-future smell, but something that reminded him of an electric fire being turned on after a long period of disuse.

'Hold still, Dookie!' he commanded, in his most authoritative voice. It might have sounded like the uncertain voice of a tetchy teenager, but it was the voice of the pack-leader as far as the dog was concerned and he respected it. Stevie grinned as his faithful subject stopped struggling and he picked up the dog's leg to inspect it.

What he saw didn't please him. Something had *burned* those two lines into Duke's coat. The odd odour was singed hair. Stevie inspected the light scratches in the middle of the bare spots on Duke's leg. *Just thorns*, he told himself.

But rose-bush scratches didn't end in a little burnt dot.

Stevie frowned. Maybe the council had sprayed the roses with some new bug killer – the kind that gave kids and dogs burns and hallucinations when they came in contact with it.

Duke tensed when Stevie ran his finger down the edge of one of the bare patches. Brown dust flaked off the ends of the hairs. Duke complained more forcefully when Stevie touched one of the scratches.

He sniffed his finger, which smelt rather like marzipan. 'I dunno what this is,' he told the dog, 'but we'll get it washed off you as soon as we get home. And we'll stick some antiseptic on it, too. Come on!'

A few minutes later, Stevie stopped wondering what had hurt Duke's leg because on the other side of the fence that ran down the alley he could hear someone talking quietly.

He stopped dead in his tracks, held his breath and listened. The voice's owner – a small boy, judging from the pitch – said something Stevie couldn't hear, then shrieked with laughter.

Stevie checked up and down the alley in case anyone was watching, then found a small gap in the fence to look through. Duke pulled on the lead a couple of times, as if he wanted to go home right now, but then settled to lick his wounds with the pink tip of his tongue, which was all he could poke through the muzzle.

For the time being, though, Stevie had forgotten his faithful follower, because in the garden on the other side of the fence was the famous vanishing boy, sitting on his swing.

And the kid, who was blond and maybe seven years old, was having an animated conversation with someone who didn't exist.

Chapter Two

Cereal Killer

While Wolfgang Stephen Warner was staring through a fence at a small blond boy talking to an invisible friend, his father was two miles away, sitting on a bench in the Memorial Park wondering where the cut on his forefinger had come from. He was leaning forward, his posture loosely mimicking Rodin's *The Thinker*, right hand supporting his chin. His left wrist rested on his thigh, the bleeding finger pointing down into the gap between his legs. On the tarmac a small red pool was gradually expanding with each bright droplet.

How did I do that? Andy asked himself, as blood steadily gathered at the point of his finger and swelled until it was large enough to fall. Then, *Why am I still bleeding? Why isn't it clotting?* There was a chance, he guessed, that he'd suddenly turned into a haemophiliac.

Wondering how long it would take him to bleed to death, Andy looked up and felt his tired eyes struggle to change focus from close to distance. The park – a great swath of neatly clipped, healthy-looking grass with a bandstand at one end and swings and slides at the other – was busy. Mums and nannies wheeled babies around the perimeter path beside which he was sitting; a handful of kids were in the sand-pit, tossing the bright yellow sand at each other; down near the bandstand a bunch of gangly teenagers, around Stevie's age, were playing an odd game that seemed to be half football, half rugby and all violent. Way across the green at the edge of the tree line the girl who had been locked in an embrace with a boy for the last half-hour was now straddling him, holding his wrists down while she worked at him with her hips.

The panorama looked wrong. Everything looked as if it had been handcrafted by someone who'd forgotten to add that little extra something. Soul, perhaps. Life. Andy didn't know.

What he *did* know was that he'd seen this park look exactly like this before. A long time ago.

'A very long time ago,' he murmured, and wasn't surprised that his throat hurt when he spoke and that his voice sounded rusty.

Another drop of blood hit the ground.

Why am I still bleeding? Andy asked himself again. 'And, better still, how the hell did I cut myself?' he added aloud, clearing his throat.

You don't want to know that, a small, still voice told him.

'Ah, the voice of the Mysterons!' Andy said bitterly. 'The voice of those who know all, see all.' He took his packet of Silk Cut 100s from his shirt pocket, stuck a cigarette in his mouth, lit it with an almost-dry Zippo, sucked hard and felt no better for it. And this was the man who swore he'd kick the habit when lighting a ciggie ceased to give him either pleasure or relief.

'Fuck it,' he said, and sucked harder. 'If at first you don't succeed, you're not doing it right.' The second blast didn't do the business either. All you got from these, he concluded, was the graveyard cough. And probably cancer. What a way to kill yourself.

Well, it's better than . . .

Andy cut the thought dead in its tracks.

'Where's my signal?' he muttered. 'All I need is my signal and I can go home.'

Andy Warner was the only one who never truly forgot. The wipe that had been done on him was the kind that aliens were wont to give their abductees: a quick and dirty job that wouldn't last. Except it *had* lasted for the others. And, to some degree, it had lasted for Andy too.

Something had happened back in the days of peace and understanding, when the world was young and everyone who wasn't high on acid or speed was high on life and love, something that didn't fit.

'Something *waaaaayyyy* bad,' Andy acknowledged. But he didn't know what it was. The others didn't even remember that much.

Good for them! Andy thought. *Lucky old them!* Because not knowing that anything had happened was far better than knowing *something* had happened and not knowing what it was. Whoever first said, 'Ignorance is bliss,' knew what they were talking about. When you were ignorant you didn't sit about in parks watching your finger bleed and waiting for a signal.

I'm fucked up, Andy thought, sucking furiously at the cigarette he'd lit from the dog-end of the last one. He glanced around the park again. The humping girl was still humping, the kids were still sand-fighting. Nothing had changed. There was no signal.

Andy blew the smoke out of his nostrils and wished he'd never become a writer. It had been a bad move or, at least, trying to be a novelist had – the computer journalism was as safe as milk. If he'd never wanted to become an author, he wouldn't have made a deeply hidden sub-directory on his computer and named it *My Novel.* If he hadn't made it, he wouldn't have forgotten about it and stumbled across it five years later.

I don't want to think about this, Andy warned himself, but it was too late to stop. He *had* wanted to be a novelist. He *still* wanted to be a novelist – not one of the breed who wrote literature and whose name lived on for hundreds of years, but a quick-buck pulp-fiction writer who got instant fame and fortune. But to be a novelist you had to have story-ideas. You had to want to tell lies over maybe a hundred thousand words. And Andy had been trained as a journalist, who wrote fact, wrote it short and then went back and made it shorter still. But the lack of ideas was the worst thing. Andy Warner, who was left-handed and therefore right-brain-dominant and supposedly creative because of this, hadn't had one good idea that might be stretched into a novel.

Except you did, didn't you? the Mysteron voice reminded.

The Mysteron was right. He *had* had a good idea.

The trouble was, he couldn't remember having had that idea or writing it down. When he stumbled across that idea five years after he'd stored it in his hidden directory, it had scared the shit out of him.

It was a single-page idea for a story that he'd thought would work well under the title *The Devil on May Street.* Five weeks ago and, according to the file's creation date, five years to the day, hour and minute from the time he'd finished writing the idea, he'd found the file again. And he'd thought, in that bemused way he had that Jacqui said endeared him to her, Oh, what have we here then, boss? and opened the file.

And pulled the lid off a box that had surely belonged to Pandora.

He didn't read it all, just the title and first line. That had been enough.

Andy shook his head and glanced around the park for his sign. It wasn't showing. He gazed down at the pool of blood – now sporting a layer of ash and two dog-ends – then at his bleeding finger. The blood was now soaking into the filter of the latest Silk Cut.

The Devil on May Street was a horror story, there was no doubt about that. Its first line had driven an icy spike up through Andy's innards and almost stopped his heart. He'd closed the file and for the rest of the day he'd sat in front of his computer, alternately shaking like a man suffering a high fever and trying to forget that the story existed.

But once the top was off the box, as Pandora would have wholeheartedly agreed, the bad stuff was out and would never go back. Not even if you laid bait in there and sat up all night waiting.

We did something terrible last night, the voice of the Mysteron said in its cold, glassy voice.

Andy nodded. He didn't need reminding of the first line. That was what had kicked all this shit into play.

I should have deleted that bloody file, Andy told himself, knowing it wouldn't have made the slightest difference.

The six of us, Andy thought. *Us six trippy hippies. We did something terrible.*

At least, that was the opinion of the man sitting waiting for a signal.

In the hierarchy of questions queuing up inside Any Warner's head, the first and foremost should have been: *Where have I been?*

But Andy didn't think this because a little old man had appeared down by the bandstand and was walking towards the gang of ball players. He looked like a giver of signals. No ordinary person came out on a sweltering day like this wearing a full-length raincoat, fedora hat and wellington boots, or chose to walk through a gang of teenagers who were all but kicking the shit out of one another.

Andy glanced at his finger, half expecting it to have healed now that the old man had appeared. Blood welled up. Andy looked back at the old man. He had hold of one of the boys by the arm and was animatedly talking to him, shouting the odds by the look of him. The boy looked contrite – or at least his stance suggested that the man held authority around there.

Andy's finger stung and he remembered cutting it on a piece of jagged glass. A piece of glass that *he'd* broken.

'Where was I?' he heard himself asking distantly. Suddenly it seemed important to know.

Over by the bandstand, the old man was tottering back the way he'd come. The kid was trailing along in his wake.

That wasn't my guy then, Andy told himself and began to think back.

He remembered waking early, kissing his wife – who was dressed in a sharp suit and ready to rock – and then – since he remembered waking up a second time – he must have gone back to sleep again. He woke for real around nine, and had crawled out of bed feeling like crap and sheened with sweat. He'd showered, shaved, dressed and gone downstairs, coughing up his lungs with the first coffin-nail of the day hanging from the corner of his mouth.

So far, so good! he told himself. *So far it's much like any ordinary day in the life of Andrew Warner, freelance computer journalist and all-round good egg.*

Jacqui had left early for a meeting in London so it'd just been him and Stevie at breakfast. Stevie had tried to tap him for a tenner and his dear old dad had refused. For at least ten minutes, anyway.

Then he'd gone into his workroom, turned on the beast with one hundred and twenty-eight megs and sat down to get stuck into his current project. *I've got to go to America next week!* he remembered with a start. *What'll happen then, when I'm not here to do this?*

Andy didn't know. What he did know was that the three weeks with IBM in Austin was likely to cause him a big problem.

What if you get called and you're not here? he asked himself.

He shook his head in frustration. *The old scalpel-sharp mind has lost its edge*, he told himself. But it was worse than that – his mind had metamorphosed from scalpel to butterfly. Andy knew this and it hurt. There was the IBM contract for one thing. That was big money and one of the best breaks he'd had for a long time. And if he couldn't concentrate on it and meet the deadline he was likely to be up shit creek with several holes in his canoe and no bailing can.

Another bright drop of blood dripped from his forefinger. Andy watched it fall as if in slow motion.

So, Andy me boyo, you went into your workroom and sat down in front of the beast. Then what?

He'd started his word processor and opened the file containing what existed of the manual. It was nothing but a rough outline at present: he was in England and the software was in Austin, Texas, hidden away behind locked doors.

I tinkered around for a time. He could clearly recall revising bits and pieces of the outline before he'd started writing a technical article for his regular column in one of the monthlies. Then he'd swapped back to the outline.

And something had happened.

He could recall thinking briefly about *The Devil on May Street.*

But forget that, he told himself quickly. *Use that sharp brain and reconstruct the day.*

It was difficult to concentrate, what with the blood, the search for the signal, the humping girl, the kids and everything, but Andy tried.

He'd sat in front of the computer. He'd written a bit. He'd smoked several cigarettes. So he'd been there maybe two hours. And then . . .

You got the urge, he told himself.

Evidently he had, but the urge to do *what*?

'Climb,' he muttered, through a mouth as dry as dust.

He'd gone to the toilet. He remembered now. He'd gone for a pee – and not because he'd wanted one. It had been one of those indoctrinated water-passings, the kind you owed to your mother because when you were a kid she'd always made you pee before you went out.

I was getting ready to go out. Andy frowned, searching his memory for the reason why.

I went back into my workroom, he continued. He could picture himself standing there, lighting a fresh cigarette and checking the pack to see if he had enough left to keep him supplied while he was out. He'd got a fresh pack from his bookcase shelf and he'd put this in his shirt pocket with the Zippo. He could recall this. He looked at his watch. It was three twenty. He got out his cigarettes again and counted how many were left.

Fourteen. He'd smoked six here, hence he'd been here maybe an hour and a half. According to the estimated tobacco consumption prior to going out, he must have left his workroom around eleven thirty. So wherever he'd been, he'd been unable to smoke.

Well done, butterfly, the voice of the Mysteron grated. *You went somewhere you couldn't or didn't smoke. That doesn't tell you where you've been though, does it?*

'Somewhere I broke glass . . .' Andy said, and an image instantly lit up in his mind.

He saw a hand – a left hand, wearing a wedding ring similar to the one on his third finger. Between finger and thumb it held a red polka-dot bandanna, similar to the one that now resided in the pocket of his jeans. As he watched, a right hand came into view and wrapped the bandanna tightly around the hand, which clenched into a fist, leaving part of the index finger uncovered and unprotected.

Andy suddenly felt cold and as if he was going to cry.

I punched out a window, he told himself.

If he thought about it, he found, he could actually *hear* the thud of his fist hitting the glass . . .

In the back door . . .

. . . and the sound the pane made as it shattered.

'Oh sheeeeeiiiiiitttt,' Andy moaned.

And began to remember.

A call had come in while he was sitting in front of his computer. Not a telephone call but a demand. It had felt a little like a wire deep in his brain had suddenly begun to glow hot. Then there had been a sensation of something snapping inside his head, the way a brand-new light switch clicked.

Andy had smiled. He'd snapped out of his slumped writing posture and sat up straight, beaming from ear to ear.

God spoke, the voice of the Mysteron said.

And that was pretty much what it felt like. As if he had received a wordless communication that contained all the information he needed.

On occasion, Andy had had dreams in which he *understood*. The kind of dream in which all the mysteries of life, death, the universe and its purpose could be clearly comprehended. This was close to the feeling he got when the light switch snapped on inside him.

Andy realized, with a growing horror, that without understanding what he was doing he had carried out someone or something else's instructions.

Except that whatever it was had seemed to have his best interests at heart. Andy felt this deep down inside himself. The task was a prophylactic. Properly carried out, it prevented the shit from hitting the fan.

For all six of us, Andy told himself. *And our kids, too.*

The fact that he didn't know the nature of the shit that might hit the fan if he didn't do as he was told was neither here nor there. The fact that it existed was enough.

But do you know the shit really exists, O razor-sharp? the voice of the Mysteron enquired.

'Oh, yes,' Andy said aloud. 'I know the shit exists, believe me. I'm the only one of the six of us who hasn't forgotten that . . .'

But when he came to put a name to the shit, he couldn't. It had something to do with that directory on his computer called *My Novel* and the file that was contained within it. And maybe something to do with the first line of that file: 'We did something terrible last night.'

Several hours earlier, when the light switch in his head had clicked, Andy had got up, gone to the toilet, returned to his workroom, lit a smoke, collected a new packet of Silk Cut 100s, put them and the Zippo in his shirt pocket and then . . .

He'd listened at the door for Stevie, closed it, picked his way across the room, opened the window, climbed on the space he'd cleared on his desk and jumped through, down to the alley alongside the house.

He'd walked from the shade of the alley into the scorching sunshine on Solby's Road and had turned left, not knowing where he was headed and not caring. He was feeling good: charged with energy and clear-headed. He'd sashayed down on to Worting Road and headed up Sarum Hill – towards the Memorial Park, in fact. The hill had made him puff a little and he'd thought: *Never mind. When this is all over we'll get ourselves fixed up. We'll quit the old cancer weed and do a little exercise. Take the Dukester out for long walks, just me and Jacques and the Dogboy*. And now he remembered having thought this sounded rather like the kind of thought a doomed man might have. *Planning to do something he knew he'd never do because there wasn't enough of his life left to do it.*

He'd turned left, then right at the traffic lights, and had followed the road onwards. Then he'd peeled off right and gone across the flat car park towards Southern Road. A Caterham 7 was standing in the car park, brand new and in British Racing Green. He'd looked it over for a few moments, drooling: the 7 was the car he'd lusted after all his adult life. *I'll have one exactly like this when the money comes rolling in*, he'd told himself, and walked on.

He could recall it all: the bumble-bee chasing him up the alley to Chequers Road; the fat woman, the underarms and chest of her dress dark with sweat, watching him bemusedly as he fled the bee; the way the sun caught the clematis in the garden of the house on Wallis Road, turning it into something gorgeous and surreal. It felt exactly as if someone had slipped a 370 microgram tab of his old buddy Dick Kemp's best acid into his breakfast and he was on his way *up*.

Chuckling to himself, Andy turned into Cliddesden Road, walked two hundred and three paces, stopped and swung to the right. And there was a house.

The house.

Cliddesden Road was a good area and the house was detached, set back from the road and almost hidden behind a tall hedge with big yellowish-green leaves. Andy would have liked to have spent some time inspecting those leaves because veins seemed to be pulsing in them, and the leaves were beginning to writhe. But he knew he had to hurry.

He checked up and down the road to see if he was being observed by any pedestrians, car drivers or window-monitors, then opened the inricate wrought-iron gates and crunched his way up the drive and into the porch.

The front door was one of those fancy affairs: solid oak lower half, stained glass leaded lights above the shiny brass letter-box. Each little pane of glass depicted an animal. An odd creature, like a were-lion, caught his eye. At the top of the door, a Victorian-style fanlight showed the name of the house: Black Rock.

He pressed the brass bell-push. Deep inside the house a mellow chime sounded. Andy knew already that no one would answer the door. No one was in.

He waited for a count of sixty-five, watching the animals in the leaded lights very carefully. He was pretty sure that whenever he took his eyes off the were-lion, the damned thing moved. He was pretty sure, come to think of it, that when he'd arrived, the were-lion had been crouched, as if ready to pounce. Now it appeared to be leaping.

He rang the bell again and rapped on the door. He smiled and began to hum a tune: Steve Miller's version of 'Motherless Children'. After another long count he went to the side gate that stood between the house and the garage. It was tall, stout and bolted from the inside. He took hold of the top of the gate, heaved himself up, and landed nimbly on his feet the other side.

He strode round to the back door. It was plain, but the upper half had four panes of bubbled glass. He rapped on one, waited, then tried the handle. The door was locked.

He glanced behind him at the garden, realized the area wasn't overlooked by other houses and pulled the bandanna from his pocket. Something fell to the step at his feet. A small square of dull, dark metal. Andy bent and picked it up. It was a magnet, one of Stevie's and last seen hanging on one of the old cast-iron water pipes in the bathroom. Andy had no memory of having picked it up.

'Aha!' he said, suddenly understanding. *You're so brilliant you even know things you don't know*, he told himself.

He held the magnet between his teeth while he wrapped his left hand in the bandanna, balled his fist and punched the lower left pane of glass as hard as he could.

The bad thing was that it *hurt*. The good thing was that the glass broke.

Andy unwound the bandanna and looked at the deep cut in his finger. He sucked away the blood and bound the wound with a tissue he found in his other pocket. Then he put his right hand through the hole he'd made and felt for the key in the keyhole.

People whose back doors had mortice locks on them *always* left the key in the lock. He did, all his neighbours did, so there was no reason why these people shouldn't.

The key was in the lock.

Andy turned it and felt up the door jamb for the alarm system's sensors.

And here we are! he told himself, finding the plastic case. He took the magnet from between his teeth, held it and stuck it to one sensor. For a man who'd never (to the best of his knowledge) broken into a house before and who knew zilch about alarms, he thought he was doing pretty well. Of course, he had no way of knowing if the magnet trick would work but he thought it would.

He walked into a big, clean kitchen, stepping over the pile of glass shards. Somewhere in here was a box of porridge oats.

Suddenly Andy began to feel anxious. If there was no box of porridge oats he was sunk. And not only himself, but the others. No oats, no safety. The sacrifice had to be made and it had to be made with oats.

He hurried over to the cupboard that looked most likely and opened the door. Pots and pans. He worked his way down the others, opening and closing them quickly. No cereal. He checked each one twice. Then he spotted the door that evidently led to the pantry.

'Bingo,' he said, and hurried over, his Nikes squeaking on the parquet floor. It was a walk-in pantry rather than a cupboard and it contained enough tinned and preserved stuff to last through a nuclear winter and probably the following spring. There were boxes of cereals of every kind imaginable, from Honey Nut Loops to Muesli Munch.

But no porridge oats.

'For fuck's *sake*!' Andy yelled in frustration. He pulled several boxes of cereal from the shelf and threw them to the floor and . . . hey presto! One small box of Scott's 'Porage' Oats, hiding behind three boxes of Frosties. Andy grabbed it and hugged it to him like an old friend.

Back in the kitchen, he set the box on the table, sat on one of the chairs and began to unlace his trainers. Blood was seeping through the tissue now and it was likely that he was going to leave some behind. He didn't think this would prove too troublesome – no one was going to bother with DNA testing for this – but he wasn't supposed to leave anything of himself.

There was a big box of man-size Kleenex on the window-sill. Andy got one, unwound the tissue from his wound, stuffed it in his pocket, then wrapped a fresh one round the cut.

He removed his Nikes and placed them on the table. He took off his socks and placed them inside the shoes. Undoing the buttons of his shirt wasn't easy without using the forefinger of his left hand, and it took a frustratingly long time. He hung his shirt over the back of his chair with his jeans and underpants.

Being naked in a stranger's house was an odd and shockingly erotic experience. To Andy's amazement, he'd grown an achingly hard erection that just *begged* for relief. He frowned at himself for a moment, then laughed. Maybe Jacqui would put him right later on when she got home. He was doing this for her, after all.

He opened the box of oats and poured some in the bottom of a dessert bowl he found in one of the cupboards. Then he took the box back to the pantry, put it where he'd found it, and stacked in front of it the boxes he'd thrown down. He went to the refrigerator and took out an unopened bottle of semi-skimmed. He poured in the milk, carried the bowl to the microwave, set the machine on full power, turned the timer to three minutes and hit the start button before returning to the other side of the kitchen for a dessert spoon.

Three minutes later, Andy Warner, housebreaker supreme and master chef, had a perfect bowl of porridge, piping hot and ready to eat.

Andy got a tea towel, picked up the hot bowl, set it down on the table and laid the spoon beside it. 'All we need now is a little sugar,' he muttered.

There was a choice of white, demerara or golden granulated. Andy went for the golden granulated and shook a little on to the surface of his porridge. When he'd replaced the bag in the exact spot he'd found it, he returned to the table, sat down, picked up the spoon, rapped it on the table three times, said, 'Who's been eating *my* porridge?' and took a mouthful.

Andy *hated* porridge. He didn't remember this until his lips had closed round the first gooey spoonful. His throat closed up, preventing him from swallowing.

It won't kill you, he told himself, but evidently his throat didn't believe him. He sat still for a long time, moving the sweet, sloppy mixture round in his mouth and trying to make himself swallow. Eventually he managed it, but by this time there were tears in his eyes.

He rapped the spoon another three times. Tiny pieces of milky cereal flew across the table.

It took a long time to finish the entire bowl.

When the deed was done, Andy laid the spoon in the bowl in the twelve o'clock position, and stood up. The table was a mess, but the ritual had been carried out and now his safety was guaranteed for an unspecified time.

He began to smile again as he dressed.

It wasn't until he was on his way out of the house that he realized he'd been quietly chanting that old Edgar Broughton Band favourite, 'Out Demons, Out!' The song was supposed to exorcize demons, but as he passed through the doorway into the sunshine, Andy had second thoughts. *What if it doesn't send them away? What if it draws them out of the woodwork?*

He paused for a moment, frowning and almost remembering. Almost, but not quite. He evidently didn't *want* to recall whatever it was. Trying to dredge up the memory felt a little like trying to drag a submarine out through your arsehole. It hurt and it didn't want to move.

Then he shivered. He felt good again, like a man who'd done an honest day's graft and was on his way home to a hot bath, a hot dinner and a hot wife.

He unlatched the gate, went out through it, crunched his way down the path to the street and left his burglary behind him.

'And that was *all*, she wrote,' Andy said bitterly. Remembering was like having a nervous breakdown. Only worse.

He lit a fresh Silk Cut and didn't even care about the blood that soaked into it from his weeping cut.

I wasn't meant to cut myself, he told himself, sucking hard on his fresh-air cigarette. *If that hadn't happened I would never have known.*

But he *had* cut himself and now he *did* know. What he had to do next was try to make sense of what he'd done. What reason could you possibly have for breaking into someone's house and eating a bowl of their porridge?

The simple fact was he'd broken into someone's house and eaten a bowl of the world's most disgusting breakfast cereal to protect himself and his family and friends from harm.

'Makes sense really, doesn't it?' he asked aloud, glancing up and down the park for his sign.

But, no it didn't make sense. None at all. You couldn't protect youself . . .

From what, *Andy? Evil? Is that what we're talking here? Ghoulies and Ghosties and all that crapola?*

. . . from *anything* by doing lunatic acts of breaking and eating. He was certain of that. Rationally, he was, anyway.

What he needed to ask himself, he realized, was had the idea come from himself or from elsewhere? He had the distinct feeling that if he were to take a coin from his pocket and toss it, it would land on the side designated 'elsewhere'.

Either the protracted use of lysergic acid diethylamide eventually got to you, just like everyone said it would, or you're being manipulated by a . . . a force?

But Andy hadn't taken acid for twenty-five years and the flashbacks, nasty though they'd been, had stopped twenty years back.

Which left the other option. Andy kept remembering that single-page file in the depths of his computer: *We did something terrible last night.*

Over on the far side of the green, the humping girl stood up and began to dance around. She was tall and skinny, wearing a pink tank-top and a short, flouncy skirt that fanned out as she spun. She had long, pale legs.

Andy sighed, still trying to assimilate the new knowledge about himself. If he'd done what he'd done this afternoon and only remembered it because of the cut, the chances were he'd done it before, too. And that he would do it again. In fact, now he thought about it, the thought of *not* being able to do it again scared him. Hadn't he just been worrying about the forthcoming trip to America? About being called to do his job while he was away?

Something's at me, he thought. And then, *I could just get up and walk away. Forget all about waiting for a red signal. Finish the networking article and e-mail it to Mr Editor and make some money. That'd be a much better idea than sticking around here worrying about things like porridge and signals.*

You could *simply get up and go home*, the voice of the Mysteron said calmly, *but waiting for the signal might be advisable. Things are pretty well fucked up as they are and it might be a good idea not to fuck them up any further until we know exactly what we're dealing with here.*

Andy nodded, still staring at the girl dancing, way across the grass. She was attractive. Not her face – he couldn't see it clearly from this distance – but the sexy way she moved.

Andy took his cigarettes from his shirt pocket and withdrew another fresh smoke. His mouth was dryer than the Sahara on a sunny day in August and when he lit up the smoke hurt his throat.

The girl suddenly quit dancing and the boy sat up, shaking his head. The girl nodded. Andy watched. Blood dripped.

The girl reached up under her skirt, pulled down her underwear and stepped out of it.

Andy didn't have much experience of underwear. He knew his

wife wore comfy Sloggi briefs to work and tiny, almost non-existent things she called wispies when she wanted to play, but that was about as far as it went. Up until now, he had been under the impression that teenage girls went for pretty much the same kind of thing as his wife but the garment the girl had just slipped out of didn't belong to either of these grades: it belonged to the genus *passion-killer*. This was one huge pair of sturdy red knickers. The girl bent and picked them up.

She raised them over her head, spun them round on her finger and let them fly away. They arced through the air, bright as Andy's blood in the sun, and fell about ten feet from her and the boy. She went back to the boy and straddled him again.

Andy didn't notice. His eyes were still fixed on the spot where the knickers had fallen. He'd received the signal for which he'd waited so long and all he had to do now was force his aching legs to get his numb arse off the bench and wander home.

Where he could drink a long cold drink, relax and, with a little luck, forget again.

Chapter Three

A Boy and His God

'Who is?' the kid on the swing asked the empty air. Then he listened, looking up in front of him to a height of what must have been six feet or more. He paddled his feet up and down and giggled coyly. 'No, I'm not,' he protested happily, 'I'm a *good* boy. My mummy says so.'

Stevie gazed in through the fence, his mouth open in an O of astonishment. This kid didn't go in for invisible friends of the same age group, apparently. Judging from the way he was looking up, his pal was a grown-up. A pretty tall one. Perhaps even a basketball-player-sized one.

After a further listening pause, the boy said confidently, 'My mummy knows *everything*,' and adjusted his grip on the swing's chains.

Stevie tried to fill in the missing half of the conversation. The first thing the invisible pal had said was evidently: *You're a bad boy!* And evidently it had been spoken in jest, since the kid hadn't batted an eyelid.

The second thing Mr Invisible had said had to be: *What does your mummy know about it?*

The kid began to work his feet so the swing tried to turn against its chains and wobbled back and forth in a juddering arc. He glanced up at Mr Invisible and said, 'I don't know.'

Stevie couldn't fill in the blank for that one. At his feet, Duke made a disgruntled moaning noise. The edges of his muzzle were drenched in foam. Stevie bent down, undid it and slipped it off. Duke immediately began to run his mouth through the grass at the foot of the fence.

'Get you a drink in a minute,' Stevie said, and turned his attention back to the boy.

'I might want to,' the boy said. 'But why can't I ask my mummy?'

Might want to what? Stevie wondered.

'She's indoors, asleep,' the kid went on, 'but I could wake her up. If I wanted to.'

'Yes I *could*,' he protested, sounding a little offended now. He listened again, then said, 'You *have* to drink. You die if you don't drink. My teacher said so and my mummy does, too. That's why people dry up and go dead in the desert. Everyone knows that.'

Mr Invisible must have launched into a set-piece then, because the kid said nothing for a long time, just stared up into thin air, a rapt expression on his face.

Duke suddenly launched himself at something that scurried through the patchy grass, and almost pulled Stevie's arm out of its socket. 'Sit down!' he hissed. Duke ignored him and dug in, heaving at the lead and making a half-strangled growling noise.

As Stevie yanked back at the lead, something dark scurried away from behind the raised clump of weed for which the dog was reaching. Stevie only caught a momentary glance of it as it dashed through the longer grass behind the clump and was gone, but it looked too big to be a rat and moved in a peculiar fashion.

The dog gave one last tug and, admitting defeat, came back to Stevie and sat down.

What was *that?* Stevie asked himself. His mind instantly replied, *It was the gobbling, of course. It came back!* and he shuddered.

'I wouldn't even have to *clean my teeth*?' Stevie heard the boy on the swing ask. He turned back to the gap in the fence and forgot about the rat, or whatever Dookie had been after.

'Do you *promise*?' the boy asked. 'No school for ever? Always playtime?'

Nice try, Stevie thought. He knew exactly how the kid felt.

On the far side of the fence, the boy nodded. 'I might do. My daddy went away.'

Stevie had had an invisible friend of his own for a while, when he was young, but he couldn't recall whether it was a boy or a girl or an animal. It had always struck him as weird that he'd forgotten all the details about his special pal other than its name: Manaymon. He tried to imagine himself having a conversation like this one with his own imaginary friend, and failed. He was pretty sure that Manaymon had been a silent, compliant friend. What was the point of manufacturing yourself an invisible pal if you had to discuss stuff with it? If it was any good, it ought to *know* what you wanted from it.

The kid on the swing's Mr Invisible was a construct of a different colour, apparently.

The boy nodded solemnly. 'I'll think about it. I promise. But would I really like being a bad boy *all* the time?'

Sure you would, kid, Stevie thought, grinning. *Who wouldn't?*

Which was when something hit him hard from behind.

If there had been time before the strong hand was clapped across his mouth, Stevie would have let out a little yelp of surprise – the collision hadn't hurt him much but it had almost scared the shit out of him.

As he was snatched off his feet, he sucked in air through his nostrils and tried to summon his faithful follower but the sound came out *oooooooooooook*. The dog looked up in surprise and to Stevie's total disbelief, began to wag his tail.

'I caught you eavesdropping, you *dirty little Dogboy*,' a voice snarled in his ear.

Stevie scraped his heel down his attacker's shin, but the soft rubber heel of a British Knight trainer wasn't something your average attacker found too disturbing. This attacker didn't even seem to notice. Stevie wriggled frantically and snapped his teeth at his attacker's palm, while he tried to work his left hand round behind him to grab the guy's nuts. The moment his teeth found a nip of skin, he was dropped. He spun round, ready to fight. Then he relaxed.

'Hiya, Wolfie Dogboy,' Johnny said, beaming. 'That scared you, didn't it?' He glanced at the palm of his hand, then showed it to Stevie: a perfect impression of Stevie's front teeth showed an angry red.

Stevie grinned and tried not to look as shaken as he felt. 'Didn't know it was you,' he said, truthfully. 'Want me to kiss it better for you?' he added, ducking casually as Johnny slapped at him.

'My mummy told me not to talk to men like you,' Johnny said, bending to fuss Duke, who was circling him and wagging furiously. 'You got my letter, then,' he noted. 'What's happening over there now? Is he doing it again?'

'He's talking,' Stevie said. 'To a very tall imaginary friend.'

Johnny nodded, shook his fringe out of his eyes and grinned, showing perfect teeth. 'He does a lot of that. They talk and then he swings. It's worth seeing when *that* happens.'

Stevie frowned. 'What do you mean?' he asked.

'You read the letter?' Johnny asked.

'Some bullshit about the kid vanishing.' Stevie nodded.

Johnny shook his head in mock sadness. 'Some people just won't believe *anything* unless they see if for themselves,' he said. 'Have you no faith?' He gazed at Stevie for a few moments and a peculiar dazed look came into his eyes. Stevie had seen this one before. It was Johnny's I've-got-a-good-idea look.

Stevie and Johnny might have been near inseparable and just about as close as friends could get, and they might have been able to read one another's thoughts, but sometimes Stevie almost hated Johnny. As Stevie had fought a voice that broke late, spots, and hair that looked like it'd been greased with Castrol XL . . . and then wrestled with shyness and blushing, he'd noticed that not all men were created equally. There were people like him (sufferers), and there were others who sailed through puberty without so much as a hair out of place (lucky bastards). And then there were people like Johnny.

Johnny had had a good clear voice before it broke and the same voice, but somewhat deeper, the day after it broke. He had never had a spot in his life. He had lustrous black hair that always looked as if it had been freshly washed. To add insult to injury, Johnny had clear blue eyes, an even-featured face and the kind of skin that always looked faintly tanned.

Stevie himself had been told that he was good-looking, but whenever he went somewhere with Johnny where there were girls, he always felt as if he was walking in his friend's shadow.

Worse still, Johnny had that crazy guy inside him. The daredevil man-of-action streak. He was mad, bad and dangerous to know, and consequently people wanted to know him very badly indeed.

When you were with Johnny you could very easily end up feeling inferior, especially when he had one of his ideas.

The last one he'd had involved the electric third rail on the railway line. He'd postulated that since you only got a shock from electricity when you earthed it, it should be possible to stand on the electric rail without dying.

'I could jump on,' Johnny had said. 'If neither of my feet provide an earth, there won't be any problem, will there?'

Stevie had pointed out that DC electricity was well known for its ability to jump gaps, that it *liked* to arc, but Johnny was going up the bank to the line, and he was going to do it now, and they could either come and witness, or he'd go alone.

There were a lot of trains running through. The closest electric rail – a dull, greasy-looking thing, boxed in on either side with wooden boards – was on the far side of the line closest to them.

'They turn off the electricity between trains,' Becky said. 'I bet they do.'

Which was why Johnny waited until there was a train approaching to make his move. Half-way through a final argument Johnny simply turned away, skipped across the line, jumped over the electric rail, turned back and yelled, 'Here goes!' and hopped up on the rail.

Nothing happened. No sparks, no body flying off leaving a trail of smoke and charring clothes, just Johnny, both his feet on the

600 volt live rail and grinning like a lunatic while to his right an express train approached at high speed.

How he was still alive, God only knew.

Stevie looked at his friend now and could almost see the circuits lighting up behind his eyes. Duke wandered back to where he'd last seen the dark thing and began to sniff.

'Yes?' Stevie asked, and watched Johnny slide back into his face. It was a weird thing to see.

'Let's see if the kid's started to swing yet,' Johnny said, and walked over to the fence.

He was still there. Still talking.

'How about this for weird?' Johnny asked, taking his eye from a knot-hole and turning to Stevie. 'We can hear him, but he can't hear *us*!' He began to yell and hammer on the fence.

'HEY KID! YOU GONNA SWING ON THAT SWING, OR JUST NATTER THE DAY AWAY? WE WANNA SEE YOU DO YOUR THING. WHY DON'T YOU ASK YOUR FRIEND FOR A PUSH? LIKE LAST TIME. YOU GOT AN AUDIENCE OUT HERE WHO WANNA BE ENTERTAINED!'

The dog looked up from his rooting, his tail between his legs and a startled look in his eyes. On the other side of the fence, the boy on the swing continued to talk to his imaginary friend as if nothing had happened.

Johnny turned to Stevie, an odd look of excitement on his face. 'Way too strange, guy!' he said.

Stevie's sensible side told him that the best thing he could do was go home and read some more *Sons and Lovers* because staying here was a sure path to disaster and possibly to gobblings, too – but Stevie had a streak like Johnny's.

This small part of him wanted letting out of the tight place inside him in which it was imprisoned; it wanted to come out and play and perhaps never go back again.

What was happening over the fence *was* way too strange.

'I wish you'd just push me,' the kid on the swing said, to the air above and beyond him. 'I *like* it when you push me!' he added, tailing off with a chiming laugh.

'Watch this, Wolfie!' Johnny whispered.

Stevie watched, wanting to run but wanting to stay even more. Duke pulled tight on the lead and began to growl.

His heart in his mouth, Stevie put his face to the gap in the fence. He was surprised – and a little disappointed – to find that nothing unusual was happening in that untidy back garden. No six-foot-plus spook was pushing the kid hard in the back; the boy was merely working at the swing. He leaned back, his feet outstretched, then leaned forward, his legs tucked beneath the seat, then repeated the process. The swing slowly began to move.

'What's so good about *that*?' Stevie asked.

'Nothing,' Johnny replied. 'Be patient for a minute, Dogboy.'

Within thirty seconds the swing was making an arc of about three feet in either direction. The metal chains clinked as they moved and the hinges on the top bar squeaked as the swing reached the top of its arc and went backwards. The boy grunted as he put all his effort into making it go higher.

'If he put a drop of oil or grease or something on those pivot pins, he'd find it'd work better,' Stevie observed, suddenly understanding that he wasn't going to see anything weird happen at all. In a flash of inspiration, he suddenly knew why they could hear the kid and the kid couldn't hear them. He was deaf.

Stevie felt cheated. He moved away from the fence and said, 'Fuck this, JK, I'm going home. I'm not even supposed to be out and if my dad finds out—'

'Wait!' Johnny implored. 'Watch!'

Stevie sighed and decided to humour his friend for a little while longer. He put his face to the gap again. The kid was swinging about six inches higher than he had been before, which was hardly a significant improvement and certainly no miracle.

It wasn't until the swing had gone back and forth a couple more times that Stevie realized something odd *was* happening. The kid wasn't vanishing, as Johnny had promised, but it *did* look as if the laws of physics were being broken.

The pivots at the top of the swing's chains were stiff, if not rusty. The kid had stopped working and was now enjoying the ride, sitting back holding the chains, his legs straight out in front of him. This meant, as Newton would have been happy to explain, that each arc the swing made should have been smaller than the last. Gravity would see to that. The swing *had* to be slowing down.

But it wasn't.

'This is where it gets really weird,' Johnny whispered, in an awed voice. 'Watch his feet.'

Stevie watched. The boy and the swing began to increase the length of the arc, accompanied by a loud *swoosh!* sound like the one the blade had made in the film *The Pit and the Pendulum.*

A while back, Stevie's mum had sat him down and warned him of the dangers of drugs. Ecstasy, she told him, could kill you first time out. Marijuana was thought by some to be even more carcinogenic than tobacco and most hallucinogenics could bend your mind so far and so quickly that there was a possibility you'd never untwist yourself. Stevie and Johnny had once smoked fifteen quid's worth of Black Lebanese in one clumsily rolled five-string joint and nothing had happened to Stevie. Now he decided that he was finally getting high, three months after the event. All this looked normal, but it couldn't be real.

Now something was happening to the boy's feet at the top of each upswing. He was wearing black canvas bumper boots – the kind with the white soles and little white rubber circle where your ankle bone stuck out. The white toe-caps were vanishing when the boy's feet were at their highest point. They reappeared so quickly that it was difficult to convince yourself they'd actually gone at all – until they reached the top of the next arc. What was even more peculiar was that each time the kid's feet hit the high spot, a little more of them disappeared.

'Too fuckin' weird, Mister Man!' Johnny cried, in a voice that was a mixture of fear and excitement. This was the first time Stevie had ever heard Johnny sound like a sheep bleating, so he guessed his friend felt much the same way about this as he did.

We're seeing the impossible happen! Stevie thought. *We're watching a miracle!*

'Harder!' the kid suddenly squeaked. He was now vanishing up to the top lace-holes of his bumper boots each time he swung forward.

'Where do you think he's going then, Dogboy?' Johnny asked, in that half-strangled voice.

'I dunno,' Stevie replied. His voice had taken on the same nanny-goat quality as Johnny's.

The kid's feet were getting wet when they were in what Stevie was coming to think of as the *other side*. They came back glistening with big jewels of moisture that flicked off, sparkling in the sunlight, as he passed the nadir of his arc. And now he was entering that place up to his knees. On the downstroke, as he fell back from the *other side* his bare legs looked wet and shiny. Stevie fancied he could see a trail of vapour left behind as the moisture steamed off the kid's legs – and whatever the wet stuff was, it was all gone by the time the kid reached the top of his back-swing and began the return trip.

The invisible someone was pushing a little harder each time: it was evident in the way the kid's legs buckled a little, then straightened, and the way the swing wobbled.

He was swinging still higher and vanishing up to his chest now. And Stevie really could see the vapour trail he left behind him as he came out.

'I want a go!' Johnny yelled.

Stevie nodded inwardly, totally unsurprised. This was Johnny's bright idea.

Two swings later, the boy entered the *other side* all the way up to his neck – and paused for a moment in that position, as if the following push was taking a while to happen.

The swing's chains reached out at an angle of sixty degrees or so then simply stopped *being*. Two feet below them, the boy's head hung back, almost inverted, a big cheery grin on his face. Each time he paused, it took a little longer for him to return.

A picture formed in Stevie's mind of what might be going on in that invisible realm. The someone wasn't a human at all, but a kind of humanoid insect with a taste for little boys. In Stevie's mind that thing was feeling the kid up with super-cold feelers, exploring his legs with a long, moth-like proboscis that unrolled from its human mouth and tasted his flesh.

The kid exited the *other side* fast. His shirt flapped and cracked in the wind and the vapour trail was as thick as smoke. The force with which he'd been pushed sent the swing's seat up as high as the crossbar so his upper body was above it. An expression of glee was glazed on to his face.

'Shit!' Johnny whispered.

The swing seemed to hold its position out over the crossbar for an impossibly long time and as Stevie watched he saw the kid's hands slip a couple of inches down the chain.

Then the swing was arcing downwards again – too fast to have been moving under gravity. Either the invisible basketball player had moved round to the back of the swing and given the kid a good hard push, or he was somehow sucking it back.

The swing tore down towards the ground like a jet-fighter with its afterburners on. As it hit the lowest point of its arc, the kid's hands peeled away from the chain, his body bowed backwards and his head missed the compacted soil by inches as the swing rose. One moment he was there, the next he was upside down, travelling vertically, and the moment after that he was gone.

'That's what happened last time,' Johnny said, sounding supremely impressed.

Stevie gazed into the garden, his mind reeling dizzily. The swing's chains were taut and stationary and reached out at an angle of almost ninety degrees to the vertical. Into nothingness. 'Jesus,' he said. It was the only word left in his vocabulary. He closed his eyes, certain that when he opened them, things would have magically rearranged themselves so that the kid was sitting on the swing again, talking to his imaginary friend. But when he looked nothing had changed.

Stevie took his face away from the fence, the faint scent of old creosote in his nostrils. A track from one of his dad's ancient albums began to play in his mind: 'Motherless Children' by someone Miller. Duke sat at his feet, his big pink tongue lolling. Johnny stood still peering through his knot-hole, his fingers splayed against the smooth boards. The entire world seemed oblivious to the travesty that was being done to physics on the far side of the fence. Johnny turned, his stance casual. 'Kinda scares you the first time you see it, doesn't it?' He grinned.

Stevie opened his mouth to say something and found he had nothing to say. He nodded instead.

Duke moaned.

'I think something calming is called for before we do anything else,' Johnny said. He pulled a pack of Marlboro from his pocket, flipped open the lid, planted a cigarette in his mouth and threw the pack across to Stevie.

They were both still close to the fence. And as far as Stevie could tell the pack was moving too slowly. He reached up and took it as it cartwheeled through the air, extracted a cigarette and tossed it back. While it was in the air, Johnny had time to take a Swan Vesta from the yellow box he now had in his hand, draw its red tip across the fence to light it, apply it to the end of his cigarette and shake it out. He threw the matches to Stevie, then reached up and plucked the pack of Marlboro from its arc.

Stevie's hands were now trembling so much that he had a lot of difficulty taking a match from the box.

'So, whaddya think, Mr Wolfgang Dogboy?' Johnny asked, exhaling smoke that looked too thick and heavy to be from a cigarette.

Stevie thought he needed to suck hard on his cigarette and get a big hit of nicotine before he turned his attention to anything else. The Marlboro would make him feel ill, he knew, but he needed *something* to steady his nerves.

He managed a little grin. 'I think I've been slipped something . . .' he said.

'Now think about slipping something else,' Johnny said, grinning. 'Like over this fence for instance. We're going in.'

'What if the kid's mother comes out?' Stevie asked.

'She won't,' Johnny said. 'If you look up the garden behind the house you'll see why she won't. There's enough empty bottles of Johnny Walker Export to fill a bottle bank. And it's my guess that Mummy's the one who's emptying them. I could be wrong though. I *was* wrong. Once.'

'And if she does?' Stevie asked.

'We'll say kiddo over there asked us in,' Johnny replied, nodding towards the garden.

'But kiddo *isn't* over there,' Stevie observed, sucking on the Marlboro and hating himself for feeling better rather than worse as each fresh whack of nicotine hit his bloodstream. If he wasn't careful he was going to end up like his dad – a walking incinerator who couldn't get through a shower without poking out his head for a top-up.

Johnny grinned, that odd expression on his face once more. 'C'mon!' he urged, and flicked away his half-smoked cigarette. Before Stevie could say a word, Johnny was scrambling over the fence.

Stevie glanced at Duke, then looked round for something to tie his lead to. Then he had a better idea: he put the dog's muzzle back on and forced the handle of the extending lead through a narrow gap in the fence. Once it lay flat on the ground, Duke wouldn't be able to pull it back.

'Three fuckin' weird,' he heard Johnny exclaim, and began to scale the fence.

Stevie's ears popped as he dropped down into the overgrown back garden. It was like being in an aeroplane that was descending rapidly – except this happened all at once and consequently the effect was greater. It hurt.

He got up. The sounds he made as he moved seemed amplified and ragged, slightly distorted. Johnny was ten feet away from him, facing the other way. His fingers were in his ears, and he was waggling them crazily. He looked as if someone had slipped Superglue on to his forefingers and he was ony now discovering the dirty deed.

I was right, Stevie told himself. *The air pressure over here is phenomenal.* And the air itself seemed charged with static electricity. It felt prickly somehow.

'You look like one of those mime artists pretending to be stuck in a glass jar!' Johnny's voice rattled against Stevie's eardrums like a rain of rice.

'I feel like one, too,' Stevie replied. His voice sounded pretty much like Johnny's but it rattled the snare-wires on his eardrums even harder. It wasn't a pleasant sensation and Stevie wondered if he'd done himself some permanent damage. And his stomach was starting to complain about the nicotine. *I wanna throw up*, he thought.

Johnny chuckled. 'Looks like we've discovered something special,' he said.

'Now what?' Stevie asked, glancing down at the red handle of

Duke's lead. It was moving as if the dog was straining against it. He knelt down and peered through the gap at the outside world. Duke was busy cropping grass like a sheep and was pulling to get at a few strands that must have smelt like the right kind. Here was another candidate for the old upchuck manoeuvre.

'Whaddya think?' Johnny said, walking towards the swing.

I think I've been drugged, Stevie thought. *Either that or I've gone crazy, or I'm at home lying on my bed asleep. Or I've stepped into the kind of magic garden you read about in fairytales.* This was an enchanted place.

It could be dangerous, Stevie thought, as he followed his friend to the frame of the swing.

Johnny suddenly turned to him. 'Yeah, it could be *very* dangerous,' he agreed.

The A-frame of the swing was sheened with moisture. Stevie hesitantly reached out to it. This was definitely not the scientific approach – anyone with half an ounce of sense would have cut off their own hand before doing something this dumb. He knew this with the utmost clarity. But Stevie *wanted* to touch the swing, in perhaps the same way that mythical sailors had wanted to hear the song of the Siren. In an *enchanted* way.

Don't! Stevie told himself, and another voice, probably that of his mother, warned: *It's the first step on to a very slippery slope!*

Stevie thought, *Fuck it, who cares?* and watched his fingers approach the misted paint, realizing distantly that not only had his bellyache gone but that he felt pretty good.

The moisture was only just above freezing and began to steam off as he touched it. When he removed his fingers, a pleasant tingly sensation ran up his arm, across his left shoulder and down his spine. He shuddered, grinning.

'This is double fucking crazy, man,' Johnny said from beside him in a dismayed tone.

Stevie turned to look. Johnny was standing in the spot below where the swing's chain vanished into thin air about three feet above him.

'The kid's head ought to be *here*,' Johnny said, and reached up.

Stevie watched, fully expecting to see his friend's hand vanish just like the kid had but it just waved in the air above his head. From what Stevie could see, there *was* no other side for it to vanish into.

'You can't get there from here,' Stevie said, and failed to fight off the fit of giggles that followed.

'You wanna bet?' Johnny bleated. 'It might be higher up than I thought.' He jumped and sliced his fingertips through the air above him in a clawing motion, as if he anticipated a ledge he could grab hold of. His hand remained in view. Stevie giggled again, certain he was going mad.

Johnny stared at him, his expression so comically distraught that Stevie felt he would die of suffocation if he didn't soon stop laughing.

'This isn't *possible*,' Johnny complained. 'I don't believe it!'

'None of this is possible,' Stevie chortled. 'Why not admit it, then just enjoy it while it lasts? Whatever it is.'

'Because I've *got* to know where that kid is,' Johnny replied. 'And I'm gonna find out even if I have to stay here all day.'

'Then listen to the voice of reason,' Stevie said, suddenly understanding that the finding of the kid was the all-important thing. *If we knew where the kid was, we'd have the answer.* 'The half of this team that owns the brain cells has an excellent idea,' he continued. 'There's evidently only one way in. The way the swing's chains went in. It might have been different when the kid went in there, but he's not on *this* side at all at the moment. The only connection between there and here is the chains. If you want to get over there, or at least feel in there for the kid, you're gonna have to climb up the chains.'

Johnny had leapt up and grabbed the chains half-way through Stevie's speech. They didn't give so much as a millimetre as they took his weight. They may as well have been solid poles of cast iron with supports every six inches. He hung there for a few moments, grimacing, then dropped down again. Now he was shaking his hands hard.

'And I was going to add that the metalwork is *very* cold,' Stevie said, watching the steam rise from Johnny's hands.

'Thanks a bunch, Dogboy,' Johnny said. He stripped off his T-shirt, took out his famous bone-handled flick-knife and cut the sleeves off the shirt. Then he wrapped them around his hands like fingerless mittens.

'Why don't we just wait for the kid to come back?' Stevie wondered aloud.

'He's five years old,' Johnny bleated, 'or maybe six. So you really think he's gonna be able to tell us what's over there? We've gotta see for ourselves what it is. And you know what *I* reckon it is?'

'Another universe? Another planet? Ghosts?'

'The stuff that drives everything,' Johnny said. 'The stuff that holds everything together. The clockwork that runs reality. The power. Maybe . . .'

'Or maybe not,' Stevie said.

Johnny shrugged. He checked his makeshift gloves, adjusted them slightly, then leapt up again and grabbed the nearest chain. 'That's better,' he said, grinning. 'No pain, lots of gain.' He swung-turned himself to face back towards the frame and began to work his legs, swinging them back and forth until he could wrap his ankles around the chain. He hung upside down, head towards the ends of the chain and looked at Stevie. 'Wish me luck,' he said.

Stevie watched as his friend inched his way along the chain towards the point where it vanished into another realm.

'Heeeeeeeeeere goes Johnny!' Johnny called, as he approached the end of the chain.

Stevie crossed the first two fingers on both hands and held them up for Johnny to see, then watched as his friend put out a hand to grab the invisible part of the chain.

It did not exist.

If Johnny had had the slightest doubt that the hole in reality had closed up all the way round, including around the point at which the chains entered the *other side*, he might have been a little more prepared. But he wasn't the doubting kind. He reached, grasped nothing, unbalanced himself then tried to grab the same stretch of nothingness, but a little further along, with his other hand.

Stevie glanced at the ground where Johnny was going to fall. It was baked mud. Better than concrete, but not as good as grass.

Johnny's feet were crossed over the chain, the back of one ankle resting on top of the one against the chain. Had he locked his ankles and supported himself on his calves, he might have been in with a chance, but there was no way he could possibly recover from this one. He wasn't going to swing upside down from the chain and work himself back up, he wasn't going to hit the ground on his feet, he wasn't even going to fall well. What he *was* going to do was swing back until he was inverted, then fall like a pile-driver, head first to the hard ground.

Stevie watched it all happen in slow motion.

What saved Johnny from serious injury was a primary, unconscious instinct for self-preservation: he put out his hands in front of him to save his face. When he hit, his elbows buckled, cushioning the impact, and his body curled up. Johnny's knees and elbows slammed into the dirt, his forehead followed and he stayed exactly where he'd landed, in the posture of a Muslim at prayer. Dust puffed up around him.

For a few moments Stevie was sure that he was either dead or unconscious. Then the jelly-mould shape began a kind of coughing chuckle and looked up.

Johnny's face was filthy and his forehead was grazed. Tears were streaming down his face. 'I bagged by doze,' he said, feeling his nostrils with his fingertips, then inspecting his fingers for blood. He wiped the tears from his cheeks with the back of his hand, leaving two dirty smudges in their place. Moving like someone with arthritis in every joint, he slowly got to his feet.

'It didn't work,' Stevie said, not certain whether to laugh or cry in relief.

Johnny glanced up at the chain. It was still steaming. 'There's gotta be a way to get in,' he said thoughtfully. 'The kid's in there somewhere and he's got to be able to get back out again.'

Unless this time he's not coming back, Stevie thought. Suddenly he wanted to be away from here, enchanted garden or not. It all felt *wrong* now. 'Come on, Johnny, let's get out of here,' he said.

'You're joking, of course!' Johnny said, punctuating his sentence by spitting dust. 'We can't *go*! Not now. It's just getting interesting.'

Stevie's heart sank. 'So what next?' he asked.

'We wait,' Johnny said, going for his Marlboros and matches. 'The kid's gonna come back in a mo. When he does, maybe we'll catch a glimpse of what's on the other side. It's gotta open up to let the little bugger out again, hasn't it?' He lit his cigarette and handed the pack and the matches to Stevie.

'And the hole might stay open long enough to go through?' Stevie asked, feeling as though he'd finally cracked. Here he was, standing in the back garden of someone he didn't know, taking seriously Johnny's intention to leave this dimension for another one.

Johnny nodded. 'It might,' he said, and took a deep, thoughtful drag on his cigarette.

Stevie lit up, took a pull on his Marlboro and felt the stomach-ache re-awaken. He didn't care. His body needed some kind of narcotic in it and to hell with the consequences.

'What if the kid doesn't come back?' he asked.

Johnny shrugged. 'The swing will, though,' he said. 'It can't stay up there like that or we'd have a modern miracle on our hands. People don't see stuff like this. It doesn't happen. If the swing stays up there, the substance of the world will have been seen to change, and whoever or whatever runs it doesn't like that because it counts as proof. Trust me, the swing'll come back, even if the kid ain't on it.'

'I wanna go home,' Stevie said, sucking on the cigarette again.

Even the smoke was different on this side of the fence: it was like inhaling talcum powder.

'So do I.' Johnny grinned. 'I'm scared shitless. But I've gotta see. And so have you. You know that, don't you?'

Stevie nodded. This was the main thing that was making him feel uncomfortable: the sense that there was a *purpose* behind all this. 'You know what'll happen if the swing comes back without the kid and we're found in here, don't you?' he asked.

Johnny nodded. 'Yup. They'll think we've done for the kid and we won't be able to prove we haven't. Every silver lining has a black cloud around it,' he said, smiling.

'Let's get the fuck out of here. At least back to the other side of the fence,' Stevie implored. The anxiety in the pit of his stomach was building. He just wanted to leave – and leave now. *While we still have a chance.*

Johnny thought about it. Then he nodded. 'You're right as usual, Dogboy,' he said. He squeezed Stevie's shoulder and nodded at the fence. 'The Dukester's probably lonely over there anyway,' he said. 'And I can't stand this bloody buzzing in my ears much longer. Every sound *hurts*. C'mon, let's go!'

They had taken two steps towards the fence when, from behind them, the swing's chains made an odd noise. Both boys turned back to see what was happening. The chains were wobbling slightly, as if whatever had hold on the *other side* was pulling hard.

It's trying to bust the chains, Stevie thought. *It's trying to pull the entire swing through.*

The chains twanged and vibrated.

Stevie grabbed Johnny's arm and pointed at the fence. 'Quick!' he shouted.

But before they could move, the air around the spot where the chains disappeared seemed to bulge and the swing shot out, steaming.

The kid was still on it, in the same position he'd been in when he'd vanished. He shrieked with laughter as the swing arced back with that deep *swoosh!* sound, leaving a graceful curve of vapour in its wake. It peaked just above the centre bar and when it began to fall again, the kid screamed, 'Yeeeeeeeeeeesssss!' in delight.

This time, the swing didn't disappear as it rose. The kid clung on tight and stayed still, chortling to himself, and when the arcs began to lessen, sat upright again. By the time the swing had slowed to a gentle back and forth movement, the vapour had gone and the damp sheen on the swing's frame had dried, leaving dull green paintwork showing.

To Stevie's relief, the air pressure dropped and the feeling of imminent electrocution vanished. He found he could hear perfectly again. On the far side of the fence, Duke gave a little, I'm-bored-with-this whine.

The boy on the swing suddenly noticed he wasn't alone. He stuck out the heels of his bumper boots and dug them into the hard ground, raising puffs of dust and slowing the swing. By the time it stopped, he'd made two little curved runnels in the ground. He peered over at Johnny and Stevie myopically, a frown creasing his forehead.

The kid's eyes must be in a terrible state, Stevie thought. He and Johnny were less than ten feet away.

'I can't see you very well,' the boy announced, in a high, clear voice. 'I left my glasses indoors. Come closer.'

Stevie glanced at Johnny, who began to walk over to the boy. He took a deep breath, sighed and followed.

'Hello,' the boy said, smiling. 'My name's Nigel.'

Johnny said, 'Hi, Nigel, pleased to meet you!' and stuck out his hand. The kid took it and gave it a shake.

Close up, Nigel looked to Stevie as if he was going to turn out to be the world's most precocious child. He spoke with a clipped, upper-class accent and managed to sound about fifty. But he hadn't sounded a bit like this when he'd been talking to his invisible playmate. About ten minutes ago he'd sounded just like an ordinary kid. Stevie stored this one away with all the other things he was going to have to consider later.

'I'm Jimmy,' Johnny told Nigel, 'and this is David.'

Nigel put out his hand for David to shake. Stevie shook it. The false names were only used when either of them thought it a good idea to keep their identities secret. That usually meant mischief was about to follow.

Johnny crouched down in front of the kid, trying not to appear threatening, Stevie thought. He did likewise.

'What're the chances of a go on your swing?' Johnny asked, getting to the point straight away, just as Stevie had known he would.

'Certainly,' Nigel said, making no move to get up. 'Do you want to be my friends? I'm very lonely all on my own.'

'Except you're *not* all on your own, are you?' Johnny smiled.

The kid looked bemused. Or, at least, did a good impression. 'I'm sure I don't know what you mean,' he said.

'Your friend,' Johnny said. 'The person you were talking to just now.'

The boy smiled, secretively.

'What's his name?' Stevie asked. 'I used to have an imaginary friend called Manaymon. When I was a kid.'

'He's going to make me see more better,' the boy said, talking like a child of his own age again.

'So, what's his name?' Stevie asked again, and shivered. Something was still going on here. It hadn't finished when the kid had returned and the air pressure had gone back to normal.

'I c'n see better than I could see once,' the kid chirped. 'He did that for me already.'

Stevie frowned. The boy's voice was losing its posh tone, too.

'My mummy says I was nearly blind,' the boy continued. 'But I'm making a ...' he squinted, searching his memory, '... markable provemunt. I'll see just like everyone else, soon,' he said.

Johnny nodded. 'And it's your invisible buddy who's doing the biz, right?'

Nigel glanced around the garden furtively. 'It's 'posed to be a secret,' he said quietly. 'I'm not s'posed to tell. If I do, *he* won't make me see proper.'

'Are you sure it's not the doctors at the hospital who're making you see better?' Stevie asked.

Nigel shook his head. 'Them doctors are worse than useless,' he said, apparently quoting an oft-repeated phrase. 'My mummy says so. They told her off. I *heard* them. They said about her bottle, that it's naughty. She shouted at them doctors. They said I'd be blinded and it's her bottle's fault. From when I was in her tummy. Them doctors said she drinked too much, but you got to drink or else you die, haven't you? And my mummy says that her bottle is her only friend 'cept me.'

'Hey, big guy,' Johnny said, 'if you're s'posed to be keeping it a secret, haven't you kind of screwed it up already? After all, you've already told us.'

The kid shrugged. '*He* said it doesn't matter because you aren't growed up proper yet.'

'This'd be your pal, right?' Johnny said. 'The invisible one who pushes you on the swing.'

Nigel smiled and nodded.

Stevie didn't much like the look of that expression. It was secretive and knowing and somehow *malicious*. He told himself that he was seeing things that weren't there, but that didn't stop the hairs at the back of his neck prickling up.

'What's his name, this friend of yours?' Johnny asked.

Nigel screwed up his face. 'He whose name shall not be spoken,' he said, nodding with each word as if reciting a piece of poetry he wasn't certain he'd properly committed to memory. 'Jaweh.'

'Yah who?' Johnny said, smiling.

'I think he's trying to tell us it's God,' Stevie said. 'It's pronounced Yavay. It's the tetragrammaton. The Hebrew for God. I had to look it up for an essay I was doing.'

Johnny looked delighted. 'So what's he look like?' he asked. 'Can I see him too?'

'I think you have to be innocent,' Nigel said.

'Kinda counts me out.' Johnny grinned. 'But I bet he'd make an exception just this once, seeing as we're your friends and everything. So what's on the other side – the place where you go when he pushes you? Is it heaven or something?'

'*He*'s there,' Nigel said. 'He talks to me.'

'God talks to you,' Johnny said, nodding. 'Right. So . . . what's he got to say for himself?'

'And what does he look like?' Stevie added.

'He's *fun*!' the kid said. 'He tickles me. On the inside. He shows me things, too.'

'What's he look like, though?' Stevie insisted, remembering that only about twenty minutes ago 'God' had asked Nigel if he'd like to be a bad boy twenty-four hours a day.

Nigel peered at him. 'He looks like *God*,' he said.

It's a fantasy, that's all, Stevie told himself. *The kid's mother is probably a drunk because she's a failed religious fanatic who thinks she's headed for hell. That's how he'd know about Jaweh. He can't tell us about where he goes, so he probably doesn't go anywhere.*

Of course, this didn't answer the question of what had happened here. If it was a hallucination, then how come Johnny was bruised and dirty? Stevie didn't know. All he wanted was to get as far away from here as possible and let his head settle.

'What's it look like over there?' Johnny said, pointing at the spot in the air where the kid had disappeared. His eyes were gleaming.

'It's nice,' Nigel replied.

It isn't because he can't articulate what he's seen, it's because he has no idea, Stevie told himself. *Johnny and I have shared a hallucination and the kid thinks we're nuts and is humouring us.*

This didn't fit either, but it felt a good deal more comfortable than the alternative.

Which is . . .

Stevie killed the thought. It was stupid even to *consider* that a half-blind boy called Nigel had found a gateway from earth to heaven and that God was curing his eyesight for him. It couldn't be God, anyway, because God would have zapped his eyes better in one go. And God wouldn't ask little boys if they'd like to go somewhere they could be bad all the time.

You're frightened! a small voice told him.

Yes, I am, he immediately answered. *Who wouldn't be? I've seen something impossible happen.*

But the fear isn't because you've seen something impossible, is it? the inner voice continued. *You're frightened of something else. Of what you're feeling inside. You're frightened of wanting to be a part of all this. Of wanting to belong, just like Johnny does. Why don't you relax and let yourself have fun for a change? Why not follow Johnny's lead?*

'OK, so if I sit on your swing, do you think Yah-hoo will give *me* a push?' Johnny asked.

'He might,' Nigel said, got up and came towards them. 'You can have a go,' he said.

Johnny looked at Stevie. The having-a-good-idea expression was still on his face, but now there was a sick-looking pallor under it. Johnny was frightened, too. 'Whaddya think, Dogboy?' he asked. 'Should I? Will it be dangerous, do you suppose?'

Stevie knew that if he showed even the slightest hint of concern, his friend would do it right away. He gave his best who-knows?-who-cares? shrug and said, 'I can't see it being dangerous because whatever was happening before has stopped and I don't think it's gonna start again. Try it if you like but I think we're wasting our time now.'

Johnny grabbed Stevie's shoulders and gave them a squeeze. 'Good try, Wolfie Dogboy, but you're gonna have to do a little more work on the old poker-face to be convincing. Here goes. Wish me luck!'

He scooted over to the swing and made a pantomime of touching various bits of it experimentally then leaping away as if he'd had an electric shock. Stevie acted bored, but his heart was hammering and he was already concocting a cover story to tell the cops and his and Johnny's parents when his friend vanished and didn't come back.

Eventually Johnny sat down on the swing, grinning back at Stevie.

'You can have a go, too,' Nigel said, from beside him.

Stevie glanced down at the kid, who was regarding him with eyes of such a pale blue they looked as though they'd been bleached. 'I think you'd enjoy it,' Nigel added, in that odd, clipped, grown-up's tone.

For a moment Stevie was convinced that Nigel hadn't said those words himself; that something was using him as a communication channel. But the kid's lips didn't move out of synch and this time there was no sly expression on his face. He looked like an ordinary kid who couldn't see very well. Somehow, that made it worse. Stevie shivered again and wished this particular day in his life was behind him.

'Nothing's happening,' Johnny said, his tone slightly surprised. Then he looked up and said, 'How about a push, Yah-hoo?'

He turned to Stevie and Nigel, pulling a stupid face, and leaned off the swing in their direction. 'Old Yah's gone shopping,' he said, in a tone that sounded like relief, and his face lit with a big sunny grin.

Beside Stevie, Nigel made the sound of disapproval that was apparently spelt *tsk! God won't mind, though*, he said to himself.

I expect he's used to people taking his name in vain by now, Stevie added, feeling his skin crawl on his back as the prickly electrical sensation began to fill the air once more. Disaster was being courted here, Providence was being tempted and challenges were being issued. If he'd been able to find his voice, he would have told Johnny to stop wasting his time. But his voice had quit on him. As had his ability to turn away.

Here it comes! he told himself, quite certain Johnny was going to be zapped by lightning.

'Come back, Yah-hoo, all is forgiven!' Johnny tempted.

When nothing happened, he looked over at Stevie and rolled his eyes.

The frame of the swing shook violently. For a moment, the ground beneath Stevie's feet seemed to have liquefied and he staggered sideways, trying to keep his balance.

Johnny was off the swing and running for the fence in an instant.

Then the tremor stopped. Johnny turned back, looking sheepish. 'Earthquake,' he said. 'A tremor, at least. Even here in northern Europe we get the odd tremor.'

Stevie nodded. It was all he could do.

'Thank fuck!' Johnny said. 'I thought old Yah-hoo had come for me!'

'Let's go,' Stevie said, noticing that weird electrical sensation had gone again. He refrained from adding *while there's still time.*

'In a mo,' Johnny said, went back to the swing and sat on it.

'You there, Yah?' he asked the spot in the air. ''Cause if you are, your friend Johnny Kane wants to come visit for a while. Deal?'

Nothing happened.

Whatever was going on had ceased. Stevie was sure of it now. His skin had stopped crawling, his back had stopped tingling and whatever it had been was all over.

Johnny frowned, pulled a face then evidently realized that he had to start the ball rolling by swinging. He pushed back and began to work, pulling hard and lying back as he swept forward and bending forward as far as he could on the return arc.

The swing's pivots complained and the chains rattled with the effort Johnny expended. It took him less than thirty seconds to work the swing up as high as the kid had been. In another few seconds he was going up above the centre bar at the peak of each arc.

'Push meeeeee!' he yelled, and leaned back like the kid had.

Holding that position, Johnny slipped in and out of the airspace into which Nigel had disappeared with no effect whatsoever.

'It's over!' Stevie called. 'Let's get outta here!'

'No way!' Johnny yelled back. 'It's cold at the top! I think the gate's going to open again. PUSH ME!'

The arc of the swing began to lessen now that Johnny had quit working. He was wasting his time as far as Stevie was concerned. Whatever had been happening had quit after the brief earthquake, or whatever it was. *It was probably God slamming the door shut when he stomped off*, Stevie thought.

'Your friend might have drived God away,' Nigel said, in his own voice. 'He might not have liked what he said. His name mustn't be spoke.'

'Never mind, eh?' Stevie said, with a grim satisfaction.

'Nothing!' Johnny yelled. And the next time he reached the top of the swing's arc, he jumped off.

As he dropped, feet first, through the area in which Nigel had been captive, he seemed to ripple slightly as if you were looking at him through water or a heat-haze. He landed on his feet, crouched against the shock, straightened up and walked back to the others, looking a little disappointed.

'Old Yah-hoo isn't much of a God, is he?' he said to the kid.

Nigel stared at his feet. 'Him's making my eyes better, so *there*!' he mumbled.

'Good for you, kid,' Johnny said. 'I hope he comes back to finish off the job. I just don't think he wants to play with the big boys. Thanks for letting me try though. And next time you speak to old Yah, you give him my regards. Tell him I'm looking forward to meeting him.' He tousled Nigel's hair and grinned at Stevie. 'Come on, let's get out of here,' he said.

'He told me he wanted you,' Nigel said to Johnny.

'Jesus wants you,' Stevie said, feeling better now that his friend had finished courting disaster.

'Well, he'll just have to get to the back of the line, won't he?' Johnny said.

'He wants *you*, too,' Nigel told Stevie. 'For a sunbeam.'

'He told you that, did he?' Stevie asked, feeling unsettled again.

Nigel nodded solemnly.

'It's cool, kid. We'll stop by again. Maybe,' Johnny said kindly.

It was a brief aberration, Stevie told himself. *Something's weird about the kid. He's not just short-sighted, he's got mental trouble, too. He's suffering from delusions and we caught 'em for a few minutes, that's all that happened. Everything's gone back to normal now, hasn't it?*

Stevie paused for a quick reality check. Everything had, indeed, gone back to normal. The air pressure felt right, birds were singing, the sky was blue, there was no shimmering patch where the kid had vanished and the swing wasn't misted. Reality had stabilized and this time it looked like it was planning to stay that way.

Stevie relaxed.

And on the far side of the fence Duke went ballistic.

The red handle of the dog lead that lay on the ground between the fence panels suddenly jumped as the slack was taken up. The dog's bark had become one continuous snarling howl. It wasn't a cat on the far side of the fence, but something that Duke thought demanded his best.

Stevie raced towards the fence, leapt at it and slammed into it, catching hold of the top with the tips of his fingers. Under normal circumstances he could have pulled himself up and been down on the other side in five seconds. But the fence was old, and when Stevie hit it his knee broke a panel and the split wood snagged his jeans. He struggled but he was stuck.

'Don't panic!' Johnny shouted from behind him. 'The Dukester's got his snout-guard on. He can't bite anyone!'

On the far side of the fence, Duke screamed. He'd borne a lot of hardship and pain during his relatively short life and he wasn't a yelping dog. A scream from this dog meant that he'd been *hurt*. Someone was attacking him.

'*Quick!*' Stevie shouted, meaning that Johnny should get his arse over the fence pronto and see what the trouble was. Johnny misunderstood and hurriedly tried to part the two halves of the fence panel which had nipped Stevie's jeans.

Slightly to the left of where Stevie was suspended, Duke whacked into the lower part of the panels with enough force to crack them. Splinters of wood flew into the garden. The dog gave a little yelp of surprise and pain.

'For fuck's sake, *hurry up*!' Stevie shouted to his friend above the fresh torrent of barking from the far side of the fence. 'Something's attacking him!'

The handle of the lead leapt as the dog charged at his tormentor. This time the panels broke and the handle vanished. Stevie heard Duke hammer away down the path, wailing like a banshee.

'Can't get this fucking fence to let go!' Johnny grunted. 'Wait, Stevie!' Stevie looked down as Johnny backed off and took a flying leap at the fence. He crashed into it and fell on his back in the dust.

But the panel to which Stevie was attacked broke, freeing him.

A little way away, Duke could be heard putting up the fight of his life. Whoever or whatever he was fighting wasn't making a sound.

It doesn't have to, Stevie thought as he scrambled to the top of the fence, *it's a one-sided battle. Dookie can't defend himself because he's wearing his muzzle. All he can do is snout-butt whatever it is.*

He leapt over the fence and landed on his feet. He glanced at the grass and froze. *Grass,* he told himself slowly, *is traditionally green.*

This grass, however, looked as if someone had just dropped a gallon can of red paint on it.

Blood! Stevie's mind informed him coolly. *You're looking at Dookie's blood.*

And yet the dog was still alive. Armageddon was taking place down in the little park.

A second later Johnny landed beside him. 'Jesus on roller-skates, Dogboy, what happened?' he gasped.

The trail of blood didn't just cover this area, it ran all the way down the alley.

'Gallons!' Johnny said. 'It *is* blood, isn't it?' he asked, jogging alongside Stevie.

But Stevie wasn't listening. He'd spotted something he recognized, and bent to scoop it up as he passed.

It was the Dukester's muzzle.

It was soaked with blood.

Around the corner came a single high-pitched *yap!* and the sound of growling and whining suddenly ceased. Stevie stopped running, his heart sinking. He could feel the blood running out of his face, feel himself starting to shake. A pair of words lit up in his mind: TOO LATE.

'Oh, *fuck*!' Johnny said, taking Stevie's arm. 'I'm sorry, man.'

Stevie drew in a breath of air that seemed too thick. The reek of fresh blood filled his nose. He gazed at the muzzle. *Why didn't you just run away, you dumb dog?*

Suddenly he saw that the muzzle wasn't off because the clasp had come undone. It was still fastened securely. It was off because the tube that held the dog's mouth shut had been torn down one side. And the nylon didn't look as if it had been severed by a knife. It looked as if it had been *burned* apart – by a surgical laser or a thin, hot point of flame. The material wasn't ragged and fraying, but sealed with heat. There were little blobs of melted nylon down each edge of the split.

What did this? Stevie asked himself, and suddenly remembered the thin burns down Duke's forelegs.

He began to run.

The thing that waited for Stevie and Johnny when they shot round the corner into the little park didn't look so much like a medium-sized black dog as it did a dead red blob.

In the centre of the largest pool of blood Stevie had ever seen the Dukester lay still, his head between his paws.

'He's dead,' Stevie said, and stopped. Tears stung his eyes.

'He's breathing,' Johnny said. 'Look!'

Stevie took two steps closer to the edge of the pool of blood and watched carefully. His dog didn't appear to be moving so much as an eyelid, let alone breathing.

'Who the fuck did this?' Johnny asked, looking up and down the empty playing field.

'I dunno,' Stevie heard himself reply, but that was a lie. He *did* know, and it wasn't so much a matter of *who* as of *what*. It was a gobbling. He was convinced that this was the truth. Tears were spilling down his face now, but inside he felt dry, empty and detached.

'It's less than twenty seconds since he stopped fighting,' Johnny said. 'If there was someone here, we should still be able to see them. Unless . . .' He tilted his head towards the nearest clump of neatly clipped bushes, put his forefinger over his lips and began to sidle away.

Stevie turned back towards the dog. Johnny wasn't going to find anyone hiding behind the bushes. The gobbling had probably lifted the end of the rubberized surface in the play area and slipped back to wherever it had come from.

Except that it couldn't possibly have been one gobbling that had done this. The thing Stevie had caught a glimpse of had been rat-sized. One thing that size couldn't possibly bleed so much blood. It must have gone home and come back mob-handed.

He strode over to Duke, not noticing the thick sticky noise his British Knights made in the congealing blood.

He squatted down beside him and put a hand on his head.

Duke's eyes opened.

Stevie jumped back in surprise, sat down in the blood and slid backwards a few inches. For a few seconds he wasn't certain whether the dog's eyes had opened at all or whether he'd imagined it.

'Dookie?' he whispered.

The dog looked up again, his ears back and his famous I-know-I've-been-bad-but-it's-this-demon-inside-me-makes-me-do-it expression on his blood-soaked face. He whined and pawed the ground in front of him, indicating that he needed a little human comfort right now, if Stevie didn't mind.

Stevie slid over to him, wrapped his arms around the dog's sticky neck, pressed his cheek to the Duke's and held him, trying to stop the tears of relief from falling.

'What's this?' Johnny asked, prodding something black with the toe of his trainer. 'Looks like a burst balloon to me.'

And that was exactly what it looked like to Stevie, too. He got up and walked over, horribly aware of the heavy dampness that clung to his clothes and skin.

He glanced back at Duke, who was either too tired or too badly hurt to get up. There was no way of telling what injuries he had without washing him down, and Stevie had already decided to carry him home, but first he wanted to see that black balloon. He had a pretty good idea of what it had once been.

He squatted beside it and picked it up. It wasn't a burst balloon – it was too heavy. It was thick and leathery and shapeless and on one side it felt slightly prickly, as if it was either coated with tiny cactus-like spines or charged with electricity that was shorting to earth through his fingers.

He held it in both hands and pulled it. It stretched easily and for quite a distance. 'It's the skin off the thing that was fighting Dookie,' he said.

Johnny frowned. 'Thing? What thing?'

'The gobbling,' Stevie said wearily. 'Size of rat, quick on its feet, climbs up kids' legs and hates dogs. Oh, and it holds about twenty gallons of blood, too, apparently.'

Johnny looked at him, his head cocked, his mouth hanging open. He took a breath, started to say something, then stopped again and shook his head. 'Tell me about it later,' he said. 'I feel as if I've just woken up from the most effective nightmare I've ever had.'

Stevie nodded. He knew pretty much how Johnny felt. He looked at the prickly skin again, then stuck it in the pocket of his jeans.

'We'd better get the Dukester home and check him out,' he said. 'I don't think he's badly hurt, just exhausted. I checked his legs and stuff and nothing seems to be broken, but there's no way of telling what else is wrong without cleaning him up a bit first. Just keep your fingers crossed that my dad isn't home yet. This is going to take some explaining and I don't have any answers.'

He turned back to the huge pool of darkening blood where Duke lay, panting now, blood dripping from his tongue. Stevie hoped it was from the gobbling and not from internal bleeding. 'C'mon, boy!' he called. 'We gotta go!'

The dog raised his head from the ground. It looked like it took a lot of doing. He made getting-up movements that came to nothing and then tried to drag himself towards Stevie on his belly. He looked pathetic and beaten and Stevie felt his heart wrench a little more.

He went over to Duke, stroked his sticky head, then carefully picked him up, holding him like an oversized baby. The dog moaned a little, but offered no resistance, just lay in the cradle of Stevie's arms, his nose tucked under his master's chin.

'Come on, JK,' Stevie said. 'He's too heavy to hold like this for long and I don't want to drop him.'

He turned and followed the track of blood back up the alley.

Chapter Four

Becky in Therapy

'When I was seven I discovered sexual fantasy,' Becky said, glancing round at Dr Williams, who sat at the head of the leather recliner just outside her line of vision. She was still a little surprised that in this day and age trick cyclists used the old leather couch and, even after six weeks of being here twice a week, she still hadn't got used to talking to someone without having eye contact.

'Carry on,' Williams said, glancing up from his notepad and looking at her over the top of what Becky called his sawn-off specs.

Gareth E. Williams was good, she'd give him that much. He might have been Welsh and his middle name might have been Entwhistle but the guy was good. In six weeks he hadn't called her a liar, become upset with her, talked down to her or become embarrassed.

But she had high hopes. Like psychoanalysts the world over, Williams would think sex was at the root of everything and Becky planned to give him a treat. She couldn't believe that it had taken twelve sessions to get from birth to the age of seven. She wasn't just surprised at how much of her early life she'd managed to recall, she was gobsmacked. When she'd first arrived here as a 'difficult child' who had 'problems' she'd had little memory of the first half of her life and it was strange and exciting how the simple act of talking had brought it all back.

She didn't tell Williams this, though, and she didn't tell him any of the things she remembered – at least, not as she remembered them. She'd embroidered some facts, erased others, invented more. She didn't know whether Williams knew this, of course, but she was certain he had suspicions because on occasion he cross-checked, referencing a lie she'd told him weeks ago.

But Becky knew that the prime requisite of a compulsive liar was an excellent memory. And, boy, did she have one of those! Her memory was what in the dictionary they called eidetic. Photographic. She had Total Recall. Now, since this therapy had begun, she could even remember the moment she had put the block on her earlier life; the moment she had sealed it all away.

'Becky?' Williams prompted, in that low, almost hypnotic voice of his.

'Oh, yeah, the sex thing,' Becky said. 'Well, I knew all about masturbation already,' she lied, 'at least I knew about the pleasure of clitoral stimulation.' Woollyams said nothing. 'I discovered masturbation at the age of five, in response to an itch. I liked it. Very much indeed.' Actually she'd first read about it in a copy of a teen magazine when she was ten and it had taken her three months to work up the courage to try it out.

'Then, at seven, I began to have these fantasies,' she continued. She had a good one prepared already. It involved her, in nothing but a nightdress and skates, and an ice-hockey team who turned up early for practice. She wasn't sure, though, whether a seven-year-old could have constructed such a fantasy and had a standby involving Prometheus, the mythical guy who was chained to a rock and had his liver pecked out daily by an eagle. She *had* heard that story at the age of seven and, for some reason, it struck her as intensely erotic. She went for this one.

'In my fantasy, Prometheus is chained down naked on a flat surface at the top of the mountain. He's young and kinda muscular and there's a big, livid scar across his belly where the eagle opens him up every day,' she said. 'And I'm standing there in front of him, drinking in his perfect body. Perfect but for the scar. He's lying there with his eyes closed, his body moist with dew and shining all golden in the early morning sun . . .'

Becky continued, half her mind on the picture that had lit up inside her head, and the other half remembering. She had sealed herself off at the age of six; put a big iron door across her memory of the early part of her life. Her mother had died. Her mother, whom she had loved more than anything or anyone else in the whole wide world. The woman who fed her, clothed her, wiped away her tears, tended her cuts and grazes, tucked her in at night had developed a brain tumour. One week her mother had a bad headache, the next she was in hospital having tests, the week after that they opened her up, peered inside, closed her again, and on the following week, Wednesday, 17 July, the angels came and put her out of her misery. That was bad enough, but . . .

'And I'm standing there, totally nude, legs spread, fucking myself with my fingers, really going for it . . .'

She glanced over at Williams, who was still writing. He looked a little flushed now. *Got you!* she thought.

'. . . and his eyes open. For a few moments he looks kinda

stunned. He's been expecting the eagle again and here's a girl coming her brains out in front of him, squeaking and moaning. I watch his cock get hard. He's huge and beautiful and I want him inside me . . .'

It was bad enough that her mother had died. But worse was to follow. Dad fell apart. Most people did when their spouse died, Becky knew: some took to the bottle (and her dad had done that, too, but not in the weeks after his darling was taken from him), some took to drugs and some to depression and let things slide. Not Derek. Her dad had taken to other things . . .

'And I'm kneeling down between his spread legs, his slick cock deep in my throat and he's making a kind of keening noise, a bit like a dog whining, and I'm still working on my clitoris with a thumb while my two middle fingers are inside me, fucking me still . . .'

The day-times were OK. Daddy was kind and loving, and he wanted to be strong for his daughter. Mostly he did an excellent job of it. He took over all the household chores without complaint and he knew how to scramble an egg and stuff a chicken. He never left her short of love or without clean and pressed clothes; he took her to school each day in his taxi and at four he'd return to pick her up and take her home again – or to a movie, or McDonald's or Pizza Hut. But the night-times . . .

'And now he's inside me, his rigid cock filling every last centimetre of me, stretching me so wide it feels like I'll split in two. It hurts, but it's a *good* hurt. The kind of feeling that rises up through you and you know that the top of your head's going to blow off when it hits . . .'

During the night-times, Derek would open up old books and read them while he chain-smoked Gitanes, filling the house with that Godawful stench. And then, when he thought his darling daughter was in bed asleep and dreaming sweet dreams, his mind began to warp and he did things.

'And I can feel his cock expanding, getting harder, pulsing,' Becky continued, quoting verbatim a passage she had read in one of the nudie magazines Johnny had found in the field beside the railway a month or so ago. The magazine's title was *Erotix* and the story was called 'Juice' by that well-known writer of erotic literature Dick H. Ardon. She'd thought the story hilarious when she'd first read it, but it seemed to have gained something in the retelling.

'And he's fucking me harder and harder,' Becky said, trying to fight off the picture of Stevie that kept popping into her mind. He was pulling a kind of mock shocked face, the way he had when she'd read the story aloud to him and it kept making her want to laugh. She wished he were here now, listening. He would have been proud of her.

'And I can tell that he's about to explode inside me,' Becky said, breathlessly, and paused as the picture of Stevie vanished and was replaced with one of her father, during one of his midnight weird sessions.

Becky's dad had not abused her. She knew that there was a good possibility Williams thought he *had*, but this was not the case. Her dad was a gentle man and a Gentleman. But back in those days, shortly before Becky had shut those big steel gates on it all, he had got strange in a major fashion.

During those midnight sessions, alone in the lounge with the lights turned down low, the television and the radio tuned to channels that gave only white noise, he had tried to bring back his wife from the dead.

And, a small voice whispered in the back of Becky's head, *I think if we examine that period a little more closely, we might discover that he very nearly succeeded.*

'Becky?' Williams prompted. 'You stopped.'

Becky thrust away the memory that was threatening to form in her mind. She didn't need to know about this right now.

'FUCKING BASTARD CUNTING SHITBAGS!' Becky shouted, at the top of her voice. That one was always good for a giggle. It wasn't an easy job pretending you had Tourette's Syndrome, it was a tough and dirty one. *But someone's gotta do it*, she thought smiling. She carried on with her erotic story as if the outburst had never happened.

'And my orgasm hits and my pelvic-floor muscles are clenching against that great hard cock, milking it and . . .' She swallowed. 'And my nails find the scar where the bird has pecked him open and digs in, hard, tearing the flesh, parting him in a lemon-shaped split. And now I've got either edge of the wound in my hands and I'm forcing him apart just as his cock is forcing me apart. And I can feel the skin tearing. He's giving me his blood. It's pulsing out around the wounds and down there, deep down inside him, I can see his liver, dark and shiny and new. I dip my head between my hands, put my lips against that organ and kiss it. And he bucks into me and as bursts of hot semen blast into me I take his soft liver between my teeth and tear it out of him.'

'Hmm,' Williams said.

'Is that a *normal* kind of sexual fantasy?' Becky asked.

The trouble with adults, Becky knew all too well, was that they wouldn't bloody well leave you alone. Her dad didn't really count as an adult, as far as she was concerned – he was simply Dad. And he was a good dad. He might have been a drunk, but he had never been a violent one and, these days, he seemed to be a happy one.

So what if he drinks? Who wouldn't? Becky thought, defensively.

'Tell me about your mother,' Williams said. 'We seem to be missing her out of this so far.'

Becky glanced at him again. He'd recovered well from the sexual-fantasy rubbish – although she was almost certain she'd managed to surprise him back there. The guy was good.

'My mother? She's still dead,' Becky said, and instantly wished she hadn't made this quip. Now that she'd said those words a memory she didn't want had come flowing back to her, like an icy flash-flood. The biggest part of her was now hearing those words spoken in the unsteady voice of her father at the end of one of those weird evenings.

'Tell me about her. Tell me what you remember of her. How you felt about her.'

Anti-social, they'd called Becky at school. Not to her face, of course. Teachers never told you *anything* to your face.

'She was my mother,' Becky said. 'I hated her guts. That's what children do.'

That one was a bit obvious, she warned herself. *You'll have to do better than that or he'll just start believing that you're simply saying the opposite of everything that's true.*

'Was she pretty?' he asked, presumably hitting her with the *jealousy* stick: her problems were rooted in her rivalry with her mother.

'She was gorgeous,' Becky said. This was true. She remembered her mother as a kind of goddess. 'She had lots of soft frizzy auburn hair. I used to bury my face in it. I can remember the softness of it and the smell of the shampoo she used. She had green eyes. Green and clear and kind.'

The school trouble had started because of Snidey Sindy Hallett. Every school year had one girl who looked like she'd turn out to be a supermodel or a movie star and Sindy Hallett was the one. The boys goggled at her, the girls sucked up to her, hoping for her cast-offs, Becky supposed, and she loved every minute of it. Sindy was already a legend in her own mind and acted like it. It made you want to throw up. Like everyone else, Sindy wouldn't leave Becky alone.

It was amazing what one little punch on the nose could do.

'Were you angry with your mother when she died and left you?' Williams asked.

Becky frowned, considering her answer. The fact was, she had been heartbroken. Anger didn't enter the equation. Why be angry with someone for something beyond their control? 'Yeah, I hated her when she was alive and I hated her even more for dying on me,' Becky replied.

'How do you feel about your looks?' Woolly said, throwing a swerve ball.

Is he wondering if I'm jealous of my mother? Becky asked herself and decided that the answer was yes.

'I'm not what they call classically good-looking,' Becky replied. There was no point in lying about *that* one. The evidence was there for all to see.

'Do you think there's anything wrong with the way you look?' he continued.

Becky shrugged. It was an interesting question and she didn't know the answer. She was just an average girl as far as she knew. Neither fat nor incredibly skinny, neither noticeably tall nor amazingly short, not exceptionally pretty but not gruesomely ugly, either.

'My lips are too thin,' she said, more for something to say than because she really thought it. 'I'm happy with my eyes and nose, but my lips are thin, I like my legs, but my feet are too big. Someone once told me I had a nice arse. He said he wanted to kiss it, then fuck it.'

It wasn't very inspired, she admitted to herself, but she couldn't get rid of that image of her dad, tears running down his face as he said, 'She's still dead!' in that anguished voice. What was the point of falling in love with anyone if it ended up like that?

'Hmm,' Williams said. 'What do you think of school?'

Becky wondered why he had abandoned his exploration of her in chronological order. There she was reliving her childhood, and suddenly he was hitting her with the big ones. Perhaps he'd known what she was up to all along and had suddenly tired of all the bullshit.

'FUCKING BASTARDING SHITHOUSES!' Becky cried, simply because she hadn't shouted for a while. According to Stevie, she was in danger of having to visit a mental hospital if she kept this up long enough. Well, fuck 'em! If they couldn't work out that all she wanted was to be left alone, let the bastards put her away.

One little punch on the nose, and two little words (*fuck* and *off*) had started all this. Becky Sharp had become an outcast. Overnight she had become the world's greatest slut (*not bad going for a virgin*, she thought), had developed a long history of mental illness and had become dangerously psychotic. Oh, and she was head of the class at lying, too.

She wasn't bullied but there were the daily taunts, the graffiti chalked on the walls and pencilled up in the toilets. Things like: *Call Becky (4214171) for a blow-job*, or *Becky Sharp fucks dogs!* Normal everyday stuff like that. She'd been clumsily set up for theft, assault, blackmail, you name it. Nothing had stuck but, as the saying goes, there's no smoke without fire.

Eventually Becky had begun to play the part. It was easier to do than to resist. And once you started, you soon got lost. Christ, you *enjoyed* it. While it was happening, that was. You also found there was a downside. It was kind of lonely being a terror queen.

'I hate school because I'm useless at the work they give me,' Becky lied, and she remembered how lonely she'd been at the beginning.

It wasn't lonely any more, though, for two reasons. The first was that she'd never owned a dog and had always wanted one. The second was because of a chance meeting in an overgrown field on the opposite side of town to where she lived.

Becky couldn't remember what she'd been doing in that field but she thought she'd just been walking and minding her own business. Back then, she'd done a lot of walking. It was the Easter holidays of the term in which she'd become *persona non grata* at school. Her dad had been out driving his taxi and she'd tired of watching television and she'd read enough SF to boggle her tiny mind. So she walked and wondered if her dad would let her have a dog to keep her company. She knew the most likely answer to the question, though: there was no one at home all day to look after a dog. Her dad would say, 'You get a dog, you've got to be there for it.'

She guessed she'd walked into the squelchy field on a whim. Or that she'd somehow been drawn to it by a kind of magnetism. Half-way up the muddy path to the big clump of bushes that marked the centre of the field, something had caught her eye.

It was black and low, and it was moving quickly. It came rushing out of the big bushes, vanished from view behind a tall grassy ridge, then pelted on to the path ahead of her, about a hundred and fifty yards away.

It wasn't until this point that Becky knew for certain that the black thing was a dog. It had looked like something else for a few moments but she couldn't think what.

The dog was coming towards her. At speed. Teeth first. And it looked angry.

For a few moments she considered running but she wasn't going to outpace that animal and, she wasn't scared of it. This was lucky, she thought fleetingly, because dogs didn't attack you if you weren't scared of them.

Most dogs, her mind added. This one looked like the exception that was about to prove the rule.

Becky crouched to await the dog, suddenly knowing why she didn't feel any fear. She'd given up. She didn't care any more. *Who gives a toss*? Becky thought, as the dog closed in on her. She wasn't aware until later that big fat tears had gathered under her eyelids and rolled down her cheeks.

Becky tried not to tense as the maddened animal crossed the final three yards. She tried to keep her eyes open so that she would see the animal hit her, but she failed to do this too.

What followed was over in a second. Becky felt nothing but a brief sensation of something heavy moving the air close to her head and her nose filled with the smell of hot *canis familiaris*.

It hit the ground behind her and carried on running – she could hear the thundering of its paws on the muddy ground.

Becky opened her eyes and turned round to see where the dog was going.

It stopped about twenty feet behind her, nosed in the grass for a few moments, picked up something and came trotting back towards her, still looking fierce and growling low in its throat.

Becky waited, still crouched. There was still a good chance that the dog would attack her, but she didn't believe it would, although its hackles were up and it was moving low to the ground.

The thing it had pulled from the grass appeared to be a bone, a nasty-looking thing, half green with mould and half covered in dirt.

He thought I was going to steal his disgusting old bone! Becky thought, and began to smile through her tears.

Someone back up in the direction from which the dog had come was yelling now, a single long word that sounded like 'Doooooooooooo'. Becky glanced over her shoulder and saw two boys hammering down the path, one yelling, the other just running. One looked vaguely familiar, Becky thought, but they were too far away to tell for sure.

'C'm 'ere, doggy,' Becky said gently, encouraging it.

The dog trotted towards her, eyeing her and curling back its lip so that she could see what a tremendous set of big white teeth it had.

'I don't want your bone, stupid!' Becky told the dog. 'I wouldn't touch if it if was the last piece of food on earth.'

'*Dookie!*' the yelling boy shouted. 'NO!'

The dog ignored him and held Becky's gaze, slinking slowly towards her, still growling, still showing its teeth. When it was a foot or so away, it paused, inched forward, gently placed the bone at Becky's feet and backed off. Then it lay down on its side and spread its legs, making a gesture of submission.

Becky duck-walked over to the dog and tentatively put out her hand.

By the time the boys arrived, Becky was gently stroking its chest.

'Jesus, I'm sorry, did he bite you?' the shouting boy said breathlessly, from right behind her. He sounded terrified.

Becky looked at him over her shoulder. She'd seen this boy at school. He was in her year, she thought. He had a thick mop of mad brown hair and was cute in a way. 'Nope,' she said. 'He was just worried about his bone. Which is strange since when he found I hadn't stolen it, he gave it to me.'

'Fuckarooney, Dogboy! The Dukester didn't bite her!' an impressed voice panted. And there was Johnny Kane, Mr Good-looking himself. In the flesh. Close Personal Friend of Sindy Hallett.

Becky sighed. 'I'd better go,' she said, reluctantly removing her right hand from the first friend she'd made in months and getting up. She felt empty now.

Johnny frowned at her, as if trying to place her.

Becky nodded. 'Becky Sharp. Gives blow-jobs to anyone who asks, fucks dogs, slut, thief and all-round loathsome person.' She turned back the way she'd come and began to walk. To her surprise, the dog got up and trotted alongside her, his tail swishing happily.

'Hey, why are you going?' the boy with the mad hair called after her.

'Ask your friend,' Becky said, without turning.

'Why's she going, Johnny?' Becky heard him ask in a loud whisper.

'I don't know, Stevie,' Johnny replied, 'but Dookie appears to be going with her.'

Stevie chuckled. 'Excuse me, madam!' he called. 'You haven't paid the rental for that dog!'

Becky stopped and turned round. The dog did a neat turn at heel, just like those show-dogs at Crufts. 'You know *who* I am,' she yelled angrily. 'You *think* you know *what* I am. *That's* why I'm going. Now call back your stupid dog and let me get out of here!'

'Dookie!' Stevie called. The dog ignored him.

Becky began to walk, the dog close to her right leg. She didn't look back until she was all the way back to the broken-down chain-link fence where she'd entered the field. She was surprised to see the two boys about twenty feet behind her. Stevie grinned and waved. Johnny shrugged.

'Bugger off!' Becky said, trying to keep the tremor from her voice and failing.

'Why do you think we don't like you?' Stevie called.

'*Because!*' Becky said. She was in danger of breaking down and she didn't want that to happen in front of some of Sindy's friends. She hurried on, the dog still at heel. Tears began to roll down her cheeks again.

Seconds later, the boys caught up with her and began to walk along on either side of her. 'I'm sorry,' Stevie said gently, 'but you're going to have to come back with us.'

'Why should I?' Becky snapped, wiping her face with the back of her hand.

'Because we like you,' Johnny said.

'Oh, you're a right double-act, you two,' Becky spat. 'Well, if you think the rumours are true, you can just fuck off now before I get angry and start clawing eyes out. Contrary to popular belief, I *don't* fuck anyone who happens by, nor do I make a habit of sucking people's dicks, so if that's what you have in mind you can *fucking well forget it!*'

'We didn't have that in mind, actually,' Stevie said. 'And some of us – me for example – don't even know the rumours—'

'And some of those who do don't believe them,' Johnny cut in.

Stevie continued, 'The reason you're going to have to come back is that Duke here, your new dog friend, is registered dangerous and isn't allowed out in public without a muzzle. If he's spotted by the police, or by the dog warden, he goes to the great doghouse in the sky. As you can see, he isn't wearing a muzzle. As you can also see, we're now standing on a public footpath and cycle lane. If a little kid appears on a bike, Dookie is apt to rush up and knock him off. He might not bite the kid, but the kid will swear he has, bite-marks to show or not. And Dookie won't come back. I tried calling him. He's taken to you.'

'And the reason we say we like you,' Johnny added, 'is because the Dookster likes you. And he likes very few people. So, any friend of the Dookster's has to be a good person and, consequently, any friend of his is a friend of ours.'

'Bullshit!' Becky said. 'You're just setting me up. You could just grab the dog's collar and drag him away.'

'He'd bite me,' Stevie said. 'He refuses to be held by the collar. Now, *please* come back with us.'

'If all that about the dog being dangerous is true, why isn't he wearing a muzzle?' Becky demanded.

'He was panting,' Stevie said. 'We were in a deserted field. I took a chance and took it off.' He pointed at the thicket where the dog had first appeared. 'It's hanging from a branch up there.'

Becky sighed. 'How can I trust friends of Sindy?' she asked.

'I don't even *know* Sindy,' Stevie said, glancing at Johnny.

Johnny held up his hands, fingers spread. 'OK, I'll admit it. I went out with her. Before Christmas this was. I went out with her for a week. Anyone can make a mistake. And I did. I'm not a close friend of hers.'

'I've seen you talking! Recently!'

'She's in my class,' Johnny said. 'And if I told you what I was talking to her about the last few times, you wouldn't believe me.'

'Try me!'

Johnny shrugged. 'You tell her, Stevie,' he said.

'I can't,' Stevie said.

When Becky looked at him, he was blushing. 'Why not?' she demanded.

'You want the truth?' Stevie asked, now bright red.

'Sure,' she said, starting to feel a little better.

'Because I lied. And when I tell you, you'll know I lied earlier and you won't believe me now,' he said, looking at the ground. 'I said I hadn't heard the rumours.'

Becky nodded and found a smile for him. 'Well, I suppose you'd have to have been deaf and blind to have escaped the rumours and the stuff on the walls in the toilets. I forgive you – maybe you were trying to make me feel better. Now tell me what you were going to tell me and make it the truth. And if I think you're lying I'll run away with your dangerous dog.'

'He told Sindy to leave you alone,' Stevie said, holding her gaze. 'He told her that if she didn't stop trying to stitch you up, he'd do the same to her.'

Becky suddenly felt a little dizzy. This had to be the king of all lies. There *were* no good people around. There *was* no one on her side. And yet she felt that Stevie was telling her the truth.

Johnny shrugged. 'It didn't do much good, mind,' he said. 'I'm still plotting my revenge.'

'But *why*?' Becky asked. '*Why* would you do that for me? You don't even know me.'

'I might not know you, but I do know what's not fair,' Johnny said, sounding embarrassed at having been found out doing a good deed. 'And I thought Sindy might listen to me.'

'Cross your hearts and hope to die?' Becky asked, and grinned when both boys simultaneously drew crosses on their chests with a fingertip and mimed slashes across their throats.

'OK,' she said, looking at Stevie. 'Now, that stuff about Dookie biting you if you tried to drag him off by his collar. Was that true?'

In reply, Stevie bent down, hooked a finger under the dog's collar and led him a few paces. The dog didn't bat an eyelid.

Not only did Becky walk back to the thicket in the centre of the field with them, that afternoon she ended up having the best time she could remember as she sat and smoked Johnny's Marlboros and hugged her new doggy friend while she watched the two boys try and fail to build a two-storey dwelling from railway sleepers and bits of corrugated iron. She spent the remainder of the Easter break with them and towards the end of that holiday she began to feel alive again – as if she'd woken up from a deep sleep filled with nightmares.

But the hate campaign against her at school continued. Even Johnny couldn't stop Sindy and her friends.

At times, the going got *very* tough.

The trouble with fiction, Becky knew, was that it spread like ripples on a pond. It swept over you, changing you into something you hadn't been before.

One single lie had started off all this nonsense.

Before Robert Creasey had claimed that Becky had dragged him into her house and subjected him to every sexual deviation you could put a name to she had merely been the girl no one noticed. Becky had no idea what she'd done to deserve this smear, but Robert had told the lie anyway. At Sindy's behest.

Becky knew this because shortly after she'd learned what Robert had said, she'd cornered him, alone, in the boys' shower room. He'd grinned at her. 'Hi!' he'd said. 'What do you want? More of what you already had?'

Becky felt her blood pressure rise to bursting point. She saw a faint burst of wavy blue dots, the way you did when you tried to crane round too far. She felt dizzy and for a moment she thought she would faint. *Brain tumour!* she thought fleetingly. *Just like Mum!*

Until then, Becky hadn't had a clue what she wanted to do. But the next thing she knew, Robert was up against the wall and she had his tie round her hand, right up by the knot.

And suddenly he didn't look so clever any more.

Becky began to twist the tie, close to his throat, enjoying the feeling of power and the way his frightened eyes began to bulge. That was how fiction could change you. It woke up demons inside you. Demons you never knew you had.

'I want to know,' Becky said, twisting the tie tighter with each word, 'why you said what you did.'

The weird thing was, she thought afterwards, that Robert didn't resist. He could have punched her or kicked her, but he did nothing at all except look terrified.

When veins began to pop out on his forehead and the colour in Robert's face started to darken, she released the pressure a little, allowing him to draw a ragged breath.

'Why'd you do it?' she asked, pulling him away from the wall and letting him back, so that his head bounced on the plaster. It was a most satisfying sound.

'S-Sindy wanted me to,' Robert hissed.

'Why?' Becky demanded, banging his head on the wall once more.

'You're a swot,' Robert said. 'Always top of the class. Always first with your hand up. Teacher's pet.'

Becky felt her jaw begin to drop and snapped it shut again. 'What else?' she demanded.

'Ray Cutts fancies you.'

'Ray Cutts? You're joking!' Becky said. Ray Cutts was *the* boy most lusted after. Becky had never spoken to him or seen him so much as glance in her direction. And she didn't particularly want him to. Cutts was a dummy of the first order and had no sense of humour. Becky had seen him in action.

'She's welcome to him,' Becky said. 'I don't want him.'

She gave Robert one more bang against the wall, turned away from him and strode out.

A minute and a half later she'd punched Sindy's nose.

And the ripples spread.

During that term the teachers took an interest in her, an interest that suggested they might have heard the rumours – and believed some of them. And Becky reacted accordingly. She stopped trying to please and started fighting back. If they wanted a bad girl, a bad girl they would have. Her work suffered. She was called aside and asked about her 'problems'. And Becky, who wouldn't believe no one *knew* what her problems were all about, let them think what they liked.

Which was how she'd 'developed' Tourette's Syndrome and ended up on the psychiatrist's couch.

At least she thought that was how it had happened. Now that

she'd started remembering her early years she wasn't quite so certain.

He tried to bring my mother back from the dead, she thought.

'How do you feel about death?' Williams asked, as if he'd tapped into her thoughts.

'Being dead is fine,' Becky replied, doing a series of facial tics. Williams couldn't see the expressions she was making, but he'd know that something was going on. And that was good because, during this period on the couch, she'd forgotten the tics that went along with Tourette's. 'It's just the end of everything, being dead. What worries me is what *might* happen afterwards,' she added.

'Do you feel there could be an afterlife?' Williams asked.

And once again Becky was a small girl, peering through a crack in the lounge door, late at night. Inside the room her dad was trying to make his magic work.

Don't, Dad! she remembered pleading silently. *Just let her rest. Gone is gone. It might not be Mum when it comes back. It might be something else.*

'I dunno,' Becky said, truthfully. 'But I sincerely hope not.'

Chapter Five

Becky Chasing Ghosts

Five minutes later, Becky skipped out into the sunny street, her session on the couch forgotten. It was summer, it was the holidays and . . .

And there's Johnny's mum! Isn't she supposed to be at a photo-shoot in London today?

Becky shook her head as the woman passed on the far side of the road. It couldn't be Katie Kane. It might look like her, but Katie didn't wear a hippy-style cheesecloth dress and no bra and she didn't wear her hair down or walk around in her bare feet carrying a posy of yellow, red and white flowers.

But it is *her. I'm sure*, Becky thought, frowning after the woman. *And if it isn't her, it's her twin sister. She even walks in the same swivel-hipped way.*

Becky crossed the road, glanced towards where she was intending to go – to Brookvale and the field where Johnny, Stevie and Dookie were sure to be – turned in the opposite direction and began to follow Katie Kane.

Katie wasn't a fast mover. You couldn't maintain that catwalk sashay at speed without looking stupid. Becky had to slow down to keep her distance.

What am I doing this for? she asked herself, and didn't have any answer. Spying on other people's mothers was a new one for her. Always supposing this *was* Johnny's mum. *Why don't you just catch her up and say 'Hi, you're looking good' and grin a bit and ask what happened to her photo-shoot*? she wondered. Katie was attracting admiring glances from the drivers of practically every passing car while no one even noticed the girl twenty yards behind her.

What is *she up to?* Becky wondered, and decided to catch up with her and ask. She increased her speed and began to close on Johnny's mother. She still had ten yards to go when Katie glanced over her shoulder and began to run.

Now what do I do? Becky asked, still walking quite quickly. It was obvious now that it *was* Katie and that Katie didn't want to talk to her. Which made Becky all the more determined to get to the bottom of whatever was going on. She began to jog.

Katie was around a hundred yards ahead now and had slowed to a fast walk, the hip-swivelling forgotten, shoulders stooped. She looked older now, like a woman who's been middle-aged for so long she's starting to bow under the pressure.

Becky shivered. There was something about this she didn't like – especially in the light of what Stevie and Johnny had told her last week about the vanishing kid and the rubbery thing that Duke was supposed to have killed. She hadn't believed any of it, of course – the rubbery skin of what Stevie had called the 'gobbling' had disintegrated when he pulled it out of his pocket, and, of course, he had washed the blood from his clothes and hosed the dog as soon as he got home. And there'd been a big storm that evening so there wasn't even any blood on the grass by the time Becky turned up. It had just been a dumb story Johnny and Stevie had concocted to give her the shivers and it hadn't worked.

Except that it *had* worked. Not when they told it, but afterwards. The story had gained a life of its own in her mind and wriggled its way into the compartment marked *fact*, perhaps because they had insisted that this time they were *not* bullshitting. And there was that recently unlocked memory of her father trying to bring back her mother with strange words and magical passes.

Why the sight of Johnny's mother dressed as a hippy should trigger off those memories though, was anyone's guess.

Ahead, Katie turned a corner, still walking fast with her head down. Becky broke into a trot and got there less than half a minute later. And there was Katie, way up ahead by the gates to the Memorial Park – further than she could possibly have got unless she could sprint quickly enough to do a sub-ten-seconds hundred metres. She wasn't even walking fast now, but had returned to that model-girl gait.

That's not possible! Becky complained. *She can't be that far ahead!*

Then she realized the truth. She was having a hallucination. It was a frightening thought and she put it out of her head before it could do any serious damage. She began to run again. If she could *touch* Katie, she'd know she wasn't imagining all this.

Katie walked past the V-shaped junction where Hackwood Road met Cliddesden Road, continued for a few paces then crossed and vanished into an alleyway that joined two streets. This was good. Becky happened to know that there was no way off that alley without coming back the way you went in or out into Cliddesden Road.

Becky sprinted and arrived at the alleyway less than twenty seconds after Katie had entered it.

Katie had gone.

Becky was out of breath and had a stitch in her side. She stood there panting and holding her waist with both hands. She could see all the way up to the other end of the alley and Katie wasn't in it. She couldn't have got out of it in twenty seconds.

Unless she sprinted, Becky told herself and began to run again, up the alley towards Cliddesden Road. The stitch felt like a red-hot poker in her side. She slowed to a trot, then a painful hobble.

It isn't possible that a forty-year-old woman could move this quickly, Becky thought. *Even if she does work out, she couldn't move this fast.*

She reached the far end of the alley, walked out into Cliddesden Road, stepped off the pavement and stopped in the centre of the quiet road. Katie was nowhere to be seen.

Then Becky frowned. When she'd glanced down towards the town she hadn't seen Katie but she'd seen someone else she knew. It had taken a few moments to register because that person wasn't who she was looking for.

Don't look back! she told herself. *Don't look back towards the park gates because what you saw isn't what you thought you saw and it won't be there when you look for it.*

But as Lot's wife would have told you, the temptation was too strong to resist and Becky looked back anyway.

And there he wasn't.

Surprise, surprise! Becky thought bitterly, and began to cry.

A moment ago she'd seen Stevie's father, Andy Warner, heading towards the park gates. It couldn't have been anyone else. Even from the back Andy was unmistakable: he had Stevie's mad hair and he'd been swaggering along in jeans and a short-sleeved shirt, the way he did when he was pleased with himself – as though his Nikes were extra bouncy. And she hadn't mistaken Andy's red polka-dot bandanna. Except he hadn't been wearing it round his neck or – in the way that made Stevie cringe with embarrassment – over his head like a pirate. It had been wrapped round his hand.

Now he wasn't there. Although he hadn't had time to reach the gates and go through them, he'd vanished.

Unless he can sprint like Johnny's mother, Becky thought, mopping tears from her face with the back of her hand. The tears kept coming. Becky kept wiping them away, wishing herself ten minutes back in time. If she'd paused for a few moments after her session and asked Williams how she was getting on or something, she wouldn't have seen Katie Kane and wouldn't have chased her and wouldn't have come to this conclusion about herself . . .

Except you would, she thought, in the voice of her psychiatrist. *You'd have seen Katie Kane and Andy Warner whatever time you left the office. You would have seen them because neither of them was a real person. Both were hallucinations, and hallucinations don't obey normal physical rules.*

The logical conclusion was that she was genuinely mad. Insane. Off the wall.

I'm mad, Becky told herself and began to sob aloud – something she hadn't done since her mother's funeral.

And now that she'd admitted she was insane, she could see that the trouble at school was probably due to her mental condition, not because she'd been picked on – she'd *imagined* it. As she'd imagined seeing her father trying to bring back his dead wife.

She'd dreamed up Stevie and Johnny's tale of the gobbling and the kid on the swing, just like she'd dreamed up the visions of Katie Kane and Andy Warner. It was all hallucination.

'*What am I going to do?*' she sobbed.

A car horn blasted.

Becky yelped and suddenly realized she was standing in the middle of Cliddesden Road, her fists clenched and her knuckles pressed against her teeth. She had no idea how long she'd been standing here wailing.

She glanced at the car. It was a black Mercedes. Inside it, a matronly woman was gazing at her with what looked like a cross between suspicion and concern.

Becky walked to the car, held out trembling hands and touched its warm bonnet with her fingertips. The car, at least, was real. Becky felt her face screw up and her lips draw back as a fresh bout of sobbing began.

'Are you OK, my dear? Excuse me? Are you all right?'

The woman was leaning out of the driver's door window.

Becky shook her head. 'I'm cuh-cuh-crazy,' she sobbed.

'You'll be dead as well if you don't soon move out of the road,' the woman said.

Becky's sobbing stopped. She looked at the woman. 'Fuck off, you stinking whore!' she heard herself shout.

'Are you sure?' the woman asked. 'It wouldn't be any problem. Really. I don't have to be anywhere in a hurry.'

Becky began to sob again. Not only had the woman *not* told her to get out of the road, but Becky hadn't sworn at her.

Apparently, the woman *had* offered her a lift home. And she had refused.

'Yes, I'm sh-sh-sure,' Becky said. 'Thank you.'

The woman nodded and withdrew her head.

Becky went back to the pavement and, through eyes blurred with tears, watched the woman drive off. It took another ten minutes for the sobbing to subside. She fished in her pocket for a tissue, dabbed her sore eyes and blew her nose. Then, when she was more or less back in control, she turned towards the alley, not because she wanted to revisit it but because she couldn't think of anywhere else to go.

What do I do? was the question that reverberated through her mind. She didn't have an answer. Go home and raid her dad's booze cabinet might be a good idea, she thought. It might not make her any more sane but surely it would take away the pain. That was why drunks became drunks, wasn't it?

It was just a pity that she hated the taste of alcohol.

Stevie would know what to do, she thought, but she wasn't sure she could face him like this. He might understand her distress and take her in his arms and hug her but she'd been carefully cultivating her hard-woman act and Stevie might run a mile if he saw what she was *really* like.

She started when a dog suddenly appeared at her ankles. It was black and about the same size as Duke, but its coat was shiny and short, and it was thinner, its muscles more defined. It looked like a cross between a black Labrador and a greyhound or whippet. The dog danced around her, wagging its tail hard.

Becky squatted down in front of it and the dog instantly put its front paws on her knees and craned up to lick her face. 'Yeeech!' she said, leaning back. It did no good. The further back she leaned, the further forward the dog came, its tongue working as hard as its tail.

'You're licking away my tears, aren't you?' Becky asked, pushing it away. 'Good dog!'

A name tag was dangling from the dog's red leather collar, but it wouldn't stay still long enough for her to read it.

'Put her down, Cindy!' Someone chuckled.

'Oh, it's Cindy, is it?' Becky said, patting its head. She looked up as the dog's owner approached and her mouth dropped open.

'Sorry,' the man called from a little way down the alley, 'we were in the park and she made a bid for freedom. Ran straight across the road!'

Becky squeezed her eyes shut and opened them again. The

man approaching her was a dead-ringer for Stevie. Except that he was older.

He squatted down in front of her, grabbed the dog's collar and clipped a lead to it. 'She likes to run off and meet people,' he explained, the cadences of his speech matching those of Stevie. He grinned. 'It's her hobby.'

'Are you for real?' Becky heard herself ask.

'Yeah, 'fraid so.' The man grinned. 'Real as real can be.' He stood up. 'You've been crying,' he observed.

Becky nodded. 'Can I ask you a question?'

'Of course you can.'

'Are you related to anyone called Warner? Stevie or Andy?'

The man chuckled. 'Yeah,' he said, 'you could say that. Related. Only distantly, though.'

Becky reached out a hand and said, 'Pull me up, would you?'

The man took her hand. His grip was firm, his hand strong. He hoisted her to her feet. He *felt* real.

'Don't worry about it, whatever it is,' the man said, sounding as if he knew *exactly* what it was. 'I'm sure it'll all work out, one way or the other, and life's too short to waste time worrying. Right?'

'Right,' Becky agreed.

'Good girl,' he said, approvingly. He thought for a moment and almost said something else, then decided against it and closed his mouth.

A picture of a call-box lit up in Becky's mind.

'I gotta fly,' the man said. 'Things to do. Nice to have met you!' He glanced down at the dog. 'C'mon, Cind, we've got to go now.'

The dog gave a single woof, looked up at Becky briefly and then was running away, bouncing up at the man as he jogged down the alley, small change jingling in the pocket of his chinos.

I just imagined all that, Becky told herself, but she didn't believe it. The man and the dog were real. And somehow they'd made her feel better about things.

Becky thought of the telephone box again and wondered why. She walked slowly down the alley, watching her feet take one pace after another.

She stopped when, at the periphery of her vision, she caught a glimpse of colour.

Her heart sank as she turned her head to look at what lay on the footpath. She already knew that it was the posy of flowers Katie Kane had been carrying. It had been laid over a deep crack in the tarmac. A crack that Becky hadn't seen on her way up the alley.

Becky crouched beside them. The stems were wrapped in a cone of cream silk. The blooms were gorgeous colours and freshly cut. The contrast between the black tarmac of the path and the almost painful purity of the flowers made the spot look like a tiny piece of heaven, fallen from the sky.

The man with the dog put them here, she told herself. *Katie didn't come back, and I didn't see them on my way up the alley, so* he *must have done it.*

But she knew they were the ones Katie had been carrying. She didn't know their names but they looked like a mixture of orchids. They must be the exotic kind that grew only in places like Hawaii and they'd evidently cost a small fortune.

She reached out and touched one, and felt its waxy smoothness. A delicate fragrance wafted up from the posy.

'They're real,' Becky announced, nodding to herself. Why had they been set down here over this crack in the paving? It seemed significant somehow. Becky counted the blooms, touching them, one by one. There were twenty-five. All felt real.

Perhaps you can have tactile hallucinations, too, she thought, but rejected the idea. If you could have *all* your senses play tricks on you at once, you'd never know what was real and what wasn't. No one would. *Everything* could be imaginary then.

Becky looked at the crack upon which the flowers had been laid. It was a lot bigger than she'd realized. What she'd thought was shadow was actually a fissure deep into the ground.

She moved the posy away and leaned over the crack trying to see how deep it went. She could see down to a depth of about a foot, then the sides vanished into darkness. Another odd thing was that the sides looked smooth and glassy. She put her fingers to the edge of the ragged split and ran them a little way down into the hole. Beneath the gritty unevenness of the macadam, the fissure walls felt like highly polished marble – except that they were warm to the touch. She knelt closer to the hole and put her hand in up to her wrist. Then up to her elbow. The sensation was strangely pleasing – comforting somehow.

The picture of the telephone kiosk lit up again in her mind and she shuddered. Suddenly it seemed like a bad idea to be kneeling here doing this. If a movement of the earth had opened this hole since she'd walked up the alley a few minutes ago, another movement might well snap it shut again. And, now she came to think of it, the fissure *was* roughly the shape of a grinning mouth.

Becky yanked her arm out of the hole, her spine tingling, and fancied she could hear a hissing sound, like gas escaping under pressure. It died to a sigh and finished with the faintly whispered words: *You don't have to be insane . . .*

'I'm not insane,' Becky said. She knew that she'd imagined the hiss and what she'd heard afterwards. Whatever had happened had happened *internally*. She felt sick at heart, nauseous and horribly frightened, but she had no tears left to cry.

What am I going to do?

Quit worrying. Like the man said, life's too short to waste time worrying.

But the man, she was suddenly certain, hadn't existed either. It *was* possible to have tactile hallucinations. The advice had come from her own mind, just like the fissure and the orchids, and the visions of Andy and Katie. She'd played so hard at being mad that now she really was. It was a kind of method acting.

Just put the flowers back, the voice said. *And later on we'll see. You don't have to be insane . . .*

The image of the telephone box grew in her mind.

Becky took the posy and placed it back where she'd found it over the widest part of the fissure, thinking, *Let's see you get past that lot!*

She stood up, brushed off her hands and turned back towards Cliddesden Road. The image of the telephone box had given her an idea. It might not prove for certain whether or not she'd lost her marbles but it was going to make her feel a hell of a lot better for having done it.

She would make a telephone call.

Chapter Six

Katie Kool

For once in her life Katie Kane was feeling good. Not *pretending* to feel good and smiling happily because that was what was expected of happy-go-lucky KK, actually feeling good.

'Nope, feeling wonderful, actually,' she corrected herself, getting up off the weights bench in her personal gym – a tiny converted cellar in her house.

And for once she felt this way naturally, without having touched her secret stash of Momma's little helpers. 'Just those good old endorphins,' she said, tweezing the sweat-soaked leotard away from her flat belly between finger and thumb and letting it ping back. Just five miles on the exercise bike (big hills made shapely legs), the sit-ups and the cool down and she would be able to peel off this nasty Lycra thing and stand under a cool shower. It got hot in the basement in the summer.

It hadn't been an effortless wake-up-and-feel-good day, though. They never were these days. Never had been since the seventies. Since then Katie had had to jolly herself along if she wanted to end up feeling good.

She looked at herself in the mirrors as she climbed on the bike. She didn't merely look good for forty-five, she looked fabulous, even if she said so herself. In fact, if it hadn't been for the crows'-feet and that bit of crinkle starting to show where her neck met her chest, you wouldn't have been able to tell her from the twenty-year-younger version of herself.

'Oh yes you would!' she reminded herself as she began to pedal. The younger Katic had been somewhat more rounded than this one. Less defined.

'But, like they say,' she hissed from between gritted teeth, 'a healthy body breeds a healthy mind.'

This wasn't true, of course. Katie had been as fit as a matchbox full of fleas for the past five years now, and although she didn't tire easily her mind had not improved one iota, neither in clarity nor in restfulness.

Guilt was a wonderful thing.

It could keep you up nights, tossing and turning, it could haunt your day-times so that your hands trembled and your long nails got bitten down to the quick without your even noticing.

But we don't want to think about things like that at the moment, do we? Katie reminded herself.

The fact was that today, of all days, thinking about things like that was nigh on impossible to avoid.

Katie pedalled, working up to her regular speed, then trying to improve it. There was certainly something sensual in the sweaty exertion. For a few moments she considered getting off the bike, going upstairs, ringing David and telling him she wanted him, here and now. And David would leave the garage and come right home, panting for her.

On any other day, I would, she thought. *Today I can't.* Because . . .

Today was Kool Day.

The anniversary day. The day when things were put right for the next year.

Katie emptied her mind and pedalled.

Once upon a time, there was a young girl who dreamed of a bright new world, Katie had opened in the journal she'd started to keep, way back in the early eighties. *And the dream turned into a nightmare.*

It was going to be her autobiography when it was done. And it was going to be literary and marketable in much the same way as Jung Chang's *Wild Swans* had been a few years back – but for different reasons. This wasn't going to be the story of a struggle for life under the rule of an oppressive regime, but a search for happiness and the source of a woman's guilt.

Of course, the book had never been completed, it hadn't been literary and it had turned into a kind of diary in which her present-day life was entwined with her past. She still added a page here and a page there, but the thrust had been lost long ago.

The sad fact was, this woman had absolutely no idea why she felt guilty.

There was a lot of material in the journal about things she had done of which she was ashamed, but none was the source of the guilt she still felt.

Katie had spent the late sixties running drugs. Cannabis, mainly, brought back from Morocco in a Willys Jeep that shouldn't have survived one trip let alone twenty-eight. She'd flown suitcases full of Black Pak back from Pakistan and dragged them through the Nothing to Declare channel without the customs guys raising so much as an eyebrow.

Possibly because back in those days she'd been Katie Kool. Katie Relaxed. Katie No-Sweat. Back in those days she could have murdered her grandmother and gone directly to the police station covered in bloodstains and been calm enough to lie her way out of it. Back in those days Katie hadn't felt guilty about anything.

And if she wasn't ashamed of the drug running, she should have been ashamed of the robbery. Katie and a guy called Henry Williams – a graduate from Cambridge, a journalist on *Oz* (with Andy Warner, who had introduced them) and a dropout from a wealthy family – had once blazed into a branch of the Bristol & West Building Society, each wearing one half of a pair of 15-denier Pretty Polly stockings and brandishing a toy Luger, and had relieved them of almost five thousand pounds.

Weird days. But days when your blood fizzed through your veins like champagne and each new dawn signalled another twenty-four hours of adventure. Pretty much the sort of days that her son Johnny was now either starting to have or would start very soon.

But it wasn't the robbery. Katie knew that.

That wasn't the cause of *the* guilt. Or what Katie thought of as the Big Guilt. And it certainly didn't have anything to do with her sexual excesses from age fourteen until . . .

Katie slowed down. Her thighs were aching and sweat was dripping from her chin and running into her eyes. Her hands were so slippery that she could barely keep hold of the cycle's handle-grips. She'd done six miles – a mile more than she had intended.

'. . . until when exactly?' she asked aloud, letting herself roll to a halt. She mopped sweat from the frown that began to crease her face. 'CRS,' she told herself. 'Can't Remember Shit. That's what happens when you start piling on the years.'

She'd lost her virginity at fourteen. *Fourteen years, six months and two days to be precise*, she reminded herself. *In Daryl Ifould's house. In his mum and dad's bedroom on top of a red bath-sheet laid over a pink candlewick bedspread.*

She could clearly remember how the colours had clashed. It always made her grin to think that the most memorable thing about losing her virginity was how badly the red on pink had offended her eyes. The boy was called Mick. He was a year older than her, good-looking and smoked Player's No. 6. He was saving up the little green cards, too, but he'd never collected enough to buy her the hairdryer he'd promised.

Grinning, Katie got off the bike. It struck her as strange that she'd come to be so obsessed with sex after a start like that. It had lasted an entire twenty seconds and it had left her sore, bleeding slightly and completely unfulfilled. 'Great oaks from little acorns grow,' she told herself, as she sat down on the bench to do her hundred sit-ups.

Katie could remember every man she'd had between Mick and David, and there had been a lot of them. Women, too.

Katie's muscles began to protest at fifty-eight, which was earlier than usual so she guessed she hadn't slept well the previous night. That wasn't really surprising, given that today was a big day.

At the beginning, she and David had had an open relationship, so the sex stuff hadn't calmed down *then*. They'd done threesomes and had often gone out together and gone home separately, but it seemed to have made their relationship stronger. Somewhere in there, she'd fallen in love with him. And he'd fallen in love with her. Life went on being one long warm summer of psychedelic love and happiness. Then the world had changed and Katie and David had stopped having fun and started being grown-ups. And that was where the guilt came from. That peculiar period of metamorphosis, or whatever it was.

Katie could remember it to the year.

It had been 1972. *The year that Katie Kool became Katie Kane. The year our lives all changed. The year we entered the rat-race. And for Katie, the year of the Big Guilt.*

'Ohhhh,' she groaned, as she curled up from the bench for the eightieth time. Her muscles were screaming now and there were still twenty to go. It was punishment.

And I'm a masochist, luckily, Katie told herself, pulling herself up once more. *Punishment is what I need. Punishment is what I deserve.*

'What did I do in 'seventy-two?' Katie hissed as she lowered herself.

She'd got married. She'd entered the human race. Reality had set in. Apart from that, she had no idea. Except that on one level or another she had been atoning for it, whatever it was, ever since.

Today, however, was Kool Day and there were other things to think about besides punishing yourself. Having completed the hundred sit-ups, Katie got to her feet and began her cooling-down exercises. According to her watch, it was two minutes to three. The flowers were due to be delivered at three thirty. She'd been very specific about the time and Debbie at Debbie's Blooms had never yet let her down. That left her half an hour to shower, change and be ready.

Little Mrs Deceitful here had lied to her son and her husband that she'd gone to London for a pre-shoot selection today. It was a lie only in as much as she'd changed the date. The selection was tomorrow morning at ten in a room at the Strand Hotel. Little Mrs Deceitful, Charlie the stylist, Ed Binger, the MD from the advertising agency, and a gang of guys from a household-name motor-oil company were seeing fifty glamour models from which they would choose six for the oil company's next calendar.

The timing was critical. Katie had to do the honours for Kool Day, get home, collect her bags, put them in the BMW and get the flock out of here before David came home on the dot of five.

Of course, even if the timing went off properly, there was an element of danger. Johnny could come breezing in at any time. People she knew might see her while she was enacting the ritual and try to talk to her. What then?

She would deal with it. They hadn't called her Katie Kool for nothing. And, anyway, the danger added an element of excitement. If Katie were being truthful with herself she would probably admit that she planned these special days this way.

But Katie wasn't going to think about that. What she'd done each year since 1972 had worked, and she wasn't going to change a winning formula.

She glanced around the gym, turned off the lights, closed the door behind her and went upstairs.

The house was big – bought on the proceeds of her photography, a hobby that had somehow turned into a lucrative career. Good fortune had smiled on Katie Kane.

Which was handy in the light of her husband's failure to make money. Poor David had sweated his little nuts off for twenty years to make his car-sales business pay, but it seemed to be jinxed. He was stoic and never complained, but Katie knew that her success hurt him a little. She, however, was at a loss to explain why good luck always came her way.

It's because I agreed, she told herself, tossing the sweat-soaked towel into the washer/dryer. *Because I agreed to let it.*

For reasons unknown, Katie's inner guilt chose this moment to rise to a scary level. She shivered, told herself she was being silly, and put the thought out of her head. She kicked off her trainers, peeled off her soggy socks and the sweat-soaked leotard and threw them all in the machine.

She turned it on and hurried upstairs to the shower, thinking, *I wonder who you are, you lucky boy. I wonder if you'll wake up tomorrow morning thinking you've been hit by a hurricane?*

The cool water was bliss.

Katie didn't know who'd made up the rules governing Kool Day. She supposed it must have been her, since she was the only woman in the known universe who observed it. One day there had been no Kool Day and the next there had, along with all the details, procedures and etiquette.

Katie liked the part that involved flowers and she liked the deception but her favourite part was the coda.

While Katie stood in the shower, somewhere in London a young man was going about his business suspecting nothing. In Katie's mind's eye, he was in his early twenties, blond and a little skinny, but not painfully thin. He'd be good-looking, of course, and between five ten and six feet tall. With brown eyes.

Tonight, Katie would finish Kool Day by dropping half a Mandrax, swilling it down with Isle of Jura single malt then going out and picking up this guy. She would observe the last ritual of the day by taking him to her room in the Strand Hotel and showing him what they *really* meant when they said 'shagged senseless'.

Katie glanced into the mirror that formed the back wall of the shower and shrugged. 'I didn't make the rules,' she grinned, 'I merely stick to 'em!'

Her reflection grinned back at her admiringly. This woman's middle-aged body showed no signs of spread. Even gravity was being kind.

The phone rang. 'Oh, bugger it!' she said, and ground her teeth. The answering machine would get it after four rings, but the urge to leap out of the shower and run to the bedroom to snatch up the handset was strong. But she ignored it.

Downstairs, David's voice boomed from the machine, asking the caller to leave a message after the tone. This caller decided that now would be a good time to ring off.

'If it's important, they'll ring back,' she told herself, reaching for the shampoo.

The phone rang again. Katie swore. It was no good, she couldn't ignore it any longer. 'Stuff this for a game of soldiers,' she hissed, threw back the door to the shower, ran from the bathroom across the landing and into the bedroom. She snatched up the handset at the moment that the answering machine cut in, David's voice began to speak and the caller rang off.

Whoever it is will ring back in a minute, Katie assured herself, then watched herself drip on the carpet and wondered how long the damp footprints and splashes would take to dry.

The next time the telephone rang, Katie had snatched up the handset and was saying her name before the first ring had finished.

The caller sounded distraught. 'Listen, Katie,' a girl's voice said, 'I need to ask you something, it's important and I hope you won't mind me asking, and I know you're supposed to be in London and you're not, but I absolutely need to know.'

'Who *is* this?' Katie asked, her mind racing.

'It's Becky Sharp,' the girl said. 'One of Johnny's friends.'

Ohhhh, shit!

'Hello, Becky. Are you OK? You sound a little upset.'

How does she know? How did she find out?

'I'll be OK if you could just answer me a single question,' Becky said.

What's she upset about? She'll tell Johnny I'm home. And he'll tell his dad. Don't panic. Play it cool.

'You're lucky to have found me in,' Katie said. 'I'm supposed to be in London at the moment. I'm late.'

'I know,' Becky said.

Katie bit her lip before the words *Please don't tell Johnny* could leave her mouth. 'What's the problem?' she asked.

'I think I'm going mad,' Becky said. 'And there's a way you could help me to tell whether I am or not.'

Mad? Is this a joke? Something Johnny's put her up to?

'Shoot,' Katie said.

'Would you *promise* to be honest with me?' the girl asked, her voice a little cracked. And Katie heard a tiny sob. Either Becky really was in trouble or she was going to make the kind of actress who'd win Oscars.

'I promise,' Katie lied. She waved her crossed fingers in front of her face. She was beginning to get a bad feeling about this. It wasn't possible that this girl could know about Kool Day. Was it?

The bad feeling said, Yes, it certainly was.

'Cross your heart?' Becky asked.

'I do,' Katie said, waving her crossed fingers in front of her.

'OK,' Becky said, apparently satisfied. That was one of the advantages of being older, Katie decided. You weren't as gullible as this poor kid.

But, seconds later, the grin had vanished from her face and a feeling of cold, sick dread was pouring into her.

'Have you been out today, dressed in a cheesecloth dress and wearing shades and carrying a bunch of flowers?'

Katie turned round to face the bed. Where the dress lay, waiting for her to put it on. Her mouth worked, open, closed, open, closed, but no words were there to say. For the first time in her life, Katie had been caught. And she had no idea how to deal with it.

'And if the answer is yes, did you take the flowers to the

alleyway between Cliddesden Road and Hackwood Road and lay them over a deep crack in the tarmac there?'

'I'm sorry, Becky—'

'It's *important*!' Becky butted in.

Katie sighed. It sounded as if it was. But what could she do? The first and foremost rule of Kool Day was its secrecy. 'I'm sorry, Becky,' she said again, 'but I haven't been out of the house today.'

'Do you have a cheesecloth dress? A kind of hippy-style thing?'

Katie looked at the dress. It was the Kool Day dress. She'd worn it once a year since 'seventy-two. Each Kool Day.

'No,' she lied, wondering what were the chances of this girl discovering the lie. Between special days, the dress lived in a locker and the locker stayed locked. Not even David knew of its existence. It was safe.

'No,' she said. 'Used to, once upon a time. Back in the days before you were born. But not now.'

And in thirty minutes when you go out in that dress, Becky is going to be waiting in the alley for you, isn't she? Katie thought. Did it matter? Becky was a kid. She might have been a clever kid, but she was a kid all the same. If push came to shove, Katie Kool could and *would* run rings round her.

'Are you sure?' Becky asked.

Run rings, Katie? she asked herself. *Then why do you suddenly feel like throwing up? And how come Becky already knows you're lying? You've lost it! You're too old for this!*

'Sure I'm sure,' she said kindly. Then she had a bright idea. She began to feel much better.

'Have you *ever* laid flowers in that alley?' Becky asked.

'Sweetheart, I haven't got a clue what you're driving at,' Katie said. 'Look, I know I'm late, but you're distressed and—'

'Cross your heart?'

'Honest Injun. Heart crossed and everything,' Katie said. 'Now, I know I said I was in a hurry, but I can tell you're unhappy about something and I'd like you to come round here and talk to me about it. I like you, Becky, and I'd like to help you.'

Both these statements were true. But Katie *couldn't* help Becky – not today, anyway. And, as far as Kool Day went, not ever. The reason she'd invited Becky here was to get her away from the alley. It wasn't the brightest idea Katie had ever had, but it would work. She could leave the house before Becky arrived. By the time she got back, Becky would have tired of waiting and left.

'Are you sure it's OK?' Becky asked.

'Positive, sweetheart!' she said, thinking, *I'll make it up to you later. I promise.*

'Thanks,' Becky said. 'That's really kind of you.'

'Where are you now, Becky?' Katie asked, meaning to plot the girl's route from there to here and make sure she went a different way when she left the house.

Downstairs, the doorbell rang.

Fuck it! Katie thought. She put her hand over the receiver and shouted, 'One minute!' in the general direction of downstairs.

'I'm in the call-box on the junction of Fairfields Road and Cliddesden Road . . .'

Jesus! Right slap bang next to the alley!

'I thought I saw you here, not five minutes ago. And since it couldn't have been you, I'm in trouble.'

'OK. It'll take you – what – twenty minutes to walk here? I'll be waiting. I have to go. Someone's at the door. Bye, Becky. See you soon!'

Katie slammed the phone down, grabbed her dressing gown and hurried down to collect her orchids.

She saw me in the alley, ten or fifteen minutes ago, Katie told herself, as she shucked off the dressing gown and picked up the Kool Day dress. Part of the ritual was being naked beneath it since she'd been naked beneath it the first time. Katie didn't mind – she wasn't coy and she still had a body worth showing off.

What she *did* mind was that one of her son's friends had seen her in the alley. That was a nasty little fact. And it was making her feel cold and sick again.

Becky was evidently psychic. She'd seen into the future. Or the past.

'In the best possible case,' she said aloud, as she began to button up the dress. But the leaden feeling in her stomach told her otherwise. And Katie trusted her gut feelings. She didn't for a moment doubt that Becky had seen her. It was what it meant that was the problem.

What it meant was trouble. What it meant was that pay-back time had arrived. What it meant was that the biggest swindle Katie had ever worked hadn't been successful.

She gave a bitter laugh. 'And I don't even know what I did!' she said aloud.

It would be OK. Things often got a little weird around Kool Day, sometimes directly before it and occasionally afterwards, too. But that was what the annual ritual was for: to restore things to their proper order.

Katie buttoned the dress from throat to ankle in the prescribed fashion, then undid the top three buttons. The resultant gap showed just enough breast to attract attention. Then, working from the bottom up, she undid six buttons. The amount of leg on show wouldn't just attract attention, it would stop traffic. It would also allow her to run, if running became necessary. She could recall needing to run one year, but not what she'd had to run from.

What did you do, Katie Kool? Who did you lie to in 'seventy-two?

It was safer not to know. She was aware of that much. But that year was certainly the year of the Big Guilt.

And that's all you need to know, she told herself. *Forget about pay-back time, because you don't know what you did that demands a pay-back. Forget about the Big Guilt. Forget about all of it. What's done is done and there's no use crying over spilt milk. And inside half an hour it'll all be put right again.*

The cork-wedged sandals were looking pretty worn and tired now, but they felt like old friends when she put them on her feet. She wound the straps round her ankles, fastened them, then went to inspect herself in the mirror.

She looked fine. A little pale, maybe, but that was all. She grinned winningly into the mirror, checked her legs, then turned and went downstairs.

Katie picked up the posy of orchids, peered through the spy-hole, checking in case Becky had run all the way and turned up early, then let herself out of the front door.

Soon, everything would be Kool once more.

Chapter Seven

Blood

'She ain't coming,' Johnny said, from Stevie's left.

Stevie was lying on his back in the short grass, his eyes closed and the sun warming his face. He felt pretty good. Ahead of him lay plenty of holiday, his homework was done and the Honda motorbike was ready to roll.

'She said she was coming and she'll be here,' Stevie said, without opening his eyes.

'She ain't coming,' Johnny said again.

Stevie listened to Johnny take out his Marlboros and light one.

'That's five you've had since we've been waiting,' he said.

'Want one?' Johnny asked.

'Nope.'

Johnny sighed. 'You said her appointment was from two till three. We've been here waiting for the damned woman since quarter to three. It's – shit, I'm not wearing my watch. It's plenty of time later than three. Enough time for her to have got here if she was coming.'

Stevie held up his wrist between his eyes and the sun, and squinted at his G-Shock. The light hurt his eyes. 'It's half past three. Relax, she'll be here.' He sat up to look for Duke, who was in the shade of the thicket now officially known as Wanker's Paradise. He appeared to be asleep.

'Can't we just kinda start it up?' Johnny whined. 'We don't have to ride it or anything. I just want to see if it'll run.'

'It'll run,' Stevie said. 'But not till Becky gets here.'

On his right, the C90 stood, leaning on its side-stand, its paintwork – what there was of it – gleaming dully in the sun. A pleasant odour of Castrol oil wafted across from it.

The Honda, named Christine90 partly because it was ninety cubic centimetres of raw power, ha ha, and partly after Stephen King's car because you had to push it everywhere, was currently *sans* mudguards, headlight and the white plastic fairing that kept the weather off your legs. It was a long way from being a road bike, but Stevie hadn't intended it to be one. He was still six months away from being old enough to ride one on the road. Christine90 was for tearing up and down *this* field during *this* holiday. That was as far ahead as Stevie had planned his motorcycling career.

He hadn't broken the news to Johnny yet, but he was a little apprehensive about getting on her and giving her her inaugural run down the muddy path. For some reason, Johnny had got the idea that his friend was an experienced motorcyclist and Stevie had let him believe it. The fact was, he'd never sat on a moving motorcycle in his entire life.

And if he was going to hammer down the path a little way and then part company with Christine90 in a spectacular fashion, he wanted Becky to be there to see it, simply because it might turn out to be a never-to-be-repeated experience.

'You better check it'll start, at least,' Johnny said.

'I started it seventeen times this morning, after I put in the new points,' Stevie said. 'I started it twice after I'd pushed it here. If you'd been on time you'd have seen it. If I start it again there won't be any bloody petrol left to ride it. There's only a dribble in the tank now. And whose fault is that?'

'They wouldn't let me fill the can,' Johnny said. 'Just because it wasn't red,' he added in disgust. 'What difference does being red make? Bastards!'

'I'll get a sub off my dad and buy one of those proper petrol cans,' Stevie said. 'The plastic ones are only a couple of quid.'

'Did you check the kid's garden?' Johnny said, glancing at the motorcycle again.

The garden that contained the vanishing kid and his magic swing had been a constant topic of conversation since last week. Neither of them knew what had happened there. Or if it had happened at all. They had theories, of course – from mass hysteria to mistakenly ingested hallucinogenic drugs, from madness to day-time nightmares – but none quite hit the spot. What had happened had happened. Both were fairly certain of that. But neither knew why.

'Yup. I checked it on the way past,' Stevie said.

'And?'

'Same as usual. No kid.'

'Swing?'

'Still there,' Stevie said. 'And the toys.'

There hadn't been any sign of the boy since the day they'd climbed over the fence.

'Reckon he's dead?' Johnny asked, for what must have been the thousandth time.

For what must have been the thousandth time, Stevie replied, 'I reckon he's gone off on his hols with Mumsy.'

Johnny climbed on to Christine90, kicked up the stand and twisted the throttle, making motorbike noises.

'You bust anything, you fix it,' Stevie said, wasting his breath. Johnny was about as mechanically inept as it was possible to get. This, he claimed, was because he was artistic. 'Autistic, more like,' Stevie had quipped on more than one occasion. The art to suit Johnny's temperament hadn't yet been invented. Unless it was the art of demolition.

'You don't suppose that *thing*, old Yah-hoo, got the kid *and* his mum, do you?' Johnny wondered, swivelling on Christine's seat so he was sitting side-saddle.

Stevie waited for him to topple backwards into the briar patch that stood just behind him, but Johnny kept the bike on its centre of gravity, his toes resting on the ground. 'No,' he said. 'I think they went on holiday. Poor little Nigel's probably sitting on a beach somewhere in Cornwall while his mum's propping up the bar in the nearest pub.'

Johnny shook his head. 'It still hurts, just thinking about it,' he mused. 'Like someone took us out of here and stuck us in a cartoon for half an hour. Too fucking weird.'

Stevie nodded. It was too fucking weird indeed. And it had left no evidence, either, barring the odd scratches on the Dookster's legs. Scratches that just *might* have been made naturally.

But they both remembered what had happened in Nigel's back garden, which seemed even weirder. You ought to forget stuff like that after it happened. Wasn't your mind supposed to have some sort of a censor that stopped hurtful things hurting you?

And thinking about it *did* hurt.

It hurt to remember it because it wasn't right. It was something that *couldn't* have happened. Something impossible.

'It was a glitch,' Stevie said, squinting up at Johnny. 'That's what it was. But not like the Twilight Zone or anything. This only happened inside our heads. We probably didn't do any of that stuff we can remember.'

'Fuck off! That's impossible!'

Stevie shook his head. 'I went to the library yesterday and found a couple of books on weird things that can happen with your brain. Hallucinations and stuff.'

'We didn't take any drugs,' Johnny pointed out.

'You don't have to. Sometimes that kind of stuff happens naturally. Well, spontaneously, anyway. I read about this guy whose memory doesn't work. He got herpes or something and it went up his nerves and hit his brain. Now every time he sees his wife, he thinks he's seeing her for the first time in years.'

'I haven't got herpes,' Johnny countered.

'Neither have I. But there are billions of instances of people's perceptions going wonky for no reason. There was this woman in France who suddenly stopped being able to see movement. Everthing she saw was always stationary.'

'And she got run down by a truck, right?'

Stevie shook his head. 'No, but only because she can't cross the road alone any more. Can't even pour a cup of tea.'

'Was that herpes too?'

'Just happened. No one knows why. The brain is a funny thing. No one really knows how it works.'

Johnny sighed. 'So the top and bottom of it is we're mental?'

'Nah. We just had a temporary glitch. A kind of epilepsy or something.'

'Well, how come we both had it at the same time?' Johnny wanted to know.

'A good question,' Stevie said, checking his watch. It really didn't look as if Becky was coming.

'Do you know what?' Johnny said.

'What?'

Johnny didn't speak for a while. He looked a little embarrassed.

'What?' Stevie repeated.

'I hope it isn't true,' Johnny finally said.

Stevie shrugged. 'That we're mental? Or that we both had a half-hour brain glitch?'

Johnny shook his head. 'That there's a rational explanation. I hope *that* isn't true.'

'You do?'

Johnny nodded. 'I want what happened to be real.' He grinned sheepishly.

Stevie held his gaze and had one of those brief moments of understanding that sometimes happens between people who are close – an almost telepathic contact.

'I do, too,' he admitted.

It takes one to know one, Becky told herself, chewing her bottom lip.

As far as people's parents went, in Becky's opinion Katie Kane was OK. She wasn't as uptight as Stevie's mother and she was a good deal nicer than all the teachers at school. She let Johnny do more or less what he wanted and, more importantly, she'd been pleasant to Becky from the first time they'd met. Katie Kane was warm, welcoming and open. A kind of nineties version of the earth mother, Becky thought.

At least, on the surface she was.

In the beginning, Becky had been a little suspicious of Katie but that had worn off fairly quickly and she had begun to trust her.

Because Katie's good, Becky told herself. *And not just good. She's actually an expert. But now you know.*

Becky knew indeed. In much the same way as you could set a thief to catch a thief you could set a liar to catch another.

Beneath Katie Kane's warm, open exterior beat the heart of a champion fibber. She was the kind of liar who could commit first-degree murder and pass a polygraph test the following day. The kind of liar who was never found out.

When Becky had realized this, during the phone call she'd made ten minutes ago, Katie Kane had risen in her estimation. Becky had felt a surge of warmth and admiration towards Katie, the way a hobbyist carpenter might when watching a master craftsman make a perfect dovetail by eye.

It takes one to know one, Becky told herself again, rejoicing inwardly. Not that she would have put herself in Katie's league. On a scale of one to ten, Katie was closing in on the top – a good five places ahead of where Becky estimated her own position. It was a good job Katie hadn't quite reached number ten, Becky knew, because if she had Becky wouldn't have known she was being spun a yarn.

Becky still hadn't worked out what mistake Katie had made, what tiny inflection in her voice or misplaced word had given her away. But after she'd asked Katie to cross her heart and Katie had replied, 'I do,' Becky had begun to feel suspicious. Perhaps because Katie had been a little too quick to respond: as if she crossed her heart lots of times in an average month and was used to the routine.

Whatever it was, Becky had twigged. Which was why she wasn't now hammering on the door of Johnny's house but leaning up against the wall of the Lamb, hidden from view by a camper van, while she kept an eye on the approach to Cliddesden Road and Hackwood Road between which the alley ran.

Katie had asked where she was and then invited her over. To the other side of town.

Where I would be far away from where she wanted to be, Becky thought.

Becky didn't know why she'd already seen Katie arrive and lay the posy of orchids, if she was yet to come, and she tried not to think of it. Whether she'd been here already or whether she was yet to come – and Becky had seen the future – was beside the point.

The point was, Katie was coming and Becky was going to ask her for some answers. And if it so happened that Becky was way off the mark, well, it wasn't a long walk back to the office of her saviour, Woolly Williams.

If I've cracked, I'll go in and have the ECT and take the Largactil and the therapy and get better. If *I've cracked. But I don't think I have. I think there's something weird going on and I think Katie was worried that I know something.*

In the shop next to the call-box, Becky had just bought a packet of ten John Player Specials. Now she unwrapped the Cellophane, pulled the silver paper from the pack, took out a cigarette and held it between her teeth. She cursed Johnny and Stevie. It hadn't occurred to her to smoke until she'd begun to hang around with the two boys. *And now*, she thought as she struck the match, *I'm fifteen and adicted to smoking*.

Which was when Katie Kane came sashaying round the corner of Southern Road, wearing a white cheesecloth dress which showed a lot of leg, and carrying a posy of orchids.

Smiling fiercely, Becky ducked down behind the camper van.

Stevie opened his mouth wide, tracking the Marlboro's arc through the air. He ducked to the left, snapped his mouth shut catching the cigarette sideways on. The paper instantly sucked up what little moisture lay on his lips and stuck fast.

Johnny, a cigarette in his own mouth and a lit match in his right hand, guffawed around his Marlboro and punched the air with his left fist. He toppled backwards from where he was perched on Christine90 into the briar bush, the motorcycle following him.

Immediately, Stevie envisaging what little petrol was left in Christine90's tank spilling out and possibly setting fire to her, opened his mouth to yell a warning and tore strips of skin from his lips. As he dashed towards the bike, which lay on top of Johnny, the bloodstained Marlboro finally fell to the grass.

Duke, seeing what he interpreted as violence in the making, leapt from the shade of Wanker's Paradise and shot across the grass towards the motorcycle.

Johnny began to yell for help.

'Don't move!' Stevie shouted. 'Petrol! I'll get you up!' He bent forward and grabbed the bike's nearest handlebar, dimly aware of what he thought sounded like the thundering of horse's hoofs somewhere to the rear of him.

Which was when the airborne dog hit him in the back.

Stevie fell headfirst over Christine90, driving the bike back down on to Johnny.

'Ficking hull, Dogboy,' Johnny groaned, his voice muffled.

Stevie could smell the sharp odour of petrol, and, worse, smoke. He wriggled off Johnny, fought with brambles that tore at his clothing and bare arms and got to his feet. A patch of long-dead vegetation was crackling where Johnny's match had fallen. Stevie stamped it out, wrestled the bike up on to its stand, then turned to help Johnny.

Johnny got up, his face a mixture of pain and amusement. His cheeks were badly scratched and both his hands were bloody. 'You look like you're wearing lipstick,' he observed.

'You look like you've been rolling about in a bramble bush,' Stevie said, licking the blood from his lips, and added, 'Trying to get yourself burnt to death.' He stepped out of the bushes and went back to where he'd been sitting. He needed that cigarette now, bloodstained or not. It was nowhere to be seen.

'How much petrol came out?' Johnny said, glancing back at the bike.

'Just a trickle,' Stevie replied, looking up from the place where he *knew* the cigarette had fallen. 'Lucky it didn't catch. The tank would have blown.'

'Wasn't our turn to die today,' Johnny said, dabbing the blood from his hands with a tissue.

'Flash the ash again,' Stevie said. 'My fag went walkies.'

Johnny threw him another from the magic packet that never seemed to empty, no matter how many you smoked. This time Stevie caught it with his hand. 'Matches?'

Johnny handed him the box and sat down beside him.

'There's blood on this matchbox,' Stevie said.

'There's blood everyfuckingwhere,' Johnny said. 'And your lip's still bleeding. Where did that tissue go? I had it a minute ago. You got it?'

Stevie shook his head. 'I'm worried about catching something off you from this matchbox,' he said, striking a match and lighting the cigarette that was already beginning to stick to his cut lips. 'I certainly wouldn't be dabbing myself with a tissue soaked in your blood.'

'I ain't plus, y'know,' Johnny said.

'You had a test?'

Johnny grinned.

'Oh, I forgot,' Stevie said. 'You have to have had some kind of sexual contact before you need an HIV test.'

'That'd count you out then, Dogboy,' Johnny said. He thought about this for a moment and added, 'Betcha *I* can get in Becky's pants.'

'You couldn't find your way into your own pants without having your mum there to put 'em on for you every day,' Stevie said, gently peeling away the cigarette from his lips and inspecting the bloody tip. 'And, anyway, I thought you didn't fancy her.'

Johnny pulled a face. 'I might do,' he said. 'She's OK.'

'You're in love!' Stevie mocked.

'Fuck off! But you got to admit she's got good legs and a nice arse.'

'I never noticed,' Stevie said.

'Lying bastard! I've seen you drooling each time she turns her back on you.'

Stevie grinned. 'Maybe, maybe not.' He suddenly realized that his shoulder stung. He put his cigarette on the grass and gently removed a thorn. It was a big one and it had gone in deeply. Unsurprisingly the hole began to bleed.

'I'll race you into her pants,' Johnny said. 'Bet you a fiver I get there first.'

Stevie shook his head. 'I don't think Becky would want to play,' he said, but the sad fact was that even if she was open to being seduced he wouldn't stand the chance of the proverbial snowball in hell, pitched against Johnny.

'Coward,' Johnny said.

Grinning, Stevie reached down for his cigarette. It had gone. He did a double-take at the spot where he'd last seen it then checked Johnny's hand. He looked for a tell-tale curl of blue smoke.

'What's up?' Johnny asked.

'My fag's vanished again,' Stevie said.

'You smoked it, didn't you?'

'No. I put it down here.' Stevie got up and inspected the area where he'd been sitting. There were two little grey worms of ash where he'd flicked it and, nearby, the grass bore a tiny scorch-mark where he'd laid the cigarette. Of the cigarette itself there was no sign.

'The Borrowers got it,' Johnny suggested.

Or the gobblings, Stevie's mind added and he shivered.

'What's up?'

'Someone walked over my grave,' Stevie said. His skin prickled, and once again he heard the voice of the little girl: *They live all underground, down in the nasty, don't they?*

He looked up and down the field.

'See Becky yet?' Johnny wanted to know.

'I wasn't looking for her. I was checking to see if I was still in the same universe as you,' Stevie said.

'What's the time by your G-Spot?'

'Five to four.'

'She ain't coming, Dogboy. Let's face it.'

Stevie sighed. 'OK. If she isn't here by four, we'll do it anyway. Let's have another lung-rocket and this time I'll see if I can get all the way through it without losing the bloody thing.'

Crouched behind the camper, Becky dropped the remainder of her cigarette and ground it out with her shoe. Her heart was thumping and she was feeling an odd combination of anger and exhilaration mixed with relief. There *was* something odd going on here. Katie had lied to her, hence Katie was covering up for something.

In less than a minute, Katie was going to pass where the camper was parked. It was quite possible that she would glance to her right and see Becky crouched between the van and the side wall of the pub, but Becky didn't care. It would be better if she could follow Katie and see her lay the posy before talking to her, but it didn't matter. She already knew what Katie intended.

Where is she? She should be here by now! Becky thought. When Katie hadn't passed after a slow count of sixty, Becky began to worry that she'd imagined seeing her. She got on her hands and knees and peered under the van.

Katie was still a way down the road, standing on the corner where Becky had first seen her. She stood facing the pub, the sun glinting off her dark glasses. The breeze from the passing traffic made her dress billow around her and showed off her legs practically all the way up but she didn't seem to notice. She was staring fixedly ahead, her hands clenched around the posy of orchids at her chest as if she were praying.

She's frightened, Becky thought, frowning.

And so should you be, Woolly Williams's voice added on her behalf.

For some reason Becky suddenly remembered him asking her last week if she held any religious beliefs.

'Life after death, you mean?' Becky had replied. 'I fucking hope not.'

And he asked me again today, she reminded herself. *Do you think there could be an afterlife?* he'd asked. And she'd made the same sort of reply. The truth was that, yes, she *did* believe in an afterlife. She believed it because her mother had almost come back.

The weird thing was that looking at Katie reminded her of all this. It was like catching a glimpse of yourself in a mirror when you were terribly scared. Katie looked as if she was frightened that *her* father might bring back *her* mother from the dead.

You don't have *to be insane* . . .

And that wasn't the voice of Woolly Williams, replaying in her mind, but a voice she had never heard. The voice that had crept out of the split in the tarmac in the alley.

Katie was on the move, wiggling along in that swivel-hipped way of hers. Becky watched her cross the road. Katie would pass within six feet of her. Becky prepared to say, 'Hi, Katie! I called at your house but you weren't in. I thought you might be on your way here!' but Katie walked past, staring straight ahead.

This time she left a scent. Opium, Becky thought, or First. She could never remember which was which. It was a perfume that she associated with Johnny's mother, anyway.

This time Katie wasn't walking quite so quickly, more at the speed of a normal human being.

Becky followed her, keeping up easily and maintaining a gap of about fifteen feet. If Katie turned she'd see her pursuer, but who cared? Lies, like murder, as they said, would *out*.

Katie turned into the alley with Becky hot on her heels. The gap was less now – maybe nine or ten feet. Katie ought to be able to hear her footsteps closing in. But evidently she had other things on her mind. Half-way through the alley, in the exact spot where Becky knew she would, Katie stopped. Becky crept a little closer. It seemed obvious that some form of address would accompany Katie's ceremony and it might be a good idea to find out what the words were, in case Katie wouldn't answer the questions lining up in Becky's mind.

Gotcha! Becky thought, grinning.

A few feet in front of her, Katie parted the front of her dress and knelt down at the near end of the crack in the tarmac.

'Everything's cool,' Katie whispered, and nodded three times.

'Everything's cool and I'm a free woman.

'Everything's cool and I'm a free woman and you can't have what you want. Katie Kool is ahead of the game and she's called off the deal. She reneged. Went back on her word. So everything's cool on this side of the fence. Forget it, like I forgot it, and everything will be cool on that side of the fence too.'

Becky frowned as Katie rambled. She seemed to be in a trance.

She spoke in a low monotone as if repeating words in which she didn't have the slightest interest.

Or perhaps she doesn't know she's saying them, Becky thought.

'There isn't a damned thing that can be done about it,' Katie said. 'Katie Kool is the best. You don't mess with the best and expect to win, now, do you? So just chalk it up to experience and forget it. You can't touch Katie Kool. I'm a free woman. A woman who chose to forget.'

Katie waved the posy of orchids over the crack in the tarmac, outlining a shape that Becky didn't recognize. From where she stood it looked something like the movements you might make with a car's gear-lever.

And I thought I *was going crazy*, Becky told herself, a little awed by seeing someone she'd previously thought sensible and quite nice doing something like this. It was what they called obsessive compulsive disorder or something like that, Becky thought. This variant seemed to have some religious connotation, though.

Katie put down the posy on her right, in the centre of the path, and fumbled at the front of her dress. Then she reached out in front of her, her hands together like someone intending to dive. The tips of her fingers were held out over the centre of the crack at the height of her shoulders.

Becky moved silently to her right to get a better view.

A thin, shiny, steel sewing needle was pressed between Katie's forefingers. It protruded vertically, point upwards. The tip of her right forefinger was covered with a silver thimble.

'Katie Kool offers this as an example of her power,' Katie said.

A needle and thimble? Becky thought. An urge to run away and try to forget about this was creeping into her bones. On the surface it might look silly, but there was something scary about it. Something that became more frightening the longer she stood here watching.

Don't be silly! she told herself, but she kept remembering the way the crack had hissed as if gas were escaping. And the smooth sides that had felt like marble beneath her fingers. And how the hole had reminded her of a hungry mouth about to snap up its dinner.

Katie drew her hands away from the hole, then put them back, but this time the needle was in her right hand between thimble and thumb and her left hand was open and empty.

'Katie Kool offers this part of herself as a sacrifice,' Katie said.

Oh, shit! Becky thought, wincing. She tensed as Katie balled her left hand and stuck out her forefinger as if pointing the way.

'OK, it's four o'clock,' Stevie said. 'We're not waiting any longer. Becky's gonna miss it. If it's a once-only thing, tough. She should have been here.'

'*Yes!*' Johnny shouted, punching the air.

Over in the shade of Wanker's Paradise, Duke looked up enquiringly.

Stevie got up and walked over to Christine90, his heart in his mouth.

'It'll never fly, O Wolfie Dogboy!' Johnny said, joining him.

'That's what I'm hoping.' Stevie grinned.

'You're not worried, are you, my little dog-loving pal?' Johnny asked, astonished. 'You look kind of pale. You're not expecting it to blow up, are you?'

No, I'm expecting to fall off and break some bones, actually, Stevie replied mentally. 'Worried?' he said. 'Worried about what, exactly? Nothing bad is going to happen.'

Johnny grinned. 'Course not,' he said, 'because old Christine here isn't going to start and if she doesn't start, you can't fall off her and bust yourself up, can you?'

Stevie said nothing. He fished the ignition key out of his pocket with a flourish, dangled it in front of Johnny's face, said, 'You wanna go first?' then snatched it away as Johnny's hand came up to grab it.

'Bastard!'

Stevie put the key into the Honda's ignition. 'Drum-roll please,' he said.

Johnny spent twenty seconds running through his repertoire of rap-band drum noises, all of which sounded roughly the same.

The ignition light lit. Stevie's heart beat a little harder. His mouth was suddenly as dry as the Gobi desert and his hands felt as if they were going to tremble badly. He sat astride the Honda, flicked out the kick-start pedal with his foot, twisted the throttle a little way open and kicked.

Christine90 made a series of damp *phutting* noises and fell silent.

Johnny groaned, clapping his hands to his face in mock disappointment. 'Call yourself a mechanic?' he asked.

'Flooded, that's all,' Stevie said, trying to keep the tremor from his voice. 'From when she fell over, I expect.' He kicked the pedal down again, the throttle closed this time. The bike didn't start.

'If I had slow hands, I'd clap 'em, Dogboy.' Johnny chortled.

'Wait!' Stevie said. He opened the throttle all the way and kicked again.

Christine90 roared into life, revving up to a scream. The noise was deafening. Stevie let out the throttle until the engine slowed to a tick-over.

'Let's see you fly then, Dogboy!' Johnny shouted. 'And don't use all the petrol. I want a go!'

His heart hammering almost as fast as the tiny piston inside Christine90, Stevie pushed the bike off the stand and walked it to the track. He didn't want to have to do anything complicated – like making a ninety-degree turn – until he knew whether or not he was going to stay upright. He lined up the bike towards the far end of the field, the one by which Becky would be entering if she turned up now, took a deep breath and glanced over at Johnny.

'*Go!*' Johnny shouted, flinging out his hand towards the far-away fence.

You can ride a bike, and this is no different except you don't have to pedal, Stevie assured himself. *You can do it!*

He kicked the gear-shift into what he hoped was first, felt the jolt as it connected, then gently opened the throttle. To his amazement, Christine90 began to move smoothly forward at what must have been a quick walking pace. Stevie caught his balance, put his feet up on the rests and opened the throttle a little further. The bike's engine picked up, the speed increased with a jerk and the breeze began to tousle Stevie's hair. He cackled with joy. This was probably the best feeling he'd had since his eyes locked with Dookie's back at the Anstey Close Dog Rescue.

He let off the throttle, kicked the bike into second and opened her up. The speedo read twenty miles an hour, which was plenty fast enough to be travelling on rough, muddy ground. It was as bumpy as hell, it was as noisy as standing behind a jet fighter's engines, but it felt like heaven.

The end of the field was approaching a lot more quickly than Stevie had expected it to. He wound down the throttle and gently applied the brakes, hoping they were going to work before he reached the piece of broken-down chain-link that marked the field's border.

The back wheel began to slide and Stevie let off the brakes a little, yelling aloud with a mixture of glee and fear. If he wasn't going to stop in time, he was going right over that fence, the hump of vegetation that lay beneath it and out on the grassy area that lay beyond. He suddenly felt certain he could negotiate it effortlessly.

Then he realized that he *was* going to stop in time. A moment later than that, he knew that he didn't *want* to stop in time.

Go for it! he told himself, and wound the throttle open as he approached the hump.

There was a brief sensation of being pushed down as Christine90 hit the ramp, then a lightness as Stevie and the bike took to the air.

Katie stood there, the forefinger of her left hand pointing towards magnetic north and the long silver needle in her right hand pointing south.

Becky fancied she could see the air between the point of the needle and the top of Katie's finger shimmering slightly.

'My soul is my own,' Katie said in a low voice. 'My eternal soul is my own, but I give up this part of myself as a sacrifice and payment. My blood and my pain are pure. My blood and my pain absolve me of my sins and release me from my bonds. And make the most of them, sucker, they're all that you're getting,' she added, in a warning tone.

Becky listened, her jaw hanging slack.

Katie's right hand began to move slowly and steadily towards her left, and the left towards the needle.

I hate needles, Becky reminded herself unnecessarily. She had developed an aversion to them during the series of inoculations she'd had at school. As Katie's hands drew close, she tried to look away and found that she couldn't. Something in her wanted her to see this apparently.

There'll just be a little prick and it'll all be over, she told herself.

The tip of the needle came into contact with the top of Katie's forefinger and Katie paused. 'Kool Day,' she said. 'Time to seal the seals for another year.'

The point made a tiny indentation in Katie's index finger. Becky could see it as plainly as if she was right up close to Katie holding a magnifying glass over her hands. Her entire world seemed focused on that small area.

Katie didn't jab as Becky expected her to, but pushed gently. The sharp point of the needle pierced her skin and a bright bead of blood bloomed around it, gathered, swelled and dropped into the crack in the tarmac.

Becky realized she'd been holding her breath and let it go, sucking in air that suddenly tasted bad. As if something nasty was being burned close by. A bonfire of dried garden weeds, perhaps.

That wasn't so bad, was it? she asked herself.

Katie moaned.

Oh, God, Becky thought, *she hasn't finished!*

Katie pressed the needle a little deeper into her flesh, gasping quietly, then let go of it. Another droplet of blood fell into the hole, but that was all – the needle's taper had sealed the hole it had made now that Katie had pushed it deeper. The needle protruded from her finger, the eye end quivering slightly.

Suddenly Becky understood why Katie was wearing the thimble.

'Don't,' she heard herself whisper.

Katie placed the end of the thimble against the eye of the needle, her hands in perfect alignment. 'Pain,' she said, and began to push.

You didn't have to have a deep understanding of medical matters to know that if you pushed a needle into the end of your finger you were going to hit bone in very short order. Becky knew when the needle hit the bone in Katie's finger because that was the point at which Katie began to pant and mewl aloud like a wounded cat.

Becky couldn't stand to watch but couldn't tear her eyes away. *That's enough now,* she told herself. *She's done enough. She's in pain and now she'll stop. Now she'll waggle the needle free and pull it out.*

In the back of her mind, Becky began to wonder how far into the bone the needle had gone and how difficult it would be for Katie to withdraw it again. So far it couldn't have pierced the bone for more than a couple of millimetres.

In front of her Katie was gasping with each exhalation. Her chest was rising and falling rapidly and she was running with sweat. Becky could almost feel the excruciating pain in her own index finger.

Pull it out! she ordered silently. *You've done enough!*

But obviously Katie didn't think she *had* done enough. She drew a deep breath, held it and pushed the thimble hard against the eye of the needle, the muscles in her arms and shoulders bunching with the effort.

Either the needle must have been made of something stronger than steel, or Katie was able to direct the force with the utmost accuracy: it slid deeper into her finger without even flexing. It had to have gone through bone right down to the first joint by now, and still Katie pushed.

Then she let out her breath in a shuddering muted scream. Her entire body was quivering and her mouth was twisted into an agonized grimace. Blood was dripping from her finger now. Not a huge amount, but enough to form a steady supply of glittering red beads that fell into the mouth in the tarmac.

The tears that had been welling up in Becky's eyes were now flowing freely. Just watching was torture and she couldn't stand it any more. 'Stop it!' she yelled.

Katie didn't ever hear her.

'That's pain for you,' Katie hissed, from between gritted teeth. 'Take it, you fucker, because it's all you're getting.' She made a fist with her right hand, arranging it so that the top of her index finger and the thimble protruded. Then she drew back her fist to her side and hammered it round, hitting the needle hard. Blood sprayed off, flicking across the path and spattering Becky.

Becky yelped.

'Kool Day!' Katie hissed. 'And fuck you!' Then she tore the thimble from her finger, wiped it in the blood and dropped it down into the crack. She flicked the blood from her finger into the fissure after it and then did the weird sign again.

'Katie,' Becky whispered.

Again Katie didn't hear. She was inspecting the tip of her index finger. It looked nasty. It was already badly swollen and was purple where blood was welling up inside it. 'Fuck,' Katie said to herself, in a tiny shaky voice. 'That *hurts*.'

As Becky watched, feeling as if she might faint at any second, Katie opened her mouth wide, inserted the eye of the needle between the molars on the left side of her mouth and bit down on it.

Then she pulled her hand away.

Removing the needle took a lot longer than driving it in. It kept slipping out from between her teeth as she pulled and Katie had to stop to rest and, presumably, to let the pain subside. During the pauses, she flicked more blood into the fissure in the path.

The muscles in Katie's arms were well defined. Becky watched them flex and relax as, little by little, she worked the needle out of her finger. She was strong, there was no doubt about that. And not just physically strong.

Katie rested for a few seconds, gasping and keening, then bit down on the needle with her front teeth and gave one last yank.

For Becky, it happened in slow motion. Katie's finger pulled free of the needle and described an arc out over the hole in the path as if drawing a rainbow with the blood that exploded from her finger. Then she reached out with her other hand, wrapped it around the injured finger and squeezed hard as if wringing water out of a sponge.

A great deal of blood ran into the fissure, but it didn't seem to be falling naturally, rather as if it was being directed, very precisely, to a certain spot down in that hole.

The smell of burning vegetation hit Becky's nostrils again. This time the odour was a good deal more powerful. Wisps of vapour rose, curling, from the fissure.

Katie let go of her forefinger, shook the blood off her hands and spat. The needle followed the arc the blood had made, turned sharply through ninety degress and vanished into the ground, point first.

She picked up the posy of orchids, did her magical pass again and laid them over the split in the tarmac. She made a small adjustment, then nodded.

'Let's see you get past that lot!' she hissed, using exactly the same words Becky had used forty minutes or so earlier when she'd laid the posy over the widest part of the fissure.

Becky felt dizzy. *Not possible!* she told herself. But here she was, conscious and thinking. If it wasn't happening, it was the best-quality nightmare she'd ever had.

Katie got to her feet and touched her right hand to her forehead as if she had a sudden pain there. An expression of confusion swam across her features. Then, from the corner of her eye, she noticed that someone was standing beside her. She glanced at Becky, looked away, did a double-take and yelped as if she'd been stung.

'Hi, Katie,' Becky said, her voice thick with emotion.

'Oh, fuck,' Katie said, and fainted dead away.

Christine90 and Stevie must have been airborne for less than a second, but it seemed much longer. He had time enough to experience a moment of total and all-encompassing joy at having left the ground.

Then the bike hit the grass on the far side of the hump, its wheels no longer facing the direction of travel. The suspension grounded with considerable force, jarring Stevie's spine so hard it felt as if it would come out through the top of his skull. The bike bucked like a bull at a rodeo.

Stevie clung on as Christine tried to take to the air again and failed. He wrenched the handlebars to the left and leaned against the way the bike wanted to throw him. For the following three seconds he fought to stay upright, knowing he was going to fail and that when he hit the ground face first at perhaps ten or fifteen miles an hour, the bike was going to smash into his back.

By some miracle, neither of these things happened. Stevie

found his balance and skidded to a halt about three feet away from the iron railings where the pedestrian underpass went down under Churchill Way roundabout.

The engine didn't even stall.

Not quite allowing himself to believe he was still alive, Stevie kicked the shift into neutral, killed the engine and got off Christine90. He kicked down the side-stand and leaned the bike into it. Every part of him seemed shot full of adrenaline and made of jelly.

Christine90 was ticking quietly as her parts cooled. Tiny wisps of smoke curled up from gaskets that had got very hot for the first time since they'd been fitted, and thicker blue smoke drifted from holes in the patched exhaust pipe. A tiny dribble of clean engine oil ran down the gearbox casing.

You could have killed yourself, the voice of Stevie's mother said in his head.

Stevie felt his face light in a big, sappy grin. He balled his fist and punched at the sky, shouting, 'YES!'

Behind him Duke gave a woof of what sounded like approval. Stevie spun round. His dog was standing on the top of the rise that had flung Stevie into the air. He barked and glanced back over his shoulder to the field, then looked at Stevie and barked again.

'OK, I'm coming,' Stevie said. His heart was more or less back down in his chest now, and beating at its normal rate.

Duke turned and ran off into the field.

Grinning. Stevie remounted Christine90 and patted her petrol tank. 'Well done,' he told the bike, and turned on the ignition.

The motorcycle roared into life on the first kick. Stevie was still facing away from the entrance to the field, but now he felt confident enough to attempt a tight turn. He selected first gear, opened the throttle, rolled away, turned right . . .

. . . and fell off.

He lay on the ground for a few moments, then got up, started the bike again and tried once more. This time he got the hang of it. He took the hump slowly this time, then opened her up and roared back towards where Johnny was standing with Duke.

When he reached the clearing from which he'd started, he aimed at Johnny. Duke danced aside, barking.

Stevie slowed a little, then stood on the back brake pedal, locking the wheel into a skid, and whipped the bike round in a tight arc. Flinging up grass and dirt, Christine90's rear wheel described a perfect semi-circle and came to rest about four inches away from Johnny's right leg.

Johnny, of course, neither batted an eyelid nor moved a muscle.

Stevie turned off the engine, grinning. 'You can have a go now,' Stevie said. 'Get on and show me up, why don't you?'

'Bastard!' Johnny said.

Stevie pulled a face. 'What?' he said.

'You know I've never ridden one of these things before,' he said. 'You just want to see me fuck it up.'

Stevie smiled. Johnny was jealous. 'Want to know a secret?' he said.

'What?' Johnny asked, fishing his Marlboros from his pocket again.

Stevie nodded at Christine. 'I've never ridden one of these things before, either. That was my first time.'

Johnny brightened. 'Really?' he asked. 'Honest Injun?'

Stevie grinned. 'Yup,' he said, taking the cigarette Johnny offered him. 'That jump was beginner's luck. I didn't even know I was gonna try it till I got there.'

'Old Whatsisname must have been keeping an eye on you,' Johnny said.

'Old who?'

'Your friend and mine. And Nigel's. Old Yah-hoo. He whose name may not be spoken. He wants you for a sunbeam, remember?'

Stevie did remember. He plugged the cigarette into his mouth, trying not to think how good it had felt to leave the ground as though it no longer had any hold over him. *The way the kid looked when he was belting up and down on that swing, out of control*, he told himself. *That's how you must have looked when Christine90 leapt off the ground. Delirious with excitement.*

And then he could suddenly hear himself speaking. Not now, but years ago in a tiny piping voice that he didn't even remember owning. '. . . showed me how to fly! I c'n *fly*! Manaymon *said* I could fly. Mummeee!'

And the voice brought back the memory. The pictures drew themselves darkly in Stevie's mind.

He'd been in the back garden digging a hole. It wasn't in the house on Solby's Road but in the big house in East Waltham where they'd lived when he was little. He could clearly remember this hole because it was the deepest one he'd ever made. And it was the day he got banned from digging any more.

At that time, it was Little Wolfgang Stephen Warner's lifetime ambition to dig right down through the earth's crust, mine his way through the rock that he'd been told lay beneath and hit the hot stuff in the centre, just to see if it was really there. Even then he'd known he was taking on a big job, but surely it couldn't be impossible.

His holes weren't good ones: the sides caved in when he got down as far as knee-level. A bigger problem was that each time he went to bed, the hole he'd dug that day mysteriously filled itself in again.

But on this particular day he'd been doing well. He'd commandeered his dad's garden fork from the tool shed and gone down to the bottom of the garden behind the bushes. He worked all morning, loosening the earth with the big fork, then shovelling it out with a blue plastic spade he'd brought back from the seaside.

This hole wasn't just any old excavation, it was a *quality* hole. But the time he got hungry and went in for lunch, dirty and sweaty, he'd gone quite deep. When he stood in it, the ground level was at his waist.

After lunch he dug some more, working from inside the hole. By mid-afternoon he had blisters and it was starting to get difficult to climb out without pulling in the earth he'd just shovelled out. And then he'd hit a stratum of black, greasy dirt that was difficult to fork and which clung to his spade. He'd struggled with this for a while and then had sat down in the hole for a rest.

Now he thought about it, all those years later, Stevie remembered exactly how it had felt to sit in that secret place he'd excavated, cool and a little damp, the rich smell of freshly turned earth filling his nostrils. He'd felt safe and secure, at peace, like a child being hugged by its mother.

And Manaymon had begun to speak to him in a gentle voice, telling him things he didn't know. Miracles that had happened. Miracles yet to come. And Stevie listened drowsily, nodding from time to time. And then Manaymon had shown him how he could fly. It might have been real, or it might merely have been pictures – a kind of dream-vision – but for Stevie the sensation was true to life. Manaymon showed him how to sit, how to think and how to do a little wiggle to get himself airborne.

And Stevie had tried it. It didn't work at first but, in that slurred, soft voice, Manaymon patiently told him what he was doing wrong and Stevie tried again.

This time he got it right.

There was a kind of buzzing sensation that shook all through his body, then a sound like tearing and a hard jolt as if someone had punched him between his shoulder blades.

Stevie had drifted up into the air a foot and hovered, still in a sitting position, in the centre of the hole. It was an odd feeling, but he wasn't even a tiny bit frightened. After a couple of seconds of getting used to it, he began to grin. He was no longer attached to the ground. No longer a victim of that force that stopped you falling off the world. He was *free*. And it was delightful.

Stevie stood up, still floating in the hole, and looked down at his feet, grinning.

Fly away now, Manaymon had said. *Soar in the sky, as free as the birdies!*

'I don't know *how* to,' Stevie had giggled, but as soon as he'd spoken the words, he realized he *did* know how to – without even thinking about it. You just did it naturally, like scratching an itch.

Stevie rose from the hole, beside himself with glee. He elevated himself to a height of six feet or so above the level of the garden and started forward, amazed at how his attitude changed so that he was flying parallel to the ground, his feet out behind him like Peter Pan and his friends in the cartoon.

He circled the hole, leaning over to his right, then flew towards the big bush that hid him from the house. Then he slipped up over the top of it, picking up a little speed. He swooped down and skimmed his dad's wheelbarrow, then peeled off to the left and rose high above the house, so that he was looking down on it. It didn't look real any more and Stevie was amazed at how small and insignificant it seemed from this angle.

Way up in the sky over his head, two birds wheeled, riding the rising currents of warm air. Stevie slipped upwards in a wide corkscrew until he was level with them, then glided round after them, enjoying the warm air against his face and the sunshine on his back.

Then he looked down. The shock nearly made him tumble to the ground. He seemed to be *miles* high. The back garden was now the size of a postage stamp. The house looked like a model. Stevie could see the front garden, too, from here. And the road. And the big road that it joined to – the one that led into the town. And beyond that, fields of yellows and browns, all fitted together like a massive patchwork quilt made of odd shapes. Way off in the distance, Stevie could see Overton and West Waltham.

Suddenly he felt giddy. He swooped back down, levelling off again at tree-top height a couple of hundred yards down the road from his house. He swept out over a cornfield, skimming low and chortling as the corn tickled his belly, then flew up and over Mr Granger's house, three doors down from his own home, did a slow circuit of the Grangers' back garden, then fence-hopped back into his own garden where the Grangers' cat, Pookie, was sneaking up on a bird wrestling a worm from the lawn.

Stevie flew up behind the cat and shouted, 'Boo!' He laughed when the animal took off as if its tail had caught fire, and slowly glided back to his hole, positioned himself over it and let himself down.

There was another sensation of buzzing, then a breathless feeling as if someone was trying to force him into a space that he was too big to go into. He screeched and stood up, feeling heavy.

For a few moments, his body no longer seemed to fit him, then, with the merest *snap*, he was all back together again and weighed exactly as much as he had before he'd become weightless.

He chuckled aloud and scrambled out of the hole, just dying to tell his mum the brilliant news. He could *fly*! He tore up the garden path to the open kitchen door, leapt the step and skidded to a halt.

Stevie could hear his own voice ringing in his ears: '. . . showed me how to fly! I c'n *fly*! Manaymon *said* I could fly. Mummeee!'

'I'm in here,' his mother's muffled voice called from the lounge.

Stevie ran up the hall and into the lounge, the words '*Guess what!*' ready at the tip of his tongue.

'*Stevie!*' his mother yelled. 'You're filthy! Look at the mud on your boots!'

Stevie stood there panting and glanced down. There was mud around the edges of the soles, thick and black, but it wasn't the mud that caught Stevie's eye, it was the hole in the top of his boot. It was about the same size as one of the tines on the fork he'd been using to loosen the earth.

'I can *fly*!' Stevie heard himself say delightedly. But his eyes were firmly fixed to the hole. Beneath that hole, his foot felt all hot and wet.

'Manaymon showed me how to fly!' he said.

And then his mother said something strange. Something that took the wind out of his sails and replaced it with confusion. 'What did he want in return?' she asked in a snappy, *urgent* voice.

Stevie tore his eyes away from the hole in his boot. 'Nothing,' he replied, squishing his wet toes. His foot was starting to hurt now and, worse, his mother had put out her cigarette, was on her feet and coming towards him with that *look* in her eyes. The one she got when she was very, *very* upset with him. Her eyes *blazed*.

'This has got to *stop*!' she shouted. And then she was bending down, grabbing his shoulders with fingers that dug in like knives and glaring into his face. 'What did he ask you for?' she hissed. 'Tell me!'

Stevie began to cry. The best day in his life had suddenly turned into the scariest. He'd done something terribly wrong and didn't have the slightest idea what it could be.

'Tell me!' his mother yelled.

'Nothing,' Stevie sobbed. 'He just sh-showed me how to fly.'

'It's *wrong*!' his mother yelled, shaking him. 'And it's not true, either. He never gives without taking. Now tell me!'

Stevie couldn't hold his mother's fiery gaze and looked down, his eyes blurred with tears. On the top of his boot, the hole was now mended with a smeary red patch.

'Look at me!' his mother commanded.

Stevie did as he was told, cringing. His mum's breath smelled of garlic and the menthol cigarettes she smoked, but it was the mad rage in her eyes that frightened him.

'Now, tell me what he wanted!' she demanded, shaking him with each word. Her fingers dug into his shoulders like hot pokers.

'You're *hurting* me, Mummy,' Stevie sobbed, wishing he'd flown away and never come back. His mother had been angry with him many times before but he'd never seen her look anything like this. It was as if someone had crept indoors while he was flying around and magicked his mother into someone else. A kind of raving, red-eyed monster.

'What did you give him?' she hissed, her nose now less than two inches from his own and her eyes boring into him like gimlets. 'Tell me what you gave him!'

'Nothing!' Stevie cried. 'He just showed me how to fly!'

Stevie suddenly began to think that if he didn't say the right thing, she might *kill* him. Yet he didn't know what she wanted him to say. Manaymon hadn't asked him for *anything*. But his mother wasn't going to accept that explanation. He racked his brain for something to say – *anything* just as long as it would make her go back to being the kind mummy he'd suddenly lost. 'My foot hurts,' he wailed.

His mother let go of his shoulder and took his face in her hands. 'Speak!' she yelled. 'Before I have to knock it out of you!'

Stevie suddenly realized that his mother looked just as frightened as he felt. Suddenly he wanted to pee and his aching foot began to scream. He closed his eyes.

The slap that followed did four things. It made his head spin and his bladder release its contents. It made him fall over and brought his mother back to her senses.

A second later he was in her arms, sobbing against her breast as she held him to her and spoke to him in a tiny, shaking voice.

'Poor Stevie,' she said. 'Oh, I'm sorry. Poor, poor Stevie. It isn't your fault, it's mine. I'm sorry. I didn't mean it. You just scared me.'

'I'm s-sorry too, Muh-mummy,' Stevie sobbed. His boot felt heavy and hot and his foot seemed to have been removed and replaced with a fat, painful lump.

'Just promise me one thing,' she said gently. 'Just promise you'll never speak to Manaymon again. Ever.'

'I promise,' Stevie whimpered.

'And if he speaks to you, don't listen,' she added.

'Yes.'

'You mustn't because it's dangerous. Manaymon is bad. He tells lies and he offers things he can't give you.'

'He showed me how to fly,' Stevie murmured, into the damp material of her dress.

'It's all lies and tricks,' his mother said. 'And it's all my fault. But if you ignore him, he'll go away. Will you promise to do that?'

'I promise,' Stevie said. 'Why does he tell lies?' he asked.

'Because he *wants* things from you.'

'What things?' Stevie's foot now hurt so much that fresh tears were falling.

'Things you should keep for yourself.'

'My foot hurts,' he said.

And the terrible weight dropped from the end of his leg.

As it happened Stevie glanced down and saw the boot falling, turning over once in the air. When it hit the ground red liquid poured out of it in a thick little wave that sank into the pile of the carpet.

His mother gave a strangled scream.

Stevie glanced down. He suddenly understood that all this blood had come from the fork-tine-sized hole in his foot. His vision began to fade and in his ears his mother said, 'Oh, fuck, Stevie, *that* was what he wanted in exchange.'

'Earth calling Stevie. Dogboy? You all right?'

Stevie snapped out of his reverie.

'Fuck a duck, Dogboy, I thought you'd gone for good,' Johnny said, looking relieved. 'I thought you'd taken a knock on the head when you fell off the bike. I was saying about how old Yah-hoo must have been looking after you and you just kinda glazed over. What happened?'

'How long?' Stevie asked. He felt as if he'd been asleep for hours.

'How long what?'

'Was I . . . uhh . . . away. Like you said.'

Johnny shrugged. 'A minute or so. Are you OK? Only you look a bit pale.'

'I'll be fine,' Stevie said. 'I just remembered something that happened a long time ago. Something I'd forgotten.'

Johnny grinned. 'Ahh, the first ever wank!' he said.

Stevie shook his head slowly. 'Forking my foot,' he said.

'Everyone's stuck a fork in their foot,' Johnny said. 'I have. I ran a sewing machine needle all the way through my index finger once. Right in through the nail, through the bone and out the other side. My mum had to wind the handle round to lift the needle.'

Did you forget? Stevie asked himself. *Or did you just dream that it happened?* He didn't know. And he still didn't understand why his mother had been so upset about Manaymon and his flying – *which has to have been a dream, hasn't it?*

'Who was Manaymon and what did he want?' Stevie said aloud.

'You *sure* you didn't bash your head?' Johnny said, peering at him with narrowed eyes. 'What are you doing now?'

'If you had half a brain, JK, you'd realize that when people untie their shoes it's a pretty good bet they're about to take them off.'

'But why?'

'Because I remember forking my foot. My mum was angry. Not about my foot but because Manaymon, *my* invisible friend, showed me how to fly. I just had one of those moments that the Yanks call an epiphany. A moment of clarity. And even though I remember my foot bleeding and everything, it still seems like it didn't happen. So I'm going to check.'

'And what if there's no scar?'

'Then I'll conclude that what happened just now wasn't a moment of clarity, but a hallucination.'

Stevie yanked off his shoe and sock and inspected the top of his foot. 'Weird,' he said. 'I've got a scar in exactly the right place.'

'So it really happened, then,' Johnny said, yawning theatrically. 'What's weird about that?'

'What's weird is how I forgot it so completely,' Stevie said, fingering the tiny circle of discoloured skin. 'I never noticed it from that day to this.'

'Doesn't mean a thing,' Johnny said. 'No one can remember half the things that happened to them when they were kids. No one except people like Becky who have that weird memory thing, anyway,' he said, as an afterthought.

'Eidetic,' Stevie reminded him, thinking, *Your past is coming back to haunt you, isn't it?* Perhaps it was but Stevie couldn't recall anything he'd done that might be coming back to haunt him.

'My mother acted really strange,' Stevie said.

'Mine does too,' Johnny said. 'They're mothers. That's their job.'

'She got angry that I could fly.'

'What the fuck are you on about, Dogboy?'

Stevie explained.

When he'd finished, Johnny's brow was furrowed and he was reaching for his Marlboros again. 'There's something fucking weird going on,' he said.

'Give that man a cigar!' Stevie said, his spirits lifting.

The last thing that Becky expected was for Katie to faint. Becky herself had fainted a few times but had always sunk gently to her knees and landed, unhurt, in a heap. Johnny's mother keeled over backwards like a felled tree. Her head made an awful hollow *thock!* sound as it hit the path and Becky was sure she must have died on impact.

Katie lay rigid for a few seconds, an expression of surprise on her face. Then she gave a little shudder and went limp.

Fuck it! Becky thought. *She's dead and I killed her.*

Then she frowned. Katie's dress had gaped open at the thigh as she'd settled and she wasn't wearing any knickers. This didn't really surprise Becky; it certainly explained why the car drivers had been taking such an interest in Katie. Katie's pubic hair explained the odd gear-shift motions Katie had made with the posy of orchids. She'd been drawing swastikas in the air – just like the one into which her pubic hair had been shaved.

There wasn't time to think about that now, though: Becky had to see if she was still alive. She knelt beside Katie, took her wrist and felt for a pulse.

There wasn't one.

Ohmygod she's really dead, Becky thought. 'Katie? Wake up! Can you hear me?' she cried. Panic swept up to join the fear she was already feeling – and, just behind Katie's head, tendrils of stinking vapour were wafting from the crack in the paving.

This isn't happening! It can't be. 'Katie! Come back!' Becky yelled. She dropped the woman's wrist and grabbed her throat. If Katie was alive, her carotid artery should show it.

She's been down thirty seconds at least. Is she breathing? What about the blood supply to her brain?

Becky's mind was racing but her movements seemed to be slowing. It was like a nightmare.

What am I going to do?

Don't worry about it, whatever it is, the man who looked like an older version of Stevie said in her head. *Life's too short to waste time worrying. Right?*

'That's easy for you to say!' Becky snarled, but the man's words calmed her a little. She walked her fingers across Katie's throat . . .

And there it was! A pulse. Just below the rear of Katie's jawbone – further back than Becky had been feeling. It was quick and light, but it was a pulse all the same. And now she'd found the pulse she could also see that Katie was breathing in small, shallow inhalations.

'I'm gonna have to move you, Katie,' Becky said, remembering her first aid. You had to put unconscious people into the coma position. It stopped them choking on vomit or swallowing their tongue. More importantly, from Becky's point of view, it would give her a look at the damage to the back of Katie's head.

For what felt like the millionth time, she wished that someone would come up the alley.

The stench of burning vegetation suddenly ceased and the air was filled with the scent of citrus fruit. *Lemons?* Becky asked herself.

She rolled Katie into the recovery position, prised open her mouth and stuck in a finger, checking that the airway was clear. She'd never put her finger into anyone else's mouth and the sensation was disconcertingly pleasant. She caught herself wondering if one day she would put it between Stevie's lips and whether his mouth would be as soft and moist as this one.

She removed her finger and grinned. *Stevie? I've got to be kidding!*

So far, so good. Becky moved round Katie so that she could see the back of her skull. There was no blood. She slid her fingers beneath Katie's thick hair, feeling for the place where her head had hit the ground.

Katie moaned when Becky found the bump at the back of her head.

'That hurts, I bet,' Becky said, as soothingly as she could. 'Just lie still. We'll have you fixed up sooner than you can say knife.'

'Knife,' Katie murmured, then gave a pained laugh and fell silent.

*

Stevie stood on the path beside the clump of trees and bushes known as Wanker's Paradise, Duke at his feet, watching Johnny receding into the distance on Christine90. The Honda was leaving a thin blue trail of exhaust behind it, which wasn't surprising, Stevie supposed, given the state of the silencer.

What *was* surprising, Stevie thought, was that Daredevil Johnny Kane was going so gently. He didn't attempt the ramp at the end of the field, but stopped just before he reached it, got off and turned the bike round.

Duke woofed.

'You're telling me,' Stevie chuckled. 'A wimp-out if ever I saw one!'

His foot itched. Stevie tried to ignore it. Now he'd seen the scar, it had started to bug him. They called this kind of thing psychosomatic, he thought. It was something he'd given himself.

Down at the far end of the field, Johnny got back on the Honda and started to weave his way back. Duke's ears pricked up and his tail began to bat at Stevie's legs.

'When he gets here, jump up at him and knock him off,' Stevie suggested. The dog looked up at him, grinning.

Stevie now knew what had happened on the day he'd put the fork through his foot. He'd tired himself out digging, had sat in the hole, fallen asleep, dreamed flying, woken up and dug some more. That was when he'd put the prong through his foot. It was simple. The stuff about his mother being angry was true but, like kids did, he'd got the dream and the reality mixed up. He'd check it with his mum later. But it still didn't explain why the scar itched so. In the fifteen minutes that had passed since he'd put his sock and trainer back on, he'd taken them off again three times.

Johnny wobbled to a halt close by and put his feet down. Duke jumped up at him half-heartedly, but Johnny was ready for him and reached down to scratch his head.

'I didn't know you were a little old lady,' Stevie said.

Johnny grinned. 'I wasn't sure about the clutch,' he said. 'I was always under the impression you had to pull in the clutch to change gear, but when I pulled it, the brake went on. I didn't like to kick the pedal without doing *something*.'

'I thought you said you didn't know anything about motor-bikes,' Stevie said suspiciously.

'I don't know how to change gear on this one, that's for sure,' Johnny replied.

Stevie sighed inwardly. 'It's an automatic clutch. Just throttle down and change,' he said. 'As if you didn't know.'

Johnny grinned again. 'It's all new to me, honest, Dogboy,' he said, and drove off.

Christine90 picked up speed and Johnny throttled down and did a slick gear-change.

'Bastard!' Stevie yelled. Duke looked up with hurt eyes, then pawed at him. 'Not you, Dookie,' he said, crouching to hug his dog. At the west end of the field, Johnny changed gear again, did an effortless three-hundred-and-sixty-degree turn and headed back, now riding smoothly and straight. Stevie gave him the finger as he passed and shouted, 'Up yours!'

Johnny sailed by, clicked the bike into third and powered away.

'Let's go and find a stick,' Stevie told the dog. 'When he comes back we'll poke him with it as he goes by.'

He was busily constructing an image of Johnny falling off Christine90 when something caught his eye

Something red.

Stevie stopped, frowning, his eyes fixed on a patch of dandelions that shone in the sun with a yellow so pure it seemed to tickle his brain. He found himself smiling. He'd never really noticed the colour of dandelions before. *They're lovely*, he thought. But there was an odd feeling in the corner of his right eye. A feeling that wasn't yellow at all.

Stevie didn't want to look away from the happy dandelions, but something red had to be looked at. The big question of the day was: *Do you really want to see that red thing?*

Stevie decided he didn't.

To his left, Duke blundered through the tall grass, head down, as he chased a small animal – probably a field mouse, Stevie thought. He'd caught one once before.

Are you going to look, then? Stevie asked himself. The answer was no. But he found he couldn't ignore the red thing any longer and turned towards it.

It's a red rag, that's all, he told himself. It was caught on an iron stake half-way between here and the wooden pole that carried the power lines overhead.

As everyone learned at their mother's knee, red meant danger.

So, it's a sign. Is that what you're telling yourself? Stevie asked, realizing that he'd taken several steps towards the fluttering rag. He stopped. The flimsy piece of red material moved in the breeze, beckoning to him.

He shrugged. The rag had caught his attention. He *had* to go to it. If he didn't check it out now, it was going to play on his mind for the rest of the day. And part of him was going to complain that he was a coward because the only reason for not going up to the red material was because he was scared to.

'Ask yourself this,' Stevie muttered. 'What's to be scared of?'

He whistled up Duke, ace gobbling-killer, *just in case of emergency*, and strode towards the stake and the rag, feeling somehow as though he was being reeled in. What surprised him more than this sensation was that he didn't feel frightened.

Duke crashed through the long grass ahead of him, leaping into view from time to time like a dolphin arcing from the sea.

Way off to his left, at the far end of the field, Stevie could hear the distant roar of Christine90. The faint smell of Castrol oil wafted over on the breeze. Stevie felt an urge to tear away his eyes from the rag and see how Johnny was doing but it was only a distant urge. He also had a strong sense that if he took his eyes off the blinding red marker for an instant, he would lose it and miss the opportunity of a lifetime.

Duke skidded to a halt about ten feet from the stake and barked. When Stevie caught him up, the dog's hackles were raised and his tail was curled under.

'It's a bit of silk, that's all,' Stevie assured the dog. Duke looked up at him, apparently not reassured in the least.

I flew, Stevie found himself thinking, and remembered the hole in his foot. Inside his head his mother's voice repeated, *Oh, fuck, Stevie,* that *was what he wanted in exchange*. His foot began to itch, and a deep shudder ran the length of his spine. It wasn't so much an unpleasant shudder as one of anticipation.

He stood beside the dog and asked himself, *Are you sure about this?* and didn't need to reply. He was sure. It was just a piece of red silk and he was sure.

'You stay here and watch,' he said to the dog. 'Nothing bad's going to happen. I'll get the bit of rag and we'll go and look for a bull to wave it at. And if we can't find a bull, we'll wave it at JK shortly before we poke him with the stick we were gonna look for.'

The dog sat down, his ears pressed to his head.

'Coward,' Stevie admonished, and started towards the stake. Duke gave a small, warning *woof!* and shuffled backwards.

The strip of red silk material bore very familiar black polka dots. It suddenly began to look rather like a piece of his father's favourite bandanna.

As he approached, the breeze changed direction and it reached out towards him, its end curling up like a beckoning finger.

What do you want me to see so badly? Stevie asked inwardly. He tore his eyes away from the red marker and began to peer into the long grass around the pole on which it fluttered. Not because of small movements that might have been gobblings, but because something dead and very rotten was nearby. The kind of thing you smelt long before you saw it if the wind was in the right direction. Today's gentle breeze blew the disgusting reek straight towards Stevie.

But he wasn't going to let anything stop him from taking the red rag from this stake. Checking the ground ahead as he moved, he took the last six steps and reached for the flimsy red rag.

Which fluttered away from him as his fingers closed around it. Behind him, Duke whined. The scrap of material circled on the breeze, shaping itself into what looked exactly like a five-fingered fist, the forefinger extended towards a point in the long grass a yard away.

Stevie shivered, then grinned. Duke gave another whimper.

Stevie moved past the pointer. A moment later his eyes lit on a cache of several small red things, lying deep in the grass: the two cigarettes he'd lost, one with blood smeared around the filter, the other with a bloodstained tip; the Man-Sized Kleenex which Johnny had lost shortly after mopping up his blood with it; and Johnny's matchbox, covered in bloody fingerprints. Next to that lay Duke's torn muzzle.

How did they *get here?* Stevie asked himself. *Gobblings?* He felt suddenly as if he'd been lured, half hypnotized by the red rag, into a trap.

Blood, he thought. *Oh, fuck, Stevie, that's what he wanted*, his mother's voice echoed again in a distant part of his mind. *Our blood?* he asked himself, watching a tiny wisp of grey smoke curl up from one of the cigarettes. *What would he want our blood for?* At first he thought the cigarette was still alight but, in spite of the smoke, there was no glowing tip, no apparent burning. The awful stench increased.

It's the smoke that stinks, he thought, screwing up his face and trying not to breathe. But nothing was on fire. The smoke came from a different kind of consumption. Something was leaching the blood from the cigarette. The stain that Stevie's torn lips had left was vanishing slowly, its edges creeping in towards the tiny wisp of rising smoke. The paper where the blood had been was crinkled, but dry and unmarked, virginal white.

Why are you still here? Stevie asked himself, as a fresh tendril of smoke grew on Johnny's matchbox. He was sick with fear and the stench but nothing was stopping him leaving.

Stevie stayed where he was. Stuff had been happening and stuff was still happening. Whatever or whoever wanted his blood and

Johnny's had got what it wanted. Running away now wasn't going to achieve anything. Things had gone too far, had got too weird. It was too late to stop now.

And part of Stevie liked it that way.

A bigger part knew that Johnny was going to be amazingly angry if he, too, didn't get to see this new and wonderful phenomenon before it ceased and, more importantly, Stevie needed a second opinion that it was, indeed, happening. He stood up and peered back towards the top end of the field, suddenly aware that he could no longer hear the bone-rattling exhaust note of Christine90. Either Johnny had come a cropper or the bike had run out of petrol.

He couldn't see Johnny or the Honda. This meant nothing: the field was dotted with trees and bushes and Johnny could be behind one.

Above Stevie's head, something crackled with a dangerous, powerful-sounding low note. He knew what it was even before he glanced up. It was the power lines that ran across this part of the field. What he saw when he looked up, however, was not what he'd expected. Each of the four thick cables above his head was surrounded by a corona, which centred on the point at which he stood and ran, perhaps, fifteen feet in either direction. Stevie knew that power cables were sometimes supposed to give this kind of display, but he'd never seen one. He thought he remembered that the light was supposed to be blue – electric blue – but the wires above were sheathed in a buttercup-yellow light, which seemed to have a faint pale blue tinge at the edges. The coronas flexed and stretched as if they possessed an odd kind of life.

Although high-voltage power lines were known to arc, the power companies made sure they were suspended high enough not to arc down on people passing below. These lines were not very high, but they weren't National Grid lines and were, consequently, of a lower voltage. It was safe to stand under them.

At least, under normal circumstances it was.

But these circumstances are anything but *normal*, Stevie told himself as he gazed up at the pulsing, spitting lines. He glanced back towards where Johnny should be and took a step in that direction. Above Stevie the noise of the cables increased and he felt his hair begin to rise, as if drawn up by static. He took another step. The stench of the burning blood vanished, replaced by ozone, which Stevie knew was associated with lightning.

To his left, Duke got up and ran for it. No lightning struck him.

'Hey! Dogboy!'

Stevie glanced up, and there was Johnny, way up by Wanker's Paradise, waving his arms in the air.

'What're you doing down there?' Johnny yelled. 'I need you up here.'

Stevie took another pace towards him. Behind him now, the power lines crackled. The hairs on the back of his neck prickled. He took another step. Then another. The sensation of being charged with static suddenly ceased and he relaxed. *Did it!* he congratulated himself. *You did it and you're out of range now.*

He opened his mouth to call to Johnny, took another step through the tall grass – and shattered like safety glass.

No noise accompanied the blast of power that blew Stevie into his component parts, no smell, no heat. The thing that hit him was a raw force, which must have possessed the power of a medium-sized atom bomb.

In the space of one ten-thousandth of a second, Stevie ceased to exist.

'Katie?' Becky said. There was no reply. Katie had been in the recovery position for at least five minutes and her heartbeat was strong, her breathing deep and steady, but she wasn't showing any sign of waking up.

Which, at this moment, was a good thing.

Three minutes ago, Becky had noticed something that had given her an idea. Earlier, she'd told herself that if she could only *touch* Katie, she'd have proof that all this was real. Now she had a better idea.

Three minutes ago a breeze had disturbed Katie's thick mop of hair and Becky had noticed that Katie was wearing at least one silver earring – she could only see one side of her head as the other was against the tarmac. Becky intended to steal it for proof that could be verified by a third party.

Becky crouched beside Katie, convinced that the earring would be in the shape of a swastika. She knew that the Nazis had adopted the ancient mystical symbol but the swastika was supposed to ward off evil and bring good luck.

Becky gently moved Katie's hair back from her ear. She was surprised, and a little disappointed, to see that the earring wasn't a swastika but a tiny crouched figure, its knees drawn up to its chest. It looked a lot like the lucky Cornish pixies you could buy in gift shops in the West Country.

It wasn't until Becky had gently removed the earring that she saw it wasn't a pixie, either. The object, which seemed too heavy to be silver and too cold to have been against Katie's warm skin, was a devil, complete with trident, devilish grin and tiny horns. Its tail wound round its knees and along the handle of the trident, and had a tiny triangular point at the end.

Becky weighed it in her hand, feeling guilty. She fought a brief battle with her conscience, told herself that she would return the earring, then guided it towards her left ear. Becky wore jewellery only on special occasions and couldn't recall the last time she'd worn her one and only pair of gold hoops from Elizabeth Duke at Argos – and the holes in her earlobes had almost closed up. It was a painful struggle to get the stud through and when she succeeded, Becky noticed immediately how heavy it was – it made her want to tilt her head to the left – and it was so *cold*. She fancied she could feel the chill radiating out from it. It was a struggle to dismiss this as whimsy, but Becky forced herself.

But the fact of the matter is, your earlobe doesn't hurt any more, does it? Dr Williams whispered in her mind.

'Cool day,' Katie moaned. Her voice grated like a rusty gate.

'Katie?' Becky said, glancing up and down the alley once more.

'Gotta get up,' Katie whispered, and tried to move.

'What's your name?' Becky asked, still worrying about the knock Katie had taken to her head.

'Kathleen Kristine Kane,' Katie replied in a hurt voice. 'KKK. Ku Klux Klan to my friends. You can call me Katie.'

'What's your address?' Becky asked. These were the questions they asked when they medically assessed your mental state.

Katie repeated her address.

'Date of birth?'

'Twenty-ninth of the ninth nineteen sixty,' Katie responded.

Becky frowned. Katie was a good ten years adrift on that one. 'You wanna try that again?'

'No,' Katie whispered, 'I want to get up. Who cares if I lie about my age? Just get me the fuck up, will you?'

'Hold still and I'll try,' Becky asked, relieved to discover that nothing bad had happened to the inside of Katie's head.

Getting Katie into the recovery position hadn't been easy, but it had been nothing compared with trying to get her up on her feet. She flopped about on the path like a fish on a riverbank. Her neck seemed to be made of rubber and, no matter what Becky did, the left side of her face remained on the ground as if it were glued there.

When Becky managed to pull her to a sitting position, Katie turned to see who her saviour was. And when her eyes finally focused she was not best pleased to see Becky.

For starters, Katie wanted to know what the fucking hell Becky was doing there – and without pausing for a reply she demanded answers to a number of other questions, like 'How the fuck did I fall over?' and 'What the fuck happened?'

'I was hoping you'd tell me that,' Becky said mildly. She'd never heard Katie swear before and there was something strangely shocking about it.

Katie glared at her. 'Just get me back on my feet,' she said.

Becky got up, stood in front of Katie and hauled her up by her wrists. Katie staggered into her and clung on to keep herself upright. For a couple of seconds her face was against Becky's left ear and Becky was certain she was going to notice her stolen earring and start yelling about that, too. But Katie merely gave a weak giggle and said, 'We can't go on meeting like this.' When she regained her balance, she stood there, swaying slightly, a rueful grin on her face. 'You caught me,' she said.

Becky nodded.

'Now you have to let me go and forget all about it,' Katie continued.

'I can't,' Becky said. 'It's too late for that.'

Katie gave a bitter grin. 'You don't know *anything* about things being too late,' she said. 'And, believe me, you don't want to, either.'

'I just want to know why you're dressed like that – like something out of the late sixties or early seventies,' Becky said. 'And why you did what you did just now. And what all this cool day stuff is about.'

'It's better that you don't know,' Katie said. 'I'm sorry. But I can't tell you. Now, I'm afraid I've got to go. I have to be in London tonight. There's a selection happening tomorrow for my calendar shoot.'

She started towards Becky, who stood in her way, then stopped, looking agitated. When she spoke, it was with the utmost patience. 'I'm sorry, Becky. You're a real sweetheart and I love you to bits and I owe you one. But I can't tell you anything. Now, *I have to go*.'

Becky shook her head, conscious of the weight dangling from her earlobe. She no longer cared if Katie noticed it. 'I want to know what's special about the crack in the tarmac,' she said. 'And why you did what you did. And you can't go to London. You're gonna have to get your finger sorted out first.'

'Crack in the tarmac? What crack?' Katie asked, looking genuinely confused.

Becky stared at her, awarding her bonus points for her beautiful lying style. This woman was *the best*. 'It might not have occurred to you yet, Katie, but it will soon. You're looking at someone who admires you very much. Someone from the same mould.'

Katie shook her head, beaming a sunny smile. 'Don't ever say that, sweetheart,' she said. 'If there's one thing you *don't* want to be it's from the same mould as me. That's not a good thing. Trust me.'

'I twigged,' Becky said. 'While we were talking on the phone. I suddenly understood that you're capable of the kind of lying that I only aspire to.'

'Oh, *that*!' Katie said, looking relieved. 'That's nothing. I'm a terrible liar. You have to have a good memory. You're probably as good as me already.'

'Well, I'm getting pretty good at telling when *you*'re fibbing at least,' Becky said, holding Katie's gaze. 'Like when you pretended not to know about the crack.'

And there it was: judging by that look, either Katie was the world's *numero uno* liar or she didn't know what Becky was talking about. Becky's confidence deflated. 'You really *don't* know what I'm talking about, do you?' she asked, dismayed.

Katie shook her head.

'That!' Becky said, stabbing out a finger. 'Oh!' The posy of orchids lay on the right spot, but there was no gaping wound in the tarmac. There wasn't even a crack in the path to mark the point where the hole had been.

Katie glanced round at her posy then shook her head. She looked back at Becky, frowning. 'Don't tell me any more,' she said. 'Please. It's important that I don't know.'

There was a peculiar sinking feeling in Becky's stomach. 'Show me the forefinger of your left hand,' she asked.

Katie obediently held it out, a mystified expression on her face.

The last time Becky had looked at it, it had been swelling rapidly and, from its top to its first knuckle, had been black with blood. It should have been twice its original size by now and throbbing like the engine of a cruise liner.

The tip of the finger looked a little discoloured, but there was no swelling and no sign of trapped blood beneath the skin.

It's healing as you look at it, Becky told herself. *In another couple of minutes it'll be as good as new.* 'Does it hurt?' she asked. 'Can you bend it?'

Katie wiggled her finger. 'It's a bit tingly, that's all,' she said, then added, 'I was probably lying on it,' and shot Becky a glance that said, *And don't you tell me otherwise.*

'You really don't know what you did, do you?' Becky asked.

Katie shook her head. 'And I don't want to, either,' she said forcefully. 'I spent a long time forgetting. Let's just call it quits. Pretend it didn't happen at all.'

Becky sighed. 'Nope,' she said. 'I saw too much. Too many weird things. I can't forget, even if you can. I've seen the impossible happen today. Several times. And it made me feel as if I was going crazy. Or as if I was mad already. I need answers. What's cool day?'

'It's today,' Katie said.

'An anniversary?'

Katie shrugged.

'C'mon, Katie. I need to know what you did what you did with that nee—'

For a woman who'd been unconscious and injured less than five minutes ago, Katie was fast. Becky didn't even see her hand moving – just the way the muscles in her shoulders stood out like cables. The blow that struck Becky's right cheek made a sound like a starting pistol, turned her head so quickly that her neck popped and threw her off balance. She staggered sideways and caught herself as she began to feel the sting.

Katie's eyes blazed. 'I told you to forget it! Now do as I say! Don't ask questions, don't tell anyone else and, most importantly, don't remind me of *anything* I did. Not one single thing, no matter how insignificant it might seem.'

'But—'

'But *nothing*,' Katie said. 'I'm doing this for *you*! Don't you understand that? I'm doing it for you and your dad. And for Johnny and *his* dad. And for Stevie's family. And I'd be doing it for your mother too if she hadn't gone and—' Katie snapped her mouth shut. She took a deep breath and held it for a while, finally exhaling with a sigh. 'I don't remember,' she said.

Becky was shaking and her eyes wanted to fill with tears, but she fought them back. She wanted to know what her mother had done. She wanted to know what Katie thought she was protecting everyone from and she badly wanted to return the slap.

'I'm sorry,' Katie said. 'I won't expect you to forgive me, but I will explain why I did it.'

Go on, then,' Becky said, shakily. She'd wanted her voice to sound vitrolic and tough but she was on the verge of tears.

'I don't remember,' Katie said. 'I need to *not* remember. That's part of the rules of Kool Day. On this day each year I have a posy of orchids delivered to my house. And I bring them here. It keeps things on track, keeps them safe. From the moment I leave my house to the moment I get back, I don't know what happens. That's God's honest truth. I don't know what I do when I get here. I don't know what I say or feel. All I know is that it protects my family and my friends. And their families.'

'You only come here once a year, right?' Becky asked, still struggling to control her voice.

Katie nodded. Tears were glistening in her eyes too now. Her anger had vanished and she looked repentant – and, if Becky wasn't imagining it, a little scared.

'But I saw you twice. When I saw you the first time, you were still at home.'

'On the run-up to Kool Day things sometimes get a little weird,' Katie said. 'There are echoes. From long ago. From the first time. That's all I can tell you. It's all I know. It's all I want to know. Now please, Becky, I have to go. Please don't ask me any more questions. I'm begging you not to. Just forget that any of this happened.'

Katie smiled wanly as two large tears spilled from her eyes and trickled down her cheeks.

'And what if I won't?' Becky asked, pleased with the hard edge that her voice had now found. 'What if I tell you *exactly* what happened?'

Katie reached out and took both Becky's hands in her own. She squeezed them gently. 'If you do,' she said quietly, 'you'll kill me.'

Chapter Eight

Across the Elsewhere

Somewhere out in that portion of space/time to which Stephen Hawking had referred as *the elsewhere*, something was happening to a huge number of thinly scattered sub-atomic particles – and it was happening exceptionally quickly.

And I'm dead, Stevie told himself, distantly feeling himself staggering, which disproved his theory. For a few moments he knew what it would *really* feel like to have been disassembled by the *Starship Enterprise*'s transporter beam and reassembled somewhere else.

Under the circumstances, the fact that he was still on his feet was remarkable: he could neither see nor hear, nor tell which way was up.

A moment later he realized that he was stationary. And that something hard, smooth and cool was propping him up. A fraction of a second after that all his senses had returned as if they'd never been away.

What happened? Steve asked himself. Panting and trying to stay upright, in spite of the vertigo that made him feel as if the entire world was whizzing around him at an amazing speed, he pressed himself against the hard, flat surface behind him. He was no longer in the field where he'd received his electric shock or whatever it had been.

Where am I? he screamed inwardly, pushing himself away from the surface that was holding him up and staggering forward like a drunk. *It's all wrong! This shouldn't be happening. It all looks wrong, for Christ's sake!*

Parked cars were dotted along the road. Even these looked wrong but Stevie was in no state to wonder why.

There's no doubt about it, Toto, he thought crazily, *we're not in Kansas any more.*

Where he actually was, was anyone's guess. All Stevie knew was that he was at one end of a long narrow street of small terraced houses. And that the street looked achingly familiar, yet was impossible to place. It was arrow straight and must have been easily a quarter of a mile long. The never-ending terrace of houses looked to be about the same age as his own home, which meant they had probably been built in the forties or fifties.

I know this place! Stevie thought, spinning round to face the other way. *I can feel it. I can feel that it knows me, too. How the fuck do I get out of here?*

The cool smooth thing that had been propping him up was the plate-glass window of a grocer's shop. The painted gold lettering above the window read Leet's Store, which meant nothing to him.

Stevie staggered back towards the glass, remembering how cool and solid it had felt against him. He badly needed that support now in a world that seemed to have liquefied. He ached to feel that cool glass on his burning face, its smoothness against his hands. He reached out for it.

The glass was no longer cool or smooth or solid. It still looked like a plate-glass window, even as Stevie's hands passed through it, but it had become a sheet of hissing power that consumed his hands as they sank into it. He was balanced to let the window receive his weight and was tilted too far forward to keep his feet. As he fell through it he screamed.

During that long, lonely period after her mother's death, Becky had found that walking helped her think. She'd rediscovered this when the trouble had begun at school, and she'd met Stevie and Johnny while on one of her marathon walks.

Right now, walking towards the field where she was certainly going to be too late to see the maiden flight of Christine90, Becky had many things to think about. Like how she was going to tell Johnny what his mother had been doing – or if she was going to tell him at all. Like what this interlude of apparent unreality meant.

She turned off Essex Road and into Southend Road, the little devil earring swinging from her ear and her face screwed up in concentration. All she was outwardly conscious of, as she stared at the pavement a foot ahead of her, was that a left foot wearing a red Ked shoe flicked in and out of her vision, alternating with a right foot in a green one of the same style but from a different pair.

This was undoubtedly the reason that she was half-way down Southend Road before realizing that something major was happening. Something that was causing a blue light to flash along the pavement.

Becky stopped walking and looked up.

What appeared to be the entire local police force was clogging the road. Blue lights were flashing, marked and unmarked police cars were coming and going. Uniformed and plain-clothes cops bustled and scurried while interested residents stood in small knots, talking and getting in the way. The end of the road hadn't been cordoned off yet but, judging from the way things were developing, it soon would be.

What the Sam Hill is going on? Becky wondered. The activity was centred around the house that stood right next to the alley. The house where the vanishing kid lived. The house into whose back garden her friends were wont to go to see if they could find a way across to the *other side* where the great god Yah-hoo reigned.

Becky's heart sank like an express elevator. *Oh, fuck! Stevie!* she thought. *Something's happened to him!* It wouldn't be Johnny. JK lived a charmed live and never came to grief.

As she hurried towards the house and the mêlée, it dawned on Becky that although she might have lusted after JK it was Stevie she cared for. And not just as a pal.

As Becky drew close two ambulances arrived, sirens blaring. Hot on their rear wheels was a fire engine and a fire-service Land Rover.

But nothing's on fire, Becky thought.

People were hurt here. Hurt and possibly trapped. And a crime had been committed. There was no other explanation for the presence of all three emergency services.

Becky approached a small gathering of middle-aged women. 'What happened?' she asked one.

'There's been some kind of accident,' the woman said. 'We're not sure what.'

'Murder,' said the bespectacled woman next to her.

'We're not sure what,' the first woman repeated. 'But I heard someone say there was a lot of blood.'

'Could you please clear the road!' a cop with a megaphone said. 'You're blocking the way for the emergency services. Kindly move to the footpaths.'

Becky's knot of women complained but began to move. Becky left them and moved closer. At the other side of the blockage of vehicles, at the end of the road where Stevie lived, people were wandering back a few paces. For a moment, as the crowd cleared, Becky caught a glimpse of her friend from the alley, the man with Cindy, the black dog. *What's he doing here?* she thought suspiciously. *First he pops up in the alley and now he's here. What's he up to? What does he know about this?*

There wasn't much chance of cornering him and asking –

several policemen were marking boundaries which they intended to prevent the public from crossing.

I'll go the other way, Becky decided. An unmade drive ran between the back of the houses on Solby's Road and those on Raleigh Road. She'd have to nip past the cop to get into it, but if she ran she could be at the top of Solby's Road before Mr Dog-walker, even if he was about to leave the area.

Cut him off at the pass! Becky thought, and went for it.

The cop on her side of the road yelled at her and tried to grab her, but Becky dodged him and pelted up the drive.

It took less than twenty seconds to reach the top of Solby's Road. Becky combed the thinning crowd for Mr Dog-walker.

He'd gone, either into one of the houses or he'd just disappeared.

She forgot about the man, ran down the road to Stevie's house and banged on the door, hoping that Stevie would be there, that he would open the door and looked surprised to see her.

Please let him be here, she prayed.

But it was Andy Warner, not Stevie, who opened the door. His hair was a mess and he looked dazed. An unlit Silk Cut dangled from the corner of his mouth and there was blood all over his shirt. A white handkerchief was wound around the forefinger of his right hand. Blood was beginning to show through what must have been several thicknesses of material.

'What happened?' Becky asking, thinking, *Oh, no, not another one who's been sticking needles in his finger.*

Andy grinned. 'Oh, just a normal day in the life of Andy Warner. Been writing an article on networks and getting prepared for the trip to Austin. Pretty boring, really.'

'To your finger,' Becky said, nodding at the handkerchief. 'There's blood all over your shirt,' she added.

'Oh, *that*,' Andy said, his grin widening.

Becky waited, but Andy just stood there looking distant. 'Yes, *that*,' she agreed. 'What happened? You ran a needle into it?'

'A needle? No way.'

Andy had run out of words. His mind was somewhere else.

'So what happened?' Becky prompted, fighting off the urgent need to ask him how recently he'd seen Stevie. 'To your finger.'

'Oh, *that*,' Andy said, looking surprised to see the bloodstained handkerchief wrapped around his forefinger. 'I cut it.'

'How?'

'Umm . . . let's see. On something. Now what was it? A tin lid? Oh, yeah, that was it, I cut it on a tin lid. This is the second time I've cut that finger inside two weeks. Last time I caught hell from

Jacq about the blood I got on my shirt and my bandanna was ruined.'

'You threw it away?' Becky said, doubting herself once more. Then she thought: *Perhaps he's telling the truth. You saw him by the park with his polka-dot bandanna wrapped round his finger while you were chasing Katie's ghost. Katie was at home while you were doing that. And she talked about echoes on the run up to the Kool Day. Perhaps when you saw Andy, you were seeing an echo of something he'd done a fortnight ago. The shirt he's wearing now is not the shirt he had on when you saw him earlier. That one was white cotton with short sleeves. This one's blue denim.*

Andy frowned. 'Lost it. On the way back from somewhere.'

On the way back from somewhere, Becky repeated silently. *The park?*

It looked like Johnny's mother wasn't the only parent she knew who'd been practising blood rituals.

'You been out today, Andy?' Becky asked. 'To the Memorial Park, for example?'

Andy frowned at her, shaking his head slightly. 'No, not today. I don't think I have. No, I've been here today. All day. Wait a minute. A red bicycle! That was it!'

'Sorry, Andy. A red bike?'

Andy looked at her, puzzled. 'Did I say a red bike? Christ, I must have thrown a cog.' He grinned and shrugged. 'No, I haven't been out today. Been here working all day. And now you can see how hard work addles the brain,' he added.

'And Stevie?'

'He's upstairs. He was tinkering with his bike this morning when I went . . . when I started work. He was here lunch-time and I haven't heard him go out, so he must be up there now.'

For a moment Becky's heart leapt. 'Can I see him?' she asked, suddenly understanding that she'd been a fool. Stevie wasn't here. If he had been, he'd have been down here by now. Andy had been bullshitting about being home all day so he probably didn't have a clue where Stevie was.

'I'll go and get him. He won't hear if I shout, he'll have his bloody Walkman cans jammed in his lugholes. Tell you what, you can go up if you like,' he said, stepping aside.

'No, you go, Andy. I'll wait here,' Becky said. The thought she'd just had was not pleasant and it was probably unjustified, but these days there was no telling. Fifty yards down the road something nasty had happened. One of the bystanders thought someone had been murdered. And here in front of her was a man with blood all over his shirt, plenty more spattered on his Nikes and jeans and a cut finger. His knuckles were badly scraped, and if Becky had been a detective on the case she'd be wanting some better answers out of him than she'd had so far.

Andy was gone for less than thirty seconds. 'He's not here,' he announced, apparently surprised.

'OK, Andy, thanks,' she said, backing away as he came towards her. 'I think I know where he might be.' *But I hope and pray to whoever might be around, that I'm wrong.* 'See you later.'

Andy might be nutty, but he's not a murderer, Becky told herself as she hurried down Solby's Road towards the crowd of onlookers. *And Stevie isn't dead or injured.*

There was no chance of getting past the police cordon – they had taped off the road with their Day-glo plastic ribbon on which was written *Scene of Crime: Do Not Enter.*

This didn't concern Becky. At the bottom end of Solby's Road there was a disused plot where, until recently, L&M Autos had stood. The garage had moved elsewhere, leaving behind its ramshackle iron buildings and rotting Portakabins. The site was protected by a high corrugated-iron fence and securely padlocked steel-mesh gates, but Becky knew that those gates were easy to climb. The day after the garage moved out, she, Stevie and JK had scaled those gates. It was pretty dull in there – although the main workshop was easy to enter and provided somewhere to sit and smoke when it was raining.

The reason that Becky intended to scale the gates now was that the fence which enclosed the western side of the site bordered this side of the alley. Becky thought that if she could climb that fence she'd be able to get a good look into the back garden of the vanishing kid's house where the action was taking place.

All it depended on was her ability to get over the gate before the cops caught on to what she was up to.

She approached the gates, which stood ten or fifteen feet behind the throng of onlookers. The two uniformed cops manning the tape this side were busy in a heated discussion with two members of the public.

Becky leaned against the gates for a little while, choosing her moment. When everyone was looking away from her, she turned, backed off, ran five steps towards the gates and leapt at them. They made a hell of a noise when she hit them, but only one or two people turned to see what was happening. Becky clung there, the wire biting into her fingers, and the toes of her Keds pressed hard into the diamond-shaped holes in the mesh while she gazed over the heads of the crowd. Then she scrambled to the top of the gates and straddled them, wishing she'd worn her jeans instead of one of the short dresses she always wore when she went to see her shrink.

It was a ten-foot drop to the ground, but Becky had done it before without injury. She cocked her other leg over and jumped.

Her dress didn't snag on the rough edges of the mesh that ran along the top of the gates, but as she fell it billowed out and the back caught on a tie-wire about half-way down. She hit the ground on her feet with the sound of tearing in her ears.

It's a crap dress anyway, she lied to herself, more worried about how much of her would now be on display than about the dress – for which she'd paid fifty quid she didn't have.

The dress wasn't split from the mid-thigh vent to the small of her back as she'd expected it to be, which was lucky. The hem had caught on the wire, sure enough, but the dress hadn't torn as it should have. Instead, a mouth-shaped chunk was missing behind her right leg, as if a large animal with sharp pinking-shears teeth had bitten at her.

Becky remembered that Katie's fissure in the alleyway had reminded her of a hungry mouth. She turned back to the gates, expecting to see a piece of her dress flapping from the wire, but it wasn't there.

Neither was it on the ground nearby.

Becky shrugged it off. The back of her leg was stinging. She felt her thigh where the chunk of dress was missing. It was scratched and bleeding.

Blood seems to be the order of the day today, she thought, glaring up at the offending twist of rusty wire and wondering if she'd die of tetanus before next week. Her last booster had been a long time ago.

Fuck it, she thought. She wasn't going to die of tetanus. What she was going to do was hurry over to the other side of the yard and scale the fence. The important thing was to find out what the hell had happened in the kid's back garden.

The fence that bordered the alley was lower than the gates but made of corrugated iron. It was supported by concrete posts through which scaffolding poles ran, one along the top and another about two feet from the ground.

I need something to climb up, Becky thought.

She spotted an empty oil drum over by the workshop, ran to it and rolled it back to what she thought would be the premium vantage point and stood it up. She could hear voices from the garden on the other side of the alley. She listened, wondering why the emergency-services people seemed so subdued and why they were talking so quietly.

Someone's dead. Becky told herself. *Someone's dead, which is why no one's rushing about panicking.* And a tiny part of her mind had found two words and was repeating them over and over.

Stevie's gone. Stevie's gone. Stevie's gone.

But he hadn't. He *couldn't* have. Becky climbed on to the oil drum, and scraped a knee on its rusty lip. It didn't hurt, but it began to bleed. She moved forward, grabbed hold of the fence post and pulled herself upright.

She rested her arms along the iron fence's top support pole and looked down into the alley. A uniformed policeman and an ambulance man stood directly below her, staring fixedly at their feet. Apparently they hadn't heard Becky climbing up the other side of the fence less than two feet behind them. She could barely believe this.

Until she saw the *stuff* in the alley. And the *stuff* in the kid Nigel's back garden.

What the hell is *that?* Becky asked herself.

Something had happened in Nigel's garden and it was centred on the swing where Stevie and Johnny had said the kid did his vanishing act.

Four cops and two firemen stood at the back door of the house while the photographer snapped away.

The swing's tubular steel A-frame was twisted – not just out of shape but woven around itself like plaited pieces of string. The chains were shattered. Some of the links were in the alley with the *stuff.* The few links still on the swing were badly misshapen and the seat was missing. The dead Honda moped was still in the same position among the weeds on the far side of the garden but it looked as if it had been fed through a shredder. Plastic toys had been melted.

Then there was the *stuff.*

Blood.

And bits of Nigel.

Becky's mind didn't miss a beat. There was no dizziness, no sense of unreality, no sick feeling as if she might faint or throw up. Becky told herself that this was because she'd suddenly been plunged into deep shock. Somehow she doubted that.

Because this is more or less what I expected.

Either something massive had hit Nigel at incredible speed or he'd detonated. It looked as if every cell of his body had been blasted apart from every other cell. Nigel had disintegrated.

What had been Nigel was spattered over everything, leaving a thin slick of red-grey mulch here and a bright red patch of blood there. Becky could see that he had been on the swing when it had happened to him because at this point there was a two-foot diameter *Nigel-free* area.

There's too much of it for it to have been just Nigel, Becky thought. *One exploded kid couldn't have made that mess.*

Which meant, Becky realized, that others had gone, too. Probably the kid's mother, since no one had said they'd seen her leave the house. And some of that slime had once been Stevie. And Johnny. And Dookie.

'I don't believe it,' Becky whispered, climbing off the oil drum. 'Not Stevie and Johnny.'

When she got to the ground, Becky found that her legs felt rubbery, tears were running down her face and she was trembling. She bit her lip. *I'll be OK*, she told herself.

Then someone tilted the world and Becky found herself sliding off it.

'*Stevie's gone! Stevie's gone! Stevie's gone!*' Stevie heard Becky shouting. Then her voice morphed smoothly into Johnny's and Johnny was saying, '*Where's Stevie gone? Where's he gone?*' in a tone that suggested he was asking Dookie.

Stevie wasn't sure at which point Becky had arrived. At this moment, it didn't matter. All that mattered was that Stevie wasn't gone. He might have been gone until very recently but, sure as shit, he was back now.

'I'm here, you dummies!' he said.

Then he realized he wasn't but he was about to be.

Being slammed back into reality felt something like being hit by an express train with spikes on the front carrying 40,000 volts of electricity.

'Where the *fuck* have you *been*, Dogboy?' Johnny's near hysterical voice demanded.

Stevie's eyes opened. He was lying on his back in long grass beneath the power lines, which were buzzing gently. The sound of distant birdsong could be heard. Closer, he could hear Duke's panting and Johnny's ragged breathing. Johnny's face swam into view. Stevie grinned up at him.

'Where have you *been*?' Johnny demanded, his voice still pitched a tone or so too high. 'Fuck me, Mister Man, I was *worried* about you. I was up on the top track giving the bike the whip and I glanced down here and there you were, looking up at those power lines.'

'Yeah, they had a corona round 'em,' Stevie said.

'And something *happened*!' Johnny continued. 'The Dookster

was hammering away like his tail was on fire, and down where you were there was . . . I dunno how to describe it really. A kind of flash. It was so fast you could hardly see it and afterwards there was a kind of heat haze around you. And about five seconds later there was this fucking big window-busting bang. And then you were gone. I fell off the fucking bike. Wasn't looking where I was going.'

'Hurt her?' Stevie giggled.

'No. I fell in a patch of nettles. Got stung all up my left side.' Johnny waved a blood-smeared nettle-stung arm in front of Stevie's face.

'Did you see me come back?' Stevie asked.

'You joking? Old Dookie was down here sniffing for you and he suddenly took off again. I looked up and those electric lines started to flare up again and I legged it. I thought you were dead and I didn't want the same happening to me. There was another bang while I was running. Must have been you coming back. Where were you, Dogboy? Where did you go?'

Stevie sat up. 'I don't know,' he said.

'You were gone all that time and you don't even know where you were?'

'All *what* time?'

'Got to have been fifteen minutes,' Johnny said. 'Easily. Me and Dookie searched the whole field twice in case you'd got zapped and flung away.'

Stevie thought about it. None of it seemed real now. 'I was in a street,' he said. 'What's weird is I was only there about fifteen seconds. I got zapped, something happened and I staggered out of whatever it was into a street. Then I turned round, got zapped again and came back. Whole thing couldn't have taken two minutes.'

'Do you know what we're talking about here?' Johnny said, his eyes gleaming from his pale face.

Stevie nodded. 'Trouble of the highest order.'

Johnny didn't appear to hear him. 'Teleportation,' he said reverently. 'You teleported. But to where?'

Stevie shook his head. 'Leet's Store,' he said. 'Wherever that might be. It was at the end of a long straight street. Terraced houses. It all looked familiar. What are you grinning about?'

'You're bullshitting me, aren't you?' Johnny asked, looking as if he hoped Stevie wasn't.

Stevie shook his head. 'Nope. S'all true. What?'

'You really went to a place where you saw Leet's Store?'

'I just said I did, didn't I?' Stevie said.

'Wow, double motherfuckingcool!' Johnny said.

Stevie screwed up his face. 'Tell me what the hell you're on about,' he demanded.

'Well, my dad has a pal called Phil. You probably won't have heard of him but he's known him since he was our age. Phil's mum and dad used to have a shop. His surname is Leet. His mum and dad's grocery shop was called Leet's Store.'

'So I teleported there, right? But where's *there*?'

Johnny smiled so hard he looked as if the corners of his mouth might meet round behind his head. 'In the past, Stevie,' he said. 'Twenty-five years or more in the past.'

Stevie looked at Johnny's big wild grin and couldn't find anything to say.

'Leet's store was in May Street!' Johnny said, delightedly.

'Oh,' Stevie said, nonplussed.

'*May Street!*' Johnny prompted.

'You've lost me,' Stevie said.

'Don't tell me you don't know anything about May Street, Dogboy,' Johnny said.

'Give us a clue,' Stevie said.

Johnny stabbed a finger out towards the ring road. 'May Street!' he said, plainly exasperated.

'That's the ring road,' Stevie said, feeling stupid.

'C'm'ere,' Johnny said, and reached out a grimy hand. Stevie grabbed it and let Johnny yank him to his feet. Johnny glanced up at the overhead power lines as if expecting them to zap him, took Stevie's arms and dragged him a few paces up the gentle slope towards Wanker's Paradise. When he'd chosen his spot, he turned Stevie round to face the ring road again and said, 'Now you can see.'

And suddenly Stevie understood. From here you could see over the hedge, past the ring road and up towards the technical college. But the area that interested Stevie was closer, just the other side of the dual carriageway. A little stub of road spurred off Lower Brook Street, heading this way, and stopped after about forty feet. On the right-hand side of this road was the building in front of which Stevie had been standing. Leet's Store. Except that it was a car-radio shop.

No wonder I recognized it, Stevie thought and said, 'There was a road behind it. A long straight road.'

'May Street,' Johnny said, nodding. 'They knocked it down in the early seventies to build the ring road. That little stub is all that's left. You teleported about two hundred yards.'

Stevie shook his head and found that odd smile back on his face. 'I can't believe that happened.'

'Shit, man, we've had the gobbling and all its blood and the vanishing kid and now this. I *saw* you leave, Dogboy. And you know you left. Someone's trying to tell us something. We're gonna have to start believing it's real sooner or later.'

'Yeah,' Stevie said, staring over at the shop on May Street. 'I believe it happened but I just can't *believe* it happened, if you know what I mean.'

'The big question is, Dogboy, why did you go back in time?'

'I dunno,' Stevie said.

Johnny grinned, his I've-got-a-good-idea look shining on his face. 'You know what scientists do when they think they're on to something, don't you? They make an experiment. And if the experiment works, what do they do?'

'They do it again and see if it works the second time,' Stevie said.

'We gotta go back,' Johnny said. 'I've got to see this for myself.'

'You'd better think about a few things first,' Stevie told him.

'Like what?'

Stevie pointed at the stake from which the red bandanna undulated. 'See that? It's my dad's red polka-dot bandanna.'

Johnny nodded. 'You tied it up there to mark the weird spot, right?'

'No. It was already there.'

'Your *dad* put it there?'

'I don't think so. Ask me why.'

'Why, Dogboy?'

'It's covered in blood. It is at the moment, anyway.'

'That doesn't mean he didn't put it there,' Johnny said, pulling a new packet of Marlboro from his pocket and taking off the Cellophane.

'Did you go down to that spot before I vanished?'

Johnny lit a cigarette and shook his head. He passed the pack and a book of matches to Stevie.

'Neither did I. So that means that neither of us put the cigarettes I lost down there. How did they get there? The tissue you were dabbing your cuts with is there too. And the box of matches you lost. Even Dookie's torn muzzle is there. And there's one thing all those items have in common.'

'They've got blood on them, right?' Johnny said.

'Right.'

Johnny said, 'So . . . something, and it may be our man Yah-hoo or his gobblings or your Manaymon, is collecting up stuff on which our *essence* has been spilled. And this is being done . . .'

Stevie nodded. 'To open up a gateway.'

'To May Street.'

'Or whatever. Or wherever,' Stevie added.

'The question is . . .' Johnny said.

'Why,' Stevie finished. 'And the answer is . . .'

'Yah-hoo wants us for his sunbeams.' Johnny grinned.

'He's just gonna have to wait his turn,' Stevie added, smiling.

'I got a question,' Johnny said, frowning.

'You ask, 'em, I'll answer 'em,' Stevie said, feeling sunnier than he thought he had any right to feel. Something serious was going on here; something that *could be deadly*. But Stevie found that not only was he not frightened, he was eager to get on with it.

'You won't be able to answer this one.'

'Try me, JK.'

'How does your dad fit into all this shit?'

'I dunno,' Stevie said. 'But I'm gonna find out.'

'Next question. When you told me about your dad's bandanna being covered in blood, you didn't say whose blood was on it.'

'His, I suppose. It certainly isn't mine.'

'And another thing. When you said the bandanna was covered in blood, you also added, "It is at the moment, anyway." What did you mean?'

'It's fuel, I think,' Stevie said. 'The blood's like a battery or something. The gateway is using it. When I looked at my ciggie, I could see the blood vanishing from it very slowly. I thought the fag was alight, but it was the blood burning off. Weird thing was, when the blood vaporized, the paper underneath was undamaged. No heat. A bit of stinking smoke, but no heat at all.'

Johnny thought about this for a while. 'Final question,' he said.

'The great mystical Wolfie Warner reads your mind. You are about to ask: "Are we gonna try going back to May Street again?"'

'Took the worms right out of my mouth,' Johnny said.

Stevie glanced over at his dad's bandanna. 'Now?'

Johnny nodded. 'I don't think I could wait till tomorrow. Not knowing you'd been there and come back and I hadn't.'

Stevie sucked hard on his Marlboro. The nicotine hit made him feel a little dizzy. 'It might not be up to us. For all we know it'll never happen again. We might go back down there and wait and nothing'll happen.'

'Bullshit. We're *meant* to go through that gate. It's been put there using our blood. It's for us.'

'And my dad, apparently,' Stevie said.

'He ain't here so he can't come,' Johnny said. 'But we are and can. So let's do it!'

'OK,' Stevie said. 'We'll try, anyway.'

Wooh, I fainted! Becky thought as the world began to spin back into existence around her.

She was lying on her back on the cinder courtyard of L&M Autos, about ten feet away from the oil drum. She remembered the sludge of blood and flesh that had been covering everything and moaned.

It wasn't Stevie. Stevie wasn't there, she told herself. *Stevie was gone but he's back now.*

She had no idea why she should think this. The cold fact was that Stevie might have been in the kid's back garden when whatever had happened had happened. She sat up, which caused her giddiness to return. When her head settled, she began to curse silently. If the fifty-quid dress hadn't been ruined when that chunk of it got torn out, it would certainly be ruined now after she'd been lying on this oily surface.

'Someone hurt over the fence!' a voice yelled from the alley.

Great, Becky thought, getting to her feet and starting to head for the bottom of the yard. *Someone finally thought to look over the fence for more evidence.* By the time someone began to shout after her, she was squeezing through the gap in the fence and out into the Brookvale Community Centre playing field.

She ran as fast as she could past the bottom of the alley, heading for the underpass that would take her beneath the roundabout and out on the side of the dual carriageway where the field was.

Where Johnny and Stevie are supposed to be waiting for me to turn up for the inaugural flight of Christine90, she thought. Whether or not the bike would go didn't seem important any more.

In the cool of the tunnel under the roundabout, Becky stopped to catch her breath. She pushed back her hair from her sweaty brow, checked that the devil earring was still with her and inspected her knee and the back of her leg.

There was a small dried bloodstain at the back of her thigh where the fence had taken a bite out of her but although Becky felt around the area with her fingertips she couldn't find the site of the scrape.

So what happened? Did I bleed spontaneously? Did it heal like Katie's finger?

It was possible but unlikely, she thought. Especially since the cut on her knee was still there. It was no longer bleeding, and the trail of blood down her shin was dry, a scab forming on top of the graze.

Your body's OK, Becky told herself, *but are you still sane?*

She thought she was. Sane, but dealing with an insane series of events. Kids didn't detonate. Her friends' mothers and fathers didn't torture themselves to save one another and their children.

Except today they did.

Becky began to walk again. Maybe everyone else had gone mad while she'd stayed sane. That, she thought, was the classic way of telling you'd got a screw loose. *But I didn't hallucinate that mess up the alley. Or Katie. I've got her bloody earring on, for proof.*

The alternative *was* insane, though.

The alternative is that the impossible is happening.

Becky shrugged. The best thing she could do was find out what JK and Stevie had to say – although she didn't know how she was going to broach the subject of Katie while Johnny was there.

Becky walked along the path through the centre of the roundabout wondering if she should take Stevie aside, tell him about Katie and let him tell Johnny. She turned down the slope towards the tunnel that would bring her out by the field.

Just ahead of her a dog barked. She looked up in surprise.

'Dookie? What are *you* doing here?' At first she thought he had been sitting in the shade of the tunnel to keep cool, but she'd never known him to do that before, and he wasn't wearing his muzzle. He was looking agitated. Normally when he saw one of his playmates he would run up, wagging his tail like crazy, and launch himself at them. He did none of this. He barked again and trotted a few steps into the underpass, looked back, turned round, came towards her, barked and did the whole thing again.

Becky had seen enough reruns of *Lassie* to think, *He wants me to follow him.* 'What is it, Dookie?' She began to jog towards the dog.

Duke waited until she drew level with him, then licked her hand and began to trot along beside her, making an odd keening noise.

Becky ran up the slope and out on to the clipped grass that bordered this end of the field. Skid-marks were carved into the grass – at least two sets. Which meant, she guessed, that Christine90 had been running this afternoon. Maybe one of the boys had run the bike into the other. For all she knew they were lying injured somewhere in the long grass.

Duke ran ahead of her, turning and waiting on the rise of ground where the fence was down. Becky sprinted after him, her heart hammering, not just with the effort but with fear.

He led her up to where the track forked into two and she was surprised when he took the lower one – the boys usually hung around up by Wanker's Paradise. He increased his speed and Becky tried, and failed, to keep up: a stitch lit up in her side and forced her to slow.

She was half-way along the lower track when she saw them. Her heart lifted. They were both under the power lines and neither seemed in any trouble. She slowed to a trot, then stopped, pressing her fingers into the site of the pain.

Duke came back and barked at her.

'It's OK, dog,' she gasped. 'They're fine. I don't have to save them at all. There's nothing wrong.'

Standing beside a stick on which someone had tied a red flag, Stevie was pointing up at the power lines above his head. He was in profile to Becky, but kept looking away to explain something to Johnny, who stood on his far side.

Becky cupped his hands to her mouth and bellowed, 'HEY!' at the top of her voice. It was loud enough to make her eardrums tickle, but the boys didn't hear her.

Duke snout-bumped her ankles from behind, apparently in a bid to get her moving. He might have been a mongrel but the collie in him hadn't been swamped. 'OK, OK,' she said, starting to walk again. Now that the dog had rediscovered his sheep-dog genes, he was going to make the most of them, it seemed: as she walked, he nosed her ankles, keeping her going the way he wanted to go. When he wanted her to speed up he butted her and gave little growls.

'There's no hurry,' Becky said, wincing as her stitch returned.

Suddenly Duke gave up. Becky ran a few paces before she realized he was no longer hurrying her along. She looked back. He was pressed to the ground, making like a jelly-mould.

'What's wrong?' she said.

The dog didn't move, didn't look up, just stayed where he was.

Becky glanced towards her friends, who were shuffling backwards – away from what was happening to the power lines fifteen feet above their heads. *Oh, no!* she thought, watching yellow coronas form on all four wires.

'Wait!' she yelled, and began to run towards them as fast as she could, not knowing what she could do even if she arrived before anything happened to the boys. Whatever that thing was, forming up there on those wires, it certainly wasn't something she could control. *And it isn't going to be something good that's going to happen, that's for sure!* she thought, remembering the red-grey sludge in the alley and in Nigel's back garden.

'Run!' she screamed. She was less than a hundred yards away now and closing rapidly, but it was too late. The boys weren't running, they were still staggering backwards looking up at the weird yellow light around the cables. It seemed to be centred above them, trying to struggle off the wires and get down to what it saw as its dinner.

Becky saw that the boys were in the field of the power. There were auras around them: they were sheathed in that buttercup-yellow light. And the power, she knew, needed them to provide an opposite pole to jump to them. If they stayed where they were, they were going to be safe . . .

. . . and if they took a few more backward steps, they were going to fall out of the area of influence of the power and provide an earth.

'STAY WHERE YOU ARE!' she screamed.

The boys simultaneously took one large step backwards.

The flash that followed came and went in a nanosecond. Becky staggered sideways and sat down hard on the path as a tidal wave of brilliance burst into dark purple and blue shapes. She opened her eyes and found that everything looked the same as it had when she'd had them squeezed shut.

I'm blind! she thought bemusedly.

Which was when the sound of the explosion hit her.

When Becky had been little – during the September after her fifth birthday – her parents had taken her on a trip. Becky had always been fond of fireworks and, unlike most small children, didn't get frightened at those that went bang. Her dad had told her that during this trip she would hear bangs that rattled her bones. Becky had been excited. The trip had been to an Army proving ground in the middle of nowhere. Her dad had a friend in the Army who had arranged for them to be present at a demonstration of explosive power. With what felt like half the Army, a sprinkling of civilians and her parents, Becky had gone into a concrete shelter dug into the ground. There were viewing slits at ground level so you could see out, and one of the soldiers had held Becky up so she could see. She'd seen a string of cordite burn so quickly that the flash from it looked as if it was travelling in the opposite direction to the way it was really going, and she'd seen smoke grenades and Mills bombs let off. The highlight, for her anyway, had been when they'd detonated a pound of high explosive. The sound was fantastic, even from a distance. And you really did feel your ribs rattle.

But that sound didn't come close to matching this one.

This bang was all-encompassing. While it was happening, nothing existed except Becky and the bang.

When it had gone, she was deaf as well as blind. The only thing she was certain about at that moment was that the sludge, all that remained of her friends, would fall on her soon.

This time when Stevie was ejected from the gateway the dizziness and disorientation weren't so bad. He stood still with his eyes closed until the spinning sensation left him. *Must be getting used to it*, he thought, opening his eyes and turning to look for Johnny.

Johnny was about six feet away to his left, lying face down in the middle of the road, moaning gently and trying to dig his fingers into the tarmac. Stevie grinned. He knew exactly how Johnny felt.

'Don't worry,' he said, trying to keep the mirth from his voice. 'You'll feel better soon.'

'Get me outta here, Dogboy,' Johnny moaned. 'I don't like it.'

There was nothing here not to like, once you got used to being disassembled and put back together again, Stevie knew. It was just an ordinary street.

One that ceased to exist back in the seventies, he reminded himself and felt the giddiness sweep back over him. He fought it off. *It's here and so am I*, he told himself, taking a deep breath and holding it. *There's no problem.*

'Dogboy!' Johnny moaned. 'Help me!'

Stevie walked over to him and knelt beside him, taking in his surroundings. The building through which they'd materialized was, until they'd crossed, the car-radio shop. The stub of road to his right ended in a crossroads where it met Lower Brook Street and Queen's Road. He knew this area well. Except that the lower end of Queen's Road didn't look like it should: and there were old-style buildings on the west side of Lower Brook Street in what he *knew* was a new cluster of small houses.

'I'm gonna die,' Johnny groaned. 'I'm in pieces.'

Stevie laid his hand on his friend's back and could feel his body shuddering and his heart pounding. 'S'OK,' he said. 'It's the crossing that does that. It'll wear off in a minute.'

He looked down the part of May Street that no longer existed in his time. He couldn't see clearly where it led at the far end.

'How come *you*'re OK?' Johnny wanted to know, his voice muffled as he spoke into the tarmac.

He's beginning to feel better, Stevie thought. *If he's starting to worry about being outdone, he'll soon be back to normal.*

Parked cars were dotted down the street. Old-fashioned cars. And it was these that brought home to Stevie the enormity of what had happened.

You got to know about classic cars when you lived around Andy Warner. Andy had a thing about Caterham 7s – the kind of car that Patrick McGoohan had driven in *The Prisoner*. Not ten feet from where Stevie stood was a D registration 7 – which meant it was from 1966. It was in perfect condition. And it had a Lotus badge on the bonnet.

Behind it was a sparkling 1970-registered Austin; a little further down was a '65 Ford Classic. And a brand-new-looking MG Midget from 1971.

It isn't a hallucination, Stevie thought. *All this is real. These old cars are new cars. You really are back in the seventies.*

'Do you think I'll be OK if I open my eyes?' Johnny asked.

'Try it,' Stevie said, suddenly wondering where all the people were. 'You can always shut 'em again if you don't like what you see. What you're going to see is a long street full of brand-new old cars, and from the MG Midget I'd say we were in 'seventy-two. No people.'

'I don't feel so dizzy now,' Johnny said. 'I'm gonna live. Opening my eyes on five. One . . . two . . . three . . . four . . .'

'Five!' Stevie said.

'Oh, Gawd, fuck,' Johnny said.

'What?'

'My nose has been bleeding. Must have hit it on the ground when I fell down.' He pushed himself up. There was a small pool of blood on the tarmac and Johnny had a red moustache. He sniffed. 'It's nothing,' he said. 'All over now.' Then he looked down the street and his eyes widened. 'Fuckingbloodyhell in a bucket, Dogboy. We really *did* go back in time. Ohhh . . . I'm dizzy again.' He squeezed his eyes shut again.

'There aren't any people,' Stevie said, frowning. 'There should be people.'

'Fuck people, Dogboy. We can do without them right now.'

'This street has been one hundred per cent people free since we got here,' Stevie said.

'So what? Who cares?' Johnny said, opening his left eye a little. 'I'm steady again,' he announced, and opened both eyes, squinting against the light. 'If there were people they'd only want to know what the hell we were doing here. Jesus, we're in the past,' he added, impressed.

'The houses are here, the cars are here but there're no humans.'

Johnny got to his feet, staggered a little and held on to Stevie for support. 'Meaning?'

Stevie shrugged. He meant that it was possible they weren't in the past at all but in some odd mock-up of it. Perhaps they were both dead and this was some version of hell.

'Meaning?' Johnny persisted.

'I dunno,' Stevie said. 'Meaning I'm worried, I suppose.'

'It all looks safe,' Johnny said, glancing around. 'The blind's drawn in the shop. Maybe it's Sunday lunch-time and everyone's indoors eating their roast beef, Yorkshire pudding and two veg. Christ, I wish I hadn't thought about food.'

'If you're gonna puke, do it away from me or I'll be joining you,' Stevie said.

'Chill out, Wolfie, I'm OK. Let's check out this place. I bet ole Yah-hoo's here somewhere, waiting to make us his sunbeams,' he said.

'That's what I'm afraid of,' Stevie said. 'Do you think any of this is real?'

'We'll find out,' Johnny said. 'But if it's fake, it's a good fake. It looks just like it used to.'

'It was torn down before you were born,' Stevie pointed out.

'Yeah, but my mum has a book of photos of what the town looked like before they ripped out the old stuff and rebuilt. It's got a photo of May Street in it.'

Stevie giggled. He wasn't sure why. 'How do you feel?' he asked.

Johnny thought about it. 'It's weird. Considering the massive blast of power that whacked us, I don't feel burnt or sore or stiff. In fact, if you ignore the mind-crushing fact that I'm now *somewhere else* and the fact that I'm only just settling down and getting used to it, I actually feel pretty good. You?'

Stevie nodded. 'Yeah, I feel good, too. It's like the way I think we should have felt after smoking that dope we paid so much money for. I feel kind of relaxed and happy.' He felt his face rearrange itself into a big soppy grin and had to stop himself thinking, *I like it here!*

'It's good here, isn't it?' Johnny chortled. 'Let's go look at stuff.'

If a thing could be classed as having existence because it possessed a scent, the street was real enough: the odour of old vegetables and fruit hung around the store and the street smelt dusty, as if rain were long overdue.

It had substance: Stevie could feel the tarmac, the brickwork;

the plate glass of the store window was real: his fingers left greasy smears on it.

But the street had the sound of a ghost town. Stevie's and Johnny's movements seemed unnaturally loud in their ears and there was no background traffic noise, no barking of distant dogs or even any birdsong. Everything was still.

'Kinda dead around here, ain't it?' Johnny said.

Stevie turned from the window of Leet's Store, where he'd been trying to peer through the gap at the edge of the blind. 'Yeah, and I think we may well be stuck here, too,' he said. 'Last time I came, I touched this window and fell back through into the field. It was like the glass was the doorway. A big humming power source. Now it's nothing but glass.'

'Gotta wait for it to recharge, I expect,' Johnny said. 'It had to use twice the power to get us both here.'

'Either that or whatever it is intends to keep us here,' Stevie replied.

'We'll see,' Johnny said. 'I don't think I'm up to the return trip just yet, anyway. I've only just recovered from coming. Don't worry about it. Let's just have a look round. I'll go this way,' he said, pointing down the street, 'you go down to the junction there and see what's happening on Lower Brook Street. Anything happens, just yell. I'll do likewise.'

Stevie watched as Johnny loped off down the street then turned back towards the nearby junction, looking for a street sign on the brickwork above the store. There wasn't one. The next building was another shop unit, but this one was empty and had white-washed windows.

Stevie walked towards the junction. Across the narrow road to his left was the blank wall of the end house on May Street, a wooden fence, which presumably enclosed a tiny back garden, then the back garden fence and the end wall of the house on Lower Brook Street. Some kind of climbing plant was growing up the wall. It had an amazing amount of foliage and hundreds of large, pink and yellow striped flowers were blooming on it. Sweet perfume wafted across the street to Stevie and he inhaled it deeply. He started across the road to get nearer to it. The smell seemed to be taking over his entire being. It was a perfume you could drown in and die happy.

Half-way across the street, Stevie paused. A low hum of power was coming from the junction where this street met the next. He paused, looking at the crossroads and wondering whether he was about to get zapped again. Evidently the gateway was mobile.

The air at the crossroads shimmered slightly, as if he was seeing it through a heat-haze.

Either that, or this isn't the gateway at all, but a kind of electrified fence to stop us leaving May Street, Stevie thought, frowning. He felt in his pocket for something to throw at the power source and pulled out a ten-pence piece. He aimed it at the centre of the crossroads at about head-height and flung it.

There was no explosion and no flash. The coin hit the heat-haze and ceased to exist.

Which doesn't prove anything, he concluded. *The only way to find out if that's a kind of electrified cow-fence or the gateway itself is to walk into it, and I'm not about to do that.* He decided to let Johnny have the first go at this one.

Stevie continued across the road towards the flowers, moving slowly as he approached the house and trying to keep as far away from the road junction as possible. Even so, the right side of his hair began to rise as he approached the flower-clad wall, and his scalp prickled.

As he drew closer to the climbing plant, Stevie found he was no longer concerned about the power source. The perfume of the flowers filled his nostrils and the colour of the blooms was overwhelming. The plant *wanted* him. And Stevie wanted the plant to have him.

He stopped. He was right in front of the flowers now, which was strange. Last time he'd been aware of his position, he'd been half-way across the road.

The plant didn't smell any more and its flowers weren't so hypnotically gorgeous now. It was just a climbing plant, probably a clematis, he thought, the flowers of which were on their way out and a little shrivelled around the edges. Stevie frowned at it, wondering what *that* little episode had been about. He didn't have to wonder long.

Something was fixed to the wall behind the clematis, just above the height of Stevie's head. He knew what it was long before he started to pull the winding plant stems and leaves away from it. It was the street sign. 'May Street', it read.

So what? Stevie thought. *A clematis turned into a Siren to draw me over here to see this? Why?*

In the not-too-distant past, May Street time, someone had used a thin, sharp object to scratch a small swastika into the white paint under the letter 'r' in street. Next to it was a clumsily drawn arrow, pointing towards the ground.

Nazis? Stevie thought, pulling aside the plant stems beneath the arrow. Perhaps there was something else to see down here.

The stems suddenly seemed as though they didn't want him to tear at them any more. It was like trying to peel back metal rods. Stevie wasn't someone who gracefully accepted defeat, and any obstacle placed in the path of something he'd decided to do turned his resolve into steel.

And someone – or some*thing* – knew this. It was because all his attention was focused on tearing away the resistant plant that he ignored Johnny's call. If he'd stopped pulling away the plant then, the chances were he'd never have gone back to it and never have seen what was written beneath. It had been made difficult for him to ensure that he persisted.

'Dogboy, come and see *this*!' Johnny yelled.

I'm seeing something for myself, thanks very much, Stevie thought, tearing at the greenery.

There was a chalk mark on the wall under the plant. Stevie tore off leaves and flowers and saw first the number five then a two.

Fifty-two? he asked himself, still tearing at the plant. *Fifty-two what?* There was another swastika beneath the letters, and beneath that a three-letter word: Ray.

Stevie felt his heart sink. The word Ray could have been something to do with Yah-hoo wanting him for a sunbeam, but it was more likely that it was someone's name. *But I don't know anyone named Ray*. Nevertheless, a sick feeling of fear was forming in the pit of his stomach. There were two more words: *In culvert.*

Fifty-two, Ray, in culvert, he wondered. *What does it mean?*

Stevie stood up and turned away. *Probably just something that kids wrote*, he told himself, not believing it for one moment. The word Ray meant something. Something important.

'Dogboy!' Johnny called. 'Quick! You'll love this!'

Stevie turned away from the clematis, walked up to the corner and turned into the long, straight part of May Street.

Johnny was about a hundred yards away, standing beside a long-haired girl in a cheesecloth dress and a man with equally long hair wearing bell-bottomed trousers. The couple were in a passionate embrace and not paying any attention to Johnny.

Stevie jogged down the street, glancing at the houses. Most had net curtains in the windows, which made it impossible to see inside.

Johnny trotted towards him. He grabbed Stevie, giggling so hard he could barely speak. 'This is gonna come as a bit of a shock, Dogboy,' he said, between bursts of laughter. 'Try to remain cool, calm and collected. See those people?'

Stevie nodded. 'They can't see or hear us, right?' he said.

'Nope,' Johnny said. 'Just as well, because I nearly pissed myself. They came out of that house. The one where they're standing. I nearly had a heart-attack and then I realized they couldn't see me. The terrible thing is what I discovered when I went up to them.' Johnny chortled and dabbed tears from his eyes with the back of his hand. 'Look at them!' he said. 'How old are they?'

Stevie looked. It wasn't easy to tell since their faces were locked together and the man's hair was draped over the girl's face. But they couldn't have been much more than eighteen or nineteen. 'Under twenty,' he said.

'And the clothes?'

'They're hippies. I've seen pictures of my mum and dad wearing stuff like that. They used to call those trousers loons, I think.'

'He's wearing sandals.' Johnny giggled. 'And my mother's barefoot.'

Stevie looked at him. 'Your *mother*?'

Johnny emitted a short burst of laughter and panted, 'It gets worse. That guy *eating* her is your dad!'

Stevie looked from the couple to Johnny and back again in disbelief. Then he walked closer to them.

'S'OK,' Johnny said. 'They won't be aware of you and you can't influence them. Christ, you can't even touch 'em. They're like ghosts or something.'

Stevie stepped right up close to the couple, then shuffled around them, trying to see if Johnny was right. It wasn't until they broke off their kiss that he could see his friend hadn't been kidding. It was indeed his dad and Johnny's mother. They looked painfully young. Andy was razor-thin, fresh-faced, and there wasn't a line to be seen or a single grey hair. His eyes were bright and clear instead of bloodshot and bagged. Katie was slimmer and didn't have the muscle she had these days. She was achingly pretty, which she still was, of course, but the skin of her face looked new and pristine.

'Something else we didn't know about our parents,' Johnny said.

'Oh, shit,' Stevie said. 'I do hope I'm not gonna turn out to be your half-brother.'

'Jesus, what a thought, Dogboy! I'd just have to kill myself if my dad turned out to be your dad!'

The couple were facing one another now, holding hands and talking happily. Their voices couldn't be heard across the gap of time.

'Looks like they were in love,' Stevie said. 'I didn't know about that.'

'It does. And I didn't either,' Johnny agreed. 'They look kind of sweet, standing there like that, don't they?'

'So sweet you could puke,' Stevie said, grinning. 'All that's missing is the flowers that should be in their hair. Did they live here or something?'

'Not to my knowledge,' Johnny said, 'but *I* didn't know my mum had ever fucked your dad, so it doesn't mean much. I'll find out, though, believe me!'

'Yeah, I'll ask a few questions when I get back too,' Stevie said, then added, '*If* I get back.'

'You did it once, you can do it again,' Johnny said. 'I have every faith.'

An elderly woman was coming down the street towards them. A white West Highland terrier was pulling ahead on the lead she was holding. The dog reached them and Stevie automatically stood back to let the animal and its owner past. The dog sniffed Andy's leg and Andy bent to pat it. The woman glared at him but he smiled up at her and said something that looked like 'Lovely dog.'

The Westie peeled off, headed for Stevie and stopped at his feet. Its tail wagged.

'The bloody thing can see me!' Stevie said, stepping back another pace.

'Ah, the animal's sixth sense, see,' Johnny said, as the dog paused to sniff his foot. He crouched and waved his hand in front of the dog's nose. The dog followed his fingers, sniffing and looking interested.

The old woman stepped round Andy and Katie and walked into Johnny, passing through him as if he were vapour. A second later the dog was dragged through him, too. Stevie saw the woman give a someone's-walked-over-my-grave shudder at the same moment as Johnny did.

'When worlds collide,' Stevie said.

'This is too fucking weird for words,' Johnny said, standing up again. He did a double-take at the pavement in front of him. 'Hey, shit, they're going!'

Andy and Katie were walking slowly down the street towards the town, their arms around one another's waists. Stevie and Johnny stood looking after them.

'Who's Ray?' Stevie asked.

'Ray . . . There's Ray Charles. There's Sugar Ray Leonard who used to be a boxer. Ray Davies, the songwriter that Damon Albarn always wanted to be. And then there's—'

'A Ray we know,' Stevie cut in.

'Dunno a Ray. Unless you count Ray Wire from school. Only I don't know him either. Only that he's meant to be hard. The only other Ray I can think of is the guy who used be an artist and photographer. I saw a documentary about these arty types in Paris and they mentioned him. Cool name. Man Ray.'

'Oh, fuck,' Stevie said.

'What is it? Shit, Dogboy, you've gone quite pale. What's up?'

'Man Ray,' Stevie said. 'That's what's up. That *man Raymond.*'

Johnny pulled a face. 'What the fuck are you talking about?'

'Back down on the corner, where the street sign is. There's a climbing plant going up the wall. Big flowers. There's writing on the wall underneath the flowers. In chalk. "Fifty-two. Ray. In culvert", it says. Along with several swastikas. And I've been wondering about it.'

'And you've finally made sense of it?' Johnny frowned.

Stevie swallowed. 'I fucking hope not. But yes, I think I have. The Ray bit of it, at least.'

'"That man Raymond," you said. Right? So what's it mean?'

'Manaymon,' Stevie said. 'Man Raymond. When you said Man Ray, it all fell together. I was a little kid. Little kids mispronounce things. My imaginary pal wasn't imaginary at all. He was real. In some sense.'

'Some *supernatural* sense,' Johnny said. 'And you reckon that's the same Ray on the wall back there?'

'Look, Johnny, we're back in the past. That doesn't happen naturally. My dad and your mum were here, on this day, in this month, in this year, whatever year it is. There's a weird message on the wall mentioning Ray. I had an invisible friend called Manaymon – of whom my mother was shit scared, incidentally. It's got to be the same Ray.'

'And you reckon Man Raymond is the same as little Nigel's Yah-hoo?'

'He told Nigel he wanted us for sunbeams, didn't he?' Stevie said.

'Shit, man! Of course! Sunbeams! *Rays* of light, right? He was giving us a clue!'

'I dunno about that,' Stevie said. 'But it's high on my list of things to find out in the near future. Along with what the fuck else he wants. Why's he opened this gate between our now and this then?'

'Doublefuckingcool,' Johnny said, 'but what's the shit with the numbers and the culverts and the swastikas?'

'I don't know,' Stevie said grimly, but he was pretty sure he did.

It seemed like hours before Becky's sight and hearing began to return, but it was probably only minutes. During that time, the remains of her friends did not fall on her. She was grateful for that. She was also grateful that her favourite dog of all time had snuggled up against her as she lay in the tall grass.

The Dukester lay beside her shoulder, his head placed gently on her ribcage.

'Oh, Dookie, you are a good boy!' Becky said, feeling for the top of his head and patting him. Her vision was flickering and bleached, but it was coming back. There was a high-pitched whine in her ears and her voice sounded odd, but at least she could hear.

The dog gave her face a single lick, then got up, went round behind her head and started to nose at her as if trying to get her back on her feet. 'Wait a minute,' she said, rolling her head away and then having to fight off the wave of dizziness that the motion caused. 'Be OK in a minute. Just wait!'

Duke barked, the high-pitched urgent yip he gave when he was in a hurry to go walkies.

'What?' Becky asked. Her vision had stopped flickering, but she wasn't sure she was ready to get up yet.

The dog nosed her again.

The ringing in Becky's ears had now turned into a low buzz mingled with a higher-pitched crackling noise. 'Hold on!' she told the dog, trying to prop herself up on her elbows. Duke yipped and danced into her line of sight, glancing from her to the power lines and back again. It wasn't until the low buzz became a metallic rattling that Becky understood the sound wasn't in her head but was coming from the electric wires.

A moment later she was on her feet, looking up at the four cables. She didn't think she was in any danger: whatever was happening was taking place at the spot where the boys had been zapped; the racket overhead was merely the sound of it vibrating along the wires. At the spot beside the red flag the wires lit up in smoky yellow coronas.

But there's no one for them to zap! Becky thought. *Surely it can't reach me from there?*

Duke nosed at her ankles, whining now.

'OK, dog,' she said, and backed well away from the lines. Duke continued to nudge her until he was satisfied they were both out of harm's way, then he jumped up at her, wagging his tail. Becky petted him, keeping her eyes on the area where something was about to happen and wondering if she was going to be blinded and deafened again.

This time, though, she noticed something different; something that saved her eyes and ears from another hammering. A slender tracer of plasma rose from the base of the pole on which the flag fluttered; it was a ghostly grey colour and wiggled up through the air in acute angles like low-powered lightning happening in slow motion. Becky knew enough about the workings of lightning to know that something similar happened on the earth immediately before a strike. Which was why she closed her eyes and plugged her ears.

A moment later the flash came. Through her eyelids it didn't seem particularly bright and the bang that followed was certainly no louder than a large firework.

She opened her eyes the instant the flash had passed and saw something silver arc through the air, glinting in the sunshine. Whatever it was landed close to the spot where Johnny and Stevie had been zapped.

Becky looked down at Dookie. He was trembling from nose to tail. 'You can stay here if you like,' she said, 'but I've got to go over there. I've got to find out what's . . .' She paused, refusing even to think the words *what's left of Stevie and Johnny*, and finished, '. . . what's happened to the boys.'

They're dead, that's what, Dr Williams's deadpan voice said inside her head. *You're still in denial. The root of your problem is that you can't accept mortality; the fact that everything living eventually dies. It's not uncommon. Those we love from childhood, those we grow up loving; they are the ones it hurts most to lose.*

'Fuck off,' she said aloud to the voice, and began to hurry towards the red flag. Dookie followed her, keeping low to the ground.

Becky was not surprised to discover that there was no Stevie or Johnny mulch covering the area beneath the power lines. But what the hell *had* happened here?

They dematerialized, she told herself. *In pretty much the same way that Nigel did – or whoever it was in his back garden. But they did it cleanly and, hopefully, whole and living. Whoever dematerialized Nigel was making sure he never came back.*

She glanced up at the power lines and pronounced them safe for the time being. Whatever was powering these weird goings-on was evidently taking a breather.

A couple of yards away from her, Duke woofed. When she turned, he was looking up at her, his ears tilted forward – which generally signified he'd found something interesting.

'What?' Becky asked.

By way of reply, the dog nosed the thing in the grass and then looked up at her again. His tail gave a tentative wag.

The interesting item turned out to be the silver object she'd seen arc through the air after the last explosion. It was a ten-pence coin. A freezing-cold ten-pence coin that lay in the grass, steaming gently. After a minute she picked it up. It was just an ordinary ten-pence piece.

Which materialized in pretty much the same way as poltergeist activity is supposed to make things like this appear. But this isn't a poltergeist, is it?

Stevie and Johnny had been transported to somewhere else. And wherever they were, they were alive. She was sure of that. One of them, probably Stevie, had tested the escape route by flinging something into it. Johnny seldom carried money but Stevie's pockets were always shedding loose change when he sat down.

They were still alive five minutes ago, Becky thought, *so they're probably still alive now. Things get a bit weird around Kool Day, remember.*

Becky wasn't surprised that the red flag was Andy Warner's polka-dot bandanna. The one that he said he'd lost on the way back from somewhere after cutting his finger for the first time. *Last week*, Becky reminded herself. *So who found it and tied it up here? Not Andy, surely. It must have been Stevie. But why would he do such a thing?*

Because it was bloodstained. Becky knew that, because around the base of the pole there were other bloodstained things. Cigarettes. Tissues. A matchbox. Dookie's muzzle – the one that had been torn during the fight with the thing Stevie called a gobbling. Whatever was going on around here was powered by blood.

Then she stared in disbelief, her hands reaching round behind her to the hem of her skirt.

Yes, her fingers reported. There *is* a bite-sized chunk of dress missing from round here. *Yes*, her eyes confirmed. That bite-sized chunk of dress in the grass, stained with your own blood, is indeed the piece of material that would fit in the hole.

'It's impossible,' Becky said, but, as Katie Kane had insisted, you could expect the occasional oddity on Kool Day. Gobblings must have brought that bit of her dress here. Or it had teleported out of L&M Autos' yard and reappeared here. But how it got here, wasn't really the point. The point was . . . *it's* my *blood. And Dookie's blood is here. And Andy's, and some of Stevie's and Johnny's too. Like Katie said, we're all in this. And if I'm not mistaken, we all get to teleport.*

Becky wasn't sure she *wanted* to teleport.

'I *have* gone mad, haven't I?' she asked. Duke wagged his tail. At Becky's feet in the long grass, something moved. Becky screamed. She could suddenly smell the odour of bonfires that she'd last detected when she had been in the alley with Katie.

What happened next happened so fast that Becky had no time to act.

The power lines pulsed with yellow light. Duke looked up just as the tracer snaked up his back legs and round his tail. He lit up as if he were hollow glass and someone had turned on a searchlight inside him. Light flashed and he vanished. Thunder rocketed through the air.

Becky moaned.

'So what do you reckon then, Dogboy?' Johnny asked, turning back from the door whose knocker he was hammering. No one was answering. Neither of them was surprised: this was the third time they'd tried knocking; the first two times they'd run away. Now that they'd tested the house next door too, they were sure that either no one was in or that the occupants couldn't hear the knocking of people from the future. Which was odd, given that the houses were real and that they could rap the knockers.

'The sound doesn't travel back in time?' Stevie suggested.

'It doesn't have to,' Johnny said. 'We're already back here. You can hear this fucking knocking, can't you?' he added, thundering at the door with his fist. 'Surely they should hear that, even if they can't hear us!'

'They're like ghosts to us. We're like ghosts to them, I suppose,' Stevie said. 'I dunno how it works.'

The house was the one Johnny had seen his mother and Stevie's dad leave, which suggested that it was significant, that they'd been drawn to it to investigate it. They'd peered in through the lounge window, primarily trying to establish if Katie and Andy had been shacked up together, but there wasn't much evidence in the tiny room. The walls were covered in posters for concerts by rock bands that neither Stevie nor Johnny had heard of: Patto, the Groundhogs, the Edgar Broughton Band, Kevin

Ayers and the Whole World, May Blitz. There was a big poster of some bearded soldier in a beret, too, but this meant nothing to them either. Old-fashioned twelve-inch long-playing records were strewn about the floor, their covers off. Stevie spotted a Grateful Dead album and wondered if it was the same one his dad still had. He thought he recognized the Tyrannosaurus Rex cover, too. This one was called *Prophets, Seers and Sages: the Angels of the Ages*. There was a jam-packed bookcase at the back of the room beside the fireplace, but it was difficult to make out the titles. A copy of *Catch 22* was lying on a low coffee-table amongst overflowing ashtrays, empty beer bottles and huge dented cans of Jackpot 7 bitter.

'But you can hear ghosts knocking,' Johnny said. 'People are always hearing them knock or walk up and down creaky stairs and stuff. Why can't they hear *us*?'

'No idea,' Stevie said, still gazing into the ancient but modern room. 'You tell me.'

Johnny yelped and danced backwards into the street.

'What?' Stevie said, tearing his eyes from the window. He heard the front door opening three feet to the left of him. He froze, certain that his nemesis, Manaymon, was coming out to take him.

'Who the fuck's there?' asked a voice that didn't sound monstrous. 'They must fucking think I'm fucking deaf or something. Oh, my God, oh, my God. Fucking people.'

The voice bore the faintest hint of an accent that might have been West Country. Cornwall, perhaps.

I know this voice, Stevie told himself. It wasn't the voice of Manaymon, that was for sure.

The face that appeared around the door and looked straight at Stevie wasn't Manaymon's face, either. Stevie wasn't quite sure what Manaymon looked like but he knew this wasn't him. This guy was in his late teens or early twenties. His almost-skeletal face was pale, and watery blue eyes blinked behind little round steel-rimmed glasses. He was trying to grow a moustache and beard and his hair, a jumble of brown curls, cascaded over his shoulders.

He looked Stevie up and down, then his body followed his head round the corner. He was wearing battered Dunlop Red Flash trainers, a tired pair of Levi's jeans with the knees out and with flowery inserts in the lower-leg seams, which had converted them into bell-bottoms. Something that looked like egg had been spilled down the front of his yellow three-button vest.

Who do I know who looks like this? Stevie asked himself,

suddenly certain he wasn't in any danger. *I do know someone who looks just like this! Someone who's always got stuff down the front of his shirt. Someone with watery blue eyes.*

'Wow,' the guy said, in a small voice, and his face lit up in a big sunny grin.

Stevie thought about it and shrugged. 'Hi,' he replied, and raised a hand in greeting.

The hippy shook his head in wonderment. 'Auditory, too,' he said, and began to giggle as if those words were the funniest he'd ever heard. Stevie stood there, unsure if he should talk, run away or wait. He waited. Johnny was coming back now, moving slowly and cautiously like a frightened deer.

'This is far out!' the hippy said. 'Wow, am I spaced!'

'Looks like you're enjoying yourself,' Stevie said, increasingly uncomfortable because the guy was looking him up and down as if he'd fallen in love.

'Oh, this is so cool, man!' the hippy said. 'I gotta tell Davey Kane about this batch. This is some killer stuff. Never had anything like this happen before! God bless you, Dick Kemp!'

Stevie was still trying to place him. Whoever he was, he'd once been a close friend of Stevie's father and Johnny's too.

The hippy giggled. 'I can't believe my eyes! It looks so ... *solid.* You spoke, didn't you? Just a minute ago. That *was* you speaking, wasn't it?'

'Yes,' Stevie said.

'Far out! A walking, talking hally that knocks on doors!'

'What's a hally?'

The hippy frowned. 'Trick question, right? You're gonna tell me you're not a hallucination now, aren't you?'

'Not me,' Stevie said, gaining confidence. 'I wouldn't think of it.'

The hippy blinked. 'You're losing me, man,' he said. 'You gotta remember that I'm having a sensory overload here. This is the strongest acid I've run across in my entire life. You got echo on your voice. I've got reverb on mine. There're swirling patterns on the brickwork. This is power-pack acid-tripping, man.'

'What's your name?' Stevie asked.

The hippy's face took on a guarded look. 'I'm sorry, man, but I can't tell you that. I don't know who you are. I know you're dressed weird and you got those weird space-boot things on your feet and everything, but there's a chance you might be real. I've had some trips in my time, but I've never hallucinated anything like you, so I gotta be careful. Sure, I can see right through you from time to time, but, hey, I'm out of it, man. I gotta go indoors now. Sorry.'

'Hey!' Johnny called, from a little way up the street.

Stevie and the hippy both turned towards him. 'Who's that?' the hippy asked. 'I can hear him but I can't see him. Just a kind of outline. With horns. Don't like the look of it. Might be bad to stay out here.' He retreated inside his house and slammed the door.

'Where'd he go?' Johnny said, trotting back.

'He thought you were the devil and went back in,' Stevie said. 'He's tripping, on LSD. He thinks he hallucinated us. He could only see an outline of you and he thought you had horns. He got scared. They call it the horrors.'

'What did you find out?'

'I recognized him, but couldn't place him. His face looked familiar and his voice sounded familiar, too. Oh, and he knows your dad. Your dad's gonna be delighted when he finds out about this new acid our friend's got.'

'That figures,' Johnny said. 'I *knew* something had scrambled my old man's brains. You didn't get the guy's name?'

'Wouldn't tell me,' Stevie said.

'Do you think meeting him's important? Or is it just chance?'

Stevie scowled. 'I don't think *anything* around here is happening by chance. Old Yah-fucking-hoo has got his hooks into us. This is his place. His time.'

'Which would explain the house,' Johnny said, nodding.

'This one?'

'No, the one I could see just down the road. The one where old Yah-hoo lives.'

The medium-sized black dog that had just materialized outside Leet's Store was unable to stand up. Duke had entered on his belly, leading the way with the bottom of his chin, which was grazed and bleeding a little.

He tried to get up. If he'd only learned one important lesson in his entire life, it was that to be down was to be exposed and at risk. He tried again.

He was overwhelmed and terrified by the sudden and total change of odours and sounds. Everything was wrong here. He no longer knew which way was which, or one way from the other. Worse, he understood that he didn't know his way home. Suddenly there *was* no way home.

Duke lay on the ground beneath the shuttered plate-glass window of Leet's Store, quivering and panting, the movements of his chin painting a ragged, damp line of blood on the pavement. During the next five minutes he lost control of his bladder and was unable to crawl out of the pool of urine he voided and he threw up twice. Afterwards his balance began to settle and he started to detect odours.

Stevie was here somewhere, Johnny too. But there was an odour of something else; something awesomely huge and powerful. It smelled of flowers and fires and blood.

Duke lay on the pavement, trembling, and whined for Stevie.

'And here's another thing of the genus *too fucking weird*,' Stevie said, looking at his wristwatch. They hadn't yet reached the house where Johnny said Yah-hoo lived but they'd both begun to feel euphoric. 'I've got a warm fluffy feeling,' Johnny had announced, and Stevie had it too.

'What?' Johnny asked, stepping back from the window he'd been peering into.

Since they began to feel good they must have knocked on the doors and looked through the windows of twenty or so houses. Everything had become strangely interesting, even though most of the tiny lounge rooms were pretty much the same. Each interior was one of two kinds. About half the buildings were furnished from the late sixties, early seventies period, garish colours and lots of plastic, and the other half were evidently populated by old people who'd last bought furniture just after the Second World War. The big discovery was that although all the houses had televisions not one had a video recorder.

'Come here!' Stevie said. 'Watch and learn.'

Johnny came over. 'What? Your G-Spot? What's up with it?'

It took Johnny less than two seconds to realize that the watch was running fast. Either the G-Shock had thrown a wobbler or time here was passing more slowly while the watch was still tracking time from their own period.

'Jesus, Dogboy, it's gotta be going nearly twice the speed that it's meant to be,' Johnny said. 'Lookit that second counter going!'

'It's five thirty already,' Stevie said. 'How long have we been here? Ten minutes? Fifteen? Time on our side is passing at more than twice the speed it is here.'

'Maybe May Street's trying to stay fixed in time or something,' Johnny suggested. 'Trying to stop time passing so it's always here, always now.'

'Or always a little way into the future from now,' Stevie said. 'Like at the point where Yah-hoo's finished with us.'

'What the hell does he, she or it want, anyway?' Johnny asked.

'It wants to be let out,' Stevie said. 'Monsters always do. They're always stuck somewhere and they always want to be let out. Either that or it wants to be invited into our lives so it can take us over.' He sniggered. 'We're having this done to us, y'know,' he pointed out.

Johnny's face was suddenly puce with mirth.

'We're not feeling like this naturally,' Stevie continued, unable to keep the smile from his face. 'We're being softened up. Lulled.'

'I know,' Johnny said, gasping for breath. 'Hang on, I'll be OK in a minute,' he said, and burst into a fresh fit of giggles.

Stevie watched his friend struggle for control, his own mirth fading. *We're putty in its hands*, he told himself. *If he can reduce us to hysterics as easily as this, our Yah-hoo is probably going to have us for sunbeams whether we like it or not.*

'I'm OK,' Johnny said finally, wiping tears from his eyes. 'It's passed: The house I saw is just down here. I forgot we were going there.'

Stevie felt as if someone had slapped his face with a freezing hand. He'd forgotten too. Now that he remembered it felt as if something had interfered with his memory.

'C'mon,' Johnny said. He looked nervous now: his complexion had that cheesy pallor again.

Stevie could see where the house stood before he could see what it looked like. It was on the north side of the street, closest to where the overgrown field would be some time in the future. This was surely significant.

The first giveaway that the house was different was that no cars were parked within twenty feet of either side of it, and none opposite either. As he drew closer, Stevie could understand why. The house stood out like a rotten tooth in the middle of a film-star's smile.

'This is the one,' Johnny said, pointing ahead. 'I didn't come as close as this. I spotted it and came back to get you. I didn't care for the look of it.'

Stevie didn't either.

It was exactly the same design and shape as all the others but it was different in a fundamental way. It wasn't merely that it was empty or that its windows were broken or clumsily boarded over, or that the brickwork was blackened as if the building had once caught fire. There was something else. The house looked skewed, somehow, as if its perspective was wrong. Stevie had once read a book in which a haunted house was described as looking as if it were crouched, ready to pounce. This one looked as if it was in agony.

Stevie stood across the street, next to Johnny, gazing at it. A long time ago the front door had been painted black. Now the paint was peeling, showing rotten wood beneath. There was a hole in the bottom panel that looked as if it had been made by the toe of someone's boot. The letter-box surround was probably brass under the green corrosion, but the flap was missing. There was no number on the door.

'It looks bent,' Johnny said, echoing Stevie's thoughts, and another bone-rattling shiver cruised down Stevie's back.

Johnny turned to him, excitement gleaming behind the fear in his dark eyes. 'I can't quite figure out *how* it looks bent, but it's warped somehow. And you know what?'

'Yeah,' Stevie said nodding. 'I do.' He recognized the house. It was impossible but he knew it, even though he'd never seen it before. It was familiar: he knew it in the way his flesh crept, his stomach tightened. He knew it right down to his bones.

And he didn't have to look at the houses on either side of this one to figure out that this was number fifty-two.

Four thirteens, Stevie found himself thinking. The thought seemed ancient; as if he'd thought it a thousand times before. Perhaps with someone else's mind. *Four thirteens are fifty-two. That man Raymond. In culvert.*

Swastikas. Fifty-two. Ray. In culvert.

'This is the place,' Johnny said. 'I recognize it. It's like I've been here before. You've got that feeling, too, haven't you?'

Stevie nodded, looking at the gutter in front of number fifty-two. There was a drain-grating at the edge of the pavement. *In culvert*, Stevie thought.

'We've got to go in,' Johnny said. There was an odd-looking smile on his face and that dangerous look in his eyes.

'Says who?' Stevie asked, wondering if Johnny was hearing anything. *We should be getting drawn over there*, he thought. *We should be getting an urge to cross the road and walk up to the door, which should open at the slightest touch.* The fact was nothing was calling him. The house just stood there looking hurt and *wrong*.

'Says JK,' Johnny said. 'That's why the house is here. So we can go in it.'

'What if we don't want to?' Stevie asked.

'We *do* want to go inside, don't we?' Johnny asked, a hint of puzzlement in his voice.

Stevie shrugged. Yes, he *did*. He wanted to very badly. The big question *what's in there?* was rattling around inside his head, but he was reminding himself that curiosity killed the cat.

'Our end may well be inside that house,' he said.

'Fuck off, Dogboy!' Johnny said. 'Whatever's in there, we can kick its arse. And if we can't . . .'

'Precisely,' Stevie said. 'If we can't we have no idea what the cost will be. I think we should try to get home and see what develops before we go blundering in there. If it's Yah-hoo we're likely to be in big trouble.'

But Johnny didn't listen. By the time Stevie had finished his little lecture on *Safety First*, his friend was half-way across the road.

Johnny reached the front door and pushed it.

Nothing happened.

'It's locked,' he said, in surprise. He glanced up at the lion's-head knocker on the door, then back to his friend. He grabbed hold of the knocker and pulled. Stevie saw his muscles bulge. The knocker stayed where it was.

'Fuck it!' Johnny said, dropping to his knees to peer through the letter-box.

'What can you see?' Stevie asked. The absence of anything unusual was unsettling him more than a clematis-style Siren-call. There wasn't an atmosphere; the air wasn't charged; his skin wasn't crawling. *Which is exactly it*, Stevie thought. *You're not worried because it feels as if there's something wrong, you're worried because it feels right. It feels normal. It feels like you belong here. Like it's your own house.*

'I can see the hall,' Johnny said. 'Mildewed. Wallpaper in tatters. Bare boards on the floor. Two scummy-looking rugs that were furry once. The door to the lounge, which is open, the door to the kitchen, which is closed, and the door to the back room . . .'

'Which is?'

'Interesting,' Johnny said. 'It's nailed up. Someone boarded it over by the look of it. They left their hammer behind, too. And some nails. I wonder why.'

'The floorboards are probably rotted through,' Stevie said, feeling an odd *déjà vu* as if he'd said this many times before. *Whatever's in there has probably fallen through to the cellar by now*. 'Do these houses have cellars?' he asked.

'Fuck do I know?' Johnny said, still peering into the abandoned house. 'Tell you this, though. It smells like a bonfire in here. Should smell like damp, but it doesn't. I can smell something like flowers, too.' He got up and turned back to Stevie. 'Let's kick the door in,' he said.

'I've got a better idea,' Stevie said. 'Let's go back where we came from and think about it for a bit. Just let me see through the letter-box first. I wanna see if—'

'If it looks like you already know it's gonna look?' Johnny said. 'It does. Trust me. It looks so familiar to me I could have been here a thousand times before.'

'It's like the recognition is built right into your cells, isn't it?'

Johnny gave a thin smile. 'Yeah. And it's gotta be a trick. Old Yah-hoo has to be handling it. Except that it doesn't feel like I'm being manipulated. It feels normal. That's the scary thing.'

'We don't have enough information yet,' Stevie said, 'which is why I didn't want to try to break in. We've seen your mum and my dad here. And that hippy guy. What if—'

Johnny shook his head. 'Nah. I know what you're gonna say, Dogboy, but surely not!'

Stevie waited.

'You think we remember it through our parents, right?'

'It's a thought,' Stevie said.

Johnny nodded.

'We got a deal? We'll try to get back and get some information before doing anything else.'

'I want to go inside,' Johnny said.

'Door's locked,' Stevie said. *And only I know where the key is.* Johnny hadn't yet put two and two together concerning the message chalked on the wall but Stevie had. It had given the house number, the name of the house's owner or tenant, and the cryptic message: *In culvert.*

The key to the house was in the culvert.

And, for now, Stevie was keeping that to himself.

Johnny shrugged. 'OK, you look through the slot, I'll check the windows. Maybe we can get in through one of those.'

The interior of the hall was as Johnny had described it, except that he'd left out the staircase to the right. It was narrow and carpeted in something that used to be brown and could now only be described as *nasty*. Brass stair-rods that had turned green with corrosion held the carpet in place. Stevie couldn't get low enough to see up to the top stair but something was leaking up there. The greyish-fawn carpeting was glistening, as if water was seeping down through it. There was that bonfire smell, which he'd recently begun to associate with blood being burned, and a powerful scent of flowers.

Suddenly something deep in the house groaned.

'Fuck this,' Johnny said, from the front window. 'These boards might be rotten, but I can't shift them.' His voice came from the rear and to the left of Stevie, but also through the lounge door. It sounded somewhat muffled and echoed flatly in the bare hall.

'You pulling on them?' Stevie asked. 'Only you're making something happen in the back of the house, I think.'

There was pause. 'Really?' Johnny asked. 'Hang on and I'll do it again! Ready? Pulling!'

Stevie heard the sound of creaking wood again. It didn't seem to be coming from either of the front rooms, but from the bowels of the house.

'No noise here,' Johnny reported, sounding as if he was straining. 'I can't even shift this board.'

'I can hear creaking deep inside. Tell me when you stop.'

'Stopping . . . now!'

The sound ceased. 'It stopped when you did,' Stevie called.

'Well, we're not getting in through this window, that's for sure,' Johnny said. 'And the other one down here is just big jagged bits of glass. And over here these busted fuckers are just about as sharp as . . . Oh, fuck it, Dogboy.'

Stevie knew what had happened. Johnny had been just about to tell him that the bits of glass were as sharp as needles and he'd tested one with his finger while he was speaking. He knew that Johnny had applied his finger to the point with the lightest touch . . .

. . . and like the Sleeping Beauty that touch had been enough. A tiny bead of blood had welled up on the pad of Johnny's finger, and as he'd moved his hand away, perhaps rapidly because of the sudden stinging sensation, that droplet had flown from his finger and hit the pane of glass or passed through into the room beyond and made a tiny tear-shaped stain on the floor. Exactly where it had fallen didn't matter.

What mattered was the effect it had on the house.

The house made a noise that might well have been a moan. And something wet and viscous sprayed along the left-hand hall wall.

The perfume of exotic plants increased as Stevie looked at the stuff running down the wall. It looked rather like someone had taken a dessert spoon, dug it into a raspberry mousse and flicked it.

Except there's something grey and grainy in there, too, Stevie thought fleetingly. *Something like porridge. Or . . . minced-up brains.*

The house sighed.

'Fuck,' Johnny said, from behind and to the right of Stevie.

'Someone just splattered a load of gunk into this room. It's horrible, man!'

Something in the hall gave a *crack!* and there was a hiss like a burst water main. A moment later a powerful spray flew from a dozen different directions simultaneously. The air in the hall and up the stairs filled with a grey-pink mist and every surface was coated with a slick mulch, which ran down the walls and stairs and pooled on the boards.

Something moved at the top of the stairs. Stevie couldn't see it, but he could hear it shifting up there. He tore his eyes away from the letter-box and yelled over his shoulder to Johnny, 'I think now would be a good time to leave.'

There was no reply.

Somewhere in the distance, a dog began to howl.

'Johnny?' Stevie glanced back through the letter-box: a slow, thick river of mulch was rolling slowly down the stairs now. Whatever was at the top of the stairs sounded like it was getting ready to come down.

All this from one drop of blood, Stevie thought wildly. *What did we do?*

'JOHNNY?'

The howling animal sounded like it was getting closer now.

Dookie? His dog's name ricocheted around inside Stevie's head, while he peered through the letter-box stalling until he'd seen it. The thing moving up there was Manaymon, also known as Yah-hoo. To glimpse it might result in his turning to stone, but it was too late to stop now. He *had* to see.

The high-pressure sprays of mulch ceased as if a tap had been turned off. The fine mist began to clear from the air. In the sudden silence that followed, the sound of the viscous liquid, flowing and dripping, sounded horribly loud.

And what would this little boy like for Christmas? a friendly voice asked inside Stevie's head. He instantly felt warm and secure. For a moment he was a small boy sitting on the knee of a department store Santa in a tinfoil grotto while his mummy waited outside.

Anything you want, you can have! I know you've been a good boy all year and now you can choose your reward. What'll it be, Stevie?

'I think we'd better . . . run away.' Stevie had no idea what he meant.

The thing at the top of the stairs creaked. Mulch trickled down ahead of it.

Perhaps a bike?

The top stair thumped and the next groaned. Stevie looked up as the thing came slowly down.

It was a bike.

A Honda C70.

Not a sparkling new bike, but an ancient, twisted heap of rust, rolling on buckled wheels. Its bearings squealed as it bumped slowly down the stairs, its rusted rims picking up a coating of grey-pink mulch.

Not my bike! Stevie told himself. *That's not my bike!*

But it was a bike he knew. The weeds hanging from the spokes and front forks gave it away.

It came slowly towards him, staying upright of its own volition. Manaymon wasn't supporting it.

This is the bike you wanted, the voice chimed merrily. *I know you've been lusting after it!*

It was the bike Stevie had seen in the vanishing kid's back garden. Suddenly he had a pretty good idea of the answer to the question that had bugged him and Johnny since they'd seen Nigel vanish on his swing. *What would happen to Nigel if he swung up into the other side and never came back?*

It had happened.

And the mulch was the result.

The bike hit the bottom stair, bounced down into the hall and disintegrated.

Moaning, Stevie dragged his eyes from the letter-box, found his feet, turned and yelled at Johnny. 'Come *on*! *Run!*'

Johnny looked like a statue. His arm was outstretched to one of the jagged panes of glass, his index finger resting lightly on a sharp point. Blood was seeping from his finger and running down the remains of the pane, but it was only getting half-way before it was burning off, leaving grey curls of acrid smoke that drifted into the house.

'*Johnny!*' Stevie yelled.

His friend didn't move. Stevie went closer and understood why. Johnny couldn't hear him. He was listening to the voice of Manaymon and smiling. As Stevie spoke to him again, he nodded and said, 'Yes,' in a small voice.

The mulch was seeping out from beneath the front door now and flowing slowly along the path, steaming.

Duke skidded to a halt a little way away from Stevie and began to howl. He was frothing at the mouth, his tail was curled under and his ears were back against his head.

'Dookie?' Stevie said, more surprised that he ought to have been – he'd been hearing him barking for quite a while now.

Duke gave a sharp bark and pointed in the direction he'd come from.

'I'm *trying*!' Stevie said. He wheeled round to grab Johnny's hand and yank it away from the glass, and was shocked when the dog leapt at him, growling. 'Get down!' Stevie said, and found himself staring into the dog's big white grin. 'I have to get him off!' Stevie said.

Duke snarled, pushing all his weight against Stevie, who tottered back a few steps.

Then the dog was off him, and sniffing at Johnny's ankles. He nosed at them, apparently trying to get him moving.

'Dookie!' Stevie called, and the dog looked back at him, gave one wag of his tail, then showed Stevie his teeth again. As Stevie watched, the dog, almost on his belly, circled Johnny, sniffing the ground and making an odd, frightened, keening noise.

His proximity apparently broke Johnny out of his trance. He looked over his shoulder at Stevie, tears in his eyes. 'I'm stuck, Dogboy,' he said. 'Paralysed. I can't move my arms or legs. My finger got pricked and this icy feeling went up my arm. Then it went numb. And the other one. And my legs. They're all frozen. It's using my blood and something's talking to me. I don't like it.'

'Don't listen,' Stevie said. 'We'll get you off there in a minute.'

Duke glanced up at Johnny's arm, then turned and slunk away, his tail curled under. When Stevie started forward, the dog barked at him sharply and flashed his teeth again.

'What the fuck's he doing, Dogboy?' Johnny asked, his voice pitched a full tone above normal. Stevie had never heard his friend sound so frightened and wondered if Johnny's luck had finally deserted him.

Duke made another low circuit around Johnny, then backed off again, this time going towards the trail of slime oozing from beneath the front door. He stopped at its edge, sniffed once, straightened up, then leapt over it and trotted down the road.

Stevie watched the dog slink away, his heart breaking. 'He's too frightened,' he said. 'He can't handle it.'

'You gotta get me off of here, Dogboy,' Johnny said. 'Help me, Stevie, for God's sake!'

As Stevie moved towards him, feeling as if he were wading through thick, icy water, the dog turned. Stevie stopped and watched. Duke pelted back towards them at top speed. A fraction of an inch before touching the stream of mulch he sprang forward, his top lip drawn back in a snarl and his mouth wide open. For a moment he was arcing through the air, then his mouth was around

Johnny's wrist and time paused. Then something shifted the ground beneath Stevie's feet and he was falling.

A moment later he was lying in the gutter, his left cheekbone throbbing where it had hit the kerb-stone. About five feet from him, Johnny was on his back on the pavement and Duke was sprawled across him like a rug.

Stevie's first thought was that his dog had sacrificed himself to save Johnny. His next thought cancelled that one: the Dukester was trying to get up. Johnny's hands were flapping at his sides and his feet were twitching.

A lump was already forming on Stevie's cheek as he got to his feet. 'That worked, then,' he heard himself say, glancing at number 52 May Street. He did a double-take. There was no red-grey mulch spreading from beneath the door. Frowning, he walked up to it, knelt and looked through the letter-box. The hall was in the same condition as it had been when he'd first seen it. There was no trace of Johnny's blood on the sharp point of broken glass, no smell of butchered bodies or exotic flowers. *It's as if none of it ever happened.*

'Fucking dog bit me,' Johnny moaned, clutching his arm. He waved his wrist in the air. Duke's teeth had torn two lines in his flesh on each side. It didn't look like a bad bite, but it was bleeding a little and Stevie could see several dents in Johnny's wrist where the dog's teeth had made contact but not punctured the skin. Duke glanced up at Stevie, that *I'm a bad dog* look on his face again.

'I think he was trying to save you,' Stevie said.

'From what?' Johnny demanded, glaring from Stevie to the dog and back again. 'I was just stood there looking through the window at that empty room.' He got up, scowling at the dog.

'You really don't remember?' Stevie asked.

Johnny gave an exasperated sigh. 'Yes, Dogboy,' he said in a parody of patience. 'I *do* remember.'

'You were just looking, right?'

Johnny nodded. He glanced back at the dog, who looked up at him hopefully, then laid his head down again, averting his eyes.

'Look at your forefinger. Right hand.'

Johnny looked. The expression on his face changed from irritation to surprise. 'Oh,' he said. 'It's cut.'

'You touched the glass and pricked your finger. You were stuck there. Dookie got you off it.'

'Really?'

'Cross my heart.'

Johnny shook his head. 'I don't remember anything,' he said, clutching his wrist. 'Shit, Dogboy, I think we should get out of here and regroup. My brain's going.' He crouched and called the dog over. Duke shuffled towards him on his belly. 'S'OK, old mate, I'll let you off this time,' Johnny said, and patted his head. Duke wagged his tail a little.

'The Dukester says he's sorry,' Stevie said.

'Yeah, it'll be all right,' Johnny said. 'Let's see if we can get the fuck out of here, Dogboy. I've had enough. I feel like someone's edited a bit out of my memory and I don't care for the feeling. How are we going to get back?'

Stevie was almost certain that something would happen as they walked away from the house, that a force-field would stop them leaving the area or that the house itself would wake up again and Manaymon would come out after them. This didn't happen.

But Duke didn't want to go back towards Leet's Store. He wanted to go the other way down the street. At first he tried to round the boys up, running rings around them and poking them with his nose, sheep-dog style. Then he sat down, whined and refused to move.

'What's wrong?' Stevie asked, trying to drag him along by the collar.

'There's something up there,' Johnny said, pointing, 'and Dookie's not fussy about meeting it.'

The something prowling in front of Leet's Store looked like an Alsatian-sized dog but it was moving like a cat. Its sinuous, muscular gait reminded Stevie of a captive tiger pacing up and down in its cage.

'OK, Dookie, you lead,' Stevie said, letting go of his collar.

The dog looked relieved. He barked and trotted off in the other direction. Stevie and Johnny followed him, glancing back at the distant animal. It didn't look as if it would give chase: it was just padding back and forth along the frontage of the store, as if guarding it.

'Do you think that if we'd gone into that house and looked out of its back windows, we'd have been able to see over to the field where we started from?' Johnny wondered. 'Or is it *all* nineteen seventy-something?'

'I dunno,' Stevie said. 'I don't think you can get anywhere else in whatever year this is but May Street. When I went down towards Lower Brook Street, the end of the road was sealed off with one of those force-field things. I chucked a ten-pence piece at it and it flashed out of existence. Maybe it reappeared in the field at the point where we got zapped over here.'

The Dukester had stopped and was looking back over his

shoulder. In front of him was a chain-mesh fence that ran across the end of the road and down to the right. Behind the fence was a small playground containing swings, a climbing frame and a huge cast-iron rocking horse that could seat six children.

Somewhere in that playground was the gateway they had to walk into. Stevie could feel it from here, still twenty feet away. The proximity of the power source made the hairs on the back of his neck and his arms start to rise. A feeling of nausea crept up on him.

'This playground looks like the one on the Brookvale Green,' Johnny said. 'Except there's tarmac here instead of that rubbery surfacing.'

The playground wasn't much used: large tufts of grass and clumps of weed had sprouted through the surface and turned the borders to rough grass. The rocking-horse ride was rusting and the swing seats looked damp and rotten.

'I feel sick,' Johnny announced. 'It feels as if it's siphoning you off, doesn't it? Like it's sucking away at your atoms even from here.'

Stevie glanced back up the street. It was impossible to see if the creature was still patrolling outside Leet's Store and from this distance he couldn't pick out *the* house from all the others. Nothing looked special. Nothing looked amiss. But something *felt* wrong.

'I dunno . . .' Johnny said, shaking his head. He looked pale and glassy-eyed.

'You don't know what?' Stevie asked, certain his friend was going to throw up. Blood he could stand, but the sight and smell of vomit was something else.

Johnny swallowed noisily. 'If . . .' he said.

Stevie looked away, taking in his surroundings. He estimated that the modern-day roundabout was less than forty feet from where he'd so recently leapt into the air with Christine90 under him. It seemed like weeks ago, rather than an hour at most. The roundabout and the patch of grass where he'd landed weren't there now, of course: off to the right beyond the playground's chain-link fence there was another long street – probably more of Lower Brook Street.

'. . . I can hack it,' Johnny finished.

'Going through the gate?' Stevie asked, glancing back at Johnny, whose cheeks were now tinged yellow-green. 'It gets easier,' he promised, glancing around the playground and wondering what was wrong. As he moved, he saw something from the corner of his eye. The playground didn't seem quite as deserted as he'd first thought. There was something in one of those clumps of grass at the far perimeter of the fence.

Something that sparkled, white and blue.

Stevie kept his eyes fixed on the area where he was certain he'd seen movement, but not a blade of grass trembled.

'I'm having hallucinations,' Johnny said thickly. 'I think it's this bastard power source causing it. I just saw something pop up over there. Out of that hole in the ground. Right-hand corner of the tarmac. It twinkled like a little star.'

Stevie again saw something pale blue flicker at the periphery of his vision. When he looked back nothing was there and there was nothing near the hole Johnny had pointed out.

'We're gonna have to go in there,' he said finally. 'It's the only way.'

'I know,' Johnny said, 'but that doesn't mean I like it any better.'

The gate set into the tall fence had a rusted padlock, which meant they were going to have to climb over. Under normal circumstances it would have been an easy climb, but with Johnny in this condition it might be complicated.

And the Dookster can't climb so we'll have to carry him and leave ourselves exposed going over the top.

Johnny began to retch. 'I'm OK,' he said, after a bit. 'Nothing came up. Dry heaves.'

'Good for you,' Stevie said, risking a glance and finding his friend was telling the truth. 'Where's Dookie gone?'

The dog was a little way off to his left, pawing at a clump of grass growing through the bottom of the fence and nibbling off the tips of the blades.

'We're either going to have to carry him over or kick a hole in the fence,' Stevie said.

'If we had a lever we could bust the hinges off the gate,' Johnny said, brightening at the suggestion of vandalism. 'But we haven't.' He gave the bottom of the fence a gentle kick. It rattled noisily. Duke looked up from his grazing.

'There's a rusty-looking bit at the bottom corner,' Stevie pointed out. 'We should work on that, I reckon. Wanna start?'

'Stand back, Dogboy,' Johnny said, swaggering up to where Stevie stood. He drew back his leg and gave the gate an almighty kick. Duke went back to grazing, which Stevie supposed meant he couldn't smell anything dangerous.

On the fourth kick, the chain-link started to give. On the fifth, it began to pull free of the metal frame. On the sixth, Johnny made a hole just about big enough to get his foot stuck into. And his foot stuck into it.

Which was when Dookie gave a small yap of surprise and then went ballistic.

Stevie turned from where he was watching Johnny fall backwards in slow motion towards the dog.

Duke threw himself against the fence, teeth snapping and foam flying from his mouth as he clawed frantically at the links.

On the inside of the fence, standing on top of a clump of grass and peering at Duke as if it had never seen a dog before, was Stevie's least favourite mythical creature.

A gobbling. *A gobbling that had come up from the nasty.* And, just like the little girl had said, it was all teeth and claws. It stood in a bow-backed hunch, its misshapen sloping head tilted to one side as it calmly studied the dog's fury. Its short muscular arms ended in slender hands that each had four fingers tipped with long black claws. Its crouched back legs looked as if they had been stolen from a rabbit and redesigned for war. Its taut skin was currently purple-black, but it was changing, lightening, taking on a red colour, and flexing its claws like a cat.

Stevie tried to shout a warning to Duke, but his mouth wouldn't work. All he could do was stare at the abomination and tell himself, *It looks just like I thought it would.*

The gobbling's head swivelled round towards Stevie. It grinned, showing a mouthful of Tyrannosaurus Rex-style teeth, then glared at him with glittering eyes.

Its colour was devil-red now. It flicked out a long, pointed tongue, tasting the air like a lizard, then glanced at the ground by its feet and snatched up a worm. It held it, writhing, in the air above its head and its jaws began to work. Stevie could clearly hear the sound of its teeth grating together. Dark drool trickled from the sides of its mouth.

'What *is* it?' Johnny yelled.

It's the friend of the thing Duke killed down on the playing field, and it wants its revenge, Stevie thought, but his mouth still wouldn't work.

Duke was howling and biting at the fence like murder on four legs. It rattled and shook and dirt flew from the thicket as the dog dug, but the gobbling didn't seem concerned. It watched Duke, tilting its raked-back head from one side to the other. Then it struck.

Its right hand flashed out in a long swipe, but the dog dodged back as the creature's claws met the chain-link fence.

Suddenly Stevie understood where the mysterious burn-marks

had come from: the gobbling's claws were hot. When they raked across the fence, a shower of orange sparks cascaded off leaving behind tiny jagged trailers of grey smoke.

'Get out of there, Dookie!' Johnny yelled.

The gobbling swiped again, missed, then threw itself against the fence. Duke snapped at its claws but it reached the top of the fence inside two seconds, then leapt down at the dog. Dookie danced away and there was a second when both dog and gobbling seemed frozen in mid-air.

What followed happened in a blur: rapid movement, a little smoke, a shower of sparks. Duke fell badly, hit the ground on his tail and curled over on to his back, the gobbling fixed to his head. He wriggled violently, found his front feet, heaved himself up and gave an almighty shake.

The gobbling burst.

The air was suddenly red with flying blood. Stevie put up his arms over his face as the wave hit him.

And then it was over.

'A ten-gallon gobbling by the looks of it,' Johnny observed drily, pushing his blood-soaked hair back from his face.

But Stevie was already on his way to where Duke was struggling to get up. The fall had hurt him: he was dragging himself along by his front legs. His back legs weren't working and he turned to Stevie, looking helpless. His teeth were red and he'd lost a few clumps of hair. The edge of his right ear had a nick in it and his right eye was half-closed. His chest was covered in tiny hairless strips with those thin burn-marks in the middle. He was panting hard.

Stevie knelt beside him, and felt down his back and around his hindquarters. Duke managed a feeble wag, which was a good sign that his spine wasn't broken. Stevie couldn't feel anything wrong with the dog's hind legs either – although he whimpered when Stevie touched the right one. Maybe a sprain, Stevie thought. He was probably exhausted – like he had been the last time he took on a gobbling.

'He all right?' Johnny said breathlessly. 'I've checked around the playground but there aren't any more. There *is* that hole in the corner, though. I found a lump of brick and stuffed it down.'

'I think he'll live. We might have to carry him, though. You went over the fence?'

'Yeah. The gate's over at the back. It gave me the heaves again. Fucking thing has its own gravity. Tries to suck you in. I'll go and kick the fuck out of the fence again. I'll make a hole big enough to slide the Dukester under if he can't walk. Did he hurt his legs?'

As if in answer, Duke stood up – on three legs. He held the right hind one off the ground and the left was quivering, but at least he was up.

'Brilliant!' Johnny said. 'Now let's get out of here.'

Chapter Nine

Rainy Day Tales: Goldilocks and the Worms

It was raining hard. According to the long-range forecast summer was over. A low was approaching from the North Atlantic and another, behind that one, was waiting its turn. Thunder was grumbling in the distance and Duke was lying on Stevie's feet.

Stevie wasn't aware of the thunder or the weather report. His attention was focused on the local paper, the *Gazette*, which lay open on his lap. The double murder, of the vanishing kid, seven-year-old Nigel Greenaway, and his mother, thirty-seven-year-old Joyce Greenaway, was front-page news, just as it had been in the national papers the previous day, and on the television news reports. Southend Road was now world famous. The television journalists had knocked on everyone's door, looking for new angles to the story, and the papers had done the same thing, but they were looking for big-sales dirt on Joyce Greenaway.

So far she'd been described as: *Single Mother, Joyce Greenaway*; *Pretty Young Mother Joyce Greenaway*; *Hard-drinking Joyce*; *Ex-Kissogram Girl Joyce*. Her ex-husband had been tracked down and interviewed by the police, the TV news and the papers, but he had been in Inverness for the last three years and didn't have a single bad thing to say about his wife.

The most interesting thing was that no details had been released of the murder, except that Nigel and Joyce had been 'viciously slaughtered in their own home' by what some of the papers were calling 'a knife-wielding maniac'. But, as Becky had so rightly pointed out, they couldn't very well say that the woman and her son had been liquidized, could they?

According to the *Gazette*, detectives from all across the south were still looking for the killer. Stevie sincerely doubted they were looking for an eight-foot-tall insectile god called Manaymon and also known as Yah-hoo.

The police were still waiting for the thin teenage girl 'they thought might be in possession of vital information' to come forward. Stevie thought they were going to be waiting a long time.

In Andy's workroom across the hall, something fell over. Andy swore. Stevie listened to the stream of invective until it tailed off. Andy hadn't been happy since the day of the killings. And Stevie thought he knew why. It wasn't because he was the murderer everyone was looking for, but because he knew, on some level, that he was involved. And that if he wasn't yet, he was likely to be soon.

Stevie was sure of this because something else in today's *Gazette* suddenly made sense when tied in with Becky's tale of Katie Kane's weird Kool Day ritual. Becky would be here soon and he wanted to hear her thoughts on the piece in the paper.

He flicked through the *Gazette* to the article that took up half of page thirty-four. The headline said: *Goldilocks Strikes a Fifth Time!* and the sub-heading read: *Serial Cereal Eater Sought by Police.* The article was about a wacko burglar who broke into people's houses and did nothing but make a bowl of porridge and, apparently, eat it. Messily.

Over the past six weeks, the lunatic had broken into houses in Wallis Road, Stocker Close, Anstey Close (the house owned by the people who ran the dog rescue where Stevie had got Duke), Cliddesden Road and now Bounty Road. A small map of the area was printed under the first slab of text, the houses in question marked with little flashes. There had been damage to one or two doors and tables had been left with porridge spattered all over them, but otherwise the burglar had stolen nothing.

But he might have cut himself once or twice, Stevie thought, remembering the print of Andy's trainer in the cigarette ash on his desk, and the open window. The article didn't mention the dates of the previous break-ins but the new one had happened two days ago – on the day that Nigel and his mum had been killed and Stevie, Johnny and Duke had visited May Street. On the day Becky had seen Andy covered in blood and with his finger bound up. The burglar had entered the house on Bounty Road after breaking a pane of glass in the back door, the article said. It added that there wasn't thought to be a connection between this series of burglaries and the killing.

Not a direct one, anyway. But you can bet your bottom dollar that there's some *kind of connection. My dad's Goldilocks. He's gotta be.*

It was a sobering thought. Stevie and his friends had had a lot of those in the past few days. And had gathered several questions that needed answers. If his mother had been home, Stevie would have started already, but she was off on yet another trip on behalf of the civil service and wouldn't be back until later. And Andy just hadn't been in the mood.

But Becky had hot news, she'd said when she'd phoned earlier. And she'd be round soon.

Everything's changed since we first saw that kid vanishing. Stevie thought. *Even Becky.* When you materialized into a field and suddenly Becky was hugging you and crying on you and kissing your mouth and blabbering about how she'd thought you were dead, you knew that something had changed pretty radically. And when you found that not only did you like the feel and the taste of Becky but you had a hard-on for her that felt like it would tear its way out of your jeans, you knew that things were never going to be the same again.

She only hugged and kissed you because Johnny was busy trying to puke, Stevie told himself, but he couldn't believe it. He didn't know what it meant yet but he was going to find out. Oh, yes!

'Dad?' Stevie called at the door to his dad's workroom. The Dukester limped out of the lounge and flopped on the floor behind him. He'd been to the vet and had allowed himself to be X-rayed. He'd chipped a bone and, according to Mr Meegan, had probably sprained his leg, too. The prognosis was that he'd be fine in a few days and Stevie was to wrap half an aspirin in cheese and feed it to him for the pain if necessary. This wasn't as easy as it sounded: Duke ate the cheese and spat out the pill.

'Can't fucking find any fucking thing these days,' Andy muttered, from the far side of the door.

'Dad?' Stevie called, knocking at the door.

'What?' Andy said. 'I'm busy.'

'You OK?'

'Do I sound like I am?' Andy answered. 'I've lost a scuzzy board. And I've lost my Swiss Army knife. And without that . . .'

'Can I come in?'

'Yeah, you might as well. Everything else in the universe has been in here this morning. I've got gremlins or something. Something's buggering everything, that's for sure.'

Stevie opened the door. The blind was down and it was fairly dark in the room – just the way Andy liked it when he was working. His huge monitor was showing a page of text. The room smelt peculiar: it wasn't just the stench of a billion cigarettes having been smoked in here but other, less familiar odours. There was the scent of an air freshener or kitchen cleaner, and a chemical smell that Stevie couldn't place.

'Shit,' Andy said, and Stevie finally spotted him. His father was crouched under his desk, his bare back facing Stevie. He was wearing a pair of shorts that looked like they'd last seen the washing machine in the early eighties and his faithful Nikes were on his feet. His back was scratched – not the kind of scratches he might have got while making love with Jacqui (who was pretty vicious, judging by some of the damage Stevie had seen on his dad's back) but lots of small criss-crossed ones, as if he'd crawled through brambles or something.

'What is it?' Andy asked, scrabbling at the detritus beneath his desk.

'Nothing much,' Stevie said. 'Thought I could help you look for whatever it was.'

'How much?' Andy said.

'How much what?'

'Do you want?' Andy looked over his shoulder and gave a grin that looked savage. His eyes glittered darkly from the shadows.

In that moment, Stevie could clearly picture his father breaking into people's houses and eating their porridge. Andy looked as if he was not just skating close to the edge but had one foot over the void with the other soon to follow.

'The fact is, my son, you only ever offer your assistance when you want money. So how much? I'm a practical man so shall we say a fiver? You find the scuzzy board and the money's yours. Petrol for the bike, I expect. Right?'

'I need a proper petrol can,' Stevie said, loath to turn down an offer of money, even though it was the last thing on his mind. 'This scuzzy board – is it an Adaptec one?'

'Of course.'

'It's on top of your monitor.'

'That's two fifty,' Andy said, grunting as he shifted something heavy out of his way. 'The other two fifty is for the knife and the lighter. And I think I'm gonna get there first. Have you noticed anything odd, Stevie?'

'How do you mean?' Stevie asked guardedly.

Andy held his gaze long enough to make Stevie uncomfortable. 'You'll think I'm crazy,' Andy said, smiling.

It wasn't a nice smile. It was a frightening smile. The kind of smile you'd expect to see on someone who was crazy already.

'Course I won't,' Stevie replied. 'No more than usual anyway.'

Andy snorted, sounding a little more like the old Andy. 'You lost anything recently?' he asked.

Stevie frowned. 'Don't think so. Why?'

Andy sighed. 'Call me a silly old fool, if you like, but it seems to me that since we had that murder down the road everything's *changed*. Stuff keeps vanishing, for one thing. I've lost both of my bandannas. And the scuzzy board. And my Swiss Army knife. And without that I can't get the little plug out of the bottom of my Ronson lighter so I can fill it up. And I can't even find the bloody lighter. The Zippo I had is lost, too. Haven't seen it for days. You haven't got a light, have you?'

'Nope,' Stevie said, patting his pockets. 'Hold on. Yes. I have.' He pulled out Johnny's book of matches and waved them at his dad's back.

On his hands and knees, Andy struggled out from beneath his desk and stood up, moving like a man who'd suddenly become very old indeed. 'You're a hero, kiddo,' he said, swivelling his chair round to face Stevie, then slumping down in it. His pack of Silk Cut was in his hand. Either it had materialized there or Andy had been clinging to it like a life-line while he'd been under the desk. He opened the pack and took out a cigarette, then looked at Stevie, took out another and threw it across to him. Stevie caught it and looked at his father questioningly. Andy was one of those parents who taught one thing and did another. He'd spent his entire life forbidding Stevie to smoke, now here he was handing out cigarettes.

'You sure you're OK, Dad?' Stevie asked.

'You've got matches,' Andy said. '*Ergo*, you smoke. I did my bit and taught you how smoking would kill you. You're a big boy now. You have your own decisions to make. And your own mistakes, too . . .'

'Look, Dad—'

'Light her up, kid, and pass the matches. It's not like I'm asking you to have sex in front of me or anything, is it? It's just a cigarette. You smoke when you're out so you can smoke in here.'

Andy wanted a heart-to-heart. Stevie could tell that much. He knew the signs. And since Andy was in an odd mood, it was worrying. He put the Silk Cut in his mouth, lit it, sucked hard and threw the matches to his dad.

'What I'm trying to say here, Stevie, isn't easy for me, OK? What I'm trying to say is this: I'm proud of you. You turned out to be a nice kid. A nice *guy*. And I'm impressed. Your mother and I must have done something right . . .' He tailed off.

'Thanks,' Stevie said.

'And you've worked miracles with that killer dog of yours.'

'Thanks,' Stevie repeated.

'And now you're not a kid any more. Not in my reckoning, anyway. You're a young man. And . . . I'm pretty damn thrilled how you turned out.'

'You said,' Stevie said. 'What else did you want to say?'

Andy tilted back his head and blew a smoke ring. 'In this life,' he said, 'you're gonna run up against things that'll tax you. You're gonna run up against badness. Badness with a capital B. You're gonna meet lust and avarice and pride and—'

'The other deadly sins,' Stevie said. 'Envy and sloth and what-have-you.'

Andy ignored him. 'If anything big hits you, I'm here to help. I'll do what I can. I know I can be a tetchy old bastard, but I love you, Stevie. Pretty much the same way as you love that dog, I should think. And you know how you'd feel if something happened to old Dookie? Put a power of ten on it and that's how I'd feel if something happened to you. That's all. Message over.'

He knows, Stevie thought. *He knows all about the gate and Raymond and number 52 May Street.* 'What brought this on?' he asked, wondering how much to tell his father.

Andy sighed. 'Everything's changing,' he said. 'And since that murder happened ... well, it brings it all home to you, all that stuff about how fragile life is. Could have been you down there.'

'What else?' Stevie said.

'Just stuff. It's like the weather's changed, only inside me. Then there's the stuff that's vanishing.'

'At least one of bandannas vanished before the murder,' Stevie said. 'I think the other probably vanished on the day of the murder. Your scuzzy card wasn't missing at all and your Swiss Army knife is probably on the floor here somewhere among all this junk.'

Andy wasn't listening. 'I have to go away soon, to America.'

'I know.'

'I won't be here for you,' Andy said meditatively.

'I'll be fine,' Stevie said. 'Everything will be fine.'

'I'm sure it will.' Andy nodded. 'You know what happened today? For the first time ever?'

Stevie shook his head.

'A cat came in here and shat in the corner. It's like ... a sign. An omen. It came in while I was working and I didn't even realize it had been until I smelt the stench.'

'And you were here all morning?' Stevie asked, glancing at the desk for fresh footprints. I would be in the next issue of the *Gazette* if Andy had been out and about, Stevie was sure.

'Yeah, I've written almost three thousand words since I got up,' Andy said.

Stevie nodded. 'What's that smell?' he asked, certain now that his dad had gone free-form again. Andy often did this when his mind was on his work – just flitted from subject to subject like a butterfly, without realizing you'd have difficulty following him. *I'm safe on the small matter of May Street, by the look of it*, he thought.

'Flash Excel,' Andy said. 'Used it on the carpet after I'd cleared up the cat shit.'

'The *other* smell,' Stevie said. He might not have been able to see fresh footprints on his dad's desk, but there was something he *could* see.

He's been lying to me, Stevie told himself in surprise.

Andy's lighter lay on his desk beside his keyboard with the little metal screw-in stopper that belonged in the bottom of the lighter and his Swiss Army knife, the screwdriver blade open. Just beyond that little lot was the can of lighter fuel.

'Can't smell anything else,' Andy said.

'Chemical smell,' Stevie said, getting up. Suddenly he *had* to know if the lighter had been filled.

'Where you going?' Andy said, tensing.

'Need to butt the ciggie in the ashtray,' Stevie said, picking his way through the junk on the floor to Andy's desk.

'Oh, look!' he said, planting the cigarette end in the ashtray and snatching up the old Ronson that Andy only ever used in here. 'Here's your lighter. And your knife. Strange, the lighter stinks of fuel! Looks like you've filled it up already.' He pressed down the button. It lit – with a vengeance. Andy had overfilled it and the body of the Ronson lit, too. As did Stevie's hand.

He flung it down and batted his hand against his jeans. On the floor beside Andy the lighter was still burning and a small area of carpet around it was ablaze where the fluid had leaked from the lighter. Stevie stamped out the flames then dropped to his knees to retrieve the lighter.

Which was when he got his first good look under Andy's desk. Suddenly he knew exactly what the odd chemical smell was. The carpet underneath the desk was covered in a thin coating of white powder. Andy hadn't been on his hands and knees searching for his missing things at all. He'd been using the red, yellow and white puffer bottle that was half hidden behind the flatbed scanner that lived down there. The bottle contained derris dust, a garden pest killer. Stevie leaned under the desk, picked up the bottle and read the front. 'Kills Caterpillars, Flea, Beetle, Raspberry Beetle, Pea and Bean Weevil, Sawfly and Other Insect Pests', it promised.

'Can I ask a dumb question?' Stevie said, getting up. Andy was peering at the bottle of derris dust as if it was the first time he'd ever laid eyes upon it.

'Sure,' Andy said, frowning.

'What kind of pests do you have in here? Fleas? Bean weevils?'

Andy shrugged. And looked at his feet.

'Dad, it's about an inch deep in insect killing powder under your desk. And you're gonna sit here breathing it in. This is not good stuff to be sitting in. *Why* did you put it there?'

'I don't really know, to tell you the truth,' Andy muttered. 'It seemed like a good idea at the time.'

'What's all this about, Dad? I need to know.'

Andy sighed. 'Worms,' he said. 'We've got worms. Another fine development in our sad little lives.'

'Earthworms, you mean? Or tapeworm or ringworm?'

Andy looked up at him. To Stevie's astonishment tears were glistening in his eyes. 'Dad?' Stevie said. His mother cried; he cried; his dad did *not* cry.

'Big worms, Stevie,' Andy said. 'Huge worms. Impossible worms.' Two large tears spilled from his eyes. He turned away and viciously stubbed out his cigarette. When he turned back he had a fresh Silk Cut in his hand and his lighter in the other. He lit up again, then wiped his face with the back of his hand.

Watching him, Stevie felt as if someone was twisting his innards. He wanted to ask Andy about his relationship with Katie, about the break-ins, about his mental condition, about May Street but 'You OK?' was all that came out.

Andy nodded. 'Just fine, kiddo,' he said, sniffing.

'You wanna tell me about the worms?'

Andy shook his head. 'I can handle it,' he said. 'If you hit them between the segments with a knife, they die. I tried stamping on them, but it didn't work. You have to catch them between the segments and avoid their mouths. Killed one earlier. Thought the dust might kill off the eggs, if they laid any. Or catch the larvae before it grows big.'

'They're imaginary, aren't they?' Stevie said, hopefully. 'Hallucinatory worms.'

'I can't remember,' Andy said. 'I can't remember anything just recently.' He shrugged and seemed to forget all about the worms. 'So, you gonna run Christine90 again today?' he asked, brightening.

'If the rain stops,' Stevie said carefully. 'Do you think you could answer me a couple of questions?'

'Sure, kiddo, fire away.'

'Do you remember when May Street was there?'

Andy grinned. 'Yeah, course I do. Why do you ask?'

'Did you live there?'

Andy's brow creased. 'No. What a weird question. You've seen all the photos in the album. I lived in Soper Grove till I married your mum. Then we got lucky moneywise and moved to Cuckoo Close, to the big house. You remember that, don't you? When things got a bit tight, we came here.'

'Did you know anyone who lived there?'

'Why the sudden interest?' Andy asked.

Even in this light Stevie could see the gates closing around Andy. He wasn't going to get anywhere here, that was for sure. 'We were down there the other day, by the car-radio shop, and Johnny told me about the street that used to be there. He said his mother could remember it. He thought he'd heard her say she knew someone who lived there.'

'Ahh, Katie,' Andy said, nodding.

'You and mum used to be friends with her and Johnny's dad, didn't you?'

'Once upon a time, long ago,' Andy said. 'Those times are long ago and far away. Lost in the mists.'

'How come you two don't keep in contact with them any more?' Stevie asked.

'You know how it is,' Andy said. 'You settle down and get into your own life and let things slide.'

'You liked them both?'

'We had good times,' Andy said thoughtfully. 'But it was another life. Another existence. The world moves on. Look, Stevie, take this fiver and go get your petrol can, or whatever it was you wanted. I'm all behind now. I've got lots of work to catch up with.'

'Now the worms have gone,' Stevie tested, smiling.

'Worms?' Andy said. 'What on earth are you talking about?'

'Clothes, all freshly laundered and ironed,' Becky announced, standing on the threshold of Stevie's front door and holding up two plastic carrier bags. 'Yours are in the Safeway bag and Johnny's are in the Sainsbury one.'

When Johnny and Stevie had been transported back to the field after their trip to May Street, Becky had been waiting and had refused to let them go home covered in blood because the police were everywhere. She'd sneaked into Stevie's house for fresh clothes, had taken them back and spirited away the ones with blood on them.

'And if you've got anything I can change into, I'd be the most grateful girl in . . . er . . . the street, I expect. I'm soaked to the skin,' she added needlessly. Her wet hair was plastered to her head and fell to her shoulders in thick damp cables, her white T-shirt had become transparent enough for Stevie to see the lacy bra she was wearing, and her faded Levi's were soaked black.

'You'd better come in,' Stevie said, taking the bags from her and standing aside. When she walked, Becky's feet squelched inside her odd-coloured shoes.

'Come upstairs,' Stevie said, 'and I'll find you something to put on.'

'You should have seen the blood that came out of your stuff,' Becky whispered, as she followed Stevie up the stairs. 'I had to wash it all on sixty degrees and do it twice before it was clean.'

Stevie went into his room, threw down the bags and began to rummage through his drawers. Becky stood in the doorway, dripping. 'It was only spitting when I left home,' she said. 'Just get me a T-shirt, and how about those little Ellesse shorts I saw you in last week? They're too small for you so they ought to be about my size.'

Stevie pulled out an ancient white T-shirt he'd bought when his parents had taken him to Greece the year before last. The word Karpathos was written on it. He dragged out the shorts from beneath a pile of socks and swimwear and handed them to Becky. 'Keep the shorts, if you want them,' he said, feeling himself blush. 'If they fit. A present. The T-shirt too.'

Becky grinned at him, mimed a kiss of gratitude and went to the bathroom to change.

Stevie sat down on his bed and picked up a computer magazine. He'd just about calmed himself down when Becky reappeared in the doorway wearing his clothes. There was a towel draped over her shoulders. 'Ta-da!' she said, posing like a *Vogue* model. 'What do you think?'

Stevie thought a variety of things he couldn't possibly say. Becky filled his too-small shorts in a much more satisfying way than he did. She had, as Johnny had noted, a remarkable behind and long, elegant legs. And Stevie was achingly aware of the movement of her breasts beneath the T-shirt.

Becky looked at him and giggled. 'I *do* love embarrassing you,' she said. 'The bathroom radiator's on so I've hung my clothes over it. If your dad comes up, he'll think we're in here fucking like a pair of rabbits.' She picked up the Safeway bag, came over and sat down on the bed next to him. He could feel the warmth of her thigh through his jeans, smell the fresh odour of her skin and the apple tang of the shampoo she'd used when she'd last washed her hair.

She rummaged through the bag and pulled out four photographs. 'I think you're gonna like this,' she said. She handed them to him but Stevie wasn't ready to think about them yet: he could still feel the soft skin of her bare arm from when it had brushed against his own as she gave him the pictures.

'Well?' Becky said. 'You'll have to excuse me if I'm talking a bit loud, but I think I'm still a bit deaf after that bloody great bang when you and Johnny got zapped away. My ears are still ringing.'

'How about your eyes?' Stevie asked. She had suffered from what Stevie thought was arc-eye – the kind of retina-burn that careless welders sometimes got. It healed fairly quickly.

Becky put her face in front of Stevie's, close enough to kiss, and stared into his eyes. 'How do they look?' she asked.

'Fine,' Stevie said, pulling back.

'They're better,' Becky said, moving away.

'You're full of beans today,' Stevie said, feeling himself flush again.

'Hey, I'm in a bedroom with one of my favourite men and I'm two items of clothing away from being stark naked. Course I'm full of beans! Now look at the photos!' She began to towel her hair and Stevie found that he either had to look away from what was happening under the front of the T-shirt or die of lust.

There were two Polaroid pictures, a passport-sized monochrome and a colour enprint. All were old and tatty. All were of the same person. A man.

'Is that him?' Becky asked, excitedly. 'I bet it is. I just *know* it's gonna be him!'

Stevie leafed through the photographs. The pictures had been taken in 1966 and 1967. The man in them wore little round steel-rimmed glasses. His goatee beard was thin and wispy, his hair a thick jumble of curls.

Stevie nodded. 'It's him,' he said. 'The guy who saw us on May Street. The hippy acid-tripper. He looks a little younger in these and his hair's shorter, but that's him all right. And I know what you're gonna tell me next, don't I?'

Becky nodded. 'Yup. That's my dad.'

'Did you know he'd lived in May Street?'

Becky shook her head. 'I had no idea. Didn't have a clue that he'd been a hippy. It's weird, really.'

'What is?' Stevie said.

Becky looked thoughtful. 'Well, these pictures weren't easy to find. We've got millions of photo albums lying around. Starting with my grandparents when they were kids, my dad and mum as babies. And there's pictures right up until both Mum and Dad left school. Then there's zilch till 'seventy-three, at their wedding. And in those they're clean-cut and short-haired. It's almost as if they'd hidden away the photos of several years of their lives.'

'You found pictures of your mum?'

Becky nodded. 'Yep. Hippy chick. Right down to her granny boots. The pictures were in my dad's secret stash place. Where he keeps the money he thinks I don't know about.'

'He stashes *money*?'

Becky grinned. 'Don't get excited. Most he's ever had there's a hundred and fifty – to my knowledge. I think he just keeps it there for Christmas and birthdays.'

'Did you bring any pictures of your mother?'

Becky's face fell. 'I could barely look at them without crying. They hurt too much. She looked so young and full of life . . .'

'Sorry,' Stevie said, and before he knew it, Becky's hand was clasped between his own.

Becky glanced at her hand, puzzled. Then she looked up at Stevie. A big smile lit her face. 'Oh, you *are* a sweetheart!' she said. 'Don't worry, Stevie, it was all ages ago. I can handle it!' Then she leaned across and kissed his cheek. 'Thanks, anyway,' she said, and squeezed his hand.

Stevie looked at her, feeling as though the scales were falling from his eyes. The recent sunny weather had brought out a scattering of freckles on Becky's face and given her a subtle tan. And Becky might have been many things but the thing she wasn't was plain. Far from it. She was exquisite.

'What?' she asked, a faint frown drawing fine creases at the corners of her eyes as she smiled.

Stevie shook his head and gave a dumb grin. 'Dunno,' he said. 'The little devil earring suits you. Gives you a whole other aspect.'

Becky gave an exaggerated wink.

'So . . .' Stevie said.

Becky squeezed his hand again and let it go. 'For a moment there I totally forgot what we were talking about,' she said, and giggled.

'Your dad the hippy,' Stevie said. 'We've got one or two photos of my parents when they were flower children. I dunno why your dad stashed his away.'

'Because he wanted them gone,' Becky said. 'Because they reminded him of something he wanted to forget. Something that started in 'sixty-six and finished in 'seventy-two. And it wasn't anything to do with my mother, because we have all those later pictures of her.'

Stevie thought about it. 'What we *do* know is that all our

parents knew one another. It's my personal bet that Johnny's dad and my mum were going out with each other, too. The six of them knew one another back in the late sixties. And—'

'And for some reason they'd rather forget all about it,' Becky said.

'Yeah, my dad shut down on me when I asked if he once knew anyone who lived in May Street. And at this very moment he's downstairs in his office sitting at his desk with his feet covered in derris dust. The stuff you put on plants to kill bugs. He thinks there are fucking great worms in there with him.'

'And *are* there?' Becky asked.

Stevie shook his head. 'I think he's cracking. I also think he's Goldilocks, the cereal burglar.'

'It'd figure. It's another ritual. Like the one Johnny's mum was doing. I bet the dates pan out, too. The day Nigel blew up Andy was covered in blood and had a cut finger.'

'Yep. And a house on Bounty Road was broken into that same day. Porridge was eaten. What's it mean? That's what I want to know.'

'They're trying to save us. At least Katie thinks she is.'

'From something on May Street?'

'Probably. I dunno. What I *do* know is that Katie's guilty of something. She's done something and she thinks she's atoning for it. What I also know is that, whatever it was, my mother didn't play. And because of it she ended up dead. Katie as much as said so. She's saving us and our parents from something.'

'What do we do?'

Becky grinned. 'We find out stuff before we do anything else. No more trips to May Steet, much as I'd like to see it for myself. Whatever it is Katie and your dad are doing, it isn't working. I suggest we play it cool and ask questions. Try to find out what we're dealing with before we try dealing with it.'

Stevie pulled a face. 'We'll be lucky. I told you my dad closed down on me when I asked about May Street. I doubt Mum will be any better. And Katie told you it'd kill her if she remembered. Which leaves Johnny's dad.'

'And mine.' Becky smiled. 'And while Johnny's dad's a man of few words, mine's a man of plenty. Especially on the days he's had a few too many. Which is almost every day.'

'Do you think a man who stashes away photos from the late sixties and early seventies is likely to sing like a canary on that very subject?' Stevie asked.

'You're reckoning without my feminine charm and guile,' Becky said, smiling sweetly.

Stevie grinned. 'Yep, you don't have a chance,' he quipped and tensed, waiting for her signature poke in the ribs with an extended knuckle. It didn't come.

'So, you come round to my place tonight, about eight. Bring Johnny with you. And we'll get Pops pissed out of his tiny skull and then we'll make him talk.'

'We'll be there,' Stevie said.

'And maybe,' Becky added thoughtfully. 'I can get him to tell me about all those times he tried to bring back Mum from the dead.'

Chapter Ten

Rainy Day Tales 2: Questions and Answers

Johnny tramped down Worting Road towards the town centre, his hands thrust deep into the pockets of his jeans in the vain hope of keeping his pack of Marlboros dry. He had purposely not dressed for the weather and was soaked to the bone. His feet were swimming inside his trainers and his shirt clung like a second skin.

The long walk in the driving rain didn't have the effect he'd hoped for. While he'd been trying to wheedle snippets of information out of his mother – who'd returned from her trip to London *glowing* – he'd fondly imagined that having the cool rain fall on him would make him feel better. It didn't. He still felt as taut as a guitar string. He'd had to leave when he could no longer stand his mother's serene smile and aggravatingly evasive answers.

Johnny stomped through a large puddle. He didn't want to see Stevie today. Or Becky. Or even the Dukester. He needed distance from them; distance would help clear his fuddled mind, help him think.

But it was doing no such thing.

'What did you do in the sixties, Mum?' he'd asked.

'If you can remember the sixties, you weren't there.' Katie had laughed.

Johnny had pretended he hadn't heard this warning. 'So, what did you do? Work?'

'After I left school, I took photos. You've seen the album covers. You know that.'

'What else?' he'd asked.

'The normal teenage stuff. Sex and drugs and rock and roll. All in excess. But don't worry. Everything's cool.'

'And then you met dad?'

'Eventually.'

'Where did you live?'

'What does it matter? Who cares? Lots of places.'

It had gone on like that until Johnny was almost incandescent with frustration. He had wanted to ask two direct questions: (1)

Why didn't you tell me you were fucking Stevie's dad? and (2) Why were you in an alley nearly naked, with a swastika shaved into your pubes, sticking a needle down your finger? But he could barely bring himself to believe that either of these things was true, let alone ask about them.

I'm all fucked up, he told himself, and part of the reason for that was being frightened that his mother might die if he made her remember that stuff. She'd told Becky that would happen and Becky had believed her.

Johnny glanced up as a truck swished by and showered him with gutter-water. He flipped the finger at it. And when the truck had gone by, he was treated to a vision.

Walking along the pavement on the other side of the road were two girls, one blonde, the other dark-haired. Both were around his own age, and struck him as being the most gorgeous creatures he'd ever seen. He glanced from one to the other and back again, unable to make his eyes rest on one for fear of what he'd be missing of the other.

They were wearing what Becky called fuck-me shoes, high and strappy, tiny skirts and had legs to die for. He glanced from the blonde's legs to the brunette's. The more he looked the more they seemed to out-do one another.

They had on cropped tops and the brunette had a navel piercing . . . but the blonde's navel was better in its natural state . . . except the piercing was more exotic.

And their breasts had the same effect. And their faces. Their lips, their eyes. Their hair.

His heart hammering, Johnny gawped as the girls passed, comparing the shapes of their bottoms and the seductive way they swayed.

Mine, he thought. *They should be mine.*

It wasn't until he'd watched them all the way down the hill to the traffic lights and then seen them turn off towards town that something important occurred to him. It was raining hard. Neither of the girls had been wet.

'Remember when we lived in the big house in Cuckoo Close?' Stevie asked his mother.

Jacqui Warner was sitting on the sofa with a large G&T in her hand. She'd been in from work for less than ten minutes and she was worn out. She'd left the house at six this morning and had driven all the way to the wilds of Kent for an unnecessary meeting, then driven the hundred and fifty miles back again. And the traffic had been *awful.*

'No "How are you, Mum? It's great to see you"?' she asked, swishing the ice cubes around in her glass.

'How are you, Mum? It's great to see you!' Stevie said, throwing himself down on the sofa.

For what was probably the millionth time Jacqui wondered why teenagers had to *fling* themselves everywhere. Why couldn't they just sit down like normal people? Jacqui tried to recall flinging herself on to her mother's sofa and couldn't. But not remembering was her forte. Cuckoo Close, however, was one thing she *did* remember.

'Yes, I dimly recall living in a house so large that when you shouted the echo returned about a week later,' she said. 'Why?'

She watched her son pull a variety of faces. 'Spit it out,' she said.

'Well, I was wondering . . .'

'Yes?'

'Where did the money come from?' Stevie asked.

Jacqui had known for a long time that this question would raise its ugly head. The things you did in other lives always came back to haunt you. *What am I going to tell him? The truth?*

'Seen Becky recently?' she asked, stalling for time. *I should have known. Once little Becky appeared on the scene, things were bound to slide.*

'She was here earlier,' Stevie said. 'Brought some old pictures round. Of her dad and stuff.'

It was going to be worse than Jacqui had thought. 'Really?' she asked, sounding bright and interested although her stomach was sinking. Jacqui had always known the truth would out sooner or later, but had hoped that it would be later. *Perhaps so late that I wouldn't even be alive to know about it.*

'Yeah. He was a hippy.'

Jacqui sipped her drink and nodded noncommittally.

'And so were you and Dad,' Stevie said. 'Right?'

'It was a long time ago, Stevie,' Jacqui said.

'Did you know him?'

No, I didn't, Jacqui wanted to say. The only person she felt comfortable lying to was herself – she was a past mistress at that. But lying to others didn't come easily so she merely nodded. *My hand's shaking*, she noted distantly.

'And his wife?'

Sure, Jacqui thought, *I slept with her, after all.* 'Yes, Jane her name was,' she said. 'I did know her. Quite well.'

'What was she like?'

'She was gorgeous. A bit like Becky. If you can imagine what

Becky will look like in another five years or so. Lots of frizzy auburn hair. Green eyes. Loving. Sweet and kind. Principled.' *And she died*, Jacqui added silently, *because of those principles, because she wouldn't deal.* Then she wondered quite what she'd meant by that. Then she forced herself to stop wondering, because there was a yawning chasm of darkness that lay just beyond memories of Jane, an emptiness that you could easily fall into and become lost for ever.

'What's wrong?' Stevie asked, and when Jacqui looked up she saw that he looked worried.

'Nothing. Why?'

'You looked as if you were going to faint or something,' Stevie said.

'Tired,' Jacqui said. 'Long day.' That old saw about the sixties, 'If you can remember them you weren't there,' was true. Jacqui had spent most of the late sixties and early seventies in a colourful blur. She'd woken up one blissful morning at the age of fourteen and a half and decided that it was about time she began to live. A fortnight later she'd kissed a boy for the first time. A week after that she'd got drunk for the first time. Six weeks later Jacqui had changed from the perfect daughter to the rebel from hell.

Two weeks before her fifteenth birthday, Jacqui had lost her virginity, in a park, to an older boy named Sebastian. And she'd found she liked sex. One of his friends had introduced her to cannabis, which she'd also liked. On her sixteenth birthday, wearing a kaftan and an Afghan, she'd taken her first tab of acid and changed her perception permanently.

It had been something of a miracle that she'd left school with five O levels at good grades and got a job in the civil service (war pensions). That lasted a year, during which she'd blitzed her mind with everything from dexedrine to stramonium, then she left work to hit the trail to India where, tired, confused and stony broke, she'd met Jane and been taken under her wing. When Jane came back from India, Jacqui came with her, to her house in Hampshire. Which was where the Magnificent Six had gathered. And where Jacqui's memory quit if she had anything to do with it.

'Anyway,' Stevie said, 'how did you afford to buy that big house?'

Jacqui shrugged. 'Your dad came into some money.' This was the truth – not the whole truth, of course, but it would suffice.

'From when his mum and dad died?'

'Yeah,' Jacqui lied. Andy's mother and father had been killed in a car crash, destitute, and a month later, her own parents had died, also broke, while on holiday in Spain. Something to do with the hot-water boiler in the apartment they'd rented not having adequate ventilation.

Stevie nodded. 'And why did we have to move out?'

'Money got tight,' Jacqui said. This was true, too. Money often did get tight when the authorities sequestered it and neither she nor Andy had thought of stashing the money for a rainy day.

'When dad left *Oz* and went freelance?'

'Round about then,' she agreed, a little relieved. Evidently Becky didn't know, either. Jacqui was surprised that Becky's father, Mr Booze-Head, had managed to keep his trap shut all this time. Becky was a bright girl, and very inquisitive too. 'She takes after her mother,' she said aloud.

'Becky?'

If she ever starts to wonder, she's going to find out, Jacqui thought, but said, 'Yes, she's a lovely girl. And she's smart.'

Stevie nodded thoughtfully.

'Do you like her?'

Stevie blushed and looked away. 'She's all right,' he mumbled.

Jacqui smiled. Becky wasn't as open and welcoming as her mother but when she forgot her woes her face lit up and you could sometimes almost believe Jane was alive again.

But she's doomed, a small voice whispered inside Jacqui's head. *You know that, don't you?*

Jacqui pushed away the insane thought. She didn't entertain such ideas these days. Not now she was grown-up and sorted out. She'd turned things round and got herself back on track. Normality was good. And whatever had gone before was over and forgotten.

'Why don't you see Johnny's mum and dad any more?' Stevie wanted to know.

Jacqui sipped her G&T. She'd managed to skate round the money thing and now Stevie was popping another corker of a question at her. The straight answer was that they'd all thought it best to go their own ways. Afterwards. *Christ, it's like living out a fairytale*, she told herself. *We split up and vow never to see one another again. We vow never to have children. We cut ourselves and mingle our blood to seal the pact. And what happens? Twenty years later we all have teenage children who find one another and team up. I knew we should have moved to America when Andy was offered that job in 'eighty-three.*

'We just drifted apart,' she said.

Stevie nodded. 'Can I ask one more question?'

'Of course,' Jacqui said, uncomfortably. Stevie was looking at her in an odd way. As if he was looking *into* her. Seeing her as she really was.

'And you promise to give me an honest answer?'

He knows!

'I might do,' she said, trying to sound playful.

Stevie nodded. 'OK,' he said. 'Is Dad OK?'

'How do you mean?' Jacqui demanded, a little more sharply than she'd intended. Dad wasn't OK at all. Dad was suffering. She'd been covering for him for the last eight weeks while she tried to convince herself that his journey into strangeness was due to the pressure he was under over the IBM contract.

'Well, he's seemed a bit distant,' Stevie said, 'and I was wondering what was bothering him.'

'Just the trip to Austin. He hates flying. He's been worrying about it,' Jacqui said, knowing her lies were transparent to her son. 'This IBM contract means a lot to him,' she continued, more to fill the silence than anything else. 'He doesn't like talking about it.'

Just recently Andy didn't like talking, period. Except in his sleep. He thrashed about in bed and complained about worms and cats and red signals. He called out for his mother. He cried. He pleaded for them not to take away his Jacqui. And when he was awake he acted as if he were Good King Paranoid himself. He skulked and listened at doors. He complained about insects in his workroom. He wrote for hours, then deleted the files. And, for the first time since she'd met him, he'd become impotent. It wasn't just the forthcoming trip he was worried about. She knew that. But she couldn't bring herself to face up to the most likely cause of all this. Even the double murder not a hundred yards away from here (*which is a sign if ever there was one*, she thought) hadn't made her face up to it.

She didn't think she *could* face it. Because of the two missing weeks.

'And that's all that's wrong, is it?' Stevie asked, sounding doubtful.

Jacqui grimaced. 'He's been having a little ... er ... personal trouble, too,' she said. 'Don't worry. It'll all work out. It's the pressure. I know we've both been a bit tetchy recently but it'll blow over.'

Two weeks were missing from the life of Jacqui Warner. She had always been aware of them – and the chasm in her mind they'd left behind – but until recently they hadn't seemed to matter. But if she wanted to get a handle on what was wrong with Andy, and why two people had been murdered just down the road, and why her husband kept turning up with blood on him and why the dog was covered in tiny burns and a number of other things, she was going to have to hurt herself. She was going to have to fling herself into that chasm and dredge up whatever lay in it.

'And nothing else is wrong?' Stevie asked.

She sipped her drink, which now tasted flat and weak. She held her son's bright, clear gaze for a few moments and shook her head. 'No,' she said, 'nothing else is wrong. Don't you worry about a thing.'

And, to her surprise, Stevie seemed satisfied.

Johnny saw the two girls again as he passed the gates to the Memorial Park, where he'd lost his virginity last summer – to Becky's arch enemy Sindy Hallett. Now, watching those two preternaturally beautiful girls sashay past the council offices in the driving rain, while remaining quite dry, it seemed to have happened to someone else. Someone that Johnny had been and was no longer. And he wished he was back there now. Those were simpler times, when he'd understood at least a little of what was going on.

They should be mine, he told himself again.

But he could live without them. Beauty, his mother always said, was only skin deep. You could forget beauty. What Johnny wanted most of all now was *clarity*.

A little way away from him, the high heels of the girls' shoes click-clacked on the pavement.

'Why aren't you getting wet?' Johnny yelled after them. But they were like the people on May Street. They could neither hear nor see him.

He turned away and ignored the ache of lust that filled his lower abdomen. Things were going screwy.

When the girls were out of sight, Johnny turned back and entered the park, not knowing where he was headed. His father's car lot was a little further down London Road and he'd come this way with half a mind to blitz in there and demand to know what was happening. But he wasn't sure his dad would know. And the girls seemed to be drawing him along somehow, as if their tracks were magnetic.

They weren't in the park. Johnny suspected they weren't here because they didn't exist. He squelched across the wet grass, ignoring the old guy walking towards him with the skinny black dog, and headed for the side gate that led out on to Hackwood Road.

Johnny was so deeply involved with the muddiness of his mind that he didn't realize where he was going until he arrived there. When he looked up, he was in the alley. The one where Becky had watched his mother perform the most weird ritual you could imagine.

'Oh, shit,' he said. He had no memory of having passed through the side gate of the park, or of crossing Hackwood Road. He was at the Hackwood Road end of the alley, about ten feet along it. Rain was hammering hard off the black tarmac but Johnny could still hear the distant tap-scrape of high heels.

Those girls led me here, he told himself, feeling as if he'd just woken up. He glanced back at Hackwood Road, where cars were swishing by, throwing up spray. The view in that direction looked wrong, as if it was too thinly painted and the colours were fading. The view up the alley towards Cliddesden Road, however, looked so real and clear it made his head ache.

He walked slowly up the alley, feeling as if this might be a trap. Although who would want to trap him, he didn't know. Unless it was old Yah-hoo. But, judging from what had happened to Nigel, Yah-hoo didn't need to trap you: if the fancy took him he just blew you to a sticky paste.

Ahead of him Johnny spotted the posy of flowers. Or what was left of them. They lay across one corner of the mouth-shaped hole Becky had described, their stems still wrapped tightly together. But they were long dead: when Johnny squatted to inspect them, they looked as if they'd been pressed. Like the ones that had fallen out from the pages of his grandmother's King James Bible when he'd picked it up. Those flowers had been in the Bible for over thirty years and had gone a nasty brown colour. These were just over a week old and had no colour at all. They showed no sign of decomposition but they looked as if the *life* had been sucked from them, leaving just a flower-shell behind. Now they were falling apart in the rain, melting away like moist rice-paper.

'Can't see any blood,' Johnny muttered. But that was hardly surprising, considering the power of the rain. For a few seconds he wondered if he should cut himself and drip some of his own blood down the mouth-shaped hole. Perhaps that would wake it up. Becky said she'd thought she'd heard the hole talking to her, promising to take away her madness, and Johnny wished someone would take away this uncomfortable muddiness that was doing him in.

'Talk to me,' he challenged, glancing up in case anyone was

watching him talking to a hole in the pavement. 'Tell me what's what!'

Nothing happened.

Johnny picked up the flowers by their wrapped stalks, glared at them, then tossed them at the grinning mouth in the tarmac.

They sailed down the hole without touching the sides – something Johnny would have bet was impossible. He shimmied closer to the hole, ready to dodge back if anything should shoot out at him. But the hole in the tarmac was merely a hole. It might have been mouth-shaped, but it had no teeth; the sides were smooth and pale. Johnny edged his fingertips into it, fighting off the feeling that it would snap shut. It was a hole, and that was all it was.

It was strange that the hole existed at all. The council *always* filled holes in the pavements before someone broke an ankle and sued them.

The inside of the hole was smooth and cool. It felt like marble, but softer. A little deeper into it, the surface became ridged: it even felt like the inside of someone's mouth. *How deep does it go?* he wondered.

He lay face down and fed his entire arm into the hole, which was deeper than he could reach. It certainly wasn't your ordinary hole in the ground, he decided. Down here the sides had a damp sponginess to them. And they felt warm. In fact, the surface he was now exploring reminded him of how the inside of Sindy had felt the first time he'd pushed a tentative finger into her.

Is that what your little heart desires? he could hear Sindy asking him breathlessly as she pushed herself against him. *Is that what you want?*

The jolt of pain that followed was so ferocious that, for a moment, Johnny thought something had bitten off his arm. He screeched and rolled back, expecting to see blood pumping from a ragged hole in his shoulder, but his arm was still there, undamaged from shoulder to elbow, elbow to wrist. It wasn't until he moved his hand that he discovered where the pain was coming from: something dragged from it across the tarmac and the agony increased fourfold.

Johnny knew what had happened long before he could open his eyes and see it. For almost a minute, he held the forefinger of his left hand tightly as he rolled on the ground waiting for the pain to abate. When he finally looked, through eyes blurred with tears of pain, the long, slender needle was still stuck firmly into his finger.

Bastard! You motherfucking bastard! he screamed inwardly.

Gasping at the black waves of agony rolling up his arm, Johnny bit down on the eye of the needle so hard that his teeth crunched, and tugged his finger back.

The needle came out more easily than he'd imagined and his finger bled more than it should have done. He made a point of not allowing the blood to get anywhere near the hole and fought off an urge to throw the needle back into it. Using his other hand, he wove the needle into his shirt. *I'm gonna stick this right into your fucking eye, Yah-hoo*, he thought.

Is that what your little heart desires? Sindy's voice replied. *Is that what you want?*

Johnny frowned. He could still hear the clacking of high heels, even though the two girls must have been miles away by now.

You can do better than that, I know, Sindy said.

'But it's gonna cost me?' Johnny said. Was this Yah-hoo talking inside his head or his muddy mind getting even muddier?

You know what you can get and you know how you can get it, Sindy whispered. *You can use me as hard as you like and I'll never be used up. Anything you want is yours for the asking.*

'Fuck off, Mister Man,' Johnny said. He wasn't clear about many things right now but one thing he *did* know was that that Sindy Hallett had never said anything like that.

I'm here for you. Remember that. Anything you want, the voice tinkled.

'I want answers,' Johnny gasped.

All the answers your heart desires are yours. You know how you can get them.

It doesn't have to hurt any more. Nothing has to hurt.

Johnny held out his swollen finger. Its tip was dark with blood. The pain increased to a point where he could barely stand it. He screwed his eyes shut and tried to speak, but could only make a small mewling noise. *Stop it fucking hurting!* he pleaded inwardly. *Just stop it hurting!*

The pain stopped instantly and was replaced by the intensely pleasant sensation of someone sucking at the tip of the finger. He could feel the teeth gently gripping the first joint, the warm, soft tongue supporting the pad, the lips that sealed his finger in the gentle mouth.

Johnny opened his eyes.

The blonde girl was kneeling in front of him, gazing at him with clear blue eyes as she sucked his forefinger. The brunette stood behind her, grinning. 'Doesn't hurt now, does it?' the brunette asked.

'I . . .' Johnny said, looking away from the blonde.

But the brunette was no longer there. And there was no blonde.

It's that easy, Johnny, the voice of Sindy whispered inside his head. *That easy. You know where to get it. You know where to come.*

Chapter Eleven

Rainy Day Tales 3: The Taxi Man

For a few moments Derek Sharp could have sworn he'd heard a timid male voice call, 'Let me out, please!' He chuckled to himself and changed down to third for the tight bend that was approaching a little more rapidly than he'd estimated. Then he braked fairly hard and flung the *Lady Jane* – an elderly FX model diesel taxi – round the corner. The tyres squealed and the cab slipped a little, but Derek caught it. The amulet that hung from the rear-view mirror jiggled a little and swung round like a dowser's pendulum, then settled.

Should have been a racing driver, Derek told himself.

'Excuse me!'

There was that muffled voice again. Derek changed smoothly back into fourth for the downhill stretch and put his foot down. The hill into Cliddesden was fairly steep and the cab picked up speed at an alarming rate. It felt pretty good to Derek. A little bumpy, perhaps, but the FX series cabs weren't built as limousines or racers. Still, they flew down hills like this one.

Something was banging behind him, a frantic kind of rapping. Derek hoped it wasn't something terrible happening to the *Lady Jane*'s rear end. He'd already had the gearbox fixed this month. Last month it'd been the generator. Just lately he seemed to be spending more than he was making on keeping the taxi running.

'Who cares?' he said aloud, and grinned. Worrying aged you before your time, his mother had said. And his mother, who'd worried about *everything*, had died young.

'Stop!' the voice said.

Derek glanced in his rear-view mirror and experienced a moment of cold shock when he saw that he had a passenger. He slowed down, glancing from the road to the man in the back seat. For a few seconds he was unable to recall picking up the fare or where he wanted to go. Then it all came back. Mr MacPherson. Fare from Axford to the Automobile Association at Fanum House. A middle-aged middle-manager, who'd had a few over a long lunch at the Candover Crown. He wore a shiny suit and a grey goatee.

Using the handle of his umbrella, MacPherson hammered on the privacy glass. Derek slowed to forty miles an hour and reached behind him to unfasten the catch.

'*Stop the cab, you fucking maniac!*' MacPherson screamed.

This was strange, because Derek was a pretty good judge of character and MacPherson hadn't struck him as the swearing or panicking kind.

Derek glanced over his shoulder. The sudden movement made him a little giddy. 'We're not there yet,' he said patiently.

'I don't *care* where we are, you *fuckwit*! What I care about is staying alive!'

Alive? What did *he mean?*

'For God's sake, man! Just stop the taxi and let me get out!'

'It's raining,' Derek observed, letting the cab slow. 'And we're in the middle of nowhere. You'll get soaked. How about I drop you off when we get to Cliddesden?' he asked politely, stifling an acid belch.

'We could be dead before we get there,' MacPherson said bitterly. 'If I'd realized you were drunker than I was, I would never have set foot inside this rusting hulk. Now, let me out!'

Derek glanced at his lucky amulet and shrugged. 'I've been driving this cab, or one very much like it, for twenty-three years now,' he said, 'and I've *never* had an accident. Not even one tiny bump or scrape. Now try to relax, we're not going to crash.'

'Stop the fucking taxi!' MacPherson shouted.

There was just no pleasing some people. Derek knew this. Sighing, he pulled up. 'If you've got a mobile you can call another cab with it from here and just sit here till it arrives.'

'I don't have a mobile. Can't you call me a cab?'

'You're a cab,' Derek said, giggling.

'I'm going to report you,' MacPherson fumed. 'By God, I'll have your license taken away from you and your driving license too!'

Derek grinned. It wasn't the first time he'd heard this particular set of words arranged in this particular way and he doubted it would be the last. Some folks just didn't know when they were in safe hands. 'I'd call you another cab, but I'm incommunicado at present,' he said. 'Had a fare last weekend who bust my phone and I'm still waiting for a replacement.'

'Release the door and let me out,' the man demanded.

Derek checked his meter. 'That'll be two pounds fifty, sir,' he said mildly.

The man gave a strangled cry but he went for his wallet, and thrust a fiver through the sliding window. Derek thanked him, gave him his change and released the door catch.

'You've got a fucking death wish!' MacPherson snarled, once he was safely outside the cab. He turned and set off down the road, splashing his way through the rivulet of brown water draining from the hill-top.

Derek got out of the taxi and called after the man, 'I haven't got a death wish. I've got a life wish. Thanks for your custom! Have a nice day!'

Already drenched, he climbed back in and reached under his seat for the bottle of Cardhu single malt that someone had brought him back from a trip abroad. After some of the throat-grating cheap blends he'd drunk, it was like nectar. He pulled the cork, raised the bottle to his lips and drank to MacPherson's very good health. For all the good *that* would do. MacPherson's time on the planet was limited. He had a blocked artery that was going to give him one hell of a heart-attack inside a month. Derek considered pulling up alongside the man and telling him, but as the guy thought he was a drunk (which Derek would happily admit) and probably also that his mind was wrecked there wasn't much point. Derek's mind, however, seemed indestructible. God knew he'd tried long and hard to wreck it.

'What the fuck do you know about anything, you piss-artist?' MacPherson would undoubtedly say if Derek tried to warn him. And Derek would have to acknowledge that he didn't know much at all. It was just that sometimes when he met people he could tell there was something wrong with them and diagnose it accurately. The problem was, of course, that no one believed a medical diagnosis from a sozzled cabby. A bigger problem was that whenever this happened Derek recalled his first ever diagnosis of a medical condition.

The moment the tiny clump of maniac cells had begun their rapid growth deep inside his beloved Jane's head, Derek had known. To make matters worse, he'd also known that she wouldn't get better. The killer blow was that he'd also intuited the approximate date of her death. He'd been out by exactly twenty-nine hours.

And that's what you get, he told himself, *for fucking around with things you don't understand.*

He reached up and ran his fingers over the amulet that hung from the rear-view mirror. The gilt coating was wearing off the diamond-shaped talisman and the tin beneath was showing through. The perfume of violets had once wafted through the tiny holes drilled in the upper half but now it was light and empty. Derek often suspected that the magical amulet was nothing more than a *Made in Hong Kong* pot-pourri that was well past its useful life, but he kept it in his cab anyway. *Something* was preventing him having an accident, that was for sure. He'd often done an entire day's work so drunk that the roads waved about in front of him; he had no memory whatsoever of some days. Either he was so good at driving he could do it unconscious, or he had the largest amount of dumb luck in the world. Or the amulet was playing a part.

Derek swilled a fresh mouthful of Cardhu around his mouth and swallowed. *Nothing I could have done anyway*, he thought. Being impotent appeared to be his punishment for his hubris: although his darling Jane's suffering had ended, his own suffering went on.

But this particular taxi-driver is still here, he reminded himself. *This guy can take anything thrown at him and bounce back, a smile on his face and steel in his gaze.*

If he were being honest about it, Derek's gaze was currently anything *but* steely. It was kind of blurred right now. Not with tears – Derek had done his share of crying; oh he'd cried an entire reservoir in his time – but with alcohol, his friend and protector. Derek Sharp was a happy drunk, which was just as well, because if he'd been a miserable drunk he would have topped himself shortly after Jane's death.

The fact was that if he stayed sober for any length of time the dark thoughts of suicide returned. So he stayed drunk, and not just for himself but for Becky. Becky, who looked so much like her mother that it sometimes twisted his heart hard enough to make him cry. Becky, whose voice had that same tone and timbre, whose vocabulary seemed to consist entirely of her mother's pet expressions. Becky, who was the only shining light in a life of darkness.

And what did you do to her, eh? he asked himself, swigging another mouthful from the bottle before replacing the cork. He gazed out past the swishing windscreen wipers into the rain. What he'd done was fuck up his only shining light in a big way. When you were not only a drunk but a drunk with clever ideas, it was easy to do: Becky had seen him trying to put some of those ideas into practice. He didn't know when or how, but he knew that this was what had happened.

He batted at the amulet. Its chain tinkled and it swung back and forth. 'You'll help me see her through, won't you?' he asked it. The fact was, Becky was improving. This wasn't what her teachers had said and it certainly wasn't what her shrink said, but Derek believed the evidence of his own eyes. Since she'd teamed up with those boys, she'd been a lot happier. And recently, he thought, she'd started to get a sparkle in her eyes that he recognized because he'd seen it in her mother's eyes, too.

Becky was falling in love with one of those kids.

Derek didn't know how he was supposed to feel about this. Most dads, he guessed, would go on the warpath, because what usually happened shortly after love was sex. And Becky wasn't yet sixteen. But underneath all her rebellion and thunder, his little girl had a sensible head on her shoulders. Even a drunk could see that. And if she wanted to get laid she would, and he wouldn't be able to stop her, even if that was what he desired. But everyone he knew had lost their virginity before the age of consent. His own Jane had forgotten she'd ever had hers by the time she was sixteen.

He shrugged and grinned. 'I guess I qualify as a poor parent,' he said aloud. 'Maybe I better find out what those kids' surnames are in case I have to go after one or the other with a shotgun. Or meet them, anyway.'

Their first names were Wolfgang and Johnny. Except Becky confused the issue by calling the one named Wolfgang, Stevie, or Dogboy, and the one named Johnny, JK. For some time, Derek had thought Becky was hanging around with five boys rather than two.

Derek's good friend MacPherson was on the outskirts of Cliddesden when the *Lady Jane* caught him up. He was paddling through a huge puddle that had gathered at the bottom of the hill.

'Oh dear,' Derek said, grinning. He swung the cab right into the middle of the road – where he estimated the deepest part of the water would be – and put his foot down.

MacPherson disappeared from view as the cab passed him and when Derek looked in the rear-view, the man was sitting in the water at the edge of the puddle looking something like a drowned rat.

'Have a nice day!' Derek called and sped away.

When Derek entered the lounge Becky got up quickly. He was so drunk that he perceived this as a swift blur of colour that reminded him of something he couldn't quite place. But it must have been something scary because he jumped and gave a little cry of surprise. He found the door jamb and clung on to it, catching his breath.

'This is Stevie,' Becky said, motioning behind her to the sofa.

Derek looked at Becky first, trying to focus his eyes, then at the kid crouched forward on the edge of his seat, his arms folded across his knees.

'Hi, Stevie,' he said, letting go of the door jamb and tottering into the middle of the room. ''S Wolfgang, right?' he said, knowing he was slurring badly and not being able to do a damned thing about it.

'Pleased to meet you, Mr Sharp,' Stevie replied.

'You too, kid,' Derek slurred, grinning. 'Been snogging with my Becky?'

The kid, blushing furiously, looked up at Becky who chuckled. 'So, what if we have?' she challenged.

'Nuffink, nuffink. 'S upta you two,' Derek said apologetically. 'Sorry I disturbed you. Honest! Sh'll I go out again?'

'Sit down, Dad,' Becky said, 'before you fall down. You hungry?'

Derek tottered towards his Norton recliner. 'Could eat a scabby monkey,' he replied. He bent to grab hold of the arm of the chair and stood still while the world revolved around him. Eventually he moved to the right position and fell back into his easy chair. For one awful moment he knew he was going to lose the better part of the bottle of Cardhu, right here on the carpet in front of Becky's guest. Then it passed.

'There's fish and chips in the oven,' Becky said. 'Can you manage them?'

Derek's stomach rolled. 'Sure,' he said, glancing at his daughter – who was gazing at the kid, who looked concerned.

'It's OK, he never throws up,' Becky said. 'He'll be all right.' She walked out of the room, leaving the kid to fend for himself.

Derek concentrated on not slurring his words: 'She thinks I won't remember when I've sobered up,' he said, slowly and clearly. 'But the sad fact is I have total recall, just like she does.' He didn't add the last bit: 'That's why I drink.' The kid was uncomfortable enough as it was. Even a drunk could see that.

'Good,' the kid said, nodding.

Derek found his kindest smile and offered it to him. 'Relax,' he said, waving a limp hand. 'You'll soon get the hang of how it works round here. Nuffink to worry about. I don't bite. I'm a happy drunk.'

The kid nodded.

'So, Wolfgang . . . or Stevie, you're German, are you?' Derek asked.

The kid shook his head. 'Everyone calls me Stevie and I'm English. My mother's grandfather was German.'

'Went to Berlin a few times in my younger days,' Derek said. 'Course it was all different then, what with the Wall and everything. Used to – smu – strike that one.' Derek almost bit off his tongue. Christ, here he was trying to build up a rapport with a kid he didn't know and he'd almost told him about the Willys Jeep and its tyres.

Becky came back and rescued him. 'Stevie's never been to Germany,' she said, setting down an overloaded plate in her father's lap. A large piece of battered cod lay on the plate, surrounded by chips. *Eat me!* the meal challenged. Until Becky put the knife and fork in his hands for him, Derek didn't think he could rise to it. Then he began to feel hungry. The cod was fresh and still juicy.

Becky wandered out to the kitchen and came back with a big glass of Scotch. The part of Derek that wasn't occupied by eating or worrying about how to befriend the kid wondered about this. Becky *never* brought him booze. She smiled at him and set the glass down on the fireplace at his feet, where it instantly began to call to him.

Derek tracked his daughter across the room, trying to keep her in focus. She sat down next to the kid and produced a pack of cigarettes, took one out, handed it to Stevie and then took another for herself.

'I told you about smoking,' Derek complained.

'And I told you about drinking,' Becky countered, grinning as she lit up.

'You're not old enough,' Derek said, around a fresh mouthful of fish.

'And you're old enough to know better,' Becky replied.

Derek looked at Stevie and shrugged helplessly. 'You keeping score?' he asked.

'Forty love.' The kid grinned.

Derek decided there was something about this kid that he liked. Couldn't quite put his finger on what it was, but the boy had *something*. 'You remind me of someone,' he said, pointing at the kid with his fork.

'Do I?' Stevie said.

Derek nodded. 'Yeah. Dunno who though . . . Someone . . . someone . . . smart. Clever. Are you clever?'

Stevie shrugged. 'Not very,' he said.

'Oh, yes, he is,' Becky said.

'Thought so,' Derek said, feeding a forkful of chips into his mouth. 'I can tell these things. What are you kids doing here, anyway? Surely you don't wanna sit with an old fart. Shouldn't you be upstairs playing that awful music Becky likes? Or are we playing Spot the Drunk?'

'We're playing Meet My Dad,' Becky said. 'You've been on about how you never get to meet those boys I'm always talking about. Now you've met half of them. The other half might arrive soon, too.'

Derek fed the last forkful of his meal into his mouth; the whisky gave it a whole new flavour. A good one. 'So, what's it to be? Trivial Pursuit? Poker? Snap?'

When his daughter grinned at him and replied, 'Spot the Hippy,' Derek should have known something unusual was going on, but he was very *relaxed* now. Which was the reason he let the remark pass and ignored the distant clanging of alarm bells that had been ringing every since he'd decided that the boy reminded him of someone.

'You kids want a drink?' he asked.

'I'll fetch us something,' Becky said, getting up. She came back with two bottles of Two Dogs and a half-full bottle of Glenfiddich. Derek topped up his glass and settled back.

In the next half-hour, while he exchanged banter with the kids and watched his alcohol-tank needle edge steadily towards Full, Derek began to suspect they wanted him to stay drunk.

'You happy, Dad?' Becky asked.

'Sure I am,' Derek said.

'Tell us about the trips to Germany,' Becky asked.

Derek found himself nodding. 'OK,' he said. ''S'long story, though.'

'We've got plenty of time,' Becky said, swigging from her bottle of Two Dogs.

Derek thought about it, then shook his head. Germany was something he didn't talk about. It was in the hope chest. The barred and locked place in his head where he stored things he hoped would go away. There were demons in there just waiting to come out to play.

He giggled. 'Fell in with a bad crowd,' he said. ''S all I can say. Someone putting out the lights or what? It's getting darker.'

'Germany,' Becky's voice echoed inside his head. 'Let's go to Germany.'

Derek looked up from his copy of *International Times*. 'What?' he asked. In the moment that she'd asked the question, Jacqui had sounded exactly like Jane. It was disconcerting and Derek suddenly felt uncomfortable.

'I said, "Let's go to Germany,"' Jacqui replied. 'We need a break. Let's take the jeep and motor down to Morocco, see our friends and take the goodies to Germany. I know a guy there. His name's Helmut. He's cool. He's got money. He'll take as much as we can lay on him.'

Derek shook his head. 'Too dangerous. We've done three runs this year. We need to cool it a bit. The narcs will be sitting up and taking notice by now and we're not short of bread.'

'Screw the narcs. We're charmed, Del, you know that. We've been through enough border posts this year and no one's so much as batted an eyelid at us yet. Andy says he'll come too, if we go. We won't get busted. We need to go, Del.'

'Why do we need to go? And why don't we just bring it back here? Germany's a bitch. I don't much fancy getting busted over there. They throw away the keys and stuff, man. France is cooler.'

'And Spain? We pass through Spain loaded each time we bring dope back. You ever seen the inside of a Spanish jail?'

'Spain's cool. If they were out to stop smugglers they'd have had us each time we went through. For chrissakes, Jacq, running dope inside your car's tyres is a trick just about as old as God. They just can't not know about that one.'

Jacqui shrugged. 'We'll get into Germany,' she said. 'We're charmed, remember?'

'It's not the getting in I'm worried about,' Derek said. 'It's the getting out again without having served a long jail sentence.'

'Look, Del, it's hardly Thailand and heroin, is it? No one's gonna machine-gun us to death if we get caught.'

'They don't do that, do they?' Derek asked, horrified.

'So they say. But the Germans don't. And we're wasting time even talking about it. We won't get busted.'

'What do the others have to say about it?' Derek said, still feeling unsettled.

'Jane doesn't want to go. She wants to stay home with Davey Kane and Katie. They're all madly in love with one another still. Although I think Katie would probably be up for it if we wanted her along. Especially if Andy's going. The four of us would be good. I can picture it. And—'

'What? And what?'

Jacqui shrugged. 'Well, Andy knows some guys who are going into production soon. Acid. They've got a trained chemist and they're promising blockbuster trips. Jane thinks we should buy in. Distribute for them. It'd be fun, she says and it'd help . . .'

Derek grinned. 'The revolution,' he said, 'I know. That's my Janie! Wants everyone to tune in and turn on. Won't rest till she's made the world a better place. Maybe we could buy up a load and dump it in the town reservoir. That'd be cool. Christ, I love that good old LSD. And you just can't get it, these days. I suppose that's why Andy's pals are going into production.'

'But we'll need some front money,' Jacqui said. 'Which is where the German trip comes in. Helmut says there's a dearth of smoke in Deutschland. Which means the prices will be high. With the profits we make we can buy in with Andy's friends.'

'OK, we'll go,' Derek said, nodding enthusiastically.

'OK, we'll go,' Derek murmured, his head lolling in a big loose nod.

'He's waking up,' Stevie said hopefully. He'd been anxious about Becky's dad since he'd gone unconscious after Becky had asked him about Germany. What worried him even more was Becky saying she'd never seen him do this before. Stevie thought it possible that Derek was suffering from alcohol poisoning. After all, they'd as good as poured a pint of Glenfiddich down him without knowing how much was in his system already. According to Becky, it was probably a lot. She didn't seem perturbed, though, wanted to wait and see what happened. Stevie just hoped that Derek didn't die while they were waiting.

'What did he say?' Becky asked, her eyes gleaming. 'Something about going somewhere? It was, wasn't it?'

'When shall we go?' Derek slurred.

'Either he's dreaming or hallucinating,' Becky whispered. 'Go where?' she said, at normal volume.

When Derek's eyes popped open, they both jumped. Derek grinned and spoke clearly. 'Marrakech, Jacq. Then to Berlin. I didn't just imagine you said all that, did I?'

'No, you didn't,' Becky said, glancing at Stevie. 'I said it.'

Derek nodded. 'I may be stoned but I'm not off my trolley,' he said.

'You reckon?' Becky asked.

Stevie gave her a worried glance. Derek was awake but he wasn't focused on either of them. Stevie didn't think he was even aware of their physical presence.

'This birdy is still in his tree.' Derek chuckled. 'No flies on this boy.'

'Who's here with us?' Becky asked.

'Andy?' Derek asked. 'Did Andy come in? He said he had a

new Kevin Ayres album he was gonna bring round. Where is he, then?'

'In this room, I mean,' Becky said.

'There's no one . . . Oh, I get it, clever clogs. You're talking about kids with funny haircuts and big shoes. There's no ghosts here, Jacq. And I haven't had a hallucination like that one since. That was a weird one-off. You're worried about me frying my brain, aren't you? I'm cool, Jacq. I haven't tripped out for nearly a month. Only done acid twice since the ghostly one. I'm sanity incarnate.'

'I'm not here,' Stevie whispered.

'And I'm your mother, by the sound of it,' Becky whispered back. 'And he's talking about seeing you in May Street. He thinks it's a month or two after that.'

'What'd you say?' Derek asked.

'Nothing. Where are we?'

'I'd just agreed to go on the trip to Morocco. You're freaking me out a bit here, Jacqui, and I wish you'd stop.'

'Am I? I'm sorry.'

Derek pulled a face. 'That grass we got off Chinky Davis is trippy. I'll put a bit less in the next joint. It keeps seeming to me that you're acting weird. Asking peculiar questions. What's worse is that every time you talk you sound exactly like Jane. If I shut my eyes, I'd think you *were* Jane. See what I mean?'

'Can't help that,' Becky said. 'It's not me doing it, it's the grass. Have you got a thing for Jane?'

Derek looked at the floor. 'She's far out,' he said. 'I like her. Everyone likes her, don't they?'

'Yeah,' Becky agreed. 'Anyway, about this trip.'

'Oh, the trip. I forgot.'

'What's the routine?'

'You should know by now. Down to Marrakech, see our pals, fill up the tyres with about ten kilos and then over to Germany to see your friend. What *was* his name?'

Becky glanced at Stevie. 'Herman?' Stevie suggested.

'No, not Herman,' Derek said irritably. 'You *are* trying to fuck me up, aren't you? Helmut. That's the guy's name. Then we offload the dope and come home clean and buy into Andy's friend's acid-making industry. See? I told you I was holding together!'

Jacqui was spooking the shit out of him now. Not only was she speaking in Jane's voice but she was asking circular questions, trying to catch him out. He had no idea why.

'Where are we, Derek?' Jacqui asked, and Derek shivered. It was like someone had crawled into Jacqui's skin and taken her over. Jacq never called him Derek. Just Del. And here she was asking where they were. What kind of a question was that?

'We're in my lounge,' Derek said, 'in my house. The house I rent from beastly Mrs Beasley. Nineteen May Street.' He glared at Jacqui, daring her to find fault.

'And how do you make money?' Jacqui asked.

'Jacqui, stop it, will you? You're doing my head in! You know all this stuff! Let's talk about your trip to Germany if you want to talk about anything. You're fucking me up. You know I'm on the dole.'

'You don't drive a taxi?'

'No. Not now. I drive a – a . . .' For one moment, during which Derek's soul froze, he didn't have the faintest idea *what* he drove. The words FX4 waited on the edge of his tongue, but that was wrong. He tried frantically to picture the vehicle he did all his trips in and couldn't. His heart began to hammer. Then it came back to him. 'A jeep,' he cried, joyously and then, like someone who had just fathered a longed-for son, added, 'It's a *jeep*!'

'You're a drug dealer, right?' Jacqui asked.

And then Derek knew. Knew why Jacqui didn't sound like Jacqui. Why she kept asking all these questions. She was an undercover narc. A woman from the drugs squad dressed in Jacqui's clothes. They'd pulled Jacqui and replaced her with a woman who bore a close physical resemblance, knowing he'd be well toked-up by the time she arrived. Knowing he'd tell her everything without even realizing he'd done it.

And as he looked into Jacqui's eyes, the room began to melt around them and the bare floorboards grew carpet. It started around the Dunlop Red Flashes on his feet and spread, outwards, thick and brown like a time-lapse film of fruiting fungi.

When his vision steadied Derek found himself sitting in another lounge. A large lounge that looked something like Jane's in Cliddesden Road, except this version was fitted and furnished with items he didn't recognize. And over there on the sofa sat two teenagers, a boy and a girl. The boy had mad hair and big fat shoes that Derek was certain he'd seen somewhere before. He recognized the achingly lovely girl straight away. It was Jane, from her green eyes to her each-one-painted-a-different-colour toenails. Except that someone had lopped five or six years from her age.

'You're a drug dealer, right?' Jane asked, and Derek found

that before the purity of her gaze, he could not lie. It was like being dragged before a goddess.

'Yes,' he said. 'You know that. Or you will in a few years. You'll find me.'

Jane looked at the boy, who shrugged and pushed back his hair. 'I don't know if he's back or not,' the boy said. Derek had the distinct feeling the boy was German and named Wolfgang, but he had no idea why.

'What year is it?' the young Jane asked.

''Sixty-nine,' Derek said. He was trembling. This younger version of the woman he rated the most beautiful being in the known universe was judging him. She'd dragged him back through time by six years to see if he was worthy. Worthy of what, he didn't know. 'Someone spiked my drink,' he mumbled. 'I'm tripping out further than I ever went before.'

'Who lives at fifty-two?' the goddess asked.

'Fifty-two where?'

'May Street,' the boy named Wolfgang said, without a trace of a German accent.

'May Street,' the girl repeated.

'I don't know,' Derek said. 'Honestly. But I can find out if you want me to.'

The girl frowned. Her face was even more lovely when her expressions changed.

'Wrong year,' the young Jane said, glancing at the boy. 'Think we can shift him?'

The boy glanced at Derek. 'I dunno,' he said. 'He doesn't seem hynotized to me. Confused, yes. but I don't think he's in a trance.'

'Do you think you could do me a big favour?' The girl smiled.

'If I can,' Derek said.

'Could you go forward a year for me?'

'I'm not quite with you,' Derek said. 'You want me to travel forward in time?'

'Only a year,' the girl replied.

Derek bit his lower lip. 'It might sound kind of dumb to you, but . . . how do I do it? I thought you were the one doing that.'

'Wish yourself forward,' the girl suggested. 'Just forget about 'sixty-nine and be in nineteen seventy. Do it.'

Derek tried. Nothing happened. 'I'm sorry,' he said. 'I can't do it. I'm still in 'sixty-nine.'

'Relax and go to sleep,' the girl said.

Derek lay back in the chair and closed his eyes.

'Comfortable?' the girl asked.

'Snug as a bug in a rug,' Derek murmured. He felt safe and

secure now. All the panic had left him. Being close to the girl soothed him in some way. Made him forget all his troubles. Made him forget the amulet.

Amulet?

'Just relax,' Jane's soothing voice said. 'You can tell us about the amulet later. For now, just relax and sleep. And when you're asleep, tell us about that man.'

'Maann?' Derek heard a disembodied voice say. A second later he realized it belonged to him. He found a smile turning up the corners of his mouth. This was far out. This was what dying and going to heaven must feel like.

'Aaam I deeaaaadd?' He felt his throat vibrate first and heard the stretched-out words a few moments afterwards. It was funny.

'You're not dead, just sleeping,' Jane said.

''Ssssss coooooool,' Derek said.

'Let yourself drift away. Away from nineteen sixty-nine. Right out into space,' Jane said.

Derek let himself fly like a kite, then spread out and slow down as he entered a warm, dark place that might have been his mother's womb for all he knew. It didn't matter where it was. All that mattered was the feeling of peace that came with it, the lack of thought that existed there.

'Zen,' Derek heard himself say. He felt as if his very soul was smiling.

'I just spoke to his dad,' Stevie said, coming into the lounge where Derek was apparently sleeping peacefully. 'He said Johnny went out this afternoon and he hasn't seen him since.'

'Try your house in case he's been there,' Becky said, pulling two cigarettes from her pack and tossing one to Stevie. 'We really ought to have him here if we can get my dad to talk.'

It took less than two minutes to establish that Johnny hadn't called at Stevie's house in person or by phone. Nor had Ben Andrews seen or heard from him. Or Brian Davies. Or Sindy Hallett. 'Do you think I'm fucking mad?' Sindy had yelled. 'I wouldn't let that sad bastard within a mile of me. Now fuck off and die!'

'No go?' Becky asked as he sat down beside her. In his absence she'd poured them a glass of Glenfiddich each. She saw Stevie frowning at his and said, 'I thought we might need to psych ourselves up a little. We've already had some shocks and if this works we're due for plenty more.'

'I think I'd like another fag before you try anything else,' Stevie said.

Becky squeezed his hand. 'It'll be all right, you'll see,' she said. 'Dad'll be OK. He's just supremely pissed.'

'And you've talked him into a hypnotic trance. And neither of us knows what we're doing.'

Becky fingered the devil earring and smiled. 'I don't think we need to start worrying until Dad's opened up to us,' she said. 'I think I can handle the trance thing. I've read stuff about it.'

Stevie watched her playing with the earring. The devil was starting to worry him a bit. Each time she did that her face grew thoughtful and distant. Either it merely helped her focus her thoughts or . . .

'The earring,' Stevie said.

Becky jumped as if she'd been shot. Then she giggled. 'I was miles away,' she said.

'I know,' Stevie replied. 'Don't laugh, but that's what's worrying me. It's just an earring, right?'

Becky frowned. 'As opposed to?'

Stevie was embarrassed to say, but said it anyway. 'As opposed to . . . I dunno . . . something from Weirdsville. Something magical.'

Becky smiled. 'I don't think you need worry on that count,' she said. 'When I first put it on, it made me feel a little strange but that was probably because I'd stolen it from Katie and it was so beautiful. It's not speaking to me or giving me special powers or anything. Honest.'

Stevie stubbed out his cigarette. 'What about Johnny?'

'He'll have to miss the good stuff again,' Becky said, the gleam in her eyes making her look a little crazy.

Stevie looked at her for a long moment. 'You know where he is, don't you?' he asked.

Becky shrugged. 'No idea,' she said.

'Yes, you have,' Stevie said, nodding. 'He's gone down the field. If I know Johnny he's currently standing under the electric wires waiting to be zapped. Or he's already gone across to May Street.'

'I didn't think he'd be dumb enough to go alone after last time,' Becky replied.

'Well, I'll let you into a secret. I wasn't gonna say because I thought you'd be mad at me. I thought Johnny might do this. I thought it because I've been fighting off the urge all week myself. I *want* to go back. I'm drawn to it. I feel the way I think a heroin user would feel when his junk ran out. I need a fix of May Street. That's it. I can't explain it any better than that.'

Becky gave a wan smile. 'My turn,' she said. 'Snap. I feel like that too and I've never even been there. And I know we all agreed to leave it alone until we found out what's going on, but I've been down there and stood under those power lines.'

Stevie took her hand. 'So've I. That's why I think Johnny won't be in any danger.'

'The door is closed,' Becky said. 'Still.'

'We're all dumb enough to go on our own,' Stevie said. 'We're all dumb enough to keep secrets from one another. To lie to one another. We'll have to stop. Because if we don't, we won't have a chance. From now on, we'll only tell the truth. Deal?'

Becky nodded. 'Deal. And I'm sorry.'

'Don't be. We've all done the same. Anyway, Johnny should be safe. And if he *does* get zapped across, he won't be able to visit number fifty-two. He can go up to it and look in, but that's all. And even though he got stuck there last time, I don't think he can get hurt. I think he's gonna have to get inside for anything terrible to happen to him.'

'Nigel didn't have to get inside,' Becky argued. 'And look what happened to him.'

'I thought of that, too,' Stevie said. 'You know what I think?'

'Yes, I do. You think that when Nigel went through the breach in reality, he was swinging right into the inside of number fifty-two.'

'I saw the rusted old Honda from his back garden fall down the stairs, didn't I? And the . . . mulch, too. Nigel was a special case. He'd already accepted he was talking to God. And God asked him if he'd like to be in a place where he could be bad and not get told off. Nigel thought it was an offer too good to miss.'

'So what's to stop Johnny getting inside the house in a similar way?'

Stevie considered it. 'It could be his lack of innocence, perhaps. It could be his cynicism. It could be lots of things. Like the ritual his mother did. Or the acts of the porridge-eating burglar, alias Andy Warner. I don't know exactly, but it's different for us. We have to enter the house of our own accord. After that, God only knows what happens and he ain't telling.'

'But Johnny can just climb through the window or something. Kick the door in.'

Stevie shook his head. 'I'm pretty sure there's only one way in. There's a key to the house. It's hidden and I know where it is. And I don't think anyone can get in there without the key. Something went to a great deal of trouble to lead me to the key so it has to have significance. And I haven't told Johnny about it.'

'If you found it, Johnny will find it too. You betcha. He'll be led just like you were.'

Stevie shook his head. 'Fifty-two is Pandora's box, Becky. But this time someone with at least half a brain has the means of opening it. And he's sensible enough to resist. When we get to the bottom of all this, we'll have some idea of how to zap fifty-two and all that's in it. I hope. Until then, the door stays closed. What we need now is information from your dad. We don't go running off trying to rescue Johnny.'

Becky nodded. 'OK. And you're not going to tell me where the key is, right?'

'Right.'

She grinned. 'Pretty good idea, Stevie. I wouldn't be able to resist. We'd better get back to Dad before the booze starts wearing off. I've never seen him weird-out like this before and it might never happen again.'

Stevie took the cigarette she offered him and lit it. In the distance thunder grumbled and rain began to lash against the windows with renewed vigour.

'Come on, you motherfucker!' Johnny shouted up at the power lines. He took two steps backwards, caught his foot in the undergrowth and fell over into brambles and stinging nettles. Off to the west, lightning flickered through the bellies of dark clouds.

For a few moments Johnny let the driving rain sting his face. He'd long since given up worrying about being wet. The rain wasn't cold and he'd been soaked to the skin since the afternoon. None of this mattered. What did was getting his head clear.

The only clear thought that Johnny had was that Yah-hoo was at the bottom of it all. This was all Johnny needed to know. Yah-hoo and his cast of gobblings and big cats and hallucinogenic girls.

And Johnny wanted to talk to him face to face. And to do that you had to get to number fifty-two May Street where he lived.

'For the time being,' Johnny hissed, clutching the little silver cross in his pocket.

It's that easy, Johnny, the voice of Sindy had whispered inside his head back in the alley. *That easy. You know where to get it. You know where to come.* And Johnny did know where to go. But it wasn't going to be easy. Not for Yah-hoo and his little bunch of friends. Johnny hadn't gone straight to the field after leaving the alley, he'd gone home to prepare.

No one had been in when he'd arrived. This made things easier. He went upstairs to his parents' room. His mother's jewellery box stood on the dresser. She never wore the little silver cross, but Johnny knew it was in there somewhere. He emptied out the contents of the box, sorted through the tangle of strings of pearls and chains and bracelets until he found the cross. He knew you were supposed to have faith for stuff like this to work and he thought he wasn't a Christian. What he was, was anti-Yah-hoo and he decided that was about as Christian as you'd have to be in an extreme case.

This little silver cross was going to go straight into Yah-hoo's right eye. Always supposing he had two eyes. Or any eyes at all. If not, Johnny would think of some other place to shove it. Wherever would do most damage.

In the kitchen his mother kept a large selection of huge knives she seldom used. Johnny chose the biggest, sharpest, most evil-looking one, then he realized he had no way to carry it so changed it for a slightly smaller one. He got the salt-cellar from the larder because he half remembered something about throwing salt in the devil's eye. Then he filled a plastic Coke bottle with tap water and thought about blessing it, but as he knew only priests could make water holy he cursed it instead: *By the power invested in me by the power company, may this water burn the living daylights out of any devil, demon or supernatural force which comes in contact with it.*

Then he made the secret sign of the swastika.

His feet suddenly felt as if they were made from sponge-rubber but he went into the lounge, and chugged down some Chivas before he left the house.

For the first hour, things had gone swimmingly. When he got to the point under the power lines that he now thought of as 'the gate' he could feel the power, prickling against his scalp as it built.

Johnny had stood there, in the driving rain, waiting patiently to see the plasma aura build up on the lines, but after twenty minutes, when nothing had happened barring the odd buzz and crackle, he began to wonder if the gate was ever going to open.

Ten minutes later he lay down in the wet grass under the lines. Five minutes after that, he'd fallen into a deep, dreamless sleep.

When Johnny woke up he had no idea how long he'd been asleep but it was dark now so it had been a long time. Up on the power lines nothing was happening.

He spent the next few minutes trying to use a box of damp matches to light a damp Marlboro, then gave up and threw the cigarettes away. Then he decided that the problem was that the rain had washed the blood off the items stashed near the red polka-dot bandanna flag and the gate had nothing to use as a power source. He retrieved his cigarette packet, pulled the big knife from the carrier bag, nicked the end of his finger and dribbled blood across the cigarettes. Then he placed the pack in the cache with the other soggy things.

Still nothing happened.

Which was when thunder began to roll and Johnny finally ran out of patience.

'Motherfucker!' he yelled, from his place in the brambles. He was dimly conscious of a new batch of hurts on his back, but he didn't care. The more blood he oozed, the more likely it was that the gate would power up. He eased himself to a sitting position just in time to see a multi-fingered fork of lightning flash to earth to the west. This time, the thunder followed almost instantly.

'Now I'm gonna get struck by lightning,' he muttered, finding his feet and staggering back to where he'd left the bag containing the knife and water. The little silver cross in his pocket dug into his thigh as if it wanted to come out to play. Johnny left it where it was. It might have given him some protection if this had been a vampire film but he wasn't going to drag it out while there was a thunderstorm going on.

The sky was rapidly turning into the most fabulous display of pyrotechnics he had ever seen. This was one big storm on its way in and it had plenty to say.

'Awesome!' Johnny said, feeling his head clear for the first time in what seemed like an age. His hand stole into his pocket and wrapped itself around the cross.

The air began to smell clean and pure as the storm rolled in, and Johnny shivered. Lightning flickered down and hit the field. During the deafening roar that followed, his feet tingled a little.

A moment later, Johnny's skin began to crawl and the hairs on his head started to creep. From the cloud overhead hail battered down. Knowing what was going to happen next, Johnny reached up for the sky.

'Here we *go*!' he yelled, as the blast hit him.

Derek suddenly sat up straight in his chair. 'Here we *go*!' he yelled.

Neither Stevie nor Becky saw the lightning flash, but the massive crack of thunder shook every window in the house. You didn't just hear it, you felt it deep in your chest.

'That was thunder and a half,' Becky said, glancing from Stevie to her dad and back again. Derek was rigid and his eyes were open, but he was off on another planet. *Or in another time*, she thought. 'That *was* thunder, wasn't it?' she asked Stevie. 'And not the other thing it sounded like?'

'Thunder,' Stevie said. And as if to back him up another clap rocked the house.

'Dad?' Becky said.

Derek stared ahead. *He's not anyone's dad where he is*, she thought. *It's too early*. 'Derek?'

'Yes?' Derek said, gazing straight ahead.

'We've got to talk. Can we do that?'

'Yes, Jane.' A tiny smile creased the corners of Derek's mouth. 'I'm glad to,' he said.

'Glad?'

'Glad that times don't pass. That all time happens simultaneously. I'm glad you're still alive somewhere in that tangle of time-streams.'

Becky shook her head at Stevie. 'Can you answer me some questions, Derek?'

'Yes. Of course,' Derek said, in that odd flat tone.

'What year are you in?'

''Sixty-nine.'

'OK. Well, when I snap my fingers, you'll be in nineteen seventy. January the first. Just after the twelfth strike of Big Ben. OK?'

Derek frowned and bit his bottom lip. 'I don't wanna go.'

'To Germany? Or to nineteen seventy?'

'Not Germany,' Derek said. 'The – the other place . . .' He closed his eyes and leaned back in his chair, then hugged himself as if he was cold. His bottom lip trembled and he drew a shuddering breath.

'He can't even bring himself to say it,' Stevie whispered, awed.

Becky didn't hear, her attention was fixed on her father. He'd done her nothing but kindness and he'd tried not to burden her with his own suffering. He was a good man who didn't deserve what had happened to him. He didn't deserve to be hurt any more. But she was going to have to hurt him. There was no other way.

'It'll be OK,' Becky said, her heart breaking. 'No harm will come to you. You're safe.' But she wasn't sure he would be. Katie had said she'd die if she found out what had happened. That might apply for all the others, too. Stevie's mum and dad. Johnny's. And who knew what else would happen?

'I know what you're thinking,' Stevie said, 'because I've thought it myself. But listen. None of this is our doing. We're getting fall-out from something they did years ago. Something they've kept secret. And it isn't just smuggling hash back from Africa or buying into an LSD factory because they thought they were going to change the world. It's something worse. They're responsible. If it causes them pain, it's hardly our fault.'

'That doesn't make me feel any better about doing it,' Becky said.

'Me neither. But we're gonna have to be hard. Needs must when Yah-hoo's in the driving seat.'

Becky sighed. She lit a cigarette, took a deep drag and turned back to her father. Tears were leaking from the corners of his closed eyes.

'Derek?' she asked.

And Derek heard her voice. 'Here we *go!*' he hissed quietly, glancing up at the doorway to make sure his daughter wasn't there. Once or twice, during these midnight sessions, she'd appeared there like a tiny wraith. Derek was pretty sure she'd been sleepwalking, and as soon as he'd spotted her, he'd stopped what he was doing and taken her back to her bed. He didn't think she remembered in the mornings. Becky had been well under since Jane's death and a few episodes of sleepwalking weren't terribly surprising, or her weight-loss or withdrawal.

But you won't have to worry for much longer, my little darling, Derek thought, glancing at the doorway again. *Your mum is coming home. My beloved Jane is coming back.*

The living room was lit by four fat candles, one at each point of the compass. The television was turned to a station that had ceased broadcasting. The stereo radiogram was turned to short-wave between stations, increasing the white-noise. The static hiss was necessary.

Derek had the amulet's chain in his hand. His talisman, swinging in a circle about eighteen inches from the floor, had been prepared in exactly the way he'd been taught. At midnight, he'd coated its exterior with a mixture of fresh blood, spittle, semen and some tiny snippets of Jane's hair. Just before she died he'd cut a lock from what was left on her poor head and had taken it home, tied it up in black silk ribbon and put it in a photo album.

He had the routine down to a fine art now. In the ninety days since his wife departed, he'd worked this magic every day. And now, on the ninetieth day, the spell was working.

He'd heard Jane's voice.

It was tiny, almost lost in the hiss from the stereo and the television, but it was there. Jane was alive and his persistence had paid off. He'd opened a portal between this life and the next.

'Come back to me, Jane,' he whispered, and made the shape of a swastika over the space on the carpet. The space where her body would appear.

'Derek?' Her voice came and went on the cresting waves of static.

'I'm here, lover,' he said. 'Come back to me.'

Beneath the swinging amulet something began to happen. At first it looked like a tiny spot of heat-haze, but this rapidly focused and coloured into a small ball of showering blue sparks that looked as if they were trapped inside a transparent sphere.

The amulet began to smoke, giving off a stench of singeing hair and smouldering blood and semen. In Derek's hand the chain became hot.

The ball of blue sparks burst and scattered, dancing across the carpet and showering over Derek's bare knees like sparks of molten metal from an arc welder. It hurt, but Derek didn't flinch. The chain was burning his hand now, but he kept moving the amulet in the figure of a swastika.

'Derek!' Jane's voice called.

And just above the carpet in front of him, something transparent seemed to push up, stretching the empty air as though it were a rubber glove into which a hand was being forced – except that it was roughly the size and shape of Jane.

Derek didn't hear the creak as the door opened, but after a few moments he became aware of being watched and glanced up. Becky was there, standing in the doorway in her little white nightdress, her hair tousled and her face pale. He hands worked at one another as if she were washing them and she was chewing her lower lip, but her eyes were dark and distant.

Derek looked away, neither knowing nor caring if Becky was awake. If she was, she was going to see a miracle. If she was frightened now, she would be joyous soon when he mother was back with her.

'Darling!' Derek called.

'Can you hear me?' Jane asked, her voice clearer now. The sound of static seemed to be fading, as if Jane's signal was strengthening. Her shape could be seen now, still stretching and working at the air, but the transparent thing was undoubtedly his wife – or it would be when she finished coming back. She raised an arm, her unformed fingers splayed like a flipper. Derek felt intense heat radiating from it as it passed by his face.

'It's wrong, Daddy,' Becky said. 'It's wrong!'

The pain in Derek's hand was tremendous now. His flesh was smoking where the hot chain was in contact with his skin. It didn't matter: he could get it fixed later. When Jane was back. He would happily lose that hand if only he could help her complete her journey.

'It's *wrong*!' Becky cried. 'Stop it, Daddy!'

Derek glanced up at his daughter. Her hands were buried in her hair and her elbows were pressed together in front of her like a shield. Only one of her eyes was open.

'Be all right!' Derek called to her, his voice thin with pain. 'Mummy's coming home! Mummy's coming home!'

Mummy was almost back. The stretchy part of the air had now settled. What lay before him on the carpet, head to his right, feet to his left and belly right in front of his knees, was Jane, face up. She was still transparent so that he could see the carpet through her, but her shape was steady and perfect. Inside her, a deep red smoke was swirling, thickening. In another two or three minutes she would be back.

'It *hurts*!' Jane said, through the static hiss.

Hurting me, too, Derek thought, *but it'll be over soon. And we'll be back together!*

'Stop it, Daddy!' Becky called. 'She can't come back from Heaven! It isn't allowed!'

'It is this once!' Derek snapped. 'God made an exception for me!'

'It's not right!' Becky sobbed.

'It *is* right, it's your *mother*, for fuck's sake!' Derek yelled, gritting his teeth against the pain.

And there she was, whole now, but not quite finished. Jane's body was now almost solid, her skin still faded pink, her eyes pale and her hair translucent, but she was nearly there.

The pain in Derek's hand was unbelievable. The smoke rising from his fist was being drawn down to Jane as was the vapour from the amulet.

At his knees, Jane began to writhe. Her body thrashed and shuddered, her hands clawed the air and her feet drummed noiselessly on the carpet. Her pale eyes rolled and her mouth opened in a silent scream.

'You're hurting her, Daddy! Let her go!'

'Another minute,' Derek yelled. 'Just another minute. She'll be fine!'

The scream was terrifying. Amplified by the stereo and distorted by the static, it twisted something in Derek's soul.

'Hold on, Jane!' Derek sobbed. 'Hold on!'

'Stop it, Daddy! Stop it!'

A second later, Derek experienced the agony that his wife was feeling. It made the burning in his hand and the ache in his heart pale into insignificance. But Derek didn't let up, didn't stop. She was so near.

And in front of him, Jane began to turn inside out, churning out from her centre and folding over herself in a mess of muscle and bone.

Derek yelled and let go of the amulet, which fell on the spot where her navel had been.

And Jane was gone. Gone as if she'd never been there in the first place. It was just him and Becky again. And Becky was curled up on the floor in the doorway, her eyes clamped shut, her fingers stuffed into her ears.

Derek went to her, shocked, empty and in pain. In his mind rang the words, *The devil giveth and the devil taketh away.*

'Derek?' Becky called. 'Dad?'

'The devil giveth and the devil taketh away,' Derek murmured. His eyes opened. He gave a sigh and sat up. He peered at Becky and then at Stevie.

'You all right, Dad?' Becky asked worriedly. 'You took bit of a turn there.'

Derek didn't answer. He was looking at Stevie. 'I know why I recognized you now,' he said.

Stevie glanced at Becky.

'You got drunk and fell asleep,' Becky said. 'You went into a kind of trance.'

'I know,' Derek said pointedly. 'But I sobered up! And I remember. I remember everything.' He glared at Stevie. 'I remember Andy Warner, for instance. I thought you looked familiar. You're his son, aren't you? I should have known it'd come to this.'

'Come to what?' Becky said, when Stevie didn't speak.

Derek shook his head. 'Get out,' he said to Stevie, then turned back to Becky. 'And your friend Johnny. Davie Kane's son, right? Dave and Katie?'

Becky nodded.

'Christ I must have been sozzled for the past year,' Derek said. 'I couldn't even put two and two together.' He glanced back at Stevie. 'You still here?' he asked. 'You going to wait until I throw you out?'

'Dad!' Becky said.

'They're gonna bring nothing but trouble, the two of them,'

Derek said. 'You pair have kicked up a shit-storm already. And when you get together with the other little son of a weasel God only knows what'll happen. Becky, your friend here goes *now*. And you aren't to see him again. Trust me on this one. For once in my life, I know what I'm talking about.'

'And we both know what you're talking about,' Stevie said.

'You don't know you're alive, kid,' Derek snarled. 'And you certainly don't know how much shit you're gonna let loose if you don't pack it in now. Now get out and don't meddle with things you don't understand. I can probably fix the damage you've done. The damage the three of you've done. But I'm warning you, if you fuck around any more it'll be out of my hands. And I'll give you a one hundred per cent solid gold guarantee that you'll regret it if that happens. Now you, kid, git! And you, young lady, I want to talk to you.'

'I'm not going if you're going to hit her!' Stevie yelled, blushing furiously.

'And if he goes, I'm going with him!' Becky challenged.

Derek heaved a sigh. 'You're your mother's girl and that's a fact,' he said, and his face lit in a weary grin. 'Stevie boy, for your information, I've never laid a finger on this girl in anger. Ask her.'

'He hasn't and he won't now,' Becky told Stevie, without taking her eyes off her father. 'But you'll have noticed that he's not terribly polite when he sobers up.'

Stevie said, 'I don't care about polite. I just want to know what's going on.'

'Ask your dad,' Derek said. 'Or your mother. Better still, ask Katie Kane.'

'We did,' Becky said.

'And they told you exactly what I'm going to tell you. Just these four words. Leave well enough alone.'

'But—'

'No buts. It's all over. *Finito*. I'm going to bed. You, Mr Warner, are going home. And you, Ms Sharp, are staying here. That's it. And, like I say, leave it alone. Message received and understood?'

Becky glanced at Stevie, pulled an it's-hopeless face and nodded.

Stevie got up.

So did Derek. 'I'd like to say it's been nice meeting you, Stevie, but I'm afraid it hasn't. Nothing personal, mind. It's just that you're from the wrong side of town, so to speak. I won't expect to see you again and I won't expect you to see my Becky. You can do what you like with the Kane boy but not with Becky. Got that?'

Stevie nodded, glowering.

Derek gestured at his daughter. 'See him to the door, kiss him goodnight for the last time and come back. When you're in bed, I'll lock up. I gotta get a drink.' He wandered into the kitchen.

'You can come back to my place if you want,' Stevie said, at the front door. 'No one will mind.'

Becky shook her head. 'It's OK,' she said. 'I'd better stay here and keep an eye on him. He was mumbling about my mum while he was in his trance or whatever it was. I expect it's brought it all back to him.'

'But you'll be safe?'

'Yes. He's all fuss and bluster on the outside but inside he's a sweetheart. And, besides, I might even be able to get him to open up. You never know.'

'Hasn't that kid gone yet?' Derek yelled, from the kitchen.

'You'd better go. I'll see you tomorrow.'

'But you're grounded, aren't you? You're not supposed to see me,' Stevie said.

'He won't remember in the morning, I bet,' Becky said. 'And even if he does, what can he do about it? He's out all day, working. And you're forgetting that Becky is a rebel with a capital R.' She grinned, pulled Stevie to her and kissed him. 'Go on now, go!' she said. 'I'll see what I can discover!'

Chapter Twelve

The Birds

The following morning, Johnny turned up at Stevie's house on the dot of nine o' clock. This should have told Stevie that things were not as they should be – outside school days, Johnny never got up before ten – but Stevie was still asleep when the doorbell rang and it took his mind a good hour to start firing on all cylinders.

'What are you doing here?' Stevie said, peering at his friend through eyes still heavy with sleep.

'What a greeting, Dogboy!' Johnny grinned. 'It's a beautiful morning. I woke up early so I thought I'd come round and drag you out of bed.'

'It's raining,' Stevie complained, gesticulating at the street. Johnny looked as if he'd stood out in it all night. He was drenched. He was also *glowing*. He looked like someone had charged him up.

'It's easing off now,' Johnny said. 'You gonna let me in or what? I could do with borrowing a few clothes.'

Stevie stood back from the door. 'Be quiet,' he said. 'The old farts are still asleep.'

'Where's Dookie?' Johnny wanted to know.

'He's on my bed asleep. I'm surprised he didn't run round howling his head off when you rang the bell, but he didn't.' Stevie closed the door and followed Johnny into the kitchen.

'Any chance of some brekkie?' Johnny said, striding across to the kettle and filling it. 'I'm so hungry I could eat a rancid horse.'

'Got no horses, rancid or otherwise,' Stevie said. 'Can do some eggs and bacon in a mo', if you like. Make the tea. OK?'

'Good as done, Dogboy!'

The bathroom was directly above the kitchen. Half-way through brushing his teeth, Stevie paused. The noise he was sure he'd imagined was real.

This is a first, Stevie thought, listening. *Something good must have happened.*

Down in the kitchen Johnny was singing quietly to himself.

In all the years Stevie had known him, he had never heard Johnny hum, let alone sing. He mouthed the words during hymns in assembly in the mornings and didn't even sing along to his favourite CDs.

And now he came to think of it, Johnny had looked happy this morning. He didn't have a naturally smiley-happy face, and since they'd escaped from May Street, he'd looked like he was carrying the cares of the world on his shoulders.

Stevie kicked his dressing gown into the corner of the bathroom and flitted back to his bedroom, covering himself with his hands in case his parents suddenly came out of their room. Duke looked up at him as he entered, gave a half-hearted wag, then put his head between his front paws and sighed.

Stevie sat down and hugged him. 'What's wrong, hound?' he asked. 'Johnny's downstairs. Don't you want to see him?'

The dog gave a long, tired moan and looked dolefully at Stevie.

'You OK, boy?' Stevie asked, pulling on his pants and searching for his socks. Stevie knew that dogs had off days just like everyone else, but he would have expected Duke to crawl downstairs to greet Johnny even if he'd been on his last legs. Johnny was his number one pal, second only to Stevie himself. 'Where's Johnny? Wanna go find Johnny?' he encouraged. But all Duke could manage was another feeble wag.

'If you've dug up something horrible and green from the garden and eaten it, I'll thank you not to upchuck it in this room,' he said, pulling on a shirt. 'You come downstairs and puke in the garden.'

Duke replied with another theatrical sigh.

The smell of frying bacon wafted up the stairs as Stevie went down. This was another first. Johnny couldn't cook and refused even to try. Now he was in the kitchen frying up a storm. There were four eggs in the big pan along with the bacon and all the yolks were intact. And Johnny had cut mushrooms and tomatoes into slices, too. He'd even used the chopping board.

'You're not ill, are you?' Stevie asked.

Johnny grinned. 'Just hungry. Couldn't wait for you. Hope you don't mind. Want fried bread too? Your tea's on the table.'

Stevie sat at the table and watched Johnny work. He was damp and bedraggled but you could almost see the energy bursting out of him. He looked taller, stronger, more confident.

'So what's the secret of your success?' Stevie asked.

Johnny wheeled round, a spatula in one hand and a fork in the other. '*What?*' he said. All the humour was gone from his face and he looked angry and defensive. Then his face lit up in a grin.

'Ahh . . . you noticed,' he said, nodding. 'You know me too well, Dogboy. Well, it's like this . . . hold on. Burning.' He turned back to the pan and poked at something, then turned down the gas. 'Last night I went down the field, crossed over to May Street, went inside the old house and found the devil. Old Yah-hoo himself. And I made a deal with him.' He turned back, grinning. His teeth were yellowed with cigarette tar.

'And what did you get?' Stevie asked. The fear that had stabbed his guts was fading now that he realized Johnny was kidding.

'I got a packet of Tootie-Frooties, twenty Rothmans king size and a pack of twenty-five party balloons. And all I had to do was give him my soul in return. Not bad, huh?'

'If he'd known the true value of your soul you'd have been lucky to get a single fag,' Stevie said.

'Here it comes,' Johnny said, taking food out of the pan and putting it on two plates. 'A dog's breakfast.'

He set down Stevie's plate and went back for his own while Stevie marvelled at his friend's new-found talent. His own mother couldn't have produced a better fry-up.

'So what went right?' Stevie asked, as Johnny sat down and got stuck in. He ate like someone half starved.

'Good fortune,' Johnny said, around a mouthful of food. 'Becky coming round today?'

Stevie nodded. 'What's happened?' he asked.

Johnny smiled. 'Wait till Becky gets here. I wanna take you both down the town. Got a surprise for you. That's all I'm saying.'

'Tried to pump her dad for details last night,' Stevie said, and spent the next ten minutes telling Johnny about the drug-smuggling runs to Morocco and partner exchanges that had gone on between all their parents.

'So you didn't find out about the acid?' Johnny asked. 'Or what happened in the seventies? The stuff we wanted to know.'

Stevie shook his head. 'Becky said she'd try again but her dad was pretty upset when he snapped out of his trance. She's not allowed to hang out with us now. He called you a son of a weasel, I think.'

Johnny almost choked on his food. His entire body jiggled with mirth as he tired not to spit out the mouthful of food he was chewing. Then he had a coughing fit and sprayed most of the table anyway.

'Brilliant!' he said, getting up for the kitchen roll before Stevie could move. 'Son of a weasel. That'd be my dad, I guess. What an apt description! He *does* look a bit like a weasel when you think about it. Lucky I took after my mother, really.'

Johnny finished his meal in silence. Then he said, 'I've made a decision about May Street and all that shit, and I feel better for it.'

'You look better for it, too,' Stevie told him. 'What did you decide?'

Johnny shrugged. 'Life's too short,' he said. 'I'm fucked if I'm gonna worry about it any more. If it wants me, it'll have to come and get me. I don't give a toss about May Street or Yah-fucking-hoo. I'll just take it as it comes.'

'But you're the one who wanted to go back. You want to get inside the house and everything,' Stevie said.

Johnny nodded. 'Yeah, but when I thought about it, I thought it'd only lead to trouble. And we can do without that. I don't even wanna go back there. It did my fucking head in. I was chasing about yesterday in the pissing rain following two girls who stayed dry. I fucking *imagined* them, Dogboy. And what's worse, I touched one of them. Or she touched me. And she even *felt* real. For fuck's sake, man, I can't handle that. I'm leaving it alone.'

Stevie nodded. This sudden U-turn didn't seem at all like the Johnny he knew and loved. But he *had* been badly shaken by May Street. And *he* had been the one to get stuck on the sharp point of glass in the window of number fifty-two. But *I'm leaving it alone* wasn't like Johnny. It sounded more like the kind of thing that parents said. People who were frightened of being found out.

'But what if it won't leave *you* alone?' Stevie asked.

Johnny shrugged. 'I think it will.'

'And what if it doesn't?'

'We'll cross that bridge when we come to it, shall we? Anyways, that's enough of the weirdness. I'm having a day off. Back to Becky.'

'What about her?' Stevie asked.

'Her old man had better get used to the weasel-son being around. I'm having Becky. She's mine, so stand back and let me at her. What's wrong, Dogboy? Oh, shit, Stevie! You don't fancy her, remember?'

'And neither do you,' Stevie retorted.

'I changed my mind.' Johnny grinned.

'So did I. And I changed mine first.'

'You didn't fuck her last night, did you?'

'Of *course* I did. Not,' Stevie said.

'Well, I don't want to tread on your toes, Dogboy, but it looks as if we're gonna have to fight for her.'

'How about we let Becky make up her own mind?' Stevie said.

Johnny raised an eyebrow. 'Never thought of that one, Dogboy. But you know you don't stand a chance, don't you?'

Stevie smiled back. 'We'll see,' he said, forking mushrooms into his mouth. 'I've put out some clothes for you in my room. Dog's probably lying on them. You can have a shower too, if you like.'

'You saying I stink?'

Stevie nodded. 'Yep. If you want to impress Becky, you'd better clean up.'

'It's a deal,' Johnny said, getting up.

'So tell me,' Stevie called after him. 'How did you get to smell like that?'

Johnny tensed in the doorway. Stevie saw his posture change as his muscles tightened. 'Long story, Dogboy. Tell you when Becky gets here,' he said, and left the room.

Stevie sat at the table, listening to the shower run in the room above and wishing he had a cigarette to smoke. Something was awry. The only way Johnny could have ended up here so early, as wet and hungry as he'd been, was from staying out all night. Which meant that he'd been in the field, trying to get zapped across to May Street.

And he's going to take Becky away from me, he thought.

Maybe Johnny had been to May Street last night. And if he got there, what did he do? Stevie couldn't concentrate on Johnny because he kept thinking of Becky. He'd seen the way she looked at Johnny when she thought she wasn't being observed.

'Shit,' Stevie muttered, frowning. Johnny was better-looking from head to toe. He was clever, witty and sharp. If Johnny wanted to charm Becky away from him, Johnny would. That was the top and bottom of it. And it hurt.

Upstairs the noise of the shower ceased. Stevie heard Johnny get out of it, slide its door shut. Then the bolt shot back on the bathroom door and Johnny walked along the landing.

The question you have to ask yourself is this, Stevie thought. *Are you going to let a girl break up your friendship with Johnny?*

'Oh yes,' he said finally. 'I *am*.'

'Stevieeee?' Johnny called from upstairs. His voice was faint, as if he was trying not to make too much noise. 'Stevie!' Johnny repeated, his tone more urgent.

'Coming!' Stevie called back, and took the stairs two at a time.

He burst into his bedroom and stopped. Johnny was naked,

standing with his back against the wall, his arms raised above his head. The jeans that Stevie had left out for him dangled from his right hand.

Pinning him against the wall, one paw on each of his hips, was Duke, wearing his famous white grin. His eyes were fixed on Johnny's.

'What's going on?' Johnny whispered. Duke growled and his lip curled back that extra quarter-inch.

'Get down, Dookie!' Stevie commanded. The dog glanced at him – with something like rage in his eyes – then turned back to Johnny, pushing harder against him.

'DOOKIE!' Stevie yelled. 'GET DOWN! NOW!'

'Help me, man!' Johnny pleaded. 'He's gonna bite me. I didn't do anything to him. Honest.'

Duke glowered at him, his snarling louder.

'Hold still,' Stevie said. He grabbed the dog's collar and yanked him away.

In the second that followed, Stevie's friend and protector attacked him. It was over so quickly that all Stevie saw was a blur of black dog and white teeth accompanied by a drawn-out howl of rage. He felt the teeth connect with his right forearm in a dozen different places.

By the time Stevie had got out a yell, Duke was cowering on the floor at the foot of the bed. In what felt like slow motion after the speed and shock of the attack, Stevie turned his head to look at the damage to his arm. He could still feel Duke's teeth against his skin. The word *hospital* bounced around in his mind along with the astonishing phrase, *Dookie bit me.*

Even more astonishing was the fact that Stevie's arm was unmarked.

'Fuck, man,' Johnny said. 'You hurt?'

Stevie stared at his arm. It was damp with spittle but there wasn't so much as a scratch. 'Not a mark,' Stevie said.

On the floor Duke had curled himself into a trembling ball. He glanced up as Stevie approached then averted his eyes. Stevie sat down beside him and lifted the dog's head. 'It's OK,' he said gently. 'It doesn't matter. I know you didn't mean it.'

Dookie's shuddering increased.

'He's not well,' Stevie explained. 'He wouldn't come down when I got up to let you in. Or when I told him you were downstairs.'

'There's something wrong with him, that's for sure,' Johnny said. 'He was asleep when I came in. Next minute I'm up against the wall and he wants to tear my guts out.'

Duke gave a pathetic whine. This was new too. He never complained, not even when you stood on his paws. Stevie had only ever heard him whine in excitement. 'If he doesn't get better I'll have to take him to the vet,' he said.

'Just stay here while I get dressed, will you?' Johnny said, pulling on the jeans. 'I don't want to go through that again. I thought I was dead for a minute.'

Stevie cuddled his dog. When Johnny went downstairs, Stevie waited, still soothing Duke. After a few minutes his trembling began to subside. Stevie told him to stay there and relax, kissed the top of his head and went down after Johnny.

'It was pretty much like you might expect,' Becky said, as they strolled towards the town centre. 'I told him I needed to know stuff, he told me to leave it alone and let it settle. I tried to tell him what I knew. He wouldn't listen. Then he went to bed.'

'And what did he say this morning?' Stevie asked.

'The weather's clearing up,' Becky replied, glancing up at the sky. 'He said to give him a week. If I was still bothered by anything then, he'd see what he could do.'

'Better than nothing,' Stevie said.

'It's all over anyway,' Johnny said. 'What's happened since the day that old Nigel copped his lot and we went to May Street? Fuck all, that's what.'

'My dad's going mental.'

'Yeah, Stevie,' Johnny grinned, 'but he's been doing that ever since I've known him. He's not exactly Mr Average, your dad, is he?'

'Sure,' Stevie agreed, thinking of Katie Kane, who wasn't exactly Mrs Average either.

'Our parents are all burned-out acid trippers,' Johnny said. 'That's the reason they're all weird.'

'But what about—?'

'Forget all about it,' Johnny cut in. 'Today we rest from the supernatural and craziness. Today is JK's day.'

'So why *are* we going down town?' Becky asked. 'What's the big surprise?'

Johnny grinned. 'Wait and see!' he said. 'First we go to Nicholson's.'

Five minutes later, Becky and Stevie followed Johnny through the door of the newsagent's in the New Market Square. Becky dug Stevie in the ribs. 'If he's come here to buy porno mags, I'm off,' she whispered, giggling.

'I heard that,' Johnny called back over his shoulder and headed towards the counter.

'Fags,' Becky said, nodding.

Johnny stopped at the counter and glanced back. 'What do you want? Black Russians? Cocktails? Greek? You name 'em.'

'Twenty Marlboro Lights if you're buying them,' Becky said.

'You're offering to buy me a packet of Black Russian?' Stevie asked. 'They're so expensive.'

'And horrible too,' Becky said.

'But they don't half look flash,' Johnny and Stevie both said together.

'Can I help you?' the shop assistant asked.

'Twenty Marlboro Lights, twenty Sobranie Black Russian and twenty Pallas, please,' Johnny said. 'We're having an international smoking day today.'

He paid the assistant, handed Stevie and Becky their cigarettes and headed for the exit.

'Where did he get the money?' Becky whispered.

Stevie shrugged. 'I expect he'll tell us in a minute.'

But Johnny wouldn't say. Johnny wanted to go window shopping. Stevie and Becky trailed along behind him.

He walked straight past Dixon's, which was impossible for Stevie. Whenever he went by he experienced an overwhelming urge to stop and see which new computers they had on sale.

'Where's Becky?'

Stevie broke out of his day-dream of having a faster computer than his dad and looked up. Johnny was there, but Becky wasn't.

'There!' Johnny said, pointing at a shop nearly fifty yards away. 'You're window shopping for hardware, she's lusting after clothes. Let's go see what she's gawping at,' Johnny said, and hurried away, Stevie following.

'So, what are you coveting?' Stevie asked, as he stopped beside Becky.

'That skirt,' Becky said, pointing at a dummy wearing a minute black skirt and cropped top made of something stretchy and fluffy. 'And I like the top. And you'd have to have those shoes to go with it.'

'Those black ones? High heels?' Stevie asked. 'I didn't think you liked high heels.'

'Not at that price. They're ninety-five quid,' Becky said. 'Good quality, though. Bally, see.'

'Oh, yeah,' Stevie said, pulling a face at Johnny. Johnny rolled his eyes.

'Skirt's almost a hundred quid,' Stevie said, in a tone of disgust. 'And what's the ticket on the top say? I can't see it from here.'

'Eighty-five,' Johnny said.

'There's about ten quid's worth of material in that, that's all,' Stevie said.

'It's Donna Karan, you dummy,' Becky said. 'Her new cheapo off-the-peg line.'

'What size are you?' Johnny asked.

'Ten.'

'Shoes?'

'Four.'

'OK,' Johnny said, turning away.

'Hey, where are you going?' Becky called after him.

Johnny didn't reply, and went into the shop.

Becky grabbed Stevie's wrist. 'He *isn't*!' she asked excitedly. 'Is he?'

'Looks like it,' Stevie said, pressing his nose to the glass. Johnny was striding up to an assistant, looking like he often bought expensive clothes for women.

'Where would I wear something like that?' she asked.

'Film premières, showbiz parties. That kind of thing,' Stevie said. 'You know, when you're out on the town with people like Johnny Depp and Keanu Reeves.' He peered through the glass. The top and skirt were being wrapped. The shoes were in a box on the counter.

'Where did he get the money?' Becky asked, her eyes gleaming.

'I dread to think,' Stevie said, feeling his stomach fill with lead. Johnny was buying Becky expensive clothes and Becky was reacting just as he'd anticipated.

'What's wrong?' Becky asked.

Stevie shrugged.

'Tell me,' she insisted.

'This morning, before you arrived, Johnny told me he'd made up his mind that you were going to be his.' *And he's working on it right now. And I don't stand a chance.*

'And what did you say?'

'I said it was up to you. It's not like we're going out or anything, is it? *Is* it?'

Becky smiled sadly and shook her head, but Stevie wasn't sure if that meant *No, we're not going out*, or *You poor sad thing for thinking I'd be charmed by Johnny*. And there was no time to ask because Johnny was on his way out of the shop, carrying Becky's present in a big carrier bag.

And, of course, Becky flung herself into Johnny's arms and smothered him with grateful kisses.

'Can't wait to see you in it all!' Johnny said, clinging to Becky. He looked over her shoulder and winked at Stevie. 'Come on,' he said, letting her go. 'Let's go and buy Stevie that computer. Race you there!' he said, and ran off.

Stevie caught up with him and grabbed him before he could get through the door of Dixon's. He swung him round. 'No!' he said.

'What's the matter, Dogboy? I know you want it.'

'The money, Johnny,' Stevie said.

'What about it?' Johnny asked. 'Who cares about the money?'

'You've just spent nearly three hundred quid on Becky. This computer's knocking on for three grand. You haven't got that kind of money.'

Johnny smiled. He'd got all the yellow off his teeth, Stevie was surprised to notice. Sometimes he looked so good you just wanted to kill the bastard. 'Who says I haven't?' he said.

'I do!' Stevie said.

'What's going on?' Becky said, trotting up with her bag clutched to her chest.

'He's trying to buy me that,' Stevie said, pointing at the computer in the window. 'And I think he's going to use a stolen credit card to get it. '

Johnny looked surprised. 'What makes you think that, Dogboy?' he asked.

'How else would you be doing it? You haven't even got a bank account.'

'Actually, I have,' Johnny said, 'but there's no money in it. About ten quid, I think. And there's a trust fund set up.'

'You can't get money from the trust fund, so where did you get it?' Stevie demanded. 'The only other way I can think of is stealing it.'

Becky glanced down at the bag. 'You didn't, Johnny,' she said, 'did you?'

Johnny looked pained. 'I can't believe you'd even *think* it,' he said. 'This is supposed to be my day and it's all going fucking wrong. Dookie tries to eat me alive and my two best pals end up thinking I'm a master criminal or something.'

'So where'd the money come from?' Becky asked. 'Come on, JK, just tell us where you got it.'

'I don't want to.'

Becky took his hand. 'Don't sulk, sweetheart,' she said. 'We were having such a lovely time.' She stood on tiptoe and kissed his cheek. 'Just give us a hint so we're comfortable that we're not enjoying the proceeds of someone else's labour.'

Johnny sighed. 'Oh, OK,' he said.

Stevie watched closely. The sigh and the slight smile that went along with it looked wrong – as if Johnny had rehearsed it. Maybe he had mapped all this out when he was lying out in the field all night. *Or on May Street.*

'It does involve theft, I'm afraid,' Johnny admitted. 'Week before last. I stole a fiver from my mum's purse. It's not the first time I've done it and I doubt it'll be the last. I think she knows anyway. I buy fags with the money, as you guys know.'

'And?' Stevie said.

'And I went and bought twenty Benson & Hedges and had two quid and a few pence left. Normally I'd have bought Cokes or saved the rest towards more fags. This time I was in the grocer's near Stevie's house and I bought two Lottery scratch cards. Second one won me a tenner. I used it to buy ten more cards and had two winners. One was another ten quid. The other was bigger.'

'How much bigger?'

Johnny grinned. 'Enough to cover Becky's clothes and this here computer and still have a lot left. Fifteen big ones.'

'Fifteen grand? *Jesus*, Johnny!' Stevie said.

'So, instead of pinching fivers from my mother's purse, I'm gonna put them back, one by one.'

Becky was still frowning. 'And how did you get hold of the money?' she asked. 'They don't pay out that much in the shops where you get the tickets.'

'Had to go to the Lottery headquarters,' Johnny said. 'Went yesterday. That's why I wasn't around. I had to hitch there because I didn't have any money and I was on the road most of the night trying to get back.'

'They didn't pay you in cash, surely?'

Johnny shook his head. 'Tried for it. That's why it's been so long coming. They'd only do me three in cash. Got the rest by cheque. Came down here last night when I'd got home and fed the cheque into the bank's ATM. I'm wealthy and the Milky Bars are on me. Satisfied?'

Stevie nodded. 'Good for you.'

'Lucky boy!' Becky said, and kissed Johnny's cheek again.

'So are you gonna let me buy you this new computer, or what?' Johnny said.

'Didn't you ought to hold on to the money?' Stevie said. 'I can live without it.'

'Fuck you, Dogboy, you're having it whether you want it or not. Then we'll shop some more. Then we'll go eat, then I'm taking you both to the movies. And then . . . uhh . . . how about getting drunk?'

'Sounds wonderful,' Becky said, taking his hand.

She was still hanging on to Johnny as they walked down the slope that led out of the town centre and back towards Stevie's place. They hadn't quite shopped till they dropped, but they'd come close. They now all had expensive lighters to go with the cigarettes and Johnny had bought himself an entire wardrobe of clothes, computer games and a ghetto-blaster, six pairs of Levi's for Stevie, and an assortment of footwear and sexy undies that Becky had suddenly decided she liked.

It looked to Stevie like money could indeed buy you love – no matter how many bags Becky carried, she still hung on to Johnny. He tried hard to ignore the small stabs of jealousy.

They paused at the kerb just outside the shelter of the covered walkway to let a stream of cars pass. It was spitting with rain still, but there was plenty of blue in the sky off to the west.

'So, we'll dump all this stuff at your place, Stevie, then go to the pictures, right?' Johnny said, sounding confused. It was the third time he'd asked this since they'd left Burger King, which was about three mintues' walk away.

'That's the plan,' Becky said, glancing at Stevie.

Stevie grunted in agreement. He wasn't quite sure what the expression on Becky's face meant. If it was 'I'm sorry, Stevie, but I changed my mind about you', she wasn't going to find any sympathy here. Stevie showed her his teeth in his best humourless grin. Becky looked away, that odd expression still on her face.

'I think we should use a cab,' Johnny said, sounding as if he was having difficulty speaking.

'You ate one double whopper too many,' Stevie said. Stevie had only been able to manage a standard cheeseburger, but JK had stuffed down three double whoppers with fries – on top of that massive breakfast. 'It's addled your brains.'

'You feeling OK?' Becky asked Johnny, and Stevie saw her shudder as if someone had walked over her grave.

'He's gonna throw up,' Stevie said, staring across the road at St Michael's church. A split in the cloud had caused a beam of sunlight to hit the church so that it looked like a holy oasis in a grey, grim desert of sin.

'I'm fine,' Johnny said. 'I just don't like the look of that fucking church. All those gravestones.'

'Everyone dies,' Becky said. 'It's just a matter of when. And everyone in that chuchyard died last century or before.'

Stevie looked over at the crumbling tombstones. You could see inside some of the long, raised ones that looked like caskets. Two small birds were perched on top of a weather-beaten cross, their heads turned sideways. They looked as if they could hear everything and were listening and learning.

'Where are we going?' Johnny said, glancing from Stevie to Becky and back.

'My place, Mr Memory,' Stevie said. 'Then to the movies. Got that?'

Johnny grinned. 'I dunno what's up with me,' he said. 'Lack of sleep, probably. Your place. What about a taxi?'

'We'll walk,' Stevie said. 'Come on, quick, before the road fills up again.'

They were half-way across the road when Stevie heard an odd kind of fluttering sound behind him. He turned round quickly, almost dropping his bags.

'What was that?' Becky demanded. She sounded frightened.

'Where are we going?' Johnny asked.

'Sounded like wings flapping,' Stevie said.

High in the sky above him, he could see two small birds circling. They were a long way away, but Stevie was suddenly sure they were the sparrows that had been sitting on the cross in the churchyard. It couldn't have been them making the noise, he decided: they wouldn't have had time to have climbed that high.

'C'mon, let's *go*, guys,' Johnny said. 'These bags are weighing me down. And I don't like those graves over there.'

Becky gave Stevie that odd glance again and began to hurry along after Johnny, who had crossed the road to be as far away from the churchyard as possible. Stevie glanced up at the wheeling birds again, then jogged after his friends.

Chaos broke out the moment he caught them up and fell into step with them. The next thing he knew, he was in agony and falling. He had to reconstruct the rest.

What must have happened was that Johnny began to yell and flail his arms about. Shopping bags flew everywhere. Becky ran two steps, her bags gone and her hands high in the air as she tried to protect her head, tripped and sprawled across the wet pavement. One of Johnny's hands caught Stevie in the throat in a swift, backhand karate cop and Stevie was certain he was going to die. The ground came up and hit him. His forehead bounced on the tarmac as his throat turned to fire and refused to let him breathe.

And the air was filled with the sound of Johnny shouting and the beating of wings, then footsteps as Johnny ran.

It was a good thirty seconds before Stevie could get up. Becky lay ahead of him, face down on the pavement, her hands over her head. A jumble of clothes, shoes and underwear had spilled from her bags. Stevie's new Levi's lay in the gutter.

He ran over to Becky, ignoring the gathering of interested bystanders, who watched carefully from the far side of the road.

Becky yelped when Stevie took her wrist, then relaxed. 'They gone?' she asked.

''S all right,' Stevie said, around what felt like broken glass in his throat. 'Gone.'

Becky got up. There was a graze on her right cheek and tears in her eyes. 'Birds,' she said, taking his arm and clinging to it. 'Birds. I heard 'em.'

'Damnedest thing I ever seed,' a high voice grated from behind them.

Stevie turned round. A tiny, ancient black man in an old suit and a wide-brimmed hat stood there. He had bow legs and a walking stick. A gold watch-chain dipped across the front of his waistcoat. 'I be hearin' of gulls raidin' people for food,' the man said, 'but I never, in *aaaalla* my born days, seen a man attacked by sparrows. Just the two of dem but, man, did dem fight!'

'Birds,' Becky said.

'Vicious little tings, dese were,' the black man said. 'Your frien' mus' be one mighteee bad person.' He leaned on his stick for a time, weighing up Stevie. Then he nodded. 'I'd stay away from that *friend* of yours, if I was you, boy. Him's hexed for sure. Take heed, boy! And you look after that pretty girl of yours or you'll both be lustin' after dem bad tings too. Take heed!'

Stevie stared open-mouthed at the man, who turned round and wandered off towards the town.

'Where'd he come from?' Becky said.

Stevie shrugged. 'I've got a better question. Where's Johnny gone?'

He was less than two hundred yards away, hiding in the pedestrian underpass that ran under Timberlake Road. They found him sitting against the tiled wall, his arms wrapped round his drawn-up knees, and his face buried in them.

'You OK?' Stevie called, as he and Becky approached. His voice echoed off the walls.

'I puked,' Johnny mumbled. 'Can't believe it.'

'Are you hurt?' Becky said, squatting down beside him.

Johnny looked up. There were at least half a dozen smears on his face where thin rivulets of blood had run down from his hair. 'I got pecked,' he said. 'Why did *that* happen? I never hurt a fucking dicky bird in my life.'

'Does it hurt?' Becky asked, gently parting Johnny's hair. 'Sheesh, they got you some good ones.'

Stevie peered at his friend's head. Johnny wasn't bleeding badly, but some of the cuts looked deep enough to require stitches.

'Just came at me out of nowhere,' Johnny said. 'Swooped down and fluttered round me, pecking like fuckery. Do you get rabid birds?'

'I dunno, but you should go to hospital and get these cuts looked at,' Stevie said.

'Fuck off, man, it's my *day*. I ain't going to hospital. I'll be all right.'

Becky sighed, stroking Johnny's hair. 'You could do with a tetanus booster at least.'

'Had one last year,' Johnny argued. 'I'll be OK. If they're gone.'

'Johnny, I've got to ask you something,' Stevie said.

'OK, man. Fire,' Johnny said. 'Anyone got a Kleenex?'

Becky found him a tissue and Johnny blew his nose and dabbed his eyes.

'Have you been back?' Stevie asked.

'Back where?'

'May Street. We need an honest answer.'

Johnny glared at him. 'You need an honest answer, do you, Dogboy?' he said angrily. 'Why? Do you think I always lie to you or something? You think I'd lie to you, you *fuckwit*!'

Becky laid a hand on his arm. 'Steady,' she said. 'He's just asking.'

Johnny pulled off her arm. 'I thought you were my *friends*,' he spat. 'I thought you *trusted* me. Well, you can fuck off. The pair of you! Go on, leave me! I'll be OK. What the fuck do I need you two for, anyway? You're both sad bastards and you can just go get fucked!'

'Did you?' Stevie persisted.

'What do *you* think? You tell me, you bastard!'

'Just tell us the truth,' Becky said.

Johnny glared from Stevie to Becky and back. 'Truth: I won the money on the Lottery. Got it? Truth: I did not go back to May Street. You can forget the movies and just fuck off and leave me alone. I wanna talk to someone who believes me when I'm telling the truth.'

'We believe you,' Becky said, gently taking Johnny's hand. 'We just want to help you. We want to figure out what's going on. That's all.'

Johnny nodded. 'Sure you do,' he said. This time he didn't shake off Becky's hand. He smiled at her. And she smiled back.

That's it, Stevie thought. He wasn't sure if he was still rattled by the bird attack, the pain in his throat or the way Becky was looking at Johnny. What he did know was that he didn't believe Johnny and he didn't stand a chance of convincing Becky that Johnny was lying.

'I've had enough of this shit,' he said. 'I'm going home. You want him, you have him. And the best of luck to you both. I hope you'll be very happy together.' He strode off down the underpass.

'Stevie!' Becky called.

Stevie turned round, his heart in his mouth.

'You left your clothes and stuff,' she said.

Stevie turned and walked away.

Half-way down Flaxfield Road, he turned back to see if his friends were coming after him. They weren't. He was just about to head for home when something caught his eye.

High in the sky, centred directly over the underpass in which Johnny and Becky were still sitting, two crows circled.

I'm gonna have to go back, Stevie thought. *Back to May Street and see if I can undo whatever he's done.*

Chapter Thirteen

The Devil on May Street

'Good morning, Captain Allan Mills speaking,' the tinny voice said, over the sound of jet-engine whine and the rumble of wheels. 'As you can see we're just taxiing to the end of the runway. Sorry about the hold up but we've been cleared for take-off. The cabin staff will show you the safety video now. I'll be speaking to you again later. If you'd just like to sit back and relax we'll be airborne in just a couple of minutes. I do hope you enjoy your flight with us today.'

Andy failed to understand how *anyone* could enjoy something which involved the word 'airborne'.

At least IBM had bought a first-class ticket for him, which meant he could stretch out his legs while he was puking.

The plane made the tight turn on to the main runway and jolted to a halt. Andy stared unseeing at the safety video. If the plane fell almost seven miles out of the sky, the last things he'd be needing would be a flotation jacket and an emergency exit.

'We're nearly twelve minutes late already,' a disgruntled American voice said from behind him. Andy didn't know who the man was addressing and didn't care: he didn't dare turn round because once he was on an aeroplane his sense of balance took a hike and the slightest movement of his head made him horribly dizzy.

A member of the cabin crew came towards him. 'You buckled in, sir?' she asked.

Still staring resolutely at the little video screen in front of him, Andy leaned back and showed the girl that not only was he buckled in, but he was buckled in so tightly that the belt hurt his hip-bones. And when the seat-belt lights finally went out this was one passenger who wouldn't be releasing his belt.

At least not until the drugs kick in, Andy thought grimly.

He wasn't sure what they were. He'd had a stash of Librium in a jar in the larder, left over from a long-ago series of anxiety attacks, but when he'd gone to get some the jar had been empty. Jacqui swore she'd had nothing to do with their disappearance, but Andy doubted Stevie had been at them. Jacq must have been popping the odd one or two on her bad days. And in the last three months she'd had a lot of those. Andy had continued the frenzied search and, in the bottom of the plastic Tupperware box that served as the medicine chest, had discovered a small brown canister of red pills. They'd been prescribed so long ago that the print had worn off the label. He had tipped them into his hand: Seconal, he hoped. They were sedatives. Downers. Chill-out pills. He put the canister in his pocket.

In the toilet at the airport, the place he always waited between going airside and his flight being called, Andy had taken two of the red pills, estimating that if they took around twenty minutes to start working, then they'd kick in just as he got on the plane. Ten minutes after taking the first two, he'd taken two more, just to be on the safe side.

So far nothing had happened.

The cabin began to vibrate as the engines powered up and the plane began to roll. Andy gripped the arms of his seat and squeezed his eyes shut. The plane gathered momentum and pressed Andy gently back into his seat. He braced himself for the inevitable collision.

Then the jumbo lifted its nose. Andy's balance reeled as he was tilted back. The juddering lessened, signifying that the plane was airborne. It banked left and the Seconal kicked in. Andy opened his eyes and grinned, feeling his blood pressure settle and his heart begin to slow.

The seat-belt lights pinged and went out. He was only briefly conscious of the big fluffy wave rolling towards him from the direction of the red pills.

'OK, Dad, let's see what you know,' Stevie said, settling himself into Andy's high-backed chair and hitting the 'on' switch.

Andy had anticipated that someone was going to play with his computer while he was away and had set a password in the machine's BIOS chip, which now halted and invited Stevie to *Enter Password.*

Stevie frowned. Then he typed *Jacqui.*

Password Incorrect, the BIOS warned.

Stevie hit Return and entered *Andy*. That didn't work either.

Stevie, he typed. Then he swore and had to shut off the machine and start again as he'd exceeded his maximum amount of failures. Next time he tried *Kate, Jane* and *Becky*, and had to start the machine again.

By the time he'd spent half an hour typing in the names of all Andy's known friends and associates, he was beginning to think this had been a bad idea. His mother and father must have arrived at Heathrow by now and he didn't think Jacqui would stay there long. Andy was so terrified that he could barely string two words together so he wouldn't want to go to the restaurant and eat. Stevie's mother would simply drive up to the doors and let Andy out or park and go in with him, have a cup of coffee and come back. Which, at best, gave Stevie another forty minutes.

Stevie had just rebooted the computer for what seemed like the millionth time, when Duke scratched at the door. Stevie's face lit up.

Enter Password, the computer demanded.

Duke, he typed.

'You can't come in here, dog,' he yelled over his shoulder. 'There's lots of poisonous stuff on the floor.'

Password Incorrect.

On the other side of the door, Duke gave a low moan.

'I'm sorry, Dookie, but it's no go. I won't be long.'

Stevie hit the Enter key and typed *Dookie.*

The Password Dialogue Box vanished and the machine re-entered its starting-up routine.

'Yes!' Stevie yelled, punching the air.

Twenty seconds later he was presented with a Windows 95 desktop screen that could have won an award for being the most untidy and confusing screen in the universe.

'What am I looking for?' Stevie asked himself. 'Quick. Hurry.'

He opened several recent letters that Andy had written. Then he did an extended search for any file or document containing the word 'Stevie'. Nothing.

What next? He typed the word 'porridge' into the Search slot and hit Return. After an agonizing wait he discovered that no files contained the word 'porridge'.

'Now what?' he asked, glancing at his watch. Andy's flight had surely been called now, which meant his mother was on her way home. If the motorways were clear she could be home in less than twenty-five minutes.

Stevie brought up the Search window again, typed in the words 'May Street' and hit Return.

He heard movement.

He cocked his head and listened, trying to filter out the hum of the computer's fan and the elongated clicking noises of its hard disks as they were searched. *Something rustled*, he thought.

Stevie thought of the worms his dad had laid powder to kill and shivered. There was no further sound. He swivelled round in his seat and peered around the gloomy room. If anything was in here there were a hundred or more places it might be hiding.

Behind Stevie, the computer stopped clicking. But he didn't turn round to see if any files containing the chosen words existed because over by the door he thought he'd seen something move. He was looking at a gap about three inches wide between two empty cardboard boxes and the room was darkened, but Stevie was almost sure he'd seen something.

Suddenly he wished he had a knife.

Jacqui Warner pulled into Fleet services, hoping that David Kane would be there. He wasn't terribly dependable, or he hadn't been when she'd been going out with him, but things changed, so he might have changed, too. She doubted it, though. The last time she'd seen him – two years ago in Tesco – Dave had been constructing one of his alternate-world fantasies. In this one, his car-sales business was booming and he was driving a brand new Porsche Carrera twin-turbo.

Of course, Jacqui had fallen for it. She would still be believing it now except that she'd seen Dave loading his shopping into an ancient Austin Allegro.

The only one of the six who'd come out of the seventies and done well for themselves was Katie. Katie, who'd evidently had the foresight to stash away the money. Katie, who'd built up her photography business from zilch, using her good looks and feminine charm. Katie, who'd been responsible for . . .

Don't even think that, she told herself. *You have no idea what Katie did or didn't do. She's probably as fucked up over all this as you are. And the rest of us.*

This was one of the things she hoped she was going to find out from meeting Dave. Like why she'd been so unsettled this year. Like what had happened to her during those two missing weeks all those years ago. It might hurt, but it couldn't be any worse than the way she'd been feeling since Christmas. It felt rather like someone had been eating biscuits in her mind and now her brain couldn't settle because of the crumbs that had been left behind.

Jacqui was frightened. She'd woken at six this morning with the words *Oh, fuck, we've all had kids!* rolling about in her mind. Why that simple sentence should make her so unsettled, she didn't know.

Jacqui pulled into a space close to the restaurant area, stopped the engine and pulled the keys from the ignition. She'd known that Johnny Kane existed from the moment Katie became pregnant, so that was no shock to her. It'd given her a few uneasy moments the first time Johnny had walked into her house all pally with Stevie. That they'd found one another at school was no big surprise or that they'd teamed up. Once upon a time the two boys' parents had been so close that they were never quite sure in whose arms they were going to wake up.

The real shock had come when one day Becky had waltzed in. If there had been one true *love* of Jacqui's life, it had been Jane, Becky's mother. And here she was again, reincarnated. Jacqui had felt a face-slap shock of pure love and had pushed it away, because of the greater shock that the three were together. Becky, Johnny and her Stevie, for whom she would glady die. It meant something and Jacqui didn't know what. Except that trouble was involved.

Jacqui got out of the car, locked it and strode towards the restaurant. It was Sunday lunch-time and when she walked in the Carvery was busy. On the periphery of her vision, away to the right, someone stood up. Jacqui glanced over and there was Dave, tall and slender and as handsome as he'd ever been, although his forehead was now a good three inches higher than it once had been.

They came together in the centre of the room like something out of a romantic movie, Jacqui with tears in her eyes and Dave, arms wide with a broken smile quivering at the corners of his mouth.

She fell into his arms and pressed her face against his chest as he hugged her to him. Everything still fitted, exactly as it used to; each pressure point, each dip was still there, still in the right place.

'Oh, Davey,' she murmured, her fingers feeling his wide back. 'You came.'

'It was an offer I couldn't refuse, Jacq,' he said. 'It's just a pity we had to wait until the shit hit the fan.'

It wasn't until after his second vodka that Andy realized he might have overdone the Seconal. The pills had taken their time to get started and then levelled off, leaving him feeling as if he could manage a drink. But the doped feeling began to increase: the second pair of tablets had taken even longer to get started than the first. Andy spent a few moments just sitting and feeling good. Then he began to wonder about the nature of Seconal. It wasn't a bog-standard barbie. There was something else about it. He searched his mind.

Seconal, he remembered, was a sedative-hypnotic. Andy grinned. *If someone waved a watch in front of my eyes, there's little doubt that he or she could put me in a trace. Or get inside my paaants.* He snorted and giggled, then he yawned and stretched out in his seat. *You are under my power*, Andy told himself, waving the wrist with his watch on it in front of his eyes. Someone to his right was looking at him worriedly. 'It's a self-winder,' Andy explained to the pretty girl across the aisle, only half conscious that his voice was slurred. 'You gotsta waggle your arms to make it wind.'

You are feeling sleepy, Andy thought, still waving his wrist up and down in front of his face. And then, *I'm damned if it isn't fucking well working, I* do *feel sleepy. What a surprise*!

An even bigger surprise was that he could no longer hold up his wrist: his arm had grown far too heavy.

And now the surprises multiplied. Andy felt a part of his mind go to sleep. And for some reason he'd become paralysed. It seemed that although his body had gone to sleep it had forgotten to close his eyes. Andy shut them himself and felt his jaw slacken. He opened them again, but his jaw stayed where it was.

Fuck, this is weird, he thought. It was also enjoyable. Andy couldn't remember having felt this good in years. He felt just fine. For a moment he wondered if he was going to die of an overdose but concluded that if dying was this easy and comfortable, he could go ahead and die.

But Andy didn't die. He began to remember.

Stevie kept very still for a long time. Whatever was on the far side of the room had either fallen asleep, vanished, or hadn't been there at all. But Stevie knew he wasn't going to be able to turn back to the computer and forget all about it without checking it out first. However, he didn't want to check it out. He wished Duke was in here with him.

'Dookie?' he called.

The dog scratched at the far side of the door.

'Wait there, I'm coming to let you in,' he said. 'And when I open the door, I want you in here as fast as you can move. Got that?'

Duke scratched at the door again and whined.

Stevie took a deep breath and stood up. There was no way he could get across to the door quickly – there was too much junk in the way. He had a better idea. 'Wait there, dog,' he called, leapt up on the desk and yanked on the cord that worked the blind. He could go out through the window and come in the back door. And pick up a big knife from the kitchen before he came back in here. His dad reckoned that if you hit those worms between the segments, they died.

I'm as crazy as he is, Stevie thought, as the blind went up. The room was suddenly flooded with bright, sunny day-time. The quick change in the level of light hurt his eyes, but it hurt the thing over by the door even more. Whatever it was gave a small shriek, which was followed by the kind of cracking noise you heard when you poured warm water over a tray of ice cubes. Except this was a lot louder.

On the far side of the door, Duke barked, a high yip of anxiety.

It's dead. The light killed it, Stevie thought, but he got out through the window anyway.

He ran round to the back gate, let himself in and sprinted up the path to the back door, where Duke met him, wagging his tail and grinning. Stevie patted his head, selected a large steak knife and stalked up the hall to the study. He listened briefly, then turned the knob and pushed open the door. Duke limped into the room and Stevie followed him, the knife at the ready.

Duke found the worm first. By the time Stevie got to where it was, the dog's hackles were raised and he was growling. Stevie had to use all his strength to pull him away. There was no danger: even the dog should have been able to see that. The worm – or whatever it was – was dead.

As Stevie had thought, the light had killed it. Whatever had been inside the thing had vaporized or shrivelled away or something, leaving behind only a segmented chitinous shell.

It wasn't really a worm at all. It was more like an elongated beetle or a huge millipede. The segments of the black exoskeleton were almost three inches in diameter, but there weren't any legs. The thing's skeletal head looked rather like that of a moth, except that it had a huge, armoured lower jaw with a sharp top edge.

You could lose a hand if one of those bit you, Stevie thought, still finding it difficult to believe what he was seeing. About three feet of the worm had slid out of the wall that joined this room to the hall. He estimated that a whole worm would probably be about eight feet long. That meant the other end of it should be in the hall, which it wasn't.

Stevie poked with his shoe at the segment that was half in and half out of the wall. It snapped off easily. He crouched to examine the wall and found exactly what he'd anticipated: there was no hole in the wall but a round section of the worm's exoskeleton could be seen protruding from the wallpaper. The thing had entered the house at this point from . . .

Another dimension? The past? Down in the nasty with the gobblings?

... from somewhere else. From the elsewhere.

Stevie shuddered.

Duke pushed himself forward to sniff at the remains, his ears back and his tail between his legs. He glanced up at Stevie then slunk out of the room, favouring his hurt leg.

Stevie glanced back at the computer. The Search window had found something. He went back to the screen and sat down in front of it.

The Devil on May ... the Find window said, the dots indicating that the title was longer. There was a single file on Andy's machine with the title *The Devil on May Street.* It was at the lower end of several sub-directories deep in the bowels of the second hard disk drive. It looked as if Andy had placed it there out of the way.

But it didn't matter where it was now that Stevie had found it. All he had to do was double click on the tiny icon in the Search window and the document would open.

The question was, did he really want to read it?

The answer was *no*, but Stevie knew he was going to have to read it anyway. He placed the mouse pointer on the icon and clicked the button twice.

'You have to make me remember,' Jacqui said across a steaming cup of black coffee. She'd taken the remaining Librium from the bottle this morning, while Andy was still packing, and had swallowed them just before she'd left to drive him to Heathrow. They'd kicked in on the drive here but now they'd kicked out again and there were no more where those had come from. But after all this was over there would be. There would probably be Largactil, too, or whatever it was they gave on psychiatric wards these days.

David smiled at her. It wasn't a happy smile. 'Do you really need to know?' he asked. 'Perhaps it'd be better if we all went down without knowing. All we have to know is that the card house we built is about to fall.'

'You don't know, either, do you?' Jacqui asked, astonished.

David shook his head. 'Only parts. And so do you, whether you're admitting it to yourself or not. And do you know why you're starting to remember?' David reached across the table, took her hand and squeezed it gently. 'It's because the spell's worn off, darling. Because the Sleeping Beauty has woken up. The forgetting was part of the deal. But none of us kept it. We did all the right things for a while, but then we forgot. And when you've forgotten what you shouldn't do, you can't remember you're not supposed to be doing it, can you?' He shrugged. 'Our fault entirely. It was what we asked for. I'm sorry, honey, but everything falls down in the end. Castles made of sand and all that.'

'Davey, I have no idea what you're talking about,' Jacqui pleaded.

'Then why are the tears in your eyes about to overflow? What's to be sad about? Don't bother investigating if you can't remember. Just let it lie.'

'What did we do wrong, Davey?'

'We had kids. All of us.'

'I don't understand,' Jacqui said, but a part of her did. The part that was causing the icy-cold knife to turn in her guts. The part that was lighting up a mental picture in her head of an egg being cracked open with a hammer.

David hitched a breath. 'I don't know what we're going to do, Jacq. I really don't. I just wish I'd died back in 'seventy-one.'

She watched his eyes fill with tears, which he tried and failed to blink away. Suddenly he was on his feet, dragging her out of her seat. 'Gotta get out of here,' he muttered. 'Need some air.'

In the car park they fell into one another's arms and stood there, crying, unable to speak.

Andy was mentally singing his own revised version of Sinatra's song, now named 'Strangers on the Flight'. Outside his warm, dark cocoon, he could hear the gentle whine of the engines, the sound of air rushing by at five hundred and fifty miles an hour and the occasional *bing!* of someone summoning a member of the flight crew. All this was soothing in its own strange way.

Even the way Andy was moving backwards in time was soothing. It was a new experience for him, but Andy wasn't the type of person who worried about new experiences. In his time he'd tried everything he could. He'd slept with every possible combination of humans, taken every hallucinogenic substance known to man and most of the opiates, too. He'd scuba-dived off the Great Barrier Reef, had even bungee-jumped off a bridge in New Zealand, and had crashed more cars than most people had had hot dinners. In comparison moving back in time was a piece of cake.

From the moment it had started Andy had known it was going to be an enjoyable experience. In his mind he was floating down through layer upon layer of soft, cotton-wool-like history, going deeper and deeper.

And where we stop, no one knows, he thought, smiling inwardly because smiling physically had become impossible. Andy was feeling so good that he didn't even care about the drool that was running from the right-hand corner of his mouth and soaking through his shirt.

I'm asleep, that's all, he assured himself. *Or in a deep hypnogogic state. Neither in the land of the waking nor the land of the sleeping.*

And then something hit the plane.

And a moment later Andy wasn't even *in* the plane. Had *never* been in the plane. Had never been in a plane in his life, in fact.

Oh, shit, I'm in 'seventy-two again, he thought, as the mist cleared from his head.

The word processor had loaded the document called *The Devil on May Street* but Stevie wasn't at the screen. He was perched on the corner of his dad's desk, with one of his dad's Silk Cut in his mouth and a lighter in his hand. He'd promised himself he'd read the document as soon as he'd smoked the fag, but he had the distinct feeling that everything was going to change after he'd read it and that nothing would ever go back to normal again. He wasn't sure how he felt about that.

Except that there isn't a choice, he told himself, and lit the cigarette. *If you're going back to May Street, you have to know everything you can find out about it before you go. Things have changed already. They're not going to change very much more for reading a page or two of something your dad wrote five years ago. What are you frightened of?*

'Finding out why Andy's Goldilocks,' he said aloud. 'Finding out what Katie does.'

Stevie sighed and settled himself in the chair. He took a deep drag of the cigarette and looked up at the page.

We did something terrible last night, Andy had written. These six words were the first paragraph of what looked like a page of the novel Andy was always saying he was going to write. It was a good first line.

Last night the six of us murdered a man, not knowing who he really was; not knowing that what he said was the truth. We killed him in cold blood. Murdered him merely because we were frightened that he would murder us if we didn't do something to prevent it.

And last night in May Street, with this man's blood on our hands, we made a pact. A pact between the six of us. And the devil himself.

Jacqui sat in the passenger seat of David's BMW, dabbing her eyes with a tiny lacy handkerchief. For once in her life there were no tissues in her handbag and all David had been able to offer was a scrap of rag with a slender, oily stripe on it where he'd wiped the car's dipstick after checking the oil level. He was now back inside the service area getting her 'something to blow her nose on'. The gallant act seemed pathetic in the circumstances.

And what are the circumstances? Jacqui asked herself. *You don't even know what's going on, do you?*

She didn't. But it wasn't going to stay that way for long. She could feel this. Her missing fortnight was on its way back to her. Somewhere, deep in her mind, that two-week period was beginning to surface. It felt like the hulk of a sunken liner, into which air was now being pumped in an attempt to raise it. And now years of sand and weed and the carapaces of long-dead marine life were sloughing off the decks as the ship began to rise.

When David opened the driver's door, Jacqui yelped in fear. Then she began to cry again.

He got in, turned to her and pulled her to him.

'Remember Raymond?' he whispered.

Jacqui nodded against his chest. She did remember Raymond, but only in a series of blurred images. And she remembered Stevie, covered in mud, running from the garden one summer's day a long time ago. Stevie yelling excitedly that Manaymon had shown him how to fly, while blood pumped from the hole the garden fork had made in his wellington boot. And she remembered how frightened she'd been. And how hard she'd hit him.

David laughed bitterly. 'Just goes to show how wrong you can be about people,' he said. 'And we were just about as wrong as it's possible to get. How much can you remember?'

'Not much,' Jacqui said, concentrating on the hard warmth of his chest and hoping it would take away the sick feeling building in her as her sunken ship, the *SS Missing Fortnight*, floated slowly up through the dark green water.

'You're going to have to,' David said. 'We're all going to have to. It'll kill us, I think, but we must. I can feel it starting to come back to me. Whenever it's tried before, I've stopped it, but this time . . .'

'I can feel it too,' Jacqui said. 'David?'

'Yes, sweetheart?'

'Do you think there's a God?'

David gave that bitter laugh again. 'I'm certain there is,' he said.

'Do you think he'll save us?'

David didn't speak, but through his chest she could feel the shaking of his head.

'We were bad, weren't we?' Jacqui said. 'I know that. I've known it all along.'

'We were very bad,' David said. 'We committed the sin of hubris. We thought we could take on the gods and win.'

'What are we going to do?'

David shook his head again. 'I don't know,' he said. 'First we have to let ourselves recall. After that we can try to figure out what to do.'

'You don't think there's anything we *can* do, do you?' she asked.

'No, I don't. I think the game's already been played. It was won while we were looking the other way. But I could be wrong. I *hope* I'm wrong.'

'So do I,' Jacqui said. 'I really do.' She dabbed away her tears and blew her nose.

After a time, David sighed. 'It's coming back,' he said. 'It's almost here for me.'

'Me, too,' Jacqui said. 'It'll kill us, won't it?'

'That'd be about the best we could hope for,' David replied.

'And the worst?'

David didn't reply.

And it no longer mattered because for Jacqui it was starting to be the seventies again.

Chapter Fourteen

The Fly in the Ointment

Back in the dark ages, when the world was young and love was free and you could see Pink Floyd and Blind Faith in Hyde Park for no money at all, the Jane's Gang, as the six-strong core of the local psychedelic movement had called themselves, ran into trouble finding somewhere peaceful to drink. George, the landlord of the Feathers, had quickly caught on that the odd smell that accompanied visits by the Jane's Gang wasn't just the reek of patchouli oil but the stench of substantial quantities of Black Lebanese hashish.

After being barred from the Feathers, they'd moved to the Pear Tree, which had a landlord who didn't care how much of it they smoked. Unfortunately the pub was the stamping ground of every horny-handed navvie and bricklayer in the area, and although they were happy to see Jane, Katie and Jacqui in their flimsy dresses and granny boots, they took exception to the long-haired nancy boys who accompanied them. The uneasy relationship between the locals and the new kids on the block finished one Friday night when three of the drunken navvies picked up Andy and threw him out through the pub's plate-glass front window. He suffered no injuries, but he got the message. The gang moved on.

Eventually they'd settled in the Royal Exchange, which was about as downmarket as the Pear Tree but quieter. The few regulars here were mostly drunks and the landlord welcomed the new trade, turning a blocked nose to the odd smells and a blind eye to the strange trade in items wrapped in tinfoil or sealed in ziplock baggies.

Life was sweet. Andy commuted between there and London for work and pleasure, and between London and Marrakech for another kind of work and pleasure. The Jane's Gang came and went; the relationships between its members came and went until almost all possible combinations had been tried. Love was made, peace was made, cakes baked with cannabis were made and a good time was had by all. The days passed in a psychedelic blur of fun.

Somewhere in that blur, Andy had hooked up with a guy named Dick and his little gang of revolutionaries. Dick made the world's best LSD and the Jane's Gang bought into the set-up. The world seemed to be crying out for good acid. Suddenly they had so much money they didn't have time to spend it. Andy bought a huge house in Cuckoo Close, right out in the wilds. Jane bought and crashed a series of exotic cars. David invested in a series of businesses that went bankrupt, then invested in more. No one knew what Derek did with his share of the money.

Life was just about as good as it could possibly be.

For a time.

The fly that landed in the ointment belonging to the Jane's Gang *should* have been a drugs-squad officer or a sharp-eyed tax man. It should have been an angry parent or a bunch of customs officials with a warrant. But it wasn't.

To Andy and David, who were in the pub testing Dick's latest batch of acid, it looked like a cyclops dressed as a teddy-boy from the fifties. It had a big quiff of slicked-back black hair and was wearing a blue drape-jacket, drainpipe trousers and crêpe-soled shoes of the kind that Andy's dad called brothel-creepers – the uppers were blue suede. It wore a frilly dress-shirt with a black bootlace tie beneath its open jacket, the cuffs and collar of which were black velvet.

The thing arrived, apparently out of nowhere, and stood looking at them with its one bleary eye. It swayed a little as it glared at them.

David turned to look at Andy, his mouth open in a perfect O and mirth in his eyes. Andy glanced at the hallucination, then at David. 'Far out!' he said. Then they burst into an uncontrollable fit of giggles.

The cyclops stood there, swaying slightly, watching them laughing at it.

David chortled. 'Are we both seeing the same thing? A cyclops?'

Andy nodded.

'What do you think you're looking at, fuckface?' it asked, in a thick voice.

'Dunno,' Andy said, noticing for the first time that that thing was holding a pint of bitter.

The cyclops shook its head. 'Neither do I,' it said. 'What I'm lookin' at looks human, but I think something's gone seriously fucking wrong with it.'

'Snap!' David yelled.

The creature ignored this. 'How about one of you women give me a cigarette?'

Andy looked at David. His eyes were streaming. 'Hear that?' he said. 'It called us women! Give it a straight, man! It deserves one!'

David found a pack of cigarettes and took one out. Still shaking with mirth, he held it out.

The cyclops smiled. 'You ladies shouldn't be laughing,' it said, its voice suddenly dangerous. It took the cigarette, picked up Andy's Zippo and lit it. 'You'd soon stop finding everything so funny if I were to follow you home and fuck your pretty girlfriends,' it said. 'You're lucky I'm not in the mood.'

'Too drunk, I guess,' Andy chortled. 'Can't get it up, probably.'

Which was when the cyclops' patience ran out. It smashed its glass down on the table behind which Andy and David were sitting.

The thick bottom of the glass hit the table with such force that it sounded as though a gun had gone off.

Both Andy and David stopped laughing. The glass of beer, which was full to the brim, was undamaged. There wasn't even a crack in the glass. The contents had not spilled. The surface of the table was dry and clean. Andy looked up at the cyclops, which now had two eyes in roughly the right places.

'I'm not too drunk to fuck and I'm not too drunk to scotch it up with you two women,' the teddy-boy said.

'You mean you want a drink?' David ventured.

'Mix it, arsehole. Scotch it. I mean *fight.* Either you both come outside with me now and we settle our differences, man to man, or you bring your little girlies round to my place and let me fuck their arses.'

'What girlfriends?' Andy said. 'We don't have any.'

'I've seen 'em in here, half naked,' the man said. 'They're all dying for it. They wanna be fucked by a *man*, not a skinny little length of string.'

David nodded. 'OK, we'll bring them round to your place, then,' he said.

'Fifteen Wexfield Road,' the man said. 'Name's Raymond. Ray to you. Ray Edmundson.' He held out a huge hand towards Andy, who took it. It felt like a block of mahogany. He shook it firmly and was surprised when the man didn't put the squeeze on his fingers. 'Bring them round at midnight,' Ray said. 'You can watch me fuck them if you want.'

'Sure,' Andy said, nodding and wishing the man away.

'I'll bring Katie's camera,' David said, trying to keep a straight face.

'Just bring a quick dialling finger,' Ray said. 'They're gonna need an ambulance after I'm done with them.' He picked up his drink and walked away.

Andy and David looked at one another. David shook his head. 'A shared hallucination,' he said. 'That's all.'

'It's freaked me out,' Andy said. 'I don't feel comfortable here now. Let's go over to Jane's. Or down to Derek's place. That'd be cooler.'

'OK. I'm with you, man.'

The moment they stepped out into the street Andy was yanked round and pushed against the wall of the pub. His head bounced off the brickwork and a white flare lit up before his eyes. Something that felt like fishhooks dug deep into his pectorals. The pain was tremendous and he cried out.

Suddenly there was a large, olive-skinned face in front of his own. 'Don't fuck with me,' Ray said, right into Andy's mouth. 'Do anything you like, but don't fuck with me. We made a deal. Did we make a deal?'

'You're hurting me,' Andy gasped.

The pain in his chest immediately increased. 'And I'll rip your tits right off you,' Ray hissed. 'Did we make a deal?'

Andy nodded.

'Let him go, man!' David yelled. 'Put him down!'

'Say it. I wanna hear you say it!' Ray said.

David launched himself at the man and was casually batted aside.

'We made a deal,' Andy gasped.

Ray pushed him harder against the wall. 'And no one welches on deals they make with me. Got that?'

'I've got it,' Andy moaned.

'Then never forget it,' Ray rasped. 'You know what happens to people who double-cross me? They end up in hell. If you don't keep your part of the bargain, you die.'

Neither Andy nor David saw Raymond Edmundson again for so long that they more or less forgot about him. On the odd occasion David would crack a joke about screwing someone so hard they were going to have to dial three nines, but out of sight was out of mind. To Andy it seemed as if his expanded mind had blown up a small-time drunk into something he wasn't – something a good deal more significant. That happened, Andy knew. When you were on acid, weird things happened. A while back he'd taken a trip with Jacqui and both of them had become telepathic. For a helpless, amusing and sometimes scary seven hours they'd shared *everything* their minds contained. Since then, Andy had been a little bit more in love with her than he had before. He suspected the feeling was mutual.

Life went on, the deals kept rolling, the police and the drugs squad seemed incapable of following their noses back to the suppliers and the money kept rolling in. Yet Andy had the distinct feeling that time was running out.

It might just have been well-placed paranoia: since the Jane's Gang had moved into the Royal Exchange the pub had caught on with the local heads and not only were the local freaks, hippies and bikers using it, but people were travelling in from Reading and Andover. On weekdays after eight thirty you were lucky if you could find a table and at weekends it was quite possible you wouldn't get in at all. And when you got that many alternative-lifestyle people in one place, the old guard sat up and took notice. In recent weeks there had been one or two busts outside the pub and Andy had no doubt that drugs-squad officers were frequenting the place posing as cool guys 'n' gals. The Jane's Gang weren't dealing there, of course, but they weren't buying there either, and that was the kind of thing to arouse suspicion in PC Plod.

Things were changing. Part of Andy's mind was aware that time was marching on and he wasn't comfortable about the direction in which he suspected it would go.

He only began to be certain of the direction in which time was marching when Raymond appeared on an unnaturally quiet Tuesday evening in the Royal Exchange. This coincided so neatly with the first presence of the entire core membership of the Jane's Gang that afterwards, Andy was sure that Ray had somehow known they were all going to be there and had been biding his time until that day.

'Oh, fuck,' he said, as the big man came in through the door.

'Is it that man Raymond?' Jacqui whispered.

Raymond stood on the threshold, glancing around.

He's looking for me and David, Andy thought.

Raymond noticed them, gave a curt nod and a short smile, then strode over to the bar.

'He doesn't remember us,' David said, sounding relieved. He grinned. 'He doesn't have a fucking clue who we are. His brain's pickled.'

'Keep your fingers crossed that it stays that way,' Andy said, watching Ray's broad back as he stood talking to the barman.

Derek looked up from the paper he'd been staring at. He looked bemused, which wasn't surprising since he'd whacked a good hit of morphine in his arm less than an hour ago. 'What happened?' he asked.

'Guy at the bar,' Katie said, nodding in Raymond's direction. 'He's the guy who wants to fuck me and Jane and Jacq so hard we'll need an ambulance. Remember?'

Derek shook his head. Then he frowned. Then he smiled. 'Oh, *him*. I know him.'

'You *what*?' Andy said.

'Ray,' Derek said. 'I met him in the Goat a while back. He thinks he's a cross between Elvis Presley, Jerry Lee Lewis and Bill Haley. He's got 'hate' tattooed across *both* sets of knuckles. He's nuts, but he's OK.'

'He *hit* me,' David complained.

'And he nearly tore off my pecs,' Andy added. 'He might be a lot of things but one thing he isn't is OK.'

Derek shrugged. 'He bought me a drink,' he said. 'I thought he was harmless.' He glanced over at Jane. 'That amulet,' he said.

Jane frowned. 'The mystical and magical amulet? The old tin thing that smells of flowers?' she asked.

Derek nodded, in what seemed like slow motion. 'He gave it to me.'

'Amulet?' Katie said.

Jane grinned. 'An old tin container on a chain. Diamond-shaped thing. It's probably supposed to have something smelly inside it, lavender or something, but it's empty. Still smells quite nice, though.'

'I was robbed,' Derek complained. 'Again!'

'Again? He robbed you before?' Andy asked.

'He's talking about the burglary now,' Jane said.

Andy nodded. Derek's place had been turned over the previous week and there had been a major panic because everyone thought it was the drugs squad's work. The house was clean, but it probably hadn't been the police anyway – the thief or thieves had walked off with a lot of clothes and a hacksaw and had left the plug-hole in the bath clogged with short black hairs. No one yet knew what it meant and it would be some time before they found out about the money missing from the stash in their warehouse.

'And the other thing he means,' Jane continued, 'is that he was promised a genuine magical amulet.'

'It *is* magical,' Derek insisted.

'Has it done anything magical?' David challenged, tearing his eyes away from Raymond.

'Yes,' Derek said. 'It's continued to smell good, man. It's empty and it smells good. And . . .' he tailed off, 'what else does it do, Janie?' he asked.

'It protects its owner from death,' Jane said.

'Right,' Derek said, a big dopey grin on his face. 'And I'm not dead, am I? It works, man.'

'And it'll bring back folks from the dead, too, if that's your desire,' Jane said, grinning. 'I was thinking about trying to find Hendrix's corpse. Or his ashes or whatever.'

'And that man Raymond gave it to you?' Jacqui asked.

Derek nodded. 'He's harmless,' he said. 'Talks a lot of shit, but he's cool.'

Andy looked at David and rolled his eyes.

'Don't look now,' Jane said quietly, 'but the amulet man is on his way over.'

'Just ignore him,' Andy suggested, his heart sinking. 'Perhaps he'll go away.'

'We could leave,' David said.

'Leaving sounds good,' Jacqui replied, but it was too late. Raymond was between their table and the door. As one person, the Jane's Gang fell silent and all found other places to look.

Raymond stood there, watching them, his pint glass in his right hand and a hand-rolled cigarette in his left.

With the tip of his finger, Andy flicked specks of ash from his section of the table, conscious of the man's gaze on him. Raymond was so close, he could even *smell* him. He reeked of bonfire smoke and rotting vegetation. Beneath that, almost swamped by the heavy odours, was a sweet smell that Andy couldn't identify. He could feel his muscles tensing as he waited for the *thwack!* of Ray's glass on the table.

The silence stretched taut and became almost unbearable.

I'm not gonna crack, Andy thought. *I won't. I won't give him the satisfaction.*

Jacqui's hand settled on Andy's thigh. Her fingers were trembling.

'Something smells fucking weird round here,' David suddenly announced, in a voice that was presumably meant to be scathing.

'That'd be the smell of you shitting your pants,' Ray growled.

Jacqui's fingers tightened on Andy's leg.

Jane looked up. It had to be Jane, Andy later thought. Jane, to whom everyone looked for approval. Whom everyone loved. Jane, who owned them all, in one way or another. 'Why don't you just leave us in peace?' she asked, her voice level and gentle. She sounded as if the devil himself couldn't have scared her.

It's gonna be all right, Andy thought. *It'll be cool now. Jane's in control.*

'I'd love to, sweetheart,' Raymond said, 'but I can't.'

Andy looked up and found himself staring into the ashen face of David, who was grinding his teeth in silent rage and loathing.

'Why can't you?' Jane asked.

'Ask loverboy. The big girlie with the curly locks and the quick mouth that's soon gonna need dentures to replace the teeth I'm going to pull out one by one. With pliers.'

'*You* tell me,' Jane suggested.

Raymond apparently thought about this for a while. Then he said, 'OK, I will. But not because you're so sexy and sweet. Not because I'm gonna fuck you, which I am, sooner or later, but because your soul is clean and worth a thousand of these filthy fuckheads you hang around with. Because you're the only one here with an ounce of courage.'

'Go on, then,' Jane encouraged.

'Your two boys there made a deal with me,' Raymond said. 'I kept my side of the bargain. They haven't kept theirs.'

'And what *was* your side?'

Raymond grinned. 'I promised not to trash their arses.'

'In return for?'

'Them bringing you and your ladyfriends round to my place so's I could fuck you all.'

'And you're upset because they didn't keep their side of the bargain, right?'

Raymond nodded.

'But neither did you. You beat up both the boys when they left the pub. Doesn't that make you square?'

'That wasn't a beating. That was a gentle reminder,' Raymond said.

'But you hit one and hurt the other. Andy had bruises that lasted two weeks. He could barely breathe. I think you were the one who broke the agreement.'

Raymond smiled. Bitterly. And nodded. 'Cunt,' he said.

Andy could *feel* the waves of the black rage flowing out from the man. Raymond was like a thunderstorm building up to a lightning strike.

Jane shrugged. 'You lost, Ray. Now go away and leave us in peace.'

'And what if I decide not to?'

'Then we'll go away and leave you in peace. None of us wants trouble with you.'

Raymond now looked as tense as Andy felt. 'It's too late for that, sweetheart,' he rasped.

'It's never too late,' Jane said quietly.

Raymond shook his head. 'For a woman who can be so right, you're a long way off there. Sometimes it's too late before you know anything about it. One of those times is now.'

'What do you propose we do?' Jane asked.

'We forget the old deal and make a new one,' Raymond said, spitting out the words as though they were poisonous.

Andy watched the hand that was holding the pint glass. Ray's knuckles were white. *The guy's a psycho*, he thought.

'What kind of a deal?' Jane asked, as calmly as she would if she'd been trying to knock down the price of a pair of crushed velvet hipsters in Lord John on Carnaby Street.

'A deal worth having,' Raymond said.

'Can you come up with one?' Jane asked, with just a touch of disdain in her voice.

The beer glass in Raymond's right hand shattered into splinters. The thick base dropped to the floor and rolled away. The right leg of his drainpipe trousers was stained with beer. Blood began to drip from his right hand, which was now clenched against the broken glass.

But neither he nor Jane seemed to have noticed any of this. They were holding one another's gaze, Raymond glaring and Jane calm.

'Here's the deal,' Raymond breathed. 'You put me out of action for a while and I let you and yours off the hook. You fail to put me out of action, and you all meet me at midnight in the Holy Ghost ruins and let me teach you a thing or two.'

'How do you mean, put you out of action?'

'I want you to come back here this time next week, and I want you to bring as much acid as you think it'll take to get me out of my skull.'

'Acid? What acid?' Jane asked, sounding genuinely surprised.

'Don't fuck around with me,' Raymond said. 'I know all about you and your gang. You want me to start shouting it all over this pub? The Jane's Gang sells acid? Should I start shouting or do you want to start talking to me?'

Andy's heart sank even further. He didn't know how Raymond had discovered what their business was, but he could guess. He'd evidently homed in on Derek and a drunken Derek had probably spilled his guts.

'I'll talk,' Jane said. 'You want to go tripping. Is that about the size of it? All you had to do was ask nicely and we'd have laid some acid on you.'

Raymond shook his head. 'No, I do not want to go tripping. I want you to see if you can send me to hell. I want you to try to kill me with your acid. I want to you to send me to hospital. Put me in a coma. Whatever. Put me out of action.'

'Why? Do you want to die or something?'

Ray smiled. 'Oh, you won't kill me, trust me, darling. I just want to give you a demonstration. Here's the deal. You come back here next week and bring whatever you think it'll take to blow me away. Bring as much as you like. You put it on the table in front of me, I'll eat it. Then you sit and watch. If I flinch, if I throw up or scream or giggle or fall down or faint or plead for mercy, I'll never bother you again. If not, you'll have to agree to do something for me. All six of you.'

'We meet you in the Holy Ghost ruins at midnight. What for?'

'So I can show you something that'll make all your mind-bending drugs look like sherbet dabs.'

'Ghosts?' Jane asked.

Andy didn't much care for the turn this was taking. Jane had an odd, interested look on her face, and a hint of a smile played at the corners of her mouth. Ever since Derek had reported seeing the ghosts of two teenagers, from the *future*, while he was tripping, Jane had started to wonder about the supernatural. Not only did it look as if Raymond had known this somehow, it also looked as if Jane was going to be up for it.

Worse yet, the site of the Holy Ghost chapel had a long history of inexplicable happenings. The ruins stood on a plot of land behind the station. In the village of Old Basing, three miles or so away, stood the ruins of Basing House, one of the last Royalist strongholds against Cromwell. Cromwell had sacked Basing House but there had been several notable escapes. The puzzle of how these people had got away was solved when Cromwell's men found the three-mile tunnel that came out in the chapel.

Raymond grinned. 'Ghosts,' he said, rolling his eyes and chuckling. 'Echoes, girl. Of no interest. What can I show you is the *real* stuff. Not the stuff for scaring kids, but stuff that'll blow you away.'

Jane smiled and shook her head. 'And if you survive the acid without ill effect and we refuse to meet you?'

'Then you'll wish you could die and go to hell.'

'It's a deal,' she said, putting out her hand.

Raymond shook it, smearing her flesh with his blood. 'This time next week,' he said, then nodded at the rest of the gang.

'What the fuck did you do that for?' David demanded, when Raymond had gone.

Jane shrugged. 'There didn't seem to be much choice, did there? Someone told him about our connection with Dick and the acid trade. Inside two minutes he could have the entire combined south-east drugs squads on our doorsteps. And then what happens? We go directly to jail. For between six and fifteen years each. That sound like fun to you?'

'Oh, fuck,' Andy said. 'We're gonna have to clean up.'

'How did he find out?' Katie said. 'That's what I'd like to know.' She looked pointedly at Derek.

'Derek?' Jane asked. 'Why *did* he give you that amulet?'

Derek frowned. 'Look, guys, I bought him a drink once,' he slurred. 'He sidled up to me in the Goat and gave me a sob story. I bought him a couple of pints and he gave me the amulet.'

'Were you drunk?' Andy asked.

'Fuck off, Andy. How long have you known me?'

'Long enough to know what you're like when you're pissed.'

'I wasn't drunk that night,' Derek said. 'Honest. And I've never told a single soul about the acid. Janie, surely you believe me?'

Everyone looked at Jane, who said, 'I believe him. Look, guys, there's a distribution chain, right? We might not have any weak links, but there are people we deal with who have their own people and so on. Not everyone's gonna be as tight-lipped as we'd like. Fact of life: people talk. Ray could have found out anywhere. We've been doing well now for a long time. Word was always going to get out and we're lucky it didn't happen before. What we have to do now is clean up our act. Get the stuff out of our houses and into our warehouse. We should have been doing it that way all along.'

'We're not going to meet Raymond in the ruins, then?' Andy asked thoughtfully.

Jane grinned. 'How crazy do you think I am?' she asked. 'And, anyway, he isn't gonna feel up to much after next Tuesday, is he? We'll be shot of him after that. But just in case he blabs, we'll shift the acid and warn the folks in London, Amsterdam and Hamburg.'

'You're going to send him tripping?' Jacqui asked.

'Does he deserve it?' Jane replied. 'Should we vote? Show of hands. Who wants to trip him out?'

Everyone thought Raymond Edmundson deserved it.

No one thought he would turn up the following Tuesday. At nine o'clock everyone started saying what a shame it was and how much good being sent out of his skull would have done him. He was just an alcoholic who talked big and threatened people he knew he could trash, they concluded; a nobody of no significance.

The Jane's Gang began to relax. Andy rolled a couple of joints and the gang got giggly. Ray's brain was so stewed he couldn't even remember what he'd said from one day to the next. 'Pity he didn't turn up,' Katie said. 'I rather fancied him.' Everyone thought this hilarious.

And while Andy was chortling at the sound Jacqui made blowing her nose, Raymond appeared.

He was sober, and looked fit and strong. He was wearing a lime-green teddy-boy suit and green-suede shoes. There was a pint glass of what looked like water in his right hand and a chair he'd taken from another table in his left.

'Mind if I sit?' he asked.

Everyone minded, but no one said so. The acid stocks were now safely stashed in a borrowed lock-up, but the chances were that a forensic team would still find enough dust in Andy and Jane's houses to use as evidence of dealing.

Jane and Derek moved their seats to make room and Raymond put his chair in the gap and sat down. 'I'm ready,' he said. 'Thought I'd stay sober tonight so you could judge how bad I got. What did you bring?'

One microdot tab of Dick's acid was enough to blow away the brain of the most insensitive person and Andy had figured that five ought to work on Raymond, but Jane had argued that he wanted to be reduced to a blubbering jelly and thought ten would be better. David, who hadn't forgotten his bloodied nose, thought they should throw in another ten for good measure. 'What if he dies?' Jacqui had asked, but since no one had ever been known to die from the chemical effects of pure LSD this wasn't thought to be a worry. He might, of course, walk under a bus or jump from a building, but this seemed unlikely, too.

Andy placed the matchbox containing the twenty tablets in front of Raymond, who picked it up and looked inside. He didn't seem impressed.

David grinned. 'Doesn't look much, Ray, but prepare to have your entire perception of reality changed.'

'How many of these does it take?' Raymond asked.

'One will rewire your brain,' Andy said. 'I once took two and had to take a few barbiturates after about three hours to take the edge off the trip. I couldn't handle it any longer.'

'There are twenty here,' Raymond said. 'Is that a dangerous dose?'

'Enough to put you in a rubber room,' David said.

'Good,' Raymond said. He shook the tiny tablets into the palm of his hand, clapped his hand against his mouth, then put out his tongue so everyone could see the tabs were all there. Then he took a sip from his glass of water and swallowed.

'You're gonna wish you hadn't done that, man,' Derek said.

Maybe it'll knock some sense into him, Andy thought, and said, 'They'll start working in about half an hour. Inside ninety minutes you'll be walking in Wonderland.'

'And you'll be there till three weeks next Wednesday,' David assured him. 'When the pub shuts we'll take you to the park and sit it out with you. You won't be in any fit condition to find your own way there. You're going to need someone's help, believe me. For the first few hours, anyway.'

Raymond began to roll a cigarette. 'You'll be able to tell if it's working, will you?' he asked.

'Sure,' Andy said. 'You'll probably start drooling and screaming, the amount you've put away. You'll see stuff that isn't there. You won't see things that are there.'

Jane rolled a strong joint and let Raymond smoke most of it. A good spliff would accelerate the effects of the acid. Afterwards Raymond's head should feel like it was going up in a high-speed lift.

Half an hour passed, and Raymond sat and sipped his water and smoked cigarettes. The Jane's Gang waited. From time to time Andy or David asked how Raymond felt. He shrugged and replied, 'No different.'

The barman sounded the bell for last orders at twenty past ten and Raymond was still able to hold a coherent conversation. At ten to eleven the landlord came over and asked them whether or not they had homes to go to because he wanted to lock up.

Half an hour later, in the darkness of the park, Raymond said he was getting tired of waiting and wanted to know if they'd given him the real thing or whether they'd been wasting his time.

'He took the tabs at just after nine, didn't he?' David asked.

Andy nodded. He knew exactly what David was thinking: it was impossible that nothing had happened. It was now after eleven thirty. Raymond simply had to have gone up. He should have been gazing around in wonder. He should have been at least a little confused. But he just sat there and smoked and sighed with boredom.

Which means, Andy thought, *that he's now going to demand we keep our side of the bargain and go with him to the haunted ruins.*

At midnight, Raymond said, 'Well, folks, what do you know?'

'It's working?' Derek asking eagerly.

Ray shook his head. 'Nope. Nothing's happening, just as I predicted. In a while I'm going to get up and go home. You've given me the works and now it's my turn to give them to you. I'll meet you on Friday. Midnight. You know where to come. Take the art.'

Andy found he wasn't the only member of the Jane's Gang who didn't much fancy meeting Raymond in the Holy Ghost ruins at midnight on Friday. The fact that the acid hadn't worked on him had spooked everyone and they had developed various theories as to why nothing had happened, the major one of which was that 'the art' was black magic. And black magic was something no one wanted to fuck around with. Even Jane had been scared.

On Friday and Saturday nights they stayed away from the Royal Exchange. On Sunday they went to see Kevin Ayres and the Whole World at the Victoria Palace Theatre and stayed over with some friends of Andy's. On Monday there was business to do in town and they rented rooms at a hotel in the Strand. On Tuesday, the meeting with Raymond seemed long ago and far away and David and Katie flew out from Heathrow to Amsterdam to talk to their Dutch distributor, Jacqui and Jane went to Northampton to visit a couple they hadn't seen since India, Derek went to see what was happening at the lab and Andy went to interview Timothy Leary at the Hilton. He got on the train home feeling pleased with himself. He'd been last on Leary's list of interviewers and the man had taken a shine to him. He'd come away with enough taped material for a series of articles.

The feeling of elation evaporated when he stepped down from the train and on to the platform. Raymond was there, evidently waiting for him. Andy tried to blend in with the crowd of commuters, but with hair almost to his waist and dressed in dazzling colours it was hard to lose himself amongst city types in suits. Keeping low, Andy worked his way through the throng and made it to the steps without being collared. He went out past the ticket collector and stepped out into the sunshine feeling relief.

And was flung up against a wall. His head bounced off it and a bright white light flared before his eyes. He felt his shoulder bag fall and heard the thump of his tape machine hitting the ground.

'You let me down,' Raymond said, as Andy's eyes cleared.

Andy glanced down. Everything that had been in his bag was now out of his bag.

Ray's fist was still buried in Andy's T-shirt. He dragged Andy away from the wall and pushed him back, hard. People were flooding out of the station, but no one was taking any notice of what was going on here.

'Help me!' Andy cried.

And the palm of Raymond's hand whacked into his crotch. The pain was tremendous.

'Shut up,' Raymond said, holding him against the wall, 'or I'll do it again. And if I do that, the next time you feel like fucking one of those gorgeous girlfriends of yours will be somewhere around the turn of the century. Got me?'

Andy blinked back tears. He managed to nod. He glanced helplessly at the people leaving the station. No one appeared to be able to *see* what was going on under their noses.

'You let me down, little boy, didn't you?'

Andy nodded again. It felt like someone had inserted knitting needles into his testes. The pain was growing worse.

Raymond trod on the tape that had fallen from the recorder and Timothy Leary's thoughts on life, and ways and means of escaping from it, crunched under the heel of his boot.

Andy moaned. Raymond's strong hand pulled him away from the wall and thumped him back again. Andy's head hit the wall and his jaws clacked together, catching the edge of his tongue.

'Do you remember what I said would happen if you let me down?' Raymond asked.

'Yes,' Andy said.

'I said you'd wish you'd died and gone to hell. Do you wish that?'

'Yes,' Andy replied.

'Liar!' Raymond spat, and the palm of his free hand slapped into Andy's crotch again. 'You just wish I'd died when you fed me all that crap the other day, don't you?'

All Andy could do was wheeze in agony. He just wished Raymond would kill him now and get it all over and done with.

'I know you did,' Raymond said. 'But I didn't die, did I? I didn't get carted off to the loony bin, either. Nothing happened at all, did it? Say "no sir"!'

'No, thir,' Andy lisped. He swallowed blood from his bitten tongue, but it was the pain from his crotch that had brought tears to his eyes.

'You were supposed to meet me. Remember that?'

Andy couldn't speak.

'Of course you do,' Raymond said, wagging his forefinger in Andy's face in admonishment. 'And you didn't come, did you? None of you came. But never mind, because I bring glad tidings. Rejoice! Can you do that?'

Andy shook his head.

'Oh yes you can,' Raymond said, and his finger found a length of Andy's hair and wound into it until it pulled tightly. 'Say "rejoice",' Raymond said, curling his finger into his fist. Before Andy could speak he yanked downwards. A clump of hair tore from the side of Andy's head, just above his ear. The pain was tremendous. Andy cried out.

'That'll do,' Raymond said. 'The good news is this: it doesn't matter that you didn't turn up on Friday. It doesn't matter because nothing would have happened if you had. The focus of the power has changed, you see. We'd all have been wasting our valuable time.'

Andy heard another cassette break as Raymond stood on it.

'So I don't have to harm you for not coming,' he said, and grinned. 'I don't have to, but I like doing it anyway. But you're not going to hospital today though, because your uncle Raymond is giving you another chance. You assemble all your forces and bring them to the new location and I'll be happy with that. And guess what? You don't even have to come until Friday. That gives you plenty of time to get your friends ready.'

Andy moaned. At that moment he would have agreed to anything just to get rid of Raymond.

'I take it that was yes?' Raymond asked, his left hand forefinger finding another length of Andy's hair to twine round itself. He tugged gently. 'Midnight. At my new place. You listening?' He yanked a little harder. Another clump of hair was dragged from his scalp – along with some skin, judging from the agony that followed. 'Only you look as if you're not quite here with me,' Raymond said. 'That'd probably be those dumb drugs you keep taking, keeping you half asleep. Allow me to wake you up.'

Andy saw Raymond's fist bunch and tensed as the man's hand yanked downwards.

'Yes,' Andy gasped.

'Good, because I'm going to tell you where to come and I don't want you to forget. The address is fifty-two May Street. I know you know where that is because I've seen you coming and going down that way. Your pal Derek lives there, doesn't he? No need to answer that question. Just answer this one. What's the address?'

'May Street,' Andy moaned, a distant part of him wishing he had a gun. 'Fifty-two.'

'Remember it,' Raymond said. 'This is your last chance. I know you're a peace-loving man, so if you want to be able to remember what being pain-free and peaceful was like, you'd better turn up.

Because I'm not very patient and you and your friends have tested me to the limit. And that's not a thing you should do to a son of the devil. Understand!'

Andy understood.

'Close your eyes,' Raymond said, 'because I'm going to give you a little demonstration of how bad it'll feel if you don't turn up.'

Andy closed his eyes, and when Raymond's hand left his hair he tensed, certain that he was going to receive a kick in the bollocks or a punch in the stomach. Ten seconds passed, during which he was certain he was going to die of terror. A few moments later he dared to open his eyes.

Raymond was gone.

'We should report him to the police,' Jacqui said, two days later. Andy's scalp was still tender – there were two scabbed patches where his hair had been yanked out.

'Can't,' Andy said, wincing as Jane dabbed TCP on his head wounds. 'First thing he'd do is spill his guts about the acid trade. They might not believe him, but they'd sure as shit check us out. They'd ask around. Someone would finger us, I bet.'

'We could always leave for a while,' Jane said. 'The six of us. Get out of town – out of the country, even. Just pack up and go.'

'And the police would be waiting for us when we came back,' Andy said.

'Then what do we do?' Jacqui asked.

'Christ knows,' Andy said. 'What we need is someone who could take him on. Give him a dose of his own medicine. Put him in hospital for a while or something. Trouble is, we don't know anyone like that.'

'Are we going to meet him at the house in May Street?' Jacqui asked worriedly.

'What do you think?' Andy asked, raising his eyebrows.

'I thought maybe you and David and Derek could . . . y'know . . . overpower him.'

'Beat him up? Shit, Jacq, I've never hit anyone in my life. This guy is a street fighter.'

'And a master of the art, too,' Jane said. 'And a son of the devil.'

Andy snorted. 'Any self-respecting devil would disown that kind of son.'

'We should kill him,' Jacqui said.

'Nice idea, Jacq,' Andy said. 'Go fetch the breadknife and I'll go out and do it right now.'

'Isn't that rather extreme?' Jane said, smiling.

'He deserves it.' Jacqui glowered.

'He does,' Andy said. 'But I don't think it'll happen somehow. People like that don't get murdered. They just stay around for ever being a pain.'

Out in the hall, the telephone rang. Jacqui went to answer it.

When she came back tears were welling in her eyes.

'What is it?' Andy asked.

'That was Derek. He wants someone to pick him up. He's in the hospital. Several of the bones in his left foot are broken.' She began to cry.

'What did he do?' Andy said, as Jane went to Jacqui and took her in her arms.

'It wasn't what *he* did,' Jacqui said. 'It was what that Raymond did to him.'

David and Katie didn't arrive back at Jane's house until ten to midnight on Saturday. Carrying twenty-five thousand pounds in Dutch banknotes, they'd travelled back from Amsterdam by boat and passed through Customs without being pulled. The trip had been successful. David was beginning to think that the members of the Jane's Gang really were charmed.

He changed his mind about that less than three minutes after paying the taxi-driver and giving Katie a long soul-kiss of congratulation.

A tall hedge ran along the front of Jane's property and at the left of the hedge lay the short gravel drive to the house. Tonight the gates were closed and Jane's latest acquisition, a Mercedes convertible, was parked near the house. The upstairs lights were on.

'Home free!' Katie said, opening the gate and waiting for David to come in.

Which was when Raymond appeared round the side of the car. David's first thought was to run for it, but Katie had frozen and Raymond was almost on her. She gave a small shriek as Raymond grabbed the front of her dress, pulled her towards him and effortlessly kicked out her legs from beneath her. She fell face first into the gravel and as Raymond passed, heading towards David, he stamped on her lower back. Katie jolted and her remaining breath left her in a short moan of pain.

It all happened so quickly, and so quietly, that David could barely believe it was happening at all. He balled a fist and, as Raymond swept towards him, drew it back and let it fly. David wasn't a big man, and several years of regular amphetamine intake had made him matchstick-thin, but he was fairly strong and this was a good punch. He knew it, the moment he swung it. It connected squarely with the side of Raymond's jaw. The impact jarred painfully down his arm and he knew that his knuckles would be skinned, but the feeling of that blow being struck seemed like the most satisfying moment of his life.

Raymond went down like a felled tree.

'You motherfucker!' David hissed, rubbing his knuckles. He moved closer, intending to give the man a good kick in the ribs. This was a mistake. Raymond shimmied across the ground, grabbed David's leg, levered himself upright and ducked as David threw another punch, which missed.

A moment later, David's legs were entangled and he was falling. Then Raymond was on his chest, his knees pinning down David's arms. David tried to flip him off by flicking his hips up, but the man was too heavy. 'Lemme go, you fucker!' he hissed.

'You gonna shut up and listen?' Raymond asked.

'Fuck off,' David said.

Raymond reached behind him. David felt the man's hand rest lightly on his cock and balls. 'Just checking where everything is,' Raymond said, and lifted his hand. A second later, two sharp blows powered in.

David felt as if someone had taped dynamite to his dick and blown it up. His knees curled up as the agony rose to his abdomen. For the next thirty seconds there was nothing in the universe but pain.

'That's for being a naughty boy,' Raymond said. 'You didn't come to May Street last night when you were supposed to. Come to think of, you didn't turn up at the Holy Ghost, either. But I'll let you off on that count.'

David was in too much pain to understand what he was saying.

Raymond's face loomed closer. 'Can you hear me yet?' he said. 'Nod if you can.'

David nodded. Somewhere out of his field of vision he could hear gravel shifting, which meant that Katie was getting up.

Raymond twisted round. 'Stay down where I put you, lover,' he said. 'Or I'll have to put you back there again – and this time I'll break your back so you *can't* get up.'

'Run, Katie,' David croaked, and didn't see the big hand flashing down towards him. His vision flicked out and his head filled with bright lights and a high-pitched whistle. Somewhere out there in the darkness that lay beyond him, he felt a weight lift from his chest. A few seconds later, his ears cleared and he heard a slap, a sharp squeal from Katie and the sound of tearing material.

Got to get up! David thought. And then it was too late because Raymond was back, his boot on David's sternum.

When David's head cleared, Raymond was waving a wad of large-denomination guilder notes. 'I wondered why your woman was wearing a panty-girdle when she doesn't need one,' he said. 'I think you owe me this much, at least. I've left her with about half as a gesture of my goodwill.' He pressed harder on David's breastbone. 'But my goodwill is running out. And I need a penance from you two to appease me. So I'm taking your money. And the girl is going to pay in blood. You can watch. And although that'll even things out a little between us, you folks are still in my debt. You didn't keep your side of the bargain and, until you do, this stuff will carry on. And, trust me, I know how to make it worse. Now, I'm gonna say this once. You make a noise, I stamp on your throat and you never make anything louder than a squeak again. Got that?'

David nodded. He was on the point of blacking out again.

'Put your right arm up.'

David did as he was told. Something cold and metallic closed around his wrist and tightened until it bit his skin. The pressure on his chest left and he sucked in a deep breath. Raymond yanked him to his feet by the handcuff. Katie was sprawled on the gravel and at first David thought she was dead. She was still wearing her dress, but it had been torn to strips and the panty-girdle lay beside her.

'You—' he said, and Raymond's hand clamped on his mouth. Raymond dragged him to Jane's Mercedes, fastened the other cuff around the door handle and made David sit. Then he took off his bootlace tie, pulled a dirty handkerchief from his trouser pocket and stuffed it into David's mouth. He wound the tie round David's head to hold the gag in place, then pinched David's nostrils shut. 'See how easy it would be for me to kill you?' he asked, and let go. 'Sit still and watch. And learn.'

While David gazed up at the lit window in the house, willing Jane to look out and see what was going on down here so she could summon help, Raymond went over to Katie, sat her up, then pulled her to her feet. The right side of her face was grazed and bleeding and her eye was swollen. He dragged her across and sat her down beside David. She was barely conscious.

'Now, I'll tell you what I told loverboy here,' he said to her. 'I've got some of your money but I need more to balance us up. I need a blood penance. Just a simple token.'

'Haven't you hurt us enough?' Katie said thickly.

'I've hurt loverboy here enough,' Raymond said. 'I hit him in the two places it hurts most – the pocket and the crotch. But *you* aren't done with.' He felt up the lapel of his drape-jacket, then used his fingernails to tweeze out something that was embedded in the cloth.

The needle glinted as Raymond drew it out. It was almost as long as his forefinger. He handed it to Katie and warned her not to drop it, then pulled a silver thimble from his inside jacket pocket. 'You're gonna need this too,' he said, handing it to her.

'You want me to sew on a button?' Kate asked contemptuously.

Ray smiled. 'No, I want you to take that needle, insert it into the tip of your finger and use the thimble to push it down through the bone as far you can make it go. That's your penance.'

'You're joking, of course,' Katie said. She held out the needle to the side of her and dropped it in the gravel.

'It's a pity you didn't wait until I'd finished explaining,' Raymond said. 'Because now you've got yourself a big problem. If you'd been patient enough to wait, I'd have told you this. When you insert the needle, you're not to make any loud noise, and while you're doing it, to make sure you drive it in all the way, and to make sure you don't make any noise, I'm gonna be holding loverboy's nose. See, if I hold it like *this*, he can't breathe. Which means, starting now, you have about three minutes or so to find that needle and stick it in your finger before David here passes out. Three minutes after that and the oxygen starvation will see to it that his brain's never the same again. A few minutes more and he'll be a dead duck. So you'd better get searching, sweetheart.'

David was counting off seconds while Katie scrabbled about for the needle she'd dropped. He'd realized what was coming and had breathed in deeply several times before Raymond squeezed his nostrils shut. But David had never managed to hold his breath longer than sixty-three seconds, and that was before he'd begun to smoke.

Twenty-five had already elapsed.

Run away, Katie! he thought, trying to contact her telepathically. If Katie made a break for it, Raymond would run after her. But Katie didn't hear. She was trying frantically to find the needle.

Thirty-three, David counted, trying to ignore the growing urge to take a breath. *Thirty-four. Thirty-five.* The air in his lungs was gradually escaping through the handkerchief in his mouth and when that was gone there wasn't going to be any more.

Jane! Jane, where are you?

Thirty-eight, thirty-nine.

His lungs were starting to burn.

Beside him, Katie snatched at something on the ground.

She'll never do it. She hates needles. How did he know that?

Katie looked at the needle, then at Raymond, then glanced sideways at David, who rolled his eyes.

'I can't do it,' she sobbed.

'Loverboy's counting,' Raymond said. 'What are we up to now, David? Forty? Fifty?'

Katie glanced at David again and shook her head. David had seen that expression before and knew it meant: *I'm sorry, David, I can't do this, not even for you.*

The burning sensation in his lungs was increasing. In a few seconds it was going to feel like a raging inferno in his chest.

Forty-six, forty-seven. Forty-eight.

And David had an idea. All he had to do was turn his head rapidly to one side. Raymond wasn't pinching his nose hard, just enough to stop him breathing. By the time Raymond caught him again, he'd be able to keep himself going for another minute.

Katie was now looking at the needle and the tip of her finger.

Fifty-three. Fifty-four.

David snapped his head to one side and, as Raymond's fingers parted company with his nostrils, sucked in hard.

'Now that's *cheating*,' Raymond said, and hit him in the stomach.

David lost all the air in his lungs. And before he could draw another breath, Raymond's fingers closed off his nostrils. This time he held on tight and steadied David's face with his other hand.

'He's lost all his air now,' Raymond told Katie. 'You'd better hurry.'

David's ears begin to ring and the small dark spot that was growing in the centre of his brain, expanded.

His vision fading, he turned his eyes towards Katie, who was either going to kill him or save him.

Katie held out her forefinger and rested the point of the needle against it. She winced as she pushed the needle into her skin, but she didn't make a sound. A bead of blood gathered at the tip of her finger and fell.

'Long way to go yet.' Raymond's voice echoed inside David's head.

David blacked out.

*

The window was open in the master bedroom of her house and Jane heard the taxi arrive. David and Katie were chatting happily to one another as they came in through the gate and closed it behind them. Then she heard other noises as Raymond leapt out from wherever he'd been hiding and began to attack them.

All this had happened because she'd forgotten to close one window in the house, one tiny fanlight out of eighteen. One tiny fanlight, hidden behind the venetian blind in the kitchen, was all it had taken. The doors were all locked but because of that tiny mistake she might as well have left them wide open.

He'd got in – and she hadn't heard a thing.

Jane didn't become aware that someone was in her house until a strong arm took her round the neck and toppled her backwards from her chair. Her head hit the hard parquet floor and stars lit before her eyes. Then she was back on her feet, still dazed, and Raymond was glowering into her face, his nose pressing hard against her own, his breath hot on her mouth. He gazed into her eyes, then pulled back. He didn't utter a word, just buried his hands in her hair and dragged her out of the room along the hall towards the staircase. Jane knew what was going to happen. He was going to get her upstairs and rape her. But someone like Raymond wasn't going to be content just to fuck her, she was sure. He would kill her too.

He dragged her into the master bedroom and turned on the light, but he didn't throw her on the bed as she'd expected he would. He led her past it, then, with his foot, turned the wooden dining-room chair in front of the dressing table so it faced into the room. He sat her on it.

'The mirror's right behind you now,' he said, letting go of her hair. 'You won't get any help that way.'

Jane didn't know what he meant.

'You're probably wondering why I'm here,' Raymond said. 'I'm here because I know where you live. Not in terms of your address, but in terms of *here*.' He jabbed a forefinger into the centre of her chest. 'I'm here because *you're* the fly in the ointment. The leader of the gang. You're its spiritual master. You won't understand any of this now, of course, but you soon will. I'll make sure you understand.'

He reached out, curled his fingers into the neck of her cheese-cloth dress and tugged hard. Jane fell forward and was thrust back. When she looked up, Raymond had a straight razor in his hand.

'No!' she croaked.

He grinned. He pulled the front of her dress taut and sliced the razor down it. Then he closed the razor, pocketed it and ripped the dress all the way down the front. He sighed. 'I didn't think you sexy hippy chicks wore underwear,' he said, hooked his forefinger into the band between the cups of Jane's bra and pulled. The straps bit into Jane's shoulders and back and burned her skin as they stretched tight, but Raymond held her still and pulled harder. Jane cried out. It felt as if the back strap was going to saw right through her flesh rather than break but at last the clasp gave and the bra came off. Jane sobbed. She could feel blood trickling down her back.

'Quiet!' Raymond warned. 'And sit up straight or I'll show you what pain really means.'

Jane did as she was told. Raymond leaned down and planted a kiss on her lips, then grinned. 'You'd better just hope your knickers come off a little easier,' he said.

They did. But not without leaving burns on her hips and high on the insides of her thighs.

'I bet you're not feeling quite so clever now, are you?' Raymond picked up her dress, took out the razor again and sliced strips of material from it.

'Some of the others will be here soon,' Jane said.

Raymond looked up from his work. 'I hope so,' he replied. 'I really do.'

'Let me go,' she said. 'I won't say anything.'

Raymond ignored her.

'Do you want to fuck me?' she asked shakily.

Raymond sliced a long, straight strip from the dress and laid it on the bed. He didn't seem to have heard her.

Jane leaned forward, tensing. The bedroom door was open. All she had to do was spring up and run. If she could make it past Raymond, she was free. And, miracle of miracles, he'd moved a little further to her left, giving her an escape corridor about four feet wide.

'Don't even think about it,' Raymond said, not looking up from his work. 'I'd catch you before you made it to the stairs. And then I'd have to hurt you.'

Jane began to sob. Raymond seemed not to notice.

'Look,' she said finally, 'if you want to fuck me, why don't you just do it? You don't need to tie me up. I won't fight you. Just get it over with.'

Raymond looked up and grinned. 'Oh, I'm gonna fuck you all right,' he said. 'But not in the way you think.'

'What do you mean?' Jane asked. She could barely hear her voice over the sound of her heart hammering in her ears.

'You'll see.' Raymond sat down. 'Now sit against the back of that chair, nice and upright, and put your arms behind your back. Good girl. Shows off your tits to good advantage, doesn't it?' He went behind her and bound her wrists together, tied them to the back of the chair, and secured her ankles to the legs. Then he waved the razor at her and chuckled. 'You're gonna settle your deal with me,' he said. 'You bring your gang down to May Street, like you agreed, and I leave you alone. You refuse, I fuck you. I fuck you and all your cronies. I fuck you all night and all day. And I keep fucking you till you make good. No one welches on deals with me.'

He laid the cutting edge of the razor against Jane's cheek. 'See, when I say I'm gonna fuck you, I don't mean fuck in the sexual sense. You can forget that kind of fuck in ten minutes. I mean the painful kind of fuck – a gash down this sweet little cheek, for instance.' He moved the razor to her breast. 'Or I could take off a nipple. Or I could fuck you in any number of other ways. And I will. Trust me, darling. I'm up to the job. I love my work.'

He shifted position slightly. 'See, you're pure in heart, little Janie. And that's important to me. That's why we need you.'

'We?' Jane asked.

'The others, well, they're just fine, but they're not honest the way you are. They'd lie and cheat and do deals and double-cross. What you have inside you is worth a thousand of them. You're a girl in a million, Janie. It's there, in your heart.'

Jane shook her head. 'I'm no different from anyone else,' she said.

'But you *are*,' Raymond said. 'You are because you know you can't back out on your deal.'

'Fuck the deal,' Jane spat, finding her temper and losing it again. 'We only said that stuff because we thought you wanted to hurt us. And we were right, weren't we? You do mean us harm. We said those things just because we wanted shot of you. What we said meant nothing.'

'Words, once said, can't be *un*said.' Raymond smiled. 'You made a deal. In normal life you might think a deal like that wasn't worth shit, but it just so happens that with me any deal is binding.'

'If we come to May Street, you'll kill us,' Jane said.

Raymond laughed long and hard. 'Is that what you think?' he spluttered. 'Is that what you really think? Listen, honey child, I could kill you now if I wanted to.'

'Then what do you want from us?'

'You take the art,' Raymond said.

'The black art?'

'Life's what we make it,' he replied.

'What's at the house on May Street?' Jane asked. 'What's special there? What do you want to show us?'

'Miracles,' Raymond whispered. 'Power beyond belief ... Sounds like a pile of horse shit, doesn't it?'

Jane said nothing.

'Fact is, I'm not just doing this for you, I'm doing it for me, too. See, the devil's down there in that May Street house and he's charged me with a task. I don't get my paws on what I want until I deliver what he wants. And he wants you and your friends. He's always wanted you, though. Ever since you appeared in this world he's wanted you. See, I told you you were something special.'

Jane sighed. 'The devil,' she said.

'Himself,' Raymond replied.

'OK, you leave us alone, we'll come. That's a promise.'

Raymond laughed. 'He hasn't given me everything I want yet, but he has given me one or two gifts to make my work a little easier. One of those is the power of sight. I can see right through the most opaque lie. And you're lying. I know you don't mean a word of that, but there's something I can do, something I'm *gonna* to do, that'll make you say that again and mean it.' He got up and picked up the razor. 'This won't hurt a bit,' he said, and wound his fingers into Jane's hair.

Raymond lied. It *did* hurt. It hurt when he pulled her hair, but not much. He was careful as he cut it off, but after he'd gone to the bathroom and come back with a can of shaving foam and a jug of water and started to shave her head his hand started to shake a little and he nicked her scalp many times. When he turned her round so that she could inspect his work in the mirror, her face was striped with streaks of blood. And she was bald, but for the bushy swastika he'd shaped on her head. Jane looked at herself in the mirror and tears began to run from her eyes, streaking the blood on her cheeks.

Raymond turned her to face him. He looked pleased with himself. 'I should have been a hairdresser,' he said. 'Now, this is how you fuck someone good and proper ... Oops, hang on. I'll have to move you away from the mirror before I do this. Wouldn't do to end up doing it to myself too, now, would it?'

He dragged Jane and chair aside, then covered the mirror with a sheet. 'That's better,' he said, returning to where she sat. 'Now, I'm gonna fuck you. And it's going to hurt.'

Jane tensed as Raymond put his hand around her throat. One of the fingers of his other hand found the central point of the swastika he'd shaved into her head and pressed hard. Jane felt a surge of heat crawl out across her scalp and what was left of her hair prickled erect.

'Wh—' Her voice was choked off as Raymond's grip tightened around her throat. The blood pressure rose in her head and her skull felt as if it would burst open and spew out her brain. Black dots pulsed in her eyes. Before her, Raymond appeared to be concentrating deeply.

'Listen to me,' he growled. 'Listen.'

His grip tightened. Jane's lungs began to protest. And on the crown of her head, Raymond's finger seemed to be growing hotter still – more like a red-hot poker than human flesh.

'I'm giving you a gift,' Raymond murmured. 'A very special gift.'

Jane's eyes ceased to see. Dark blue shapes with yellow edges careened before her, bursting into fragments. Her ears rang and her head felt like an overripe melon in a vice. But she could still hear Raymond's voice.

'Take this,' he said. 'Take this potential. Take this potential brain tumour. Brain tumour!'

And, beneath the burning heat of his finger, a tiny spot of cold spiralled down into Jane's head.

Then his hands were off her and she was gasping and coughing and crying and all the while she could feel the cold he'd put in her. It stayed long after the sensation of burning at her scalp had gone, long after Raymond had gone and long after the pain in her throat had subsided.

And it was still there now, as she sat tied to her chair listening to Raymond working his magic on Katie and David out in the drive. A thin coil of cold, still burrowing into her like an icy worm.

'That's how you fuck people.' Raymond had laughed. 'And that's what you get when you don't do deals. If you don't follow through and keep your promise, you'll grow a nice healthy tumour that'll eat everything it sees and you'll die. I can't take it out again now that it's there, but *he* can. So you have to keep your promise, don't you? I want you there at midnight on Friday. Check the writing on the wall for instructions. Now make that promise again.'

And after she did, he'd left.

Friday wasn't merely the thirteenth, but it was a full moon too.

The Jane's Gang had arranged to meet in the Royal Exchange at ten, but Andy, Derek and David said they had a few things to take care of. When the door opened at almost eleven, only Andy and Derek were there. They were pale, and seemed too good-humoured and confident for Jane's liking.

'What you have been up to?' she whispered. She was feeling better since the cold feeling inside her head had faded and vanished, but her throat was badly bruised and she was hoarse. She was upset that she had to wear the cloche hat each time she left her house: Katie had shaved off the swastika, but Jane couldn't adjust to being bald. And there was the dark scab in the crown of her skull, too. It looked a little nasty – exactly as it would if someone had dug a dirty fingernail into her scalp. Which, Jane had almost convinced herself, was all that had happened. People couldn't give you tumours, even potential ones.

'Nothing,' Andy replied.

'And where's David?' Katie snapped.

'You're straight?' Jacqui demanded. 'Even you, Derek?'

Derek rolled his eyes. 'We gathered at my place,' he said. 'We just wanted to keep an eye on number fifty-two. All we've had is a couple of shots of whisky each for Dutch courage. David's still down there. We wanted to know if Raymond was going to be alone or if he was bringing a gang or something.'

Andy and Derek exchanged glances and sat down.

'What aren't you telling us?' Jane asked. 'Did Raymond turn up? Was he alone?'

'He hadn't arrived when we left,' Andy said, picking up Jacqui's Bacardi and Coke and sipping it. 'Either he's been inside since before we went to Derek's or he's not there.'

'Did you check for a message? The writing on the wall thing?' Katie asked.

Andy nodded. 'Nothing written on the wall of number fifty-two,' he said. 'But at the end of the street, where it joins Brook Street, instructions have been chalked.'

'It says,' Derek said, picking up his lighter and lighting up, '"Fifty-two. Ray. In culvert."'

'Meaning?' Jacqui asked.

'That the house number is fifty-two. Although how we could forget, I don't know. That this is a message from Ray, and that the message is: In culvert,' Derek said.

'What the fuck is *that* supposed to mean?' Katie snapped.

'Relax,' Andy said. 'David checked and the door's locked. The key is in the drain outside the house. The culvert. He checked that, too.'

'Which means Raymond's already inside,' Jacqui said.

Andy shrugged. 'He may have two keys. I don't really understand this key thing. If he's going to be there ahead of us, he can't put the key back in the culvert. And if he's going to be there already when we arrive, why can't he just leave the door open?'

'Intent,' Jane said. 'We have to enter of our own accord. Having to find the key and use it is significant. It means we didn't just blunder in by mistake. It means we're keeping our side of the bargain.'

'What if he's got a shotgun?' Katie said. 'He could kill us all, easily.'

'He could just as easily have killed us all already,' Jane said, touching the crown of her head through her hat, 'but he hasn't, has he? He really believes all this supernatural stuff. He's delivering us to the devil.'

Derek took Jane's hand. 'Don't worry, it'll be cool,' he said. 'Nothing will happen.'

'Yes, folks, it's cool day,' Katie said, rolling her eyes. 'Make that Kool with a K. Kool Day, the day that things get put right. The day we keep our side of the bargain and nothing happens and Raymond leaves us alone for ever. Long live Kool Day. I'll drink to that!' She raised her glass and sipped some wine.

'Katie thinks we're in trouble if we go,' Jacqui explained, needlessly.

'We're in trouble if we don't,' Andy said. 'Might as well get it over and done with.'

'I'd like to stay out of it,' Jacqui said.

'We all would,' Derek said. 'But how can we? We have to do this.'

'I just wish we could guarantee we'd be free from that bastard for the rest of our lives,' Jacqui said. 'I've never wished anyone dead before, but I wish *he* would die.'

Andy took her hand. 'He didn't attack you, Jacqui,' he said. 'But he will, if we don't do as he says.'

'Come on,' Jane said, getting up. 'It's gone eleven. Let's go back to Derek's and get ready.'

At five minutes to midnight the Jane's Gang left Derek's house and stepped out on May Street. No other people were around and the majority of the householders had gone to bed. Only a few houses still had lights burning.

'Here we go,' Andy said, a tremor in his voice.

'Let's just get it done, shall we?' David said. 'The sooner we get in there, the sooner we can get back to normal.' He turned on the torch he was carrying and shone it along the walls of the houses on the other side of the road. 'At least we'll be able to see what we're doing,' he said, and gave the torch to Derek. 'You'd better carry this,' he said.

Jane noticed the exchange of looks between the men but didn't comment.

'You got a bad back?' Katie asked David. 'You're walking funny.' She moved towards him, but David brushed her aside.

'I'm fine,' he said. 'Leave me alone.'

Jane frowned. That didn't sound like David. But they were all jittery, she supposed. None of them knew what to expect. Except that it was quite likely to turn into a scene from a horror movie: mad Raymond wanting to sacrifice them to his own personal devil. This wasn't going to happen. Jane was carrying a razor in the back pocket of her jeans and if Raymond so much as spat when she didn't expect him to, she intended to have a good crack at removing his face with it. These people were her friends and, in a way, she was responsible for them. After all, it was her that Raymond wanted. She had volunteered to go alone, but the others wouldn't let her. And if they insisted on coming, she had to try to protect them.

Raymond was wrong about my soul, she thought. *It's not pure. There's a murderess lurking inside me.*

'Here we are,' Andy said, trying to sound jolly and failing miserably.

They stopped outside the derelict house, gazing at the broken, boarded windows, at the dark front door.

'I'll get the key,' Andy said, and knelt beside the grating. It opened easily. The key was on a ledge about two feet down. In his hands it felt abnormally cold.

'So we're all clear on what we do if trouble starts?' Andy said.

Everyone nodded. The plan was to leave the door open so that if Raymond went into psycho mode they could run for it. If things went according to plan, though, he wasn't going to get a chance to go into any mode. Andy, David and Derek had it all planned.

'I'll go first,' Derek said. 'I've got the torch.'

'Check through the windows and make sure he's not in either of the front rooms before we go inside,' Andy said.

Derek shone the torch into the house. 'Nothing in either,' he said. 'Just junk.'

Andy thought he heard the house make a sound as he inserted the key in the lock. A sigh that sounded like one of satisfaction. He shrugged it off. Your mind played tricks at times like this when your body was pumped full of adrenaline.

The key turned easily. Andy pushed the door, which didn't seem to want to open and which creaked too loudly when it did.

'Well, if he's inside, he knows we're here,' Andy said, sniffing the damp, musty smell and wondering where the undertone of bonfire smoke came from.

Derek shone the torch down the hallway and up the stairs. Mildewed paper hung from the walls. Ancient light fittings dangled from lank cables. The stairway was uncarpeted and covered in grime and litter.

'Anyone know whose house this is?' Andy asked.

'It's always been like this,' Derek said. 'At least since I moved in. Guy I met in the shop said there'd been something happen here. Suicide pact between the old people who lived here.'

'Now is not the best time to start making up spooky tales,' Jacqui said.

'Here goes,' Derek said, and, hobbling on his plastered foot, entered the house. 'I'm in,' he said. Nothing terrible happened. The bare floorboards squeaked and his voice echoed in the hallway, but Raymond didn't appear with an axe and ghosts didn't materialize. He opened the door to the room at his left and shone the torch inside. Then he went in.

Andy followed him and the others gathered in the hall.

This room held only junk, as did the right-hand room.

'I can smell flowers,' Katie said.

Jane nodded. She couldn't place the other, powerful, odour that she had detected, though. It was a perfume she knew well. *Which is impossible*, she thought. Andy and Derek were in front of her now, going down the hall towards the back room. Jane already knew that that was where Raymond was. She knew it because she could feel herself being drawn to it, just as her friends were. They were drifting down the hall, like feathers on a gentle breeze.

When the front door slammed behind them, they all gave small screams, followed by embarrassed laughs.

'The draught,' David whispered, even though there wasn't one.

What there *was*, Jane noticed, was the chill in the air that all haunted houses were supposed to have. The further they went down the hall, the colder it got. She could see Derek's breath in the torch beam as he shone it on the door of the back room.

And then Derek didn't need the torch any more because the lights came on as if they were being turned up on a dimmer switch. Even though there were no bulbs in the dangling light fittings.

Jane's skin prickled and crawled.

'Let's get out of here,' Jacqui pleaded, in a terrified voice. 'This isn't right. This can't happen.'

Jane stared at the lights. She could *see* the glowing filaments inside the bulbs that weren't there. 'Perhaps we should go back outside and think about this,' she said, as Jacqui took her hand in a tight grip.

'No,' David said. 'We do what we came here to do. And, anyway, if you were to try that front door I bet it wouldn't open.'

'Please,' Jacqui said, tugging at Jane's arm.

'Stay,' Jane said. 'It'll be OK.'

'It's in here, isn't it?' Derek said, nodding at the door to the back room. 'Raymond's in there. I can tell.'

'For fuck's sake, man, I'm getting the jitters with all this mumbo-jumbo,' David said. 'Let's just walk in like we're supposed to and forget about the haunted-house-of horror tricks. It's all a set-up. That's all. Just cheap magic tricks. Open the fucking door, Del!'

Derek turned the handle, pushed open the door and stood back, as if he expected something to come rushing out at him. Jane couldn't see into the room from where she stood, but she could see the flickering red glow even as David gave a bitter laugh and said, 'Hiya, Ray my old mate,' and went in.

Derek and Andy followed him, with Katie hot on their heels. Jane led Jacqui down the hall and went in after them, her right hand deep in her jacket pocket, her fingers curled around the razor.

The room was empty. But it was hot and it stank and another of David's 'cheap magic tricks' was happening inside. This room was illuminated by the fire that appeared to be burning inside the walls. It looked as if they and the ceiling had been replaced with glass, behind which the fires of hell licked, painting the floorboards with flickering orange light.

Jane glanced behind her and saw that there was no longer a doorway. Off to her right, David was close to one of the burning walls and had taken a pen from his pocket, which he was slowly moving towards the trapped flames. The others were watching him.

The pen touched the flat, glass-like surface and, without resistance, sank through it. When David pulled it back, it was still whole and undamaged but it was glowing as though it were red hot. He knelt and touched the end of the pen to the floorboards. A small fire instantly burst into being and began to move across the floorboards in a curved track. It vanished when David stamped it out.

'Neat trick, isn't it?' a voice said from behind them.

They spun round. There was Raymond, standing half in, half out of the wall of fire. He was naked and sheened with sweat and had the largest, ugliest erection that Jane had ever seen. It was blood red, as thick as her wrist, and curved up further than his navel. It looked as if the outer skin had been removed. Thick dark veins spiralled up its shaft and the bloated end was notched and curved out into the shape of a spear head. A huge dark sac hung beneath, heavy with testes the size of golf balls. Raymond's torso was broad and muscular and he looked younger, more dangerous than a middle-aged drunk had any right to be. He was clutching a sawn-off pump-action shotgun to his chest.

'So, what did you come as tonight, Ray?' David asked. 'The devil himself? I'm sorry, but we didn't know it was fancy dress.'

As Raymond stepped out of the wall, he flickered, making Jane blink. And in the space of that blink, he changed back into the Raymond they all knew and hated so well. He was now fully clothed, but he still had the shotgun.

'Magic night tonight, I see,' David said. 'You'll have to let us know how you do that.'

Raymond chuckled and levelled the gun at David. 'Shut up or I'll blow you away right now,' he said.

'We're here,' Jane said, in a voice that sounded more confident than she felt. What she was seeing here was no optical illusion, she was certain. It was reality. Raymond hadn't been making up garbled stories about 'the art' at all. 'We kept our side of the bargain. Now you have to stop bothering us.'

Raymond turned the gun towards her. 'I stop bothering you when you leave. When you leave this place you won't see me again. For a long time. But while you're here, you do exactly as I say. If you don't, I shoot you. I have permission.'

'What do we have to do?' Katie asked.

Raymond swung the gun round and worked the slide. 'You speak when spoken to, for one thing,' he growled. 'What you have to do is take the art. Like I have. Five of you get to live, for ever if you wish. The sixth goes where she does most good. Don't worry, Katie, you're not the sixth. You're going to be the first. Tell me what you see on the floor, over by the corner to your left.'

Katie looked round. 'A chalk circle,' she said.

'You take off all your clothes and get down on your hands and knees in that circle,' Raymond said. 'And I fuck you. And the one true God fucks you. And if you survive, you'll receive. You'll become one of the six disciples.'

'You said only five of us were going to live,' Andy reminded him.

'I am the sixth. I shall be your master,' Raymond said, without taking his eyes from Katie. 'The one true God wants Jane for a sunbeam and he wants her now. Now, Katie. Take off your clothes.'

'You're joking, of course,' Katie said.

'You undress and kneel in that circle,' Raymond said. 'Or I'll shoot your legs away and I'll fuck you with the shotgun. Do it!'

Katie glanced at David.

David's face was pale and drawn. His eyes glittered in the moving light. Sweat slicked his forehead. 'Do as he says,' he said. 'We don't have any choice.'

'No! I can't!' Katie said, glancing from David to Raymond, then to the others. 'You can't just stand there and let him rape me!' she stuttered.

'Ahh, the sweet taste of betrayal,' Raymond said. 'You see, Katie, your friends know something you don't yet realize. It's better to suffer a little pain now than to suffer the pain of eternal damnation later.' He moved towards her and jabbed her in the belly with the shotgun. 'Undress!' he growled. 'Or I shoot your David. Then the others, one by one. Then you suffer the longest, most painful death you could imagine. And the longest, most agonizing afterlife, too.'

Jane watched Katie take off her jacket and throw it to the floor. Her eyes never left Raymond's as she bent to unlace her shoes, then stood and began to unbutton her shirt. The defiant *hatred* in her eyes frightened Jane. Katie took off her shirt and cast it aside, then placed her hands on her hips. 'Take a good long look at these tits, fuckface,' she spat. 'Because if I have my way, you'll never look at another pair as long as you live.'

Raymond put the barrel of the shotgun against her sternum. 'Jeans,' he said.

Katie unbuttoned and wriggled out of them, dragging her underwear down at the same time. Jane was surprised to see that her pubic hair had been trimmed into the shape of a swastika.

She got down on all fours in the chalk circle, facing the corner of the room. She moved her knees apart and arched her back, then looked over her shoulder. 'This is gonna be the worst fuck I ever had,' she said.

Raymond shucked off his jacket and shirt and undid his trousers one-handed, while with his other hand he pointed the shotgun towards the others. He was naked under his trousers. Jane gasped when she saw that he actually owned the phallus he'd seemed to have when he'd entered the room.

'While I'm fucking your Katie, I'm going to be holding the

shotgun up beneath her,' he said. 'If I hear a movement behind me, just a single movement, I'll pull the trigger. Got that?'

'Got it,' Andy said, in a small voice. The others nodded.

Raymond turned back to Katie.

And Jane saw David's hands reach behind him. Suddenly she understood why he'd been walking as though he had a bad back. He'd had something stuffed down the waistband of his jeans.

In less than a second, he had the claw-hammer out and was crossing the room with it held high.

For Jane, what followed seemed to happen in slow motion. She pulled the razor from her pocket, opened it, saw first the chrome blade flicker orange then a hand reach down and snatch it away from her.

In the centre of the room, Raymond was turning back and starting to duck. David's feet were off the ground now, bent up behind him. His hair was flying out in all directions and his mouth was open in a silent scream of rage. The hammer was on its downstroke.

And Kate was no longer on all fours, but leaping up from the chalk circle, her mouth a screaming O. Spittle was cascading from her lips. The tendons in her neck were standing out like wires and the muscles of her thighs bulged. In her hand was a long silver needle.

On the other side of the room, Andy was approaching Raymond, thrusting something black forward in front of him. As Jane glanced at the black thing, she saw a shiny blade suddenly pop out of the tip.

And Derek hobbled past her holding a breadknife over his head.

For a moment the tableau was frozen: David's feet still off the ground, his hammer an inch from Raymond's brow, Jacqui waving Jane's razor, the other men rushing in with their knives.

The hammer hit Raymond, just above his left eyebrow, and his head cracked open like an egg. Something damp splattered across Jane's face.

Then Raymond was sinking to his knees and steel was being thrust into him from all sides in a flurry of blows and slashes that seemed to go on for ever. Each new thrust brought forth a fresh jet of bright blood, each slash opened a new grinning mouth on another part of his body. As Jacqui moved across him, Jane saw the razor hit the still-erect phallus and the spray of black that jetted from it.

The last thing Jane saw before the scene disappeared was the long silver needle protruding from the pupil of Raymond's right eye.

And then she was alone in the room with the devil.

The devil stood on cloven hooves in the chalk circle, eight feet tall or more. Its flesh was red, its build slender and muscular. A thick pointed tail swished across the floor behind it; its phallus looked exactly as Raymond's had and was erect, dripping thick fluid. Two stubby horns grew from the front of its skull. Its face was oval, the chin pointed with a goatee beard of red hair. It was almost handsome. Its black eyes were awesome, its mouth large and mobile. The teeth behind the lips looked like pearl-white saw-blades.

'I want you,' it grated, and its phallus expanded and quivered.

'You can't have me,' Jane replied, trying not to look into those eyes. A part of her was responding to them, seeing something in them she needed. Something that felt like the safety only a mother could provide and only when you were a baby. Worse still, another part of her was responding to the way the thing's phallus was swelling and contracting as if it had a life of its own. It was the most disgusting thing she'd ever seen and yet a part of her was anticipating the pleasure she would surely have when she impaled herself upon it.

'You owe me,' the devil said. 'And I've wanted you from the moment you appeared on the planet. I love you, Jane. I've loved you always. I loved you as the maker loved you, but my love was tenfold. Give yourself to me and I will pay you with whatever your heart desires.'

'I don't owe you anything,' Jane said, fixing her eyes on the devil's neck so she didn't have to look at its eyes or its phallus.

'You took away my ... representative. Flicked him out of existence. He has no soul. You owe me for that.'

'I didn't touch him,' Jane said.

'But you are responsible, nonetheless,' the devil ground out. 'And I want you. I will pay handsomely. Anything you can imagine can be yours. You may act as my new representative. You may have immortality upon the face of the earth. All power will rest with you. You owe me.'

'I don't deal,' Jane said, mistakenly looking up into those dark eyes and feeling the warmth and peace in them. It was like being home at last. *It wouldn't be so bad*, she heard herself think. *If you could spend eternity feeling that good, it wouldn't be a bad thing at all.*

'It isn't a matter of dealing,' the devil said. 'It's a matter of balance. You took away Raymond. Your friends did as you silently bade them. They acted in accordance with your wishes. You brought a razor with which you intended to . . .'

I'll take his fucking face off with this if I have a chance!

Hearing her private thoughts broadcast in her own inner voice was disconcerting. Jane gasped.

The devil grinned. 'It isn't only the maker who is omniscient,' it said. 'Why do you think he worries about me so much? Why do you think I've gained such a bad name over the ages? After all, I'm no worse than the maker. You'll feel no better with him than with me. We're equals, after all. Now, about this debt.'

'I don't think I have a debt to you,' Jane said.

'You do have a debt, whether you *think* you have or not. You also have a brain tumour biding its time. Only I can remove it. Oh, the maker could remove it too, but . . .' the devil grinned '. . . he's never around when you want him, is he?'

'If I die, you won't get my soul,' Jane said.

The devil smiled. Its phallus lengthened. 'If you deal, you won't have to die at all,' it said. 'If you deal, you'll be my right hand. You'll be my Jesus. Except that I won't cut you off as the maker did. You'd be able to call on me at any time. For anything. I would love you as if I'd made you myself. You would be my master, in a way. I would be your faithful servant as you were mine.'

'I won't deal. You're trying to trick me.'

The devil shook its head sadly. It reached out and gently took Jane's hands in its clawed fingers. 'I don't trick people. There is no small print. A soul that is mine is as well off as a soul that goes to the maker. And I'm not even asking for your soul. Only for your love.'

'I'm sorry. I can't make a deal with you,' Jane said, trying not to feel the warm current that was trickling from those gentle claws and running through her body.

'I'm sorry too,' the devil said, letting go of her hand. 'You could have experienced such delights. And for eternity. I'll ask you one last time. And before you say no, I'll add that I'm now talking to each of your friends in the same way. It isn't them I want, however, it's you. But all of your friends, Katie, Jacqui, David, Derek and Andy, have accepted my offer. You'll be alone in the world from now.'

Jane shrugged. 'Sorry,' she said.

'You have made your decision. But you have not made good your debt.' The devil sounded angry now. 'The curse that Raymond laid upon you will not be lifted. And in payment for the removal of my emissary, I will have the soul of your firstborn.'

Jane sighed. 'What makes you think I'll *have* a firstborn?' she said. 'Your omniscience?'

The devil smiled. '*If* you have a firstborn,' it said, 'then I will have its soul in payment. And I will make that soul suffer endless torment. Now, sleep, my child. Sleep and rest.'

It was dark when Jane woke and for a few moments she wasn't sure where she was. Then the king-sized headache made itself known to her and she became aware of the foul stench, the sticky substance that coated her skin.

Her hips and the backs of her thighs ached. Her right breast felt sore and her pubic bone felt as if someone had whacked it with a hammer. This was normally a sure sign that she'd spent the night at an orgy.

Listening, and hearing other people's breathing, she put her hand to the floor and felt bare boards.

Where the hell am I? she asked herself, and reached down to move something that was pressing into her hip. When she first touched it, it felt like a fat vibrator, adding to her theory that there had been an orgy. But it was a torch. *A torch?* she thought. She picked it up and shone it at her naked body. When she saw the reddish-brown stuff smeared over her, she began to remember and wished she were dead.

We killed a man, she told herself in dismay. *Last night we came here, to this very room, and we killed a man. We smashed his head open with a hammer and we stabbed him and hacked at him until he was dead. And then . . .*

Jane began to sob silently. What they'd done was beyond belief. What they'd done made them worse than animals. After they'd killed Raymond, they'd celebrated. They'd all taken off their clothes and smeared themselves with Raymond's blood and juices and danced and made love to one another, in turn and together, again and again.

Jane crawled across to the nearest sleeping body and shook it. It felt like Jacqui. 'Wake up,' she shrieked. 'We've got to get out of here. Now!'

The following night, Derek had gone back to 52 May Street, one of his pockets full of nails and a can of spray paint in the other. After an hour's work, the door to the back room of the house was closed for ever, nailed tightly shut so that no one but the most determined person would enter the room. And then he painted swastikas on the door and the walls of the hall, which Jane said would complete the seal.

Since the building had stood empty for years, there was no

reason to believe anyone would want to investigate it, barring kids. And kids wouldn't easily get inside the room where Raymond's body lay.

Time began to pass.

Jane didn't mention her dream of the devil to anyone for two months, and then it was only because Katie brought up the subject. Katie had dreamed a similar dream. She owed the devil for Raymond's death. The devil would take the soul of her firstborn, she said. Katie grinned, remembering that in her dream, she'd managed to barter a better deal out of Big Red, as she called it. In return for the soul of her firstborn she would be allowed to have a successful career as a photographer.

'Of course, I had to fuck it for that,' Katie said. 'But in that dream, it was the ride of my life, I can tell you!'

All of the others had had similar dreams. No one knew what significance they held, if any. No one, including Jane herself, could clearly remember what had happened between entering the house and killing Raymond. None of them was comfortable about that. And they all wished they hadn't had to do it.

'It was an aberration,' Andy explained, on one of the last visits he'd made to her house. He and Jacqui were settling down at Cuckoo Close and seemed happy to be with one another now. 'It was just a momentary aberration brought on by the extreme pressure that Raymond was putting us under. We killed him. But he was going to kill us. It's over and we've got to try to forget it now.'

Time rolled on.

It was the forgetting that began to break up the Jane's Gang. Andy and Jacqui had settled, David and Katie had moved into a new, larger house on the other side of town from May Street. And Derek had fallen in love with Jane and she with him.

The drugs bust, when it came, was out of the blue and on a night when Andy and David were moving a substantial quantity of acid. The squad hit them all at once.

After pleading guilty on all charges, the guys got prison sentences of six years. They were out in two. Jane and Katie got six months and Jacqui was put on probation for two years.

Worse, the money was all taken away.

The three women met only once after they came out of prison. Jane called a meeting at which all three cut their fingers, mingled their blood and swore they would never have children. No one asked why they were making the agreement and no one complained. None of them wanted children, so the deal was easy to agree upon.

Time began to fly by.

As any member of the one time the Jane's Gang would have been pleased to tell you, time was a great healer. And the more that time rolled its endless river past you, the more healed you became. You began to forget the bad old days, found ways and means of setting them aside, burying them in deep, dark places you never intended to revisit.

And when you'd forgotten those things that bothered you, or reduced their perspective by your distance from them, you began to look back and smile and say how dumb you were, when you were younger, to believe such nonsense.

And then you were apt to do things you'd sworn you'd never do. Things you'd forgotten you'd sworn you'd never do. One day you'd wake up and think, *It'd be nice to have a son or a daughter*, and you wouldn't be able to come up with a single reason why you shouldn't.

Chapter Fifteen

The Return of the Fly

Andy snapped awake and experienced the terrible sensation of vertigo he always got when waking up on aeroplanes. Then he realized, with a cold shock, that he *was* on an aeroplane. His mouth felt as if someone had inserted a thick wadge of blotting paper into it while he was asleep. The glass on his seat tray was empty. He was stone cold sober.

What was worse was that he *remembered*. He now remembered everything, even the smell of Raymond's blood as he and Jacqui had rolled in it, giggling like naughty children. Even his conversation with the devil itself.

Where you promised it your firstborn, in return for being allowed to live. In return for getting away with murder.

And Andy remembered something else: the red signals. And what happened before he received those flashes of red that told him he could go home. The break-ins. The porridge-eating. His heart sank.

I did it to keep this from happening all over again. An unconscious part of me knew the time was right when Stevie and Becky and Johnny all met and became friends. Unconsciously I knew the devil would come back for what it was owed. And I worked magic to stop it happening.

He even remembered where the porridge-eating ritual had come from. Jane had summoned him to her hospital bed, the night before they opened her head. Something strange had happened. He'd sat beside her, holding her hand, while Derek went out to smoke a cigarette and Jane had begun to communicate with him without using words. He felt her place something in his mind, something heavy that settled and then felt comfortable. And then she had opened her eyes and said, 'Only you, Andy. This is only for you.'

Andy had left the hospital wondering what had passed between them.

Now, sitting on an aeroplane thirty-five thousand feet above

America, Andy knew what she had placed there. The ritual and the sign.

Why didn't it work? Andy asked himself, and remembered Jacqui telling him that Katie claimed she'd dealt with the devil and had been promised a successful career as a photographer. The terms were the same as his own and the others', too, except Jane, which was why they'd all pledged never to have children. But Andy distinctly remembered Jacqui telling him that Katie had agreed to do 'a couple of other minor things'.

Suddenly Andy thought he knew what they were. The chances were that Katie had been passed a package similar to the one Jane had passed to him, but Katie's had been passed to her by the devil.

Katie had her own ritual.

Except that it wasn't saving her family. It was doing something else. Negating what I was doing, probably.

Andy groaned. Time had run out. There were worms in his study at home. The kid down the street and his mother had been killed. And the three children of the six members of the Jane's Gang had been asking questions about the seventies and, worse, May Street. It was happening again.

But May Street doesn't exist any more. The place where the house stood is now in the middle of the ring road. They can't access it. It can't access them.

And then he remembered Derek's famous trip, when he'd met the kid from the future. The kid with the mad hair.

The kid, who sounds just like Stevie. But the kid that Derek had hallucinated hadn't been alone. He'd had a friend along. Another kid that Derek couldn't see, except for his outline. And the outline had *horns*.

Johnny? Andy thought, unbuckling his seat belt. He needed to use the phone, and he needed to use it now.

Jacqui shook her head. 'It's all wrong,' she said. The enormity of her memory was crushing her mind. She had met a devil and she had been suckered into promising it the soul of her firstborn. It had seemed like a neat trick to agree, knowing that she would never have a child. She'd made the promise, knowing she didn't intend to keep her side of the bargain. *I should have refused, like Jane*, she told herself. *I should have let it take me. Or I should have appealed to the maker. I can't believe we all did what we did.*

'You're telling me it's all wrong,' David said. His face was still pale and he was shaking. When he'd remembered breaking open

Raymond's skull with the hammer, he'd leaned out of the car and puked.

'We were promised,' Jacqui said. 'We were promised that Raymond would leave us alone, but he didn't, did he?'

'For fuck's sake, Jacq, he was *dead* after that!'

'He came back,' Jacqui said. 'Not physically, but he came back all the same.'

'He couldn't have,' David said. 'Jane told us about nailing up the door and putting the swastikas inside the house. She knew that. It was supposed to seal the house.'

'It was just one of her notions,' Jacqui said. 'She didn't know any more than we did. What Derek did in there didn't work. Raymond came back to Stevie. For almost a year, Stevie had an invisible friend. He called him Manaymon. It took me a long time to work it out, but it was a corruption of the way I sometimes referred to Raymond: that man Raymond. Manaymon.'

'You sure it wasn't just coincidence?' David said. He looked exactly how Jacqui felt: as if he wished he were dead.

'When he comes running in and tells me that Manaymon showed him how to fly? When he's dug a hole in the ground and sat in it paying his invisible friend in blood because he's put a fork through his foot without even knowing he'd done it? And I was so frightened I hit him so hard I knocked him out. We were tricked, David. We tried to trick the devil, but it tricked us, too.'

David shook his head. 'Jane was certain. The afternoon afterwards she had a moment of enlightenment, Derek told me.'

'Oh, leave it out,' Jacqui said. 'She was just another dumb hippy chick who took too much acid. Just like the rest of us.'

'She didn't deal, Jacqui. She refused, knowing she was going to die from a brain tumour. She faced the devil and refused to deal. Which is more than you and I can say.'

'Well, if she was so bloody clever, how did Raymond manage to come back to haunt us? How come we all had children, even Katie, who was supposed to be physically unable to? How come our children all met? How come Andy's going crazy and breaking into people's houses and eating porridge?'

David looked astonished.

'It's a ritual,' Jacqui said. 'I assume he thinks he's protecting us all in some way.'

The smile left David's mouth. 'Ah,' he said. 'There's something I should tell you about Katie, too.'

The plane banked and vertigo hit Andy again. He held on to the back of the seat in front until the plane levelled, then went and asked the stewardess how to make a call. First he had to warn Stevie and Jacqui. Then he had to alert David and Derek, then to contact the BA desk at Dallas and hope to hell they had a seat on a flight back to England.

He was half-way through dialling his home number when a hand hit the phone's cut-off button. Andy stared at the stubby, strong-looking fingers. They seemed familiar.

'I can't let you do that,' someone said. The voice sounded even more familiar. As he turned to look at the owner of the voice, Andy's heart kicked up a gear.

There was Raymond, large as life and twice as scary. He looked like he'd never been away. His skull wasn't smashed open and there were no sloughs of red meat hanging from his face. He was dressed in his lime-green drape-jacket, black drainpipe jeans, a white shirt and a bootlace tie. He looked tanned and healthy, and his hair was freshly greased into that familiar quiff.

'Long time no see, Andy.' Raymond grinned.

'Where did you come from?' Andy heard himself ask. It sounded like the dumb question of the decade. 'You're dead.'

'But I won't lie down,' Raymond said, grinning. 'Hey, that stewardess is watching you talking to thin air. Want me to tell you what she's thinking? She wondering if you're gonna be OK, or whether you're gonna flip completely. She's thinking of calling a male steward called Jack. He's gay. He's currently talking to a girl called Denise while he thinks about the lover he left at home. Life's grand when you're omniscient, Andy.'

'I'm glad to hear it,' Andy said, through gritted teeth. 'Now fuck off and be omniscient elsewhere. I'm busy.' He turned away and began to dial.

Again he was cut off.

'Remember how I pulled your girlie hair?' Raymond asked. 'It's so great to be back, Andy. And, yes, you were right about Katie. You've been trying to close the gate and Katie's been keeping it open. See, our spells are greater on earth than those of the maker. And Katie's a dumb fuck. You know that alley that runs between Cliddesden Road and Hackwood Road?'

Andy nodded.

'You'll love this,' Raymond said. 'I put a reality split in the ground down there, back in 'sixty-eight. It's been there ever since. Looks like a mouth-shaped crack in the pavement. Every so often someone turns their foot in it and the council fills it in, but it's back the next day.

'That hole is connected to . . . the elsewhere, I guess you'd call it. And it's rooted in 'sixty-eight and it keeps the gate open between the good old days and the present time. And there's threads running through it. You had one that led to your back garden at Cuckoo Close. It wasn't a good one, but your boy dug down and found it. And I found him, too.

'That split needs to be maintained. I was in charge of that but you and your cronies went and killed me. A deal was struck. With Katie – of course, she didn't know it then and she doesn't now. But every year she performs a ritual. She goes to that split and she feeds it her own blood and she talks a lot of mumbo-jumbo and, deep down, the part of her that does it knows that her ritual is keeping me dead and keeping the devil away from the kids and the remaining members of her gang. She's keeping everything cool, she thinks. With a capital K. The hilarious thing is, over all these years what she's *actually* been doing is keeping us folks from the past in contact with you folks in the present.'

Andy nodded. 'Bastard,' he muttered.

Raymond shrugged. 'Fair's fair, Andy,' he said. 'You guys made a deal and tricked my good friend Yah-hoo, as your kid calls him. He only did likewise to you.'

'Raymond, you're dead, aren't you?' Andy asked.

'Literally, yes. But it's a little more complex than that. I'm still alive before you killed me and I've come here from nineteen sixty-nine as my last act. It's weird doing a last act several years before one dies, I'll admit. But that's about the size of it. It's one time only, but today I am as God. And I'm here to deliver you.'

'Go whistle, Ray,' Andy said, picking up the phone again. 'If you want to deliver something, make it a letter.'

'Sorry, but you're gonna have to choose here,' Raymond said, as Andy began to dial the number again. 'You either stop phoning or I start killing.'

'If you were here to kill me you'd have done it already,' Andy said, but he cancelled the call.

'Oh, I'd love to kill you, Andy, I really would. You killed me, after all. But the thing that crazy cunt put in you stops me doing it.'

'Jane?'

'May her soul fester in the depths of hell,' Raymond spat. 'She handed you protection, big guy. Protection, unfortunately, with the maker's stamp of approval. Fuck knows how she got in contact with him, damn his eyes. I can't even stop you making that phone call.'

'Well, fuck off, then,' Andy said.

Raymond grinned. 'However, there are others here *without* protection. Watch this.' He turned away and walked towards a woman in the nearest seats. Her seat was tilted back and her eyes were closed. Raymond peered at her, then called back to Andy, 'She's dreaming about her dog. It's attacking her. Now she's dreaming about a dark force approaching her. That's pretty perceptive. Gorgeous, isn't she? I bet she makes some man very happy with those nice full lips of hers. What a waste. But Andy needs a demonstration. Watching, Andy?'

Andy saw Raymond touch the woman lightly between her eyebrows with the middle finger of his left hand. The woman jerked, then went limp.

Raymond looked at Andy, grinning. 'Oh dear, she just died,' he said. 'No more nasty dreams for her.' He turned to a seat on the other side of the aisle where a white-haired middle-aged woman was poring over a double-spaced manuscript. Her mouth tasted the words as she read them.

'Literary agent,' Raymond said. 'Big time, too!'

'Don't!' Andy said, but as the words left his lips, Raymond snapped his fingers in front of the woman's face. She looked up and Raymond touched her lightly between the eyebrows. She slumped forward and the manuscript fell to the floor, pages scattering. The stewardess, who had been walking towards Andy, glanced back and returned to the woman.

'Still want to make that call?' Raymond asked, touching the stewardess as she bent to the dead woman. He caught the stewardess and held her up by the neck, frog-marched her to the toilets, opened the door and put her inside. Then he closed the door, and wiped his middle finger across the vacant/engaged sign. 'Locked in,' Raymond called, as he came back. 'Wouldn't do to create a panic, would it?' He leaned over a sleeping businessman. 'Bye,' he said, and touched him.

'Stop it!' Andy yelled.

'You decided against making your calls?' Raymond asked, walking up the aisle and touching each person he passed.

'Yes. Just stop it!'

Raymond smiled. 'I'll make a deal with you,' he said.

'What?' Andy asked.

'You leave the phone alone and I'll leave your wife alone.'

'What are you talking about?'

'I'll let her live,' he said. 'At the moment she's sitting in Fleet services with David. She met him there to talk about what's going on. Both have remembered their past. Right now David's explaining to her about Katie's Kool Day ritual. In a few minutes they're going to decide to drive back to your place, hoping to save the children. Well, I don't think those kids are worth much. I sure don't think they're worth saving. And you wouldn't want to lose your wife *and* your child, would you? So if you don't call Stevie, I won't kill Jacqui. Stevie's dead anyway, to all intents. Might as well save what you can, mightn't you?'

Andy was horrified. 'What do you mean, "Stevie's dead anyway, *to all intents*"?'

Raymond smiled. 'You and your darling wife both promised his soul to the devil on May Street. Stevie's spoken for. You won't get him back. He can't be saved. Same goes for the other kids.'

Andy frowned. 'Then why do you so badly want me to agree not to call him? I think you're bullshitting me.'

Raymond chuckled and paraphrased Dirty Harry Callaghan. 'What you've got to ask yourself at a time like this, Andy, is this: "Did he slip a lie to me or is telling me the truth?" See, in all the excitement back there, I've kinda forgot. So do you feel lucky, punk?'

'I think perhaps I do,' Andy said, reaching for the phone again.

'I'm asking you to choose,' Raymond said. 'Your wife lives and your son dies, or your son lives and she dies. I'm right there with her now. You've already killed your son. You killed him before he was born or even thought of. There's no saving him. Why lose your wife too?'

Andy felt tears begin to gather in his eyes and couldn't be bothered to stop them falling. What did it matter if Raymond saw his pain? It was too late in the game. 'If you're there with her, you're gonna kill her anyway, no matter what I do. You don't want me to phone Stevie, hence all the stuff about him being doomed already is bullshit. If I can save one of them, I will. And if I have to make a sacrifice to do it, even if I have to sacrifice the thing most dear to me, I will. I'm tired. I've been tired a long time now and I want an end to this fucking rubbish. I've been feeling this coming for almost a year and it's been hurting me. It's been driving my wife and me apart and it's been ruining my mental health. Innocent people have died because of what we did back in the seventies. How do you think that makes me feel?'

'Damned?' Raymond asked, grinning.

'Worse. It makes me feel I'd be better off dead, Raymond, and trusting to luck what happens after that, if anything. To tell the truth, I've been feeling two big words approaching me ever since Becky teamed up with Stevie and Johnny. Those two big words are here now, Ray, lit in flashing neon. They say THE END. So, fuck you, Ray, and fuck your minor and inconsequential devil. I just don't care any more. I'll just hope that the thing Jane gave me that's protecting me from you will see I don't end up in your hands. And if I can, before I go, I'll see an end to you and your good friend from May Street.'

Tears rolling down his face, Andy punched out the number of his home. When he looked up again, Raymond was gone.

'So what do we do?' Jacqui asked David.

'We need to talk to Katie,' David said. 'We need to get hold of Derek and tell him what's happening, if he doesn't know already. And we'll have to try to contact Andy, too.'

'And then what?'

'We get the kids together. Find out what they've been up to. Which could be easier said than done. I haven't even seen Johnny since Saturday. And do you know what I think?'

'You think he's gone. You think he's been made an offer he couldn't refuse.'

'The fucking thing's come back for payment. It wants our kids. I can only hope Johnny's sensible enough to have refused whatever he's been offered,' he added, not looking hopeful.

Jacqui understood why. Johnny was Katie's son and Katie had never turned down anything she was offered.

'Look, David, this is our mess, right? We caused it. We have to save the kids,' Jacqui said. 'Now get on your car phone and call my place. I'll tell Stevie to stay exactly where he is until we get there.'

Behind them, the BMW's rear door opened and then closed again with a solid *thunk*. The car filled with the smell of bonfire smoke.

Jacqui looked at David, the hairs bristling on the back of her neck. Every muscle in her body seemed to have turned to stone. David was frozen in place, the phone in one hand, the other poised to punch out the number.

'You don't need to make that call,' a voice said from the back seat. 'It's too late. Just save your money, honey.'

Jacqui didn't want to look, but something was turning her head against her will.

The thing in the back of the car was almost Raymond, but not quite. He was transparent as if someone had placed a glass replica of him on the seat. But it wasn't a replica: this thing was breathing and moving. And colour was trying to form in the lapels of his drape-jacket.

'You're looking pale,' Jacqui heard David say, in a tight, almost hysterical voice.

'I feel, fine, Doctor,' Raymond said. 'But I happen to know

that you're not. If I were a medical type, I'd say you were about to drop dead.'

'Get out of the car, Jacq,' David hissed. 'Now.'

But as soon as he spoke the words, the central-locking buttons snapped down. And wouldn't come up again. David turned the key to switch on the ignition and stabbed a finger at the electric-window button. The window glass shuddered, but didn't move.

'Let us go!' Jacqui pleaded.

Raymond gave a low chortle of amusement. 'The woman who tries to hack off my cock with a razor expects me to let her go when I come back to visit her. Now, will one of you turn that rear-view mirror around a little. The sun's reflecting at me and you can see how it's stopping me from being entirely here. I do dislike mirrors.'

'Fuck off,' Jacqui said.

'Please, David?' Raymond said. 'Only I want to teach this woman a lesson she'll remember throughout eternity, and I can't do it until I'm all materialized. I'd do it if I could, but I'm already stretching myself. I'm up in the plane with Andy too. He sends his regards, Jacqui. I offered to let you go in exchange for your kid, but Andy says I should kill you.'

'You're in no condition to kill a fly,' David growled. 'You've been dead nearly thirty years.'

'If you'd care to adjust the sun out of my eyes, I'll show you just how dead I am,' Raymond said. 'Now do it, David.'

'Get fucked,' David hissed. 'If I had a hammer . . .' He tailed off in a moan of pain.

'You'd hammer in the morning, right?' Raymond chortled.

'. . . kill . . . you . . . all . . . over . . . again,' David hissed.

Jacqui's head swung back towards David. His hand was half-way to the mirror, but he was resisting. His hand was shuddering as he fought to draw it back. The veins on his forehead and the tendons in his neck stood out like cables. His fingers were clawed and his hand shook.

The noise, when David's arm finally broke, sounded like a rifle shot. David screamed, long and hard, but his hand wasn't released. It began to turn at the wrist until it was palm up, and it kept turning. The snap as his radius and ulna bones gave way wasn't as loud as that of his humerus, but it was audible, even above his sudden shout.

'You want to move that mirror for me, Jacqui?' Raymond asked, 'Or should I twist your friend's hand right off his wrist?'

Jacqui moved the mirror.

David's arm fell. He screamed again.

Jacqui glanced back at Raymond, who was solid now. He looked younger than she remembered. Fitter. Angrier. 'What are we going to do with you two?' Raymond asked. 'We can't take your souls now, but neither of you deserves to live.'

'Leave us alone,' Jacqui hissed. 'Just fuck off back where you came from and leave us be.'

'Soon,' Raymond said. 'But today is *my* day. Today I'm as God. And although where I come from it's still only nineteen sixty-nine and we haven't yet met, I have a score to settle with you people. And, of course, I can't let you call up Stevie or Becky or Johnny. The best way to ensure that is to kill you both, but I really can't be bothered. It'd be much more fun to leave you alive so you suffer the rest of your lives remembering how you sold your children's souls to the devil. The suffering would be so much more exquisite than a few moments of physical pain. I only wish I could be around to watch.'

'Just . . . take . . . us,' David hissed, 'and . . . leave . . . kids.'

'How noble,' Raymond said. 'But it's too late now. The deal was struck. There can't be any exchange. You did your bit and now you have to face the consequences. Now, Jacqui, pick up the phone. You need to make a couple of calls.'

Jacqui found herself turning back. She didn't want to do it, but she couldn't stop herself. She watched herself pick up the phone and her forefinger punch out the number of her home telephone. She didn't have a clue what she was going to say, but she could feel the words building up inside her.

'Stevie's busy,' Raymond said. 'You might have known that your husband was Goldilocks, but here's something you *didn't* know about him. Something he doesn't know about himself. During his time with the master, he was charged with a task he didn't remember. You'll recall he's hankered to be a novelist for some little while now, Jacqui. Well, he started a novel without even realizing he was doing it. On cue, and just as arranged, one day, five years ago, he sat down and wrote the opening. It was called *The Devil on May Street* and he wrote down what you all did at number fifty-two. And then he hid the file in the depths of his computer and forgot about it until five years later when his son met Jane's daughter. Then Andy stumbled across that file, wondered what it was and looked at it. He didn't read it all, but he didn't need to. That short piece of writing was Pandora's box and he pulled off the lid. If he'd deleted that file, none of this would be happening now. It was the alarm clock that woke up the devil you and your friends had put to sleep with your nails and your magic signs. The house was long gone, of course, but time is flexible and Katie was keeping the past in touch with the future.'

The phone had been ringing for ages now. Jacqui hoped that Stevie wasn't there. She had no idea what she was going to say to him, but she knew it would be a trick. Something that would ease the passage towards the loss of his soul.

At the other end of the line, the ringing ceased. 'Hello?' Stevie's voice said.

Jacqui tried to speak, tried to tell him not to listen to anything she said, but no sound came from her lips.

'Hello?' Stevie repeated. 'Who is that?' he said, sounding suspicious. 'What do you want?'

'Hi, Stevie, it's me,' Jacqui said. Tears began to roll down her face again, but her voice was smooth and calm, no matter how hard she trembled and how much her chest hitched.

'Hello, Mum. Did Dad get off OK? Where are you?'

'I'm with David. We both know what's going on. You've read the bit on Andy's computer, haven't you?'

There was a long silence, during which Jacqui prayed that she would die now, this instant.

'Mum, what's that noise in the background? Sounds like someone moaning.'

Beside her, David suddenly snapped bolt upright and stopped moaning. Jacqui glanced at him, her eyes streaming. 'David fell and I think he broke his wrist,' she heard herself say. 'But he'll be OK. That's not important. What's important is that you've seen what your dad wrote. You did see it, didn't you?'

This time the silence was longer. 'Yes,' Stevie said.

'Then you must—'

'How did you *know*?' Stevie asked. 'Where are you? I can hear traffic in the background. You said you were at David and Katie's.'

'I met David at a service area. Fleet. We have't spoken to Katie yet. Please don't talk to her until I've called her. Is Becky there yet?'

'What do you mean, "yet"? I haven't seen Becky since last Saturday.' Stevie sounded offended. 'You know that. She went off with Johnny.'

'She'll be there,' Jacqui heard herself say. 'And when she gets there, you *must* take her straight to May Street, Stephen. To the house. Do you understand?'

'May Street isn't there any more, Mum. Are you OK?'

'You know what I mean, Stephen,' she admonished. 'Just do as I say. Derek and David and Katie and I will meet you there. Just do it, OK? And, Stephen, don't take the dog. If you take him he'll fuck everything up. OK?'

Stevie sighed. He didn't sound happy. 'OK,' he said.

'Promise your mum?'

'I promise,' Stevie said.

'I'll be there soon,' Jacqui said, and rang off.

Raymond chuckled.

Jacqui tried to keep her mind clear of thought in case Raymond was able to pick it up, but she was sure Stevie would know that something was askew. For one thing, she called him Wolfgang when she was upset, never Stephen, and for another she didn't recall ever having said to him, 'Promise your mum?'

But there was no time for thought because her fingers were now dialling 999.

'Emergency. Which service do you require?'

Beside her, David yelped as Raymond took a handful of his hair and yanked his head back against the seat, exposing his throat.

'Ambulance,' Jacqui said.

A moment later another operator spoke.

'Can I help?'

'Get an ambulance to Fleet services. Southbound side. Quickly!' Jacqui heard herself say.

'The nature of the problem? A crash?'

'I'm locked in a red BMW in the car park,' Jacqui said, 'and I've just had a row with my lover. Please come quickly. We've slashed open one another's throats and we're both bleeding to death. We're both blood-type O positive.' Then she rang off and reached across the rear passenger seat. Where an open razor was placed in the palm of her hand. One by one, her fingers closed around it. David looked up her, appealing silently.

'Sauce for the goose,' Raymond said. 'You cut me with it, now you're gonna cut him with it. And, after that, you're gonna cut yourself with it. Then you can just sit here and hope to die before the ambulance arrives.'

'Don't!' David murmured.

It wasn't a matter of whether Jacqui wanted to or not, but whether she could reach the rear-view mirror with her free hand, tilt it back towards Raymond and zap him out of here before she killed David.

'The short answer is, don't waste your energy,' Raymond said. 'You can try if you like, but you'll find your other arm won't work. In fact, try this for size!'

And Jacqui's left hand was drawn across to the base of David's throat, where it clamped itself in a grip so tight her fingers hurt. David's face darkened and the big veins in his throat stood out. He made an awful strangling noise.

'Those big veins are his jugular veins, I think,' Raymond said, 'but I'm not a doctor. I think those are the ones you need to open. If you open the arteries, which I think they call the carotids, David will die before help gets here. Course, the same applies to your own neck. Depends on how much you care to live, really. Now I know I've talked about aim here, but you aren't going to be able to aim very well. Because when you arm goes up like this . . .'

Jacqui's right arm rose to her shoulder. Her muscles bunched.

'. . . you won't be able to take an aim. You'll just slash down like this!'

The downstroke was fast. The metal blade of the razor flashed in the sunlight as it whipped down and hacked across David's exposed throat just below his Adam's apple. Blood spurted. A dark hole appeared and David's breath rushed from it. A moment later Jacqui realized that she hadn't only hacked a hole in David's throat, she'd also taken off the tip of her index finger where she'd been holding him. It didn't hurt, but a lot of blood was pouring from it and, from the first knuckle up, it was gone.

And she wasn't even allowed to scream.

She drew the razor sideways across David's throat, watching the skin part and the blood pour. Then she nicked open the jugular and dark blood began to jet from it.

Jacqui watched the razor as it rose from David and turned back towards her. She felt her head tip back and the cool, sharp edge of the razor as she laid it against the delicate skin of her own throat. Jacqui pressed. It stung a little. Then, keeping the pressure steady, she pulled the razor from one side of her throat to the other, feeling the pulsing relief as her life began to drain away.

David was slumped in the driver's seat, his eyes closed, his hand clamped to his neck as he tried to staunch the flow of blood.

Leave it, David, she thought. *Let yourself go. It'll be peaceful from now on.*

She glanced into the back of the car. Raymond had gone.

That's one good thing, she told herself, as she began to feel cool. *That's a job well done if ever I saw one.*

Jacqui closed her eyes, lay back in the seat and waited to die.

Chapter Sixteen

Stevie and Becky

Stevie was sitting in front of the computer screen, smoking viciously and worrying about what his mother had said when the phone rang again. He looked at it accusingly, then snatched it up. It was going to be her again, he had no doubt.

He could near nothing but a sizzle of static. He waited a while, in case the line cleared, but there were tiny robotic voices in the far distance. Eventually he hung up. He jammed the remnants of the cigarette into the ashtray and lit another. He felt as if he might puke soon, but he was certain that smoking was keeping him in touch with reality.

She called me Stephen, he thought. *She was talking to me seriously and she called me Stephen, not Wolfgang. And how the hell did she know I'd read* The Devil on May Street*?*

But Manaymon, or the insectile basketball player we call Yahhoo might know. And either of those two – that man Raymond, slaughtered by my parents and their friends according to what's written up there on the screen, or the devil he dealt with – might have told her.

And if that sounded like fancy, all he had to do was look at the dead worm thing half in and half out of the wall. Then there was the moaning. *David fell and broke his wrist. But that isn't important*, Jacqui had said. 'Right,' Stevie said to himself, 'it was only a broken wrist, after all. Sure. What's a broken wrist among friends?' And as soon as he'd mentioned the noise, it had stopped. His mother had asked him not to talk to Katie. And she'd told him that Becky would be here soon, that he should take her to May Street and not to 'take the dog' because 'if you take him he'll fuck everything up'.

What you don't know that I do, Mr Man, is that my mother never swears in my presence. Not even when she's as wild as a tiger.

Someone, or *something*, had been putting the words into his mother's mouth. And that something was trying to talk him into going to his doom. What Stevie couldn't understand was the lack of subtlety on the part of Yah-hoo. It was almost as if it had *meant* him to become suspicious. Which meant it might be a double bluff.

Stevie realized that he wasn't feeling sick because of the cigarettes but because he was more frightened than he'd even been in his entire life.

He yelped when the telephone rang again. Then he snatched up the handset.

'Stevie!' a tiny voice said, from the centre of a wave of static.

'Dad? Is that you?' Stevie asked.

'. . . whatever you do . . . don't . . . got that? Stevie? Can you . . . me?'

'No,' Stevie said. 'Where are you, Dad? I can't hear you. Say it all again. Dad?'

'Dookie . . . doesn't . . . mirrors. Stay . . . soon . . . about . . . another eight or nine hours . . . OK?'

And the connection was cut.

'Thanks, Dad,' Stevie said bitterly. He had no idea where his father was or what his message meant. Stevie felt tears well up in his eyes but blinked them away. Crying wasn't going to achieve anything useful. He had to figure out what to do. A part of him badly wanted to fetch Duke, get a couple of mirrors and something long, pointed and sharp, and a Bible maybe, and go devil hunting on May Street.

'When they say your parents fuck you up, they don't know how right they are,' he said, in a voice that sounded so pitiful it made him want to cry again.

The doorbell rang.

A moment later, Duke whacked into the front door, barking and clawing and snapping. Then he stopped attacking it and started to whine. When he gave a series of *hurry-up!* yaps, Stevie got up and went leadenly across the room towards the hall.

Judging by the noise the dog was making, Becky had arrived.

Just like Mum said she would, Stevie thought, holding back the tears.

Stevie's tears began to fall as soon as he saw Becky's shape through the bubbled glass of the front door. It was stupid, he knew, but there wasn't anything he could do about it. For the first time in his life, he'd fallen in love. He'd thought about it all day, every day since last Saturday, a week and a day ago, when Becky had stayed with Johnny in the underpass rather than leaving with Stevie. Johnny had said he'd take her away and he had. As easily as snapping his fingers.

Stevie had gone home and waited, in vain, for Becky to call.

By the following Tuesday, the day the shop had delivered the computer Johnny had bought him, he'd known that Becky wasn't going to call him. And neither was Johnny. But each time the phone had rung, Stevie's heart had leapt and his stomach had rolled; each time the postman pushed letters through the door, Stevie had been there to receive them ahead of the dog. But she hadn't written to him, either.

He had written to her, though. During the last week, he'd written twenty letters to her. Letters that demanded explanations, that detailed his grief at her betrayal, that explained how deeply he still felt for her.

But every single one remained on the hard disk drive of his computer. He hadn't even printed one out, let alone mailed it.

And now here she was, just as Jacqui had predicted.

Stevie reached for the lock, wanting to slap her face, shout at her and tell her to get lost – to *hurt* her in return for her hurting him.

Instead, he gasped when he saw her standing there, small and frightened, her own tears streaming from her eyes. There were several scabbed scratches down her left cheek, one of her eyes had been blacked and the pale skin at her throat was dark with bruising. Her dad's magical amulet was clutched in her hand.

'Stevie,' she cried, and a moment later she was in his arms, clinging to him and sobbing while Duke danced around them, yapping with excitement.

'It was terrible,' Becky said, in a small, shaky voice. She'd settled a little now and was between bouts of sobbing. She'd been here half an hour and Stevie still hadn't found out what had happened. He'd just held her while she cried and had clumsily whispered, 'It's OK, I'm here now. You'll be all right.' But each time she'd calmed enough for him to ask what had happened she'd begun to cry again. Now, she was smoking a cigarette and sipping at the cup of black coffee he had made for her. She was still struggling to keep her composure, but at least she was talking.

She stubbed out the cigarette and held up the cheap tin amulet. 'It was my fault,' she said. 'I stole this.'

Stevie considered asking what had happened as a consequence, but let it slide. Becky would tell him in her own time.

'You stole your dad's good-luck charm,' he prompted.

She nodded and wiped away fresh tears. 'And because of that, he cuh-cuh—'

Stevie's heart sank. 'Oh, Christ, he crashed?' he asked. 'Is he OK?'

Becky shook her head. 'Coma,' she said. 'He's on life-support in the hospital. He's been there since Friday. They don't know if he'll make it. He was drunk. But he didn't crash because of that. He crashed because I stole the amulet.'

'Becky, it's not your fault,' Stevie said, knowing she wouldn't believe him and that he didn't believe it either. 'It wasn't the amulet keeping him safe, it was luck. And it was bad luck that he crashed.'

Becky looked at him with a hurt expression that broke his heart. 'I stole the amulet on Thursday night when he came home. He crashed at lunch-time on Friday, two hours after he'd gone to work.'

'You look pretty well banged about, too,' Stevie said. 'You didn't discharge yourself from the hospital, did you?'

Fresh tears gathered in Becky's eyes. 'I wasn't in the taxi,' she said. 'I didn't get like this from the crash.'

'What then?' Stevie asked.

Becky looked away from him. 'Johnny,' she said.

'Oh, fucking hell, Becky,' Stevie said. 'Johnny did *this* to you? I can't believe it. I'll kill the fucker!'

Becky touched the scabs on her cheek. 'He did this on Saturday evening,' she said, 'because I wanted to come and see you.'

'You're joking. Aren't you?'

She shook her head. 'I'd better start from when those birds attacked him and you stomped off in a huff. I wanted to come after you, but Johnny was in a state. I couldn't leave him there. I felt responsible, somehow, so I just sat and talked to him until he felt better, and then we went to my place.'

'Yeah, I'll bet you did,' Stevie said.

Becky flashed him a look, but didn't rise to the bait. 'Birds followed us. Loads of them. It was scary. But we weren't attacked again or anything. Anyway, we went indoors and my dad was away. He was running someone up to Aberdeen. Anyway, Johnny hit my dad's drinks cupboard with a vengeance. I kept asking him what he'd done. He stuck to the Lottery story but I knew it wasn't true. They don't pay out big wins in cash – I rang to ask later in the week. He got quite drunk and cheered up a bit. And then . . .'

'Yes?' Stevie asked.

Becky glanced up at him. 'He wanted to see me in the clothes he'd bought me. The little black skirt and the cropped top. The Donna Karan stuff. And the shoes.'

'And you put them on?'

Staring off into the distance, Becky nodded. 'I was drunk, I felt sexy. I gave him a little model show. Walked up and down in front of him. And he went all weird. And he kept chuckling and saying that I was his and he wanted me to suck his fingers. Well, if I was going to suck anyone's anything, I'd have wanted it to be yours—'

'But you did it anyway?' Stevie said.

'I told him I wanted to call you and get you to come round. Believe it or don't believe it. It's up to you.'

'And?'

'And he got mad. He said I was his, and no one else's, and got up and started storming about, saying stuff about how he was going to fuck me until I begged for mercy. About how he was going to make me scream. And he looked like he meant it. And do you know what? A part of me *wanted* him to. I wanted to give myself up to him, let him fuck me if wanted, or tear pieces off me. I just ached to let him have everything I own. It was like a red mist came over me and I knew I could indulge every sick fantasy I ever thought up. I could literally fuck him to death. Or we could fuck one another to death.'

'And then what?' Stevie asked.

'I knew I was being tempted. Whatever was working on me – Yah-hoo using Johnny, I guess – had found all those nasty little places in my mind. But I pushed it away. I kicked off the shoes and ran. Anyway, Johnny caught me. I slapped him and he scratched my face. And then the doorbell rang.'

Stevie shook his head.

'Johnny told me to go and open it, as if he knew who was there. And there were these two girls, one blonde, the other brunette. They looked like models or something. Tall and gorgeous. Long legs and skirts shorter than the one I had on. Made me feel like an ugly duckling. And they said they'd come to take Johnny to heaven. And he told me that he'd be back soon, and that if I phoned you he'd know. And he'd kill me, then he'd kill you. There was a big black limousine on the drive. He got in it with the girls and they drove off.'

Stevie sighed. 'You know what he's done, don't you?'

Becky nodded. 'He made a deal with Yah-hoo. Everything he wants, when he wants it. He told me that when he came back on Wednesday. It was weird, Stevie. I saw him Saturday and when he came back on Wednesday he looked ten years older. Like he'd been living at about a thousand times the normal speed. He looked weird. Worn out. Hunted.'

'What did he want this time?' Stevie asked, but he thought he knew. There was enough about Becky's mother in the chapter his father had written for him to make an educated guess.

'Well,' Becky said. 'The deal he made didn't include *everything* he wanted.'

'What was missing?' Stevie asked.

Becky sighed. 'The one thing he really *did* want. Me. At least, that was what he told me. I could save him, he said. I could save him by falling in love with him.'

'Why were you excluded from the deal?' Stevie said.

Becky shook her head. 'I don't know. But he tried to seduce me – if that's what you want to call it – because if I fell in love with him, he'd be off the hook. Or so he says.' She looked up at Stevie and said, 'But I can't do that. I can't fall in love with Johnny because I've already fallen in love with you, Stevie.' She put her arms around his neck and her head against his chest.

Stevie gently stroked her hair and said, 'Snap! Me too.' It was all he could manage.

'I was too frightened to get in contact with you,' Becky said, looking up at him. 'I thought you might hate me for going off with him like I did. And the scratches he did were deep. I thought you might go after him and try to beat him up or something and I think he wanted that to happen. When he came back on Wednesday, he told me I had to get the amulet for him and bring it to him down the field today. I wouldn't and he beat me up.' She touched the bruises on her throat. 'First he strangled me until I blacked out. When I woke up again, he was sitting on me with one of his fingers wound into my hair. And he kept tugging bits of hair out of my scalp. I've got a lot of little bald spots now. Anyway, I stole the damned thing for him. Which is why my dad crashed the taxi. And it's all my fault. *Everything*'s my fault.' She began to cry again, sobbing gently on Stevie's chest.

'It's not your fault,' Stevie said gently. 'And it's not mine or Johnny's either. It's our parents. Back in the seventies they did something terrible. And now it's up to us to sort it out.'

Chapter Seventeen

Going Back Again

An hour later, Stevie and Becky arrived at the field, Becky holding the amulet and Stevie carrying a plastic Safeway bag. Its contents didn't look impressive, but they made Stevie feel a little less vulnerable, as did the gold cross and chain he now wore around his neck. It belonged to his mother and she *always* wore it. Except for today.

Inside the bag was a dog-eared King James Bible, two small mirrors and a spray-pump kitchen cleaner bottle, which he'd emptied and filled with bleach. In his pocket was the knife Johnny had given him last Christmas.

Stevie had wanted holy water – and doubted that tap water, blessed by waving the Bible over it while he said the Lord's Prayer, would work. Nevertheless, he'd snuck out into the kitchen while Becky was drinking a second coffee and prepared two glasses, one of which he'd drunk and the other he'd forced upon Becky without telling her what it was.

And he'd brought Duke, unmuzzled. He had wondered if the dog would intuit that something was wrong and refuse to accompany them – dogs were supposed to be good at sensing trouble ahead – but either Duke was dumb or as determined as Stevie was to put this thing to bed once and for all. He seemed happy enough to come along, even though he was still limping.

Becky had refused to carry a weapon, but Stevie had noticed her check that the devil earring was still there. And she was clinging to the tin amulet as if it were the most valuable item in the universe. Before they'd left, she had gone upstairs to the bathroom. When she came down, smiling grimly, there were tiny swastikas drawn in ball-point on each of her cheeks, one in the centre of her forehead and one on either hand.

'Look!' she said, pointing up at the railway bank a couple of hundred yards ahead of them.

Stevie saw a flock of birds circling, high above it, which must mean that Johnny was up there. Stevie's heart quickened and adrenaline began to pump into him.

'What do we do?' Becky asked worriedly. 'He's bound to have seen us. He'll come down after us. He wants this amulet. Badly.'

Stevie thought about it. They'd decided that it might be a good idea to keep the amulet when they crossed over to May Street. If Johnny wanted it enough to half strangle Becky to get it, there was a chance it had some use – after all Derek had managed to drive drunk all these years and only crashed when the thing was removed from his cab. But according to his father's writing Derek's amulet had been a gift from Raymond. Which meant that it might pull strings on behalf of the enemy. That, however, was a chance they would have to take.

'We go up there,' Stevie said. 'See what he says.'

Becky grabbed his arm. 'Are you sure?' she asked, fingering her throat. Her eyes were dark and frightened.

Stevie fought off a shudder. 'We have to know what we're up against. And, after all, it's only Johnny up there. It's not as if he's suddenly turned into the devil himself, is it?'

'But he's dangerous,' Becky protested. 'He might hurt us.'

'I won't let him,' Stevie said grimly.

'I couldn't stop him,' Becky said. 'And I tried. Believe me. He's not the same Johnny, Stevie.'

'You can stay down here if you like,' Stevie suggested. 'I'll go up and talk to him. If you see him coming after you, you'll have a good head start, and it'll keep the amulet out of his way, even if something happens to me. Then you'll have to hide out until you can get help. I have a feeling my dad will be back on the next flight he can get. If I were you I'd stay clear of everyone else. I told you about my mum and David being weird, but I don't think Dad's been got at – not yet, anyway.'

'I'm coming with you,' Becky said. 'I'm not letting you out of my sight.'

Stevie thought about arguing but Becky's jaw was set. He nodded. 'OK, but let's stash the amulet and this bag in case we have to run. I'll take the knife.'

Becky nodded and found a grin for him. Then she took his face in her hands and kissed him, hard and deep. When she pulled back she looked grim again. 'Thought at least I'd get one good kiss in,' she said. 'It might be the last.'

Not really believing that his dog would take a blind bit of notice of him, Stevie told Duke to sit and stay by the bag and the amulet, then knelt in front of him and held his snout gently. 'Now you stay there and guard this stuff with your life,' he said. 'Don't let anyone touch it. Understand?'

Duke grinned a doggy grin.

'And don't move unless I call you. If I call you, I want you up that bank right away, teeth first. You got that?'

The dog gazed into his eyes. His tail gave a single wag.

'Now, do as you're told and stay.'

'He won't stay there long,' Becky predicted, as they walked towards the break in the wire fence at the bottom of the embankment.

Stevie turned back. Duke was standing now, keeping an eye on their progress and occasionally scanning the field as if he understood his instructions. 'He's doing OK so far,' he said, climbing over the single remaining strand of wire and starting up the bank. He glanced up. High in the sky, hundreds of birds were wheeling in a dark cloud. Some were pretty big. Stevie wasn't sure what they were but they were bigger than crows.

'If you look at the top of those birds,' Becky said, 'you'll see a white one, all on its own, really high up. Huge wingspan. It's an albatross. Figure *that* one out. We don't *ever* get those here.'

'And some in dreams assurèd were Of the spirit that plagued us so; Nine fathom deep he had followed us From the land of mist and snow,' Stevie recited solemnly.

Becky flashed him a grin. 'Just don't kill it,' she said.

As he crested the embankment Stevie saw Johnny, about fifty yards away to his left. He was wearing jeans and an expensive-looking black blazer. He was sitting, cross-legged, close to the nearest set of tracks at the top of the bank, facing east, towards them. It took Stevie a few moments to recognize the heaped black ring of *things* inside which Johnny was sitting.

Jesus, it's dead birds, he realized. *Hundreds of them!*

He waited for Becky to reach the top of the bank. Johnny sat there, staring towards them. Stevie saw a tiny bird swoop down from the flock. Johnny didn't look up, but as it dived towards him his right hand shot up, snatched it out of the air and made a whipping motion. Then he tossed the lifeless bird on to the heap in front of him.

'I told you he's not the same Johnny,' Becky said.

'Come on,' Stevie said, glancing back to where Duke waited down in the field. 'Let's go and talk to him.'

While they approached Johnny sat and studied his fingernails. Stevie kept the knife in his right hand, but the closer he got the less dangerous Johnny looked. In fact, he looked old and tired.

Stevie got to the edge of the ring of dead birds and squatted down. Becky knelt beside him.

'Hiya, Johnny,' Stevie said.

Johnny looked up. His perfect skin was now yellow and papery.

There was a tracery of fine creases on his forehead and at the corners of his eyes. At some point, not too long ago, a bird had managed to peck at his head because blood had run out from his hairline in three places and dried on his face.

Johnny smiled wearily. 'Hello, Dogboy. Hiya, Becks,' he said, nodding slightly. 'Got a cigarette, anyone? I'm dying for one.'

'Sorry, Johnny,' Stevie said.

Johnny barked out a bitter laugh. 'Yeah, you and me both, Mr Wolfie Dogboy. I'm losing it, I guess. I don't need to scrounge cigarettes these days. Watch.'

He raised his right hand and snapped his fingers. An open packet of Rothmans King Size appeared in his hand, one cigarette already half-way out of the pack. He did the same with his left and a bejewelled lighter appeared, already open and lit. 'Good, isn't it?' he said miserably, as he put the cigarette between his lips and lit it. He tossed the pack to Stevie, who reached up to catch it, remembering when he'd done the same thing in the alley as they peered through the fence at Nigel. It seemed like years ago.

This time, though, Stevie didn't catch the pack. With a fluttering of wings, a magpie swooped in from nowhere, caught the pack by its flip-up lid and flapped away, its wings beating hard. Stevie followed it until it was lost in the mass of circling birds.

'Never mind,' Johnny said dully. He clicked his fingers and a new pack appeared.

This time Stevie caught it. It felt as if it had just been taken from a freezer. He took out one of the chilled cigarettes and lit it with the lighter Johnny threw at him. The lighter was cold too. And very heavy.

'Keep the lighter, Dogboy,' Johnny said. 'Solid gold and real diamonds and rubies and stuff. It'll be more use to you than it will be to me.'

'Johnny?' Stevie said. 'What is it with these birds? Why are they following you around like this?'

'They know,' Johnny said. 'I don't belong here any more and they can tell that. It's something else I didn't know would happen. I'm an alien now. I'm a splinter in the world's flesh, prickling and aggravating. And the world and all its creatures want me gone.'

'But what's *happened*?'

Johnny smiled sadly. 'You need *me* to tell *you* what's happened? I went back, didn't I? I may not be up to your standard of cleverness, Dogboy, but even I could work out what was chalked on that wall. I went inside the house. Looking for relief.'

'Why didn't you tell us the truth? Why didn't you come and see me or Becky? We could have done something.'

Two large tears fell from Johnny's eyes. 'I know I should have, Dogboy,' he said. 'But I didn't want you to see me like I was. I couldn't face you. After that first time I kept feeling like my mind was collapsing. I walked and walked and found myself at the mouth in the alley. And I put my hand down it and got my mother's needle stuck in my forefinger. And the pain nearly killed me and it wouldn't stop hurting. And I could hear a voice saying: "You know what you can get and you know how you can get it. You can use me as hard as you like and I'll never be used up. Anything you want is yours for the asking." And I knew who it was, Stevie. It sounded like Sindy Hallett, but I knew who it fucking well was. It was Yah-hoo, trying to trick me into becoming his sunbeam. And I thought, I'll have you, you motherfucker. I'll bring this needle and I'll cross over to May Street and I'll stick it right in your fucking eyeball.'

Johnny drew a shuddering breath and Stevie glanced back at Becky, who gave a small shrug. She didn't know if it was the truth either.

Johnny continued, 'And I came down here and couldn't get across.'

'And you waited half the night in the rain, right?' Stevie said.

'It wouldn't let me across. I just sat in the rain under those power lines,' Johnny said. 'And eventually it worked. I went across. I checked out the wall you'd spent so much time looking at. And I thought, I know where the key to the old haunted house is. I'll pick it up and go inside for a mosey around. And I got the old claw-hammer and pulled all the nails out of that sealed-up door and I went inside. And you know what was in there, don't you?'

Stevie nodded. 'I think I do.'

'Yeah, you think on,' Johnny said. 'You don't know the half of it. It convinces you it's all-powerful, then that it's dumb. And I fell for it. I started out wanting to stick a needle in its eye and ended up making a deal with the motherfucker.'

'What deal?' Stevie asked.

'I could have anything I wanted on earth for as long as I wanted it, except one thing, in return for my soul. The one thing was Becky here. I could have anything I wanted except Becky.'

'And you accepted?' Stevie said. 'I can't believe it.'

'Oh, but I was *clever*,' Johnny said. 'I said I wanted to become immortal. And I wanted to stay immortal until I'd had enough of it and wanted to die. That way, I thought, he'd never get my soul. After all, who wants to die? And I wanted wealth. And I wanted my health. And I wanted the freedom to act as I wanted and not have to face the consequences. And I wanted cigarettes and girls and stuff all on tap. And to top it off I said I wanted to be free of the deal when I felt like it, if Becky fell in love with me. And fuck me, Dogboy, old Yah-hoo agreed to it all. Course, I didn't know then what I know now.'

'Which is?'

Johnny shook his head and wiped away tears. 'I didn't know I'd be running on a different time-stream afterwards. You can't imagine what it's like. In the past week or so, I've lived a thousand years. I've done *everything*. All in the same week of your time. I've been everywhere, done everything. I've acted out all my fantasies. I've raped, I've murdered, I've made love to so many people I can't even recall a hundredth of them. I've learned to love every perversion you could think up and some you couldn't. I've tortured people to death, I've hexed folks, I've loved them and hated them. I've learned so many things my head's crammed to bursting. I've done everything you can imagine, Dogboy. And now my time's up. I can't face any more living.'

'And you can't get out of the deal because Becky didn't fall in love with you, right?'

Johnny nodded. 'And I couldn't kill her, either,' he added.

'Jesus, Johnny, was *that* part of it?' Stevie said.

Johnny glanced at Becky, then looked away. 'Yeah. She either had to fall in love with me, or I had to kill her. Course, I wanted to make her fall in love with me. That was before I realized I wouldn't be able to cope with the weird time thing. And before I realized she was in love with you already, Dogboy. So I decided to kill her. I did my best on Thursday,' he said. 'Would have been doing her a favour, too. She's her mother's daughter, see?'

'No, I don't,' Becky cut in. 'Explain.'

Johnny sneered at her, 'You're pure. You can't be bought. Just like your mother. You can own, but you can't be owned. You're a different sort of person, Becky. A special sort. I should have killed you. Yah-hoo knows, I wanted to. But you have that steely purity locked in there somewhere, right down in the centre. I couldn't fucking do it.'

'I don't understand,' Stevie said.

'Understand this, then,' Johnny said. 'Our parents made a deal with Yah-hoo and the deal was this: he'd leave them alone if they each promised him their firstborn child's soul. Me and you, Dogboy, we're fucked. But, like her mother, Becky is a special case. You see, her mum wouldn't make the deal. She died to save Becky. Course, as I've learned, the thing you want most is the thing you can't have. Old Yah-hoo wants us all for sunbeams,

Dogboy, but he wants Becky more than anything. Or, as a poor second-best, he wants her soul off the planet.'

He turned to Becky. 'You've got the amulet?'

Becky nodded.

'I'm sorry about what I did,' Johnny said.

'Yeah, sure you are,' Becky spat. 'You tried to kill me to save yourself.'

Johnny shook his head. 'If you could see things through my eyes, you'd forgive me for what I've done, Becky. I love you. I've spent a thousand years loving you, this past week. Most of what I've done was to try to forget that. To find something to replace you. No one can stand a thousand years with a broken heart. Anyway, I'm sorry. Could I have the amulet now, please?'

'What do you want it for?' Stevie demanded.

Johnny sighed. 'It was a mistake,' he said. 'Your Manaymon gave it to Becky's dad and shouldn't have.'

'And you're delivering it back? What are you now, an errand boy?'

'It's my last chance, Dogboy. *Our* last chance. It's a long shot, but it might work. I think I know how to power it up. At the moment it isn't doing anything much, but I think I can feed it and kick it into gear. And I might be able to banish our friend with it. God knows, I want to try.'

'I'm not going to give it to you,' Becky said.

Johnny sighed and felt inside his blazer. A moment later his hand reappeared holding a huge silver revolver, which Stevie instantly recognized as a Colt Magnum Python .45.

'Ask and ye *shall* be given,' Johnny said, raised the gun at Becky and pulled the trigger. The noise was tremendous. The gun recoiled and flew out of his hand. Beside Stevie, Becky was falling forward.

No blood! Stevie's mind crowed. *There's no blood!*

And at that moment a spray of blood flew up over Becky's back, followed by something huge and white.

Johnny cackled. 'More bad luck! Just what I needed!' He had shot the thing that had soared down from the sky and was homing in on her from behind. The albatross.

Stevie pulled the quivering bird away from Becky and sat her up. She looked dazed.

'Fucker was heading straight for your skull, Beck.' Johnny grinned. 'Looks like you've got my boss worried. I guess this means he's gonna be pissed off with me. Look, I'll tell you what. Why don't all of us go over? That way you can handle the amulet and if things get bad and you get desperate, you can toss it to me and let me try to save you. Otherwise, I won't do anything. How's that sound?'

'Sounds like a shitty idea,' Becky said.

Stevie nodded. It did.

Johnny shrugged. 'Guys, I'm in this pile of shit, same as you. But I'm in deeper. And I just shot an albatross to save Becky, too. That's even more bad luck for me.'

'We'll go alone,' Stevie said. 'If you don't mind, JK.'

'And you'll come back like me,' Johnny said. 'Guaranteed. But if I come along you'll at least have a chance.'

'What can you do to help?' Becky demanded. 'You've already admitted to trying to kill me.'

'No hard feelings,' Johnny said. 'But if you take me, I can . . .' He sighed. 'I don't know *what* I can do. But I'll do what I can. That's all.'

'And if we refuse?' Stevie asked.

'I guess I kill you, Dogboy,' Johnny said, getting up. 'If there's one thing I've learned in my thousand-year week, it's that life's cheap.'

Stevie glanced at Becky, who gave a small shrug and said, 'OK, you can come along.'

Duke wouldn't let Johnny near the plastic bag containing Stevie's stuff and the amulet. As soon as he saw Johnny approaching he stood up and began to snarl.

'I should shoot him,' Johnny said, waving the long barrel of the .45 at the dog.

Stevie glanced at him and knew that Johnny was merely mouthing off. He didn't look as if he had any intention of shooting Duke, or even aiming the gun at him. In fact he looked frightened of him.

'I'll carry the bag,' Johnny said, holding out his free hand.

Duke took two steps towards him and treated him to the big white smile.

'I'll carry it, I think,' Stevie said, and Johnny didn't protest.

Duke nosed along at Stevie's and Becky's heels, preventing Johnny from walking with them. Every few seconds he looked back, as if to make sure Johnny wasn't getting too close.

As they went down the path towards the power lines, two girls appeared in a break in the fence at the south side of the field, one blonde, the other dark. The blonde began to wave.

'Who are they?' Stevie asked.

'They're the girls who came to my house and collected Johnny,' Becky said. 'Johnny? Your friends are coming,' she said.

Johnny looked up and grunted. 'My captors, you mean,' he said. 'They have a limo. They get me inside it and it drives away and when it stops I'm somewhere else. Another country. Another time. And when I get back here after months, or years, about two seconds have passed. When they call I go, whether I want to or not. Looks like they're coming to get me right now. They're angels, Stevie. Yah-hoo's angels. And now they're my guardian angels. And they look after me. I've fucked them both, every way you can fuck someone, but that was before I realized . . .'

'Realized what?' Becky asked.

The blonde called in a musical voice, 'Johnny! Take us on a trip! We want to go away with you!'

'What they were,' Johnny said.

The two girls had passed under the power lines now and were less than fifty feet away. Both looked odd against the background of the overgrown field – as if they were being lit with follow spots. They looked too well defined, too perfect.

Duke brushed past Stevie's legs and stood on the track just ahead of him, growling.

The girls stopped about ten feet away, smiling happily. 'You have to come now,' the brunette said. 'We have to go away to heaven.'

Johnny pushed past Stevie and shook off his friend's restraining hand. 'It's over,' he said. 'I've had enough. I want to die.'

Duke backed away, putting himself between Stevie and Becky and Johnny and the girls. He was growling quietly and every muscle in his body was tense.

'Awww, *Johnny!*' the blonde girl said. She looked genuinely crestfallen.

The brunette smiled serenely and said, 'And you will. But not here. Not now. You have to come now.' She beckoned.

And Johnny began to walk towards her. 'I know what you are,' he said. Then he gave a bitter laugh and raised the revolver. He glanced back at Stevie and said, 'She's a gobbling, Stevie. Can you believe that? I *fucked* two of those little black rubbery bags of blood, Dogboy. Can you imagine how that makes me feel?' and without looking back at the girl, he pulled the trigger.

The brunette exploded.

What looked like twenty gallons of blood burst into the air, soaking Johnny and the blonde. Stevie thought he saw the rubbery piece of gobbling skin fly off and fall into the long grass. Duke turned tail and ran back up the track.

And the blonde girl began to scream, long and hard.

Wiping blood from his eyes, Johnny chuckled. He levelled the gun at the blonde. 'Don't!' she shrieked. 'I'm not like that! I'm human. I'm *human*!'

'In which case,' Johnny said, 'you should know better.'

And he pulled the trigger again.

The girl didn't explode. Her head snapped back, her face vaporized and a shower of blood and brain flew from her head. She came down in the grass on the other side of the path.

'Yep,' Johnny said, in the ringing silence. 'She was human, after all.'

'What's the matter with you two wooses?' Johnny said, looking back. 'So, I killed someone, so what? One of 'em was a fucking gobbling, and the other one was someone like me. I did her a favour, Dogboy. I've sent her to meet her maker. Or Yah-hoo, whoever owns her. People die every minute of every day. What's it matter?'

Stevie held on to Becky, who was shuddering and weeping on his shoulder. 'It doesn't matter, Johnny,' he said carefully.

Johnny seemed pleased with this response. 'Right!' he said, nodding. His face lit in a grin. 'You're very sensible, Dogboy. Now, let's go on down to the power lines and cut ourselves and we can get this job over and done with. Don't worry about the body. It'll be gone when we get back. The gobblings will take care of it, just like they have with all the others I've killed.'

Stevie glanced around for Duke, but the noise of the gun had scared him and he was nowhere to be seen. He didn't feel good about this: the dog was the only thing he had that scared Johnny. Without him, he either did what Johnny wanted, or ended up with his brains leaving through the big hole Johnny would put in the back of his skull.

'You've got that knife I gave you in your pocket,' Johnny said, when they were under the power lines. He grinned. 'Oh, don't worry, I know. It's another of my gifts. Just take it out and open it and cut your finger. Let it bleed a bit on the pile of stuff over by your dad's bandanna. Make Becky do the same. We want to be sure we all get across, now, don't we?'

Stevie took Becky to the place where the cache of bloodstained cigarette butts and tissues still lay in the grass and peeled himself away from her.

'He's going to kill us,' Becky whispered.

Stevie shook his head. 'No, he's going to deliver us,' he whispered, taking the knife out of his pocket. 'He hasn't told us everything. I think there's more than one way for him to break out of his deal. And I think he's gonna get released from his bargain if he delivers you and the amulet to Yah-hoo.'

'Make a nice deep cut,' Johnny called. 'I'll be wanting to suck some of Becky's blood when you get back over here.'

'I could take this fucking knife and stick it in his eye,' Becky said, slicing the cutting edge across her forefinger.

'I've thought about it, believe me,' Stevie said. 'But he knew I had the damned thing and he'd probably know if I was about to use it and shoot me first. So I suggest we do as he says until the gun's empty.' He took the knife back from Becky and sliced the tip of his own forefinger. It stung. 'Give me your finger,' he said, and when Becky held it out, he crushed his own against it. 'Whatever happens,' he said, 'I swear to do everything in my power to protect you.' He looked at the grass at his feet because he knew that as soon as he started to say his next words he would blush. And he was right. 'I love you, Becky.'

'Look at me,' Becky said.

Stevie looked up. Becky's face was pale and beautiful. Her green eyes shone. 'I swear to do everything in my power to protect you,' she said, pressing her cut finger against his. 'And, for what it's worth, Stevie, I love you too.' She leaned up and kissed him gently on the lips.

'Less of the fucking lovey-dovey stuff, please, you two,' Johnny called. 'You're making me wanna throw up. Just bleed on the fag packets and stuff, and hurry up about it.'

Becky yelped when Johnny fired the next two shots.

Stevie wheeled round. Two large crows were falling out of the air like shot-down fighter planes.

'He's still got one bullet left,' Becky said. 'And, for all we know, the gun might be reloading itself magically.'

'It won't be,' Stevie whispered, as they walked back. 'He magicks up new packs of cigarettes. Which means they must empty as he smokes them. The same will apply to the gun. He'll either have to get a new one, or get bullets and reload once the last shot is gone.'

'Bullets,' Becky said. 'There were spent cases up on the railway track. No empty guns, though. But we can't kill him.'

'Why not?'

'Because that's what Yah-hoo wants. It'll make us like him if we do.'

Coronas were forming around the three overhead wires.

'Quick!' Johnny said.

The explosion hit them before they were ready.

Stevie felt himself dissolve as the flash blinded him.

Chapter Eighteen

Katie

Katie Kane hammered on the front door of Stevie's house for the third time and gently swore to herself. Her husband *had* to be in there with Jacqui, so why weren't they answering?

So, he's fucking her, Katie thought. *Who cares? He's welcome to do that if he wants, and he knows it. Why should they not let me in?*

The answer, as far as Katie was concerned, was *not* because they wanted to keep it secret but because they weren't in the house.

Katie took the note from David out of her pocket and read it once more.

> Katie,
>
> It's all blown up again. Andy's gone to the States and I have to do something, so I've gone to meet Jacq. Stay where you are and don't do anything until you hear from me.
>
> All my love
> David XX

Which means what, exactly? Katie thought. *Why aren't they here? And if he was meeting her because Andy had gone away, where are they?*

Katie had found the note when she'd come in this morning after a long walk. When she'd read it, she'd phoned David on his mobile. It was switched off. She'd rung his car phone, which was also switched off. So she'd come round here to find out *exactly* what had all blown up again.

It could have something to do with Johnny, she supposed. He'd stayed out all night for three nights in the last eight, and he'd been acting strangely when she'd seen him. He looked tired and was evasive when she asked him what he'd been up to. She'd guessed that he'd been out on the tiles, that he'd fallen in love – probably with Becky – and that he'd been spending his missing nights discovering the joys of sex. Although why that should prompt David to have a crisis meeting with Jacqui, she had no idea.

But you do *have an idea what it's all about, don't you?* a small voice said in her mind. *It's about* Then.

Katie knelt and pushed open the letter-box. 'Hello?' she called. 'It's me. Katie!'

The hallway was empty and remained so. 'Damn!' Katie said, and got up.

As she rose something happened inside her head. It felt as if her brain had been dislocated for a long time and now it had finally done a little twist and snicked back into place, the way a shoulder would.

Oh, that's better! she thought, and a picture lit in her mind. In it, David was bleeding badly. He was in the back of an ambulance and people were working on him in a frenzy. More people were working on another bloodied body on the other side of the vehicle.

The vision vanished. 'Shit,' Katie said. Suddenly she was certain not only that David was mortally wounded but that the answer to why this had happened – a note, perhaps, or a message on Andy and Jacqui's answering machine – was awaiting her.

Katie turned side-on to the door and elbowed the window.

It hurt, but the glass cracked. She did it again, then a third time, before enough of the glass fell out to allow her to reach through for the lock.

The lounge was empty. There was a telephone there but no answering machine. It wasn't in the hall, either. Or the dining room. Or the kitchen. Which left only the dingy room with the computer in it.

Katie walked towards the room, wondering why she had the distinct feeling that she shouldn't go inside. Perhaps her vision had been of the future and if she went into the room she would find Jacqui and David in there, butchered by some psychopath.

The resistance to her entry was almost magnetic. Katie wasn't sure if the resistance was hers or the room's but she fought to overcome the pressure and stepped inside.

Where she relaxed. It was just a dimly lit room full of clutter. Andy's den and workplace by the look of it. There were no bleeding or injured bodies here. But there *was* a big computer screen with words showing on it, a telephone *and*, on the far end of the desk, an answering machine with a red light flashing to show a message was waiting.

Katie picked her way through the junk, wound back the tape and pressed *Play*.

'Stevie? Jacqui? It's Andy. I'm in Dallas now. In five minutes I'm boarding a plane home. I'll be back in ten or eleven hours at most. Stay put until I arrive. I know what's going on. Now listen. This is *important*! Just stay put. Don't go out of the house. Don't answer the door. However much you feel you may need to do something, don't do it. Got that? Just wait there till I get back. If that's you, Jacqui, you know what it's all about. Raymond's back. The devil's calling in his debts. Christ, I just hope and pray that you get this message. See you soon. I love you both. 'Bye!'

As Katie listened, her heart began to hammer. Now that her mind had relocated itself, she *remembered.* And she remembered *everything*, right down to the last detail. She'd made a deal with the devil. It sounded crazy but she'd done it. And she'd cheated. She'd gone back on her word and she'd spent the rest of her life making sure that the devil was kept from having what he wanted. The souls of their children.

In a daze, she switched off the answering machine, reset it and slumped down in the big chair that stood in front of the computer, wishing she'd had Jane's courage, wishing she'd died long ago. Now she knew what David had meant when he'd written, *It's all blown up again.*

What about Kool Day? Why didn't it work? The next question she asked herself was more pertinent: *What am I going to do now?*

And Katie found she knew the answer to that question. There was a way. Jane had told her just before she died. Katie had made a last visit when Jane was in hospital, just after they'd opened up her head, peered inside, frowned a little and closed her up again. Jane had called her and Katie had gone. And when she'd got there, Jane was so weak, so near death that she could barely speak.

'Break your heart,' Jane had whispered. 'It's not over yet. Live your life. When it's time, break your heart and seal what you've been keeping open.'

At the time, Katie had just thought that those few words were the ramblings of a dying woman. Now that her mind was clear, for the first time in nearly thirty years – and Christ, how good it felt – those words made sense.

'Time's come,' Katie said to herself. 'The Game Over sign is flashing and it's time to pay it all back.'

She wasn't sure how she felt about this. Relief was one of the words that sprang to mind, but she was also terrified and uncertain that she could even consider doing what she had to do. She suddenly knew how a condemned man must feel while they readied the electric chair and waited for the reply to a last-minute appeal for clemency. Scared shitless, but calm, too. Dreading, but hopeful.

Did I have a good time? she wondered. *Did I do what I wanted to do? Did I have fun? Did I enjoy my life?*

The answer to all these questions was yes. Which, she realized, was the best she could hope for. There was no use in crying because she would have liked to have the time to do it all over again. If this worked, she'd be getting more than she deserved. Much more. She knew she should be happy with this.

'Fuck it,' she said aloud. 'Let's go get it done!'

Katie was about to get up when she heard the noise again. The noise she'd thought she'd heard after she'd yelled through the letter-box. A kind of heavy, rustling noise. She held her breath and listened. A few seconds later she heard it again, and over by the door, a tall metal computer case wobbled.

Sounds like . . . A cat?

She watched the case. It wobbled, steadied and wobbled again.

Suddenly Katie knew what it sounded like. It sounded like the one thing on this earth of which she was terrified. A snake. A very *large* snake. She got up and edged quietly along the desk, meaning to pass behind it. Judging from the sounds and tiny movements of the clutter in this room, it was entering through a hole just to the left of the door and coming round the room in a clockwise direction towards where she was.

And then the thing raised its head from behind a packing crate.

Katie screamed. It wasn't a snake. It was a huge, segmented black worm, perhaps four inches in diameter. It had a head like a bowling ball, half of which seemed to be composed of a jutting maw filled with tiny shark-like teeth that gleamed white in the half light. Eye sockets were indented into the top of the round head, but instead of having eyes like those of a fly, this thing had huge human eyes, with red irises.

It glared at her, swaying back and forth like an eastern hypnotist's snake, rising from a wicker basket. Katie grappled around for a weapon, found a mobile phone and flung it at the worm, hitting it in the eye. There was a flash of fire, a burst of smoke and the phone fell to the packing crate, melted.

Katie shrieked and the worm pulled back its head and whipped it forward again, making a spitting sound. Something spherical, glowing red, shot from its mouth, bounced off a piece of equipment in a spatter of heat and smoke and whacked into the desk leg, which burst into tiny flames.

It's molten lava! Katie's mind howled. Katie backed up tight to the desk. There was a window on the far side of it. If she could get it open she could escape. She stood up on the desk and scrabbled, panic-stricken, at the window. When she glanced back at the worm it had gone down behind the box again.

Katie had the window a good way open before she saw that the black thing on the outer sill wasn't a sleeping cat. It looked like the goblin that used to feature on the sides of Goblin vacuum cleaners when she was a kid. But this was black and shiny and looked heavy. *What the hell is that and who put it there?*

And the thing moved. Fast.

Katie tried to slam the window shut but she wasn't quick enough. The goblin had hold of her wrist with its tiny, sharp, burning claws. The pain was phenomenal, but Katie had never let pain stop her from getting what she wanted. The thing opened its mouth in a snarl, showing its teeth, and lunged at the inside of her wrist. It hung on, digging in its claws, but again Katie slammed the window. This time it whacked into the goblin's head, trapping it there, its sharp teeth gnashing on empty air. Katie watched the thing's head compress. It bulged on either side of the window as if it were a balloon.

'I'll give you claws!' she screamed, and lashed out at the top of the misshapen head with her own sharp fingernails. They sank in and sloughed through skin like soft rubber. The goblin shrieked and struggled, letting go of her wrist and trying to force open the window with its tiny hands.

'Fucker!' Katie said, and struck at it again. This time, she opened a gash that jetted blood and left an empty sac on her side. The thing's claws scrabbled at the window, leaving smouldering scores down the glass.

A gobbet of molten lava hit her right Achilles tendon. Katie shouted in pain, twisted round and knocked over the tower that housed the computer's works. It hit the monitor, which broke and spat sparks and flame, and Katie saw a breadknife slide from the top.

She leapt forward as the knife bounced off the edge of the desk and snatched it out of the air.

The worm raised its head just in front of her face, drew back and spat fire, but its aim was off and it missed her. On all fours, Katie lunged forward with the knife, which skated harmlessly off the thing's head. *It's armour-plated*, she thought. *But the joints in its segments have to be its weak spots.*

At the window, the goblin squealed and struggled.

Katie limped towards the worm and stabbed the knife where

the head joined the body. This time it slid in easily but Katie kept up the pressure and carried on walking towards the thing, forcing it back. She was certain that the worm wouldn't die until its spinal cord was severed, and she intended to make sure that happened.

The worm made a strangulated noise that sounded like a distressed puppy and tears filled its red eyes. 'Tough,' Katie said, pushing harder and enjoying the feeling of her muscles bulging. 'Life's a bitch and then a bitch cuts your throat!' she snarled. Behind her, glass cracked but Katie didn't look away.

As she pushed harder, the worm pushed back, but Katie hadn't spent all these years working out with no result. Each time it pushed, she matched it. Using all the strength she had, she forced the thing back to the wall and pinned it there, jabbing the knife deeper and deeper. What looked like burning spittle rolled down from the worm's maw and Katie twisted her arms away, but droplets burnt her wrists and forearms like spatters of boiling water.

Behind her, the window shattered and the goblin screeched with rage and frustration.

'Die, fuck you!' she yelled at the worm, and gave one last almighty, two-handed push.

Its eyes closed and its body relaxed.

Katie yanked the knife out of it and turned round in time to see the goblin's fingers snatch open the closure and yank the top half of its head free.

She watched the empty head fill out and grinned savagely when blood began to jet from the holes she'd scraped in its skull. It bared its teeth at her and started to climb through the broken glass. Half-way through, it gave a shudder, then reached up, but it was too late. The rips in its skin had torn apart under the pressure of the blood being pumped back into its deflated head. A moment later it had torn in half and was gone, leaving gallons of airborne blood, most of which landed on Andy's desk.

Katie walked back towards the blood-soaked, still steaming computer. 'I shan't come here any more for tea,' she said and giggled. 'Not with guests like that around, anyway.'

What she was going to have to do now, she realized, was go upstairs, dump these bloodstained clothes and put on some of Jacqui's. If she set foot outside this house looking like something from *The Texas Chainsaw Massacre* she'd be arrested before she was even half-way to where she was going. She started towards the door – and slipped in the slick of blood. Her legs shot out from beneath her and she crashed to the floor. The last thing she saw before it struck her hard on the temple was the bowling-ball head of the worm.

I'm dead now! Katie thought.

And the lights went out.

Chapter Nineteen

The Devil on May Street

Number fifty-two May Street looked exactly as it had the last time Stevie had seen it: an abandoned house with broken and boarded-up windows, and that odd quality of being skewed somehow, like a blackened, twisted tooth in a row of pearly-whites. The street was deserted and Stevie thought he recognized the cars too. It looked as if the May Street they were accessing was fixed in time, possibly to the hour or minute.

Four thirteens, Stevie thought, clutching Becky as Johnny lifted the grating to get the key. Becky was still dizzy and disorientated: it was her first crossing and she was finding it hard to keep her feet. Stevie knew what she was going through. For him, the sensation of crossing was now similar to stepping off a child's playground roundabout: you simply adjusted from movement to non-movement with a couple of braking steps. But Becky could barely function.

'It's down here somewhere,' Johnny grinned, holding the big revolver on Stevie while he groped in the drain.

Fifty-two is four thirteens, Stevie repeated to himself. *If we're three of the unlucky thirteens, who is the fourth?*

It was probably coincidence. The fact that number fifty-two was divisible by thirteen didn't have to hold any significance. But it *felt* as if it should. Stevie sighed. It was useless trying to work it out. It was useless trying to work out *anything* now. He had a Bible, a bottle of bleach, a couple of mirrors and a knife but he didn't have the faintest idea what he was going to do with them. Worse, Johnny hadn't mentioned the contents of the bag, which suggested those items were useless. He'd known about the knife, so he must know about the stuff in the bag, too.

We're just going to walk into this house and meet the devil himself, Stevie thought. *And he's going to eat us alive. We're like lambs going to the fucking slaughter.*

'Ah, here it is!' Johnny said. 'Thought for a moment I'd lost it.'

'I'm OK now,' Becky whispered in Stevie's ear. 'The devil earring went cold and I stopped feeling sick.' Then she let go of him, bent double and clapped her hands to her face. She moaned. 'God, I feel sick!'

Johnny raised an eyebrow, then rolled his eyes at Stevie. 'Women!' he said. 'You bring her in, Stevie. I don't want her puking on me. In fact, so I can keep an eye on you, take this and go first.'

He handed Stevie a standard Yale key. Stevie studied it, then said, 'You don't have to do this to us, JK, you know that, don't you?'

Johnny grinned. 'Do *what*, Dogboy? All I'm doing is helping us all out of this mess. Cross my heart and hope to die.' He crossed his heart, mimed slashing his throat and spat on the pavement. 'What's wrong, Stevie, O great Dogboy? Look, I know I'm damned. You know it, Dookie knows it and the birds know it. What I'm going to do now is get *un*damned. And I'm just making sure you don't put an end to me before I do it. You keep forgetting, Stevie, I've been around longer than you now. Much longer. Long enough to know that people will sneak up on me and do me harm. I've got no reason to believe you and Becky are any different. I'm just holding this gun on you for my own safety. Now, open the door.'

Stevie went to Becky and put his arm round her waist. She clung to him as he walked up the short path to the front door. Johnny watched from the street and called, 'Open it, man. Nothing bad's going to happen.'

Stevie put the key into the lock and turned it. He pushed the door, which creaked and resisted. The bare hall and staircase looked pretty much as it had the last time he'd been here, but the mulch – the remains of Nigel and his mother – was gone.

'Down the hall,' Johnny said, from close behind. 'You know where the room is, Stevie. The back room on the left. You've always known that, deep down. Just like I have. It's destiny or something.'

And Becky acted. One moment she was slumped against Stevie on the threshold of the house, the next she'd tensed, turned and sprung at Johnny.

Stevie wheeled round in time to see her grab Johnny's wrist and push the gun into the air. Her knee rose towards Johnny's crotch, but Johnny dodged to one side, his left hand flying out towards Becky's face.

And then it was all over. Becky fell back into Stevie, who caught her and steadied her. The amulet was in Johnny's hand. He pressed the barrel of the gun to her forehead. 'See what I mean about people attacking me?' he asked Stevie. 'For two pins I'd shoot her fucking head off.'

'Go on then, fuckwit,' Becky spat at him. 'If you think you can. Do it! Pull the trigger. Go on, let me have it! Can't, can you?'

'I come to praise Caesar, Becky, not to stab him in the back,' Johnny said angrily.

'What the fuck is *that* supposed to mean?' Becky said.

'Work it out for yourself,' Johnny snarled. 'Just turn round, go down the hall and into the fucking room before I shoot your head clean off.'

'Do as he says,' Stevie said. A glimmer of hope had lit in his heart. Johnny was rattled by Becky's attack. He couldn't shoot her because he'd been *ordered* not to shoot her. Or because, alive, she was his last hope . . .

As Stevie followed Becky down the hall, the lights came on – although the fittings were empty – and at each step the temperature dropped. By the time he was half-way down the hall, Stevie could see his breath.

'And you always thought hell was hot,' Johnny said, in a voice of amusement. 'Don't worry, things warm up in a minute. Becky. Stop. That's the door, the one on your left with the nail-marks round it. You can see where I had to scrape off the swastika before I could get in. Open the door. Follow close behind her, Stevie.'

Becky glanced back at Stevie, her face pale and her green eyes dark with fear. Then she turned the handle and pushed open the door.

Stevie winced as the dazzling fiery glow and the blast of moist heat hit him. The room stank like a cross between a rubbish tip, a lion enclosure and a bonfire. And underlying this was a sweet perfume that wound through his nostrils into his brain.

He staggered in behind Becky, grabbing her for support.

The room appeared to have glass walls, behind which the flames of a furnace angrily blasted. The floor was transparent: beneath it was the clear darkness of outer-space, its unimaginable size inspiring instant vertigo. A dazzling array of distant stars winked and twinkled in reds and blues or shone blindingly with a brilliant white light. The ceiling was perhaps thirty feet above him and appeared to be composed of smooth soil upon which exotic flowers grew in tiny clumps.

Clinging to Becky, Stevie took all this in in the moment before his gaze was drawn to the huge golden throne set in the far corner of the room . . . and the creature that sat upon it.

And suddenly he was face to face with Manaymon's boss, and the incarnation of Nigel's he-whose-name-may-not-be-spoken. Old Yah-hoo. The devil itself. The eight-foot-tall insectile basketball player incarnate.

The first thing Stevie noticed was the devil's particularly nasty-looking hard-on, a long, thick, twisted and heavily veined thing that rose up to his navel.

Yah-hoo was muscular but slender, and certainly didn't look very insectile. Its body was humanoid, the skin red and hairless, but for the red goatee beard at the tip of his chin. Its legs narrowed into hooves and a thick cable of forked tail hung over one of the throne's armrests.

Yah-hoo's face wasn't revolting, though. In fact, it was handsome. Its mouth was large and the teeth showing behind the grin were white and pointed. But it was the impenetrable dark eyes that drew Stevie's gaze.

It was as hot as a sauna in here. Stevie was already dripping with sweat and each breath of air he drew in warmed his teeth and dried his throat. He heard Johnny enter the room behind him and glanced back. Johnny winked at him and grinned.

'Welcome home,' the devil said. Its voice was deep, soft and comforting, its eyes hypnotic.

Becky grabbed Stevie's arm. The pressure of her fingers hurt. 'What do you want?' she shouted, letting go of Stevie's arm to push her hair back from her face. The devil that swung from her earlobe caught the light and glinted like a star.

'Everything I am owed. Everything that has been gifted to me,' the devil said. 'And now, my little queen, I have it.'

Stevie wiped sweat from his forehead and caught sight of his watch. The seconds were whizzing by at what looked like a billion times too fast. The minute display rose as fast or faster than the seconds, which presumably meant that for every second that passed in here, a minute went by in the real world. This seemed significant, but he had no idea why. He was finding it difficult to concentrate, which wasn't terribly surprising, he thought, since he was scared enough to shit himself.

'You've got nothing,' he said, sounding as frightened as he felt.

The devil frowned at him. 'I see you're wearing the badge of the maker. Now, that's no way to treat your host, is it?' Then it grinned. 'Ah, I see. You were hoping to *banish* me with it. Well done, Stevie Warner! You made a joke!' The devil's laughter was so loud Stevie felt it in his ribcage. The silence when it ceased was worse. 'Now let's see if you can banish me with that damned thing,' the devil whispered. 'Come here, boy. Come closer!'

Stevie couldn't move; he was currently frozen to the spot with terror, but this didn't trouble the devil. It pointed a long, clawed finger at Stevie and beckoned. And Stevie's body went towards it of its own accord.

The devil smiled. 'I have the flesh, the maker has the spirit,' it said, as Stevie stopped about six feet away from him. 'Now, boy. Let me see you banish me with your cross of the maker!'

'I can't,' Stevie heard himself say, in a pathetic voice. 'I don't know how.'

The devil grinned. 'How sad. Then why come here hoping to put me to my end? How can you possibly hope to do such a thing when you *don't know how*? Stevie, my son, my soul. The reason you don't know how is because you don't belong to the maker. You belong to me. It saddens me that you resist me so.'

'Leave him alone!' Becky yelled. Stevie glanced back and saw that she didn't look a bit frightened. She looked angry.

'Becky wears *my* emblem,' the devil sneered at Stevie.

'And you can't fucking touch me while I'm wearing it, can you?' Becky snarled. 'You know where this earring came from, don't you?'

The smile left the devil's face. It said in a voice that bore a hint of suspicion, 'Tell me, my spirited queen.'

'But aren't you supposed to be omniscient?' Becky said.

The devil waved a dismissive claw. 'I know that I'm going to enjoy fucking away your flesh until all that is left is the part of you I desire,' the devil replied, its voice low and dangerous. 'Wipe those signs off your face!'

'Make me!' Becky challenged.

'All in good time,' the devil hissed. 'Then I'll *make* you take my entire phallus down your throat and, afterwards, up your virgin anus while I claw your body apart. Tell me about the emblem.'

'You should know already,' Becky said, 'Mr High and Mighty Ruler of Hell, or whatever you're supposed to be. If you *were* omniscient, you'd know, wouldn't you? But you're *not*. Admit it! You can't even get out of this place. You're stuck in nineteen seventy-something, in this terraced house. You're no longer at large in the real world. You can't get there. All you can do is send out your demons and goblins to do your dirty work.'

'What beautiful oratory,' the demon snarled. 'But quite wrong.'

'Bollocks,' Becky said. 'You need us. All three of us. Only we can release you. Isn't that right?'

The devil shook its head. 'No, my princess, you are just about as wrong as it is possible to be. All I want is what I am owed. And for your information, my queen, my mistress of pain, I *do* know where the emblem in your ear came from.'

'Ahh, the sin of pride,' Becky said, smiling sweetly. 'So where did it come from?'

The devil drew back its lips, opened its mouth and licked the air with a black, forked tongue. 'It was a gift,' it said, 'from Jane – damn her and may her soul rot – to Katie Kane. And Jane found it.'

'Psychometry,' Becky said. 'The ability or art of divining information about people or events associated with an object solely by touching or being near to it. *The American Heritage Dictionary*, nineteen ninety-four. Now tell me who made it!'

The devil nodded and smiled. 'You will make an excellent queen,' it said. 'You are quick and vicious. You have enough of your mother in you to qualify as pure and enough of your father to be an excellent trickster. As you know, the maker made it and left it for Jane to find. You have my respect. But the boy does not. Either he tries to banish me with his little cross or I take his soul, here and now.'

'You can't, can you?' Becky said. 'If you could, you'd have done it already and saved yourself all this hassle. Why not simply do what you do and have done with it?'

'Does a cat simply kill a mouse? Your souls are mine, whether you like it or not. But I love to tease the soul from the body. I love to play. I love to cause pain and fear and play tricks. It's my delight. For example. Your little devil earring and all those swastikas you've drawn on yourself are protecting you, aren't they? Well, let's see . . .'

The devil pointed a clawed finger at Becky.

Stevie heard a whisper of movement and something green hit the left sleeve of Becky's jacket and ran up to her shoulder in a slender, sparkling thread of emerald light. Becky looked down at it . . . and the arm of the jacket burst into flame. As she tried to pull away, her hair swung into the fire on her shoulder and caught alight. She shrieked. Stevie batted out her hair, then tore the jacket off her and threw it aside.

The devil chortled.

'You bastard!' Becky spat, gingerly touching her neck. It was red where her hair had burned.

'That hurts, doesn't it?' the devil said. 'Makes you want to wipe those swastikas off your face and take out that nasty little earring.'

'Fuck off!' Becky snapped.

The devil smiled. 'Are you going to remove the earring and

wipe those ineffectual markings from your skin, or should I remove your skin? You can't imagine how badly that would hurt. Or how long I could keep your soul in your body while you suffered. I have the power over your life and your death. I can let you simmer in eternal agony if I see fit. And don't think you'd pass out from the pain. No matter how much damage I do to you, I can keep you inside your body.' It lifted a finger and Becky's right shoe caught fire.

Becky kicked it off. Like a burning rat, it skittered across the floor towards the devil's throne, hit the gold plinth on which it stood and vanished in a shower of sparks.

Before Becky could speak, her other shoe began to burn. This one didn't leave her foot when she shook it. Becky dropped to the ground and pulled it off by the heel, then stood, aimed and flung it at the devil. It winked out of existence half-way across the room.

'Does your foot hurt?' the devil asked. 'I *know* it does. I can feel it! Take off the earring.'

'No!' Becky said.

Stevie's hand had stolen into the plastic carrier bag and his fingers had found the thick, comforting weight of the King James Bible.

The devil pointed at him and hissed, 'Just try it!'

At Stevie's neck, the cross grew very hot. The gold chain burned his skin and the cross seared into the flesh in the hollow of his throat.

A line of green fire cruised up both the legs of Becky's jeans. She screamed and snatched at the zip trying to get them off before she was burned.

Stevie let go of the Bible and yanked off the cross, breaking the chain. It burned his hand, but Stevie didn't let go of it. The pain was excruciating. He glanced over his shoulder, willing Johnny to act, but Johnny merely stood at the far side of the room, his eyes fixed on the devil.

'Trial by battle!' Becky yelled, tossing her jeans aside.

And in Stevie's hand the cross cooled. The burning sensation faded.

The devil stood up. Its huge phallus pulsed; a thick dark liquid dripped from its head and glistened as it ran down the length of the shaft. Its brow drew into a crease and its dark eyes glittered. 'You fool,' it growled, in a voice that was suddenly so huge the room shook. 'You shouldn't have said that. Even the maker declines to invoke a trial by battle. Renege!'

Becky stood just in front of Stevie to his right, her back to him, the tail of her shirt stopping about half-way down the curve of her buttocks, which were clad in a pair of white cotton briefs. Her legs were long, slender and finely muscled. In that second, she was the most beautiful thing Stevie had ever seen.

'I won't,' Becky said. 'I demand trial by battle.'

'The law doesn't exist,' the devil growled, stepping down from the plinth on which the throne stood. 'Take it back!'

'Never!' Becky said. 'The law exists and you know it.'

'You do not stand accused,' the devil said, taking two steps towards Becky and towering over her. 'And therefore trial by battle cannot be invoked.'

'I don't have to be accused to invoke it,' Becky said. 'To invoke, I merely have to deny your will.'

The devil reached down and took the front of Becky's shirt in its fist and lifted her at arm's length so they were face to face. 'Then have your trial by battle!' it said, pulling her closer to him. 'Let us seal the deal with a kiss.'

Its black forked tongue slid from between his teeth, as thick as Stevie's wrist and as mobile as a snake. And it kept coming, closing the two feet between it and Becky. She leaned back, but the devil's tongue flowed smoothly towards her.

A picture lit in Stevie's mind of how far inside Becky that tongue would go. It would reach right down her throat and into her stomach, perhaps if it kept expanding at the rate it was going now, it might quite possibly go all the way through her.

The fork of the devil's tongue flicked against Becky's lips, parting them.

Stevie saw Becky's jaws being forced open and snatched the Bible from the bag and held it in the same hand as the cross, which swung from his fingers. 'In the name of the Father, the Son and the Holy Spirit, by the power invested in me, I command thee to get thee gone!' he yelled.

The devil's tongue shrank back into its mouth with such speed that it was a mere blur. It let go of Becky, who fell to the floor and rolled on her side, gasping for air. It was in front of Stevie in an instant. 'Power?' it said. 'You have no power invested in you. The maker doesn't come here. His influence does not extend to this place. Whose power?'

'*My* power,' Stevie said, angrily. 'Becky's mine, so leave her alone!'

The devil chuckled. 'I do believe I see love in those angry brown eyes of yours. You are calling on the power of love?'

Stevie nodded. 'And these,' he said, waving the Bible and the cross.

'Those are useless,' the devil said. 'Even a devout believer in the maker could not use them against me. I can see you don't believe me. Watch.'

One moment the Bible and the cross were clutched tightly in Stevie's hand and the next the devil had them. The moment after that, it was reeling away screaming so loudly that Stevie thought his eardrums would burst. Smoke billowed from the clawed hand in which the Bible and cross were clutched.

'Fuck you!' Stevie yelled, triumphantly.

Then the devil's screaming ceased. It turned back, his shoulders rising and falling and a strange sound coming through its clenched teeth. The Bible still smouldered in its hand. It took a few moments for Stevie to believe that the sound was of the devil *giggling*.

'Oh, that hurts so badly!' The devil chortled. 'You poor boy. It was worth a try. And you showed spirit, too. You and Johnny will make wonderful representatives for me on earth. My two angels of death. Just think of the fun you'll have!' Its voice fell. 'If you survive,' it growled. 'Without your friend here calling trial by battle it would have been easy. But she refuses to take back the challenge, so trial by battle it must be. And if I lose you all to Armageddon, so be it. You see, Stevie, trial by battle has never been called before. Not with me. It is reserved for the final day. When the maker thinks he's strong enough to overcome the greatest thing he's ever made. The one thing he made that bested him. The reason he doesn't call it is because it's assured mutual destruction. On the day of Armageddon, *everything* ends. No more humans or animals, demons or angels. Maker or devil. And now Becky has called it. I don't know if she's called it on her own behalf or through the will of the maker. If the maker speaks through her, everyone is lost. If she speaks for herself, she's mine. As are you. And now the time has come. So let it begin!'

The devil threw the Bible and cross into the air. Both shattered like glass and the shards began to fall like feathers. Then the tiny pieces burst into flame. What hit the night-sky floor of the room looked like a sprinkling of gold dust. It shimmered for a second, then vanished.

And the devil clapped his hands.

Something hard hit Stevie and suddenly he was nowhere.

It was two in the morning when the alarm went off, signalling to Staff Nurse Judy Rotenberg that the man in intensive care had gone flat-line.

But Derek Sharp wasn't dead, Judy saw, as she hurried back

into the ward from the nursing station. He was out of bed and standing in the middle of the ward, looking like a cross between the Invisible Man from the old television series and an Egyptian mummy. He had lost an eye and had multiple fractures of the skull. His jaw was broken in three places and wired up, his right arm was plastered, the fingers of his left hand were splinted and both his legs were encased in plaster too. Add to that a serious liver bleed that had required surgery, intestinal damage and that he had been in a deep coma, and what you had was a guy who should have been dead.

'What do you think you're *doing*, Derek?' was all that Judy could think to say as she ran up to him. 'Back to bed,' she said. Thank God Nancy and Elizabeth were hurrying towards her. Both her colleagues looked as gobsmacked as she felt.

'I gotta tell her,' Derek said, taking another stiff-legged pace forward. His voice was barely audible – not surprising since, until a couple of minutes ago, a machine had been doing his breathing for him.

'You can speak later. You're not strong enough now,' Nancy said, taking one of Derek's arms. 'How did he do this?' she asked Judy.

Derek took another pace. 'Phone,' he mumbled. 'Got to tell Becky. All I've got. She's all I've got.'

'You can't go anywhere,' Judy said. 'You'll hurt yourself even more.'

'Important,' Derek breathed. 'Very very very very important. Got to tell Becky.'

'You tell us, we'll tell Becky,' Judy said, glancing at Nancy.

'Becky's your daughter, isn't she, Derek?' Nancy said. 'We'll tell her for you. You have to get back in bed.'

'Urgent. Life or death. Got to tell her,' Derek whispered.

'What do we tell her?'

'Don't give him back the amulet. That's all. Don't give it to him or he'll win. It'll be all over.'

Stevie flicked back into existence standing against a steel barrier on a high hill. Way below him a huge city of low-rise buildings shimmered beneath a baking sun. Long straight roads ran down between the buildings as far as the eye could see. Other roads crossed the city. Way off, Stevie could see a small area of skyscrapers. To his right, the sea sparkled in the hazy distance.

'Where am I?' he asked aloud, turning to find Becky standing next to him. He wasn't surprised to find that she was still dressed only in a shirt and a pair of white briefs.

'We're at Griffith Park Observatory,' Becky said, nodding towards a domed building to Stevie's right. 'Los Angeles, California.'

'Wow,' Stevie said. 'What happened? I thought we were ...' He tailed off. He couldn't remember where they'd been until now although he had a feeling that it had been somewhere not half as beautiful as this.

'We were there, now we're here,' Becky said, taking his hand. Her nails grazed his palm just a little too hard.

'I'm awake, anyway.' Stevie grinned.

'You've always wanted to come to LA,' Becky said. 'I know that.'

Stevie nodded. It was one of his secret ambitions: to live somewhere where it never really got cold. Somewhere that ice and snow didn't plague your life in January. Somewhere where *everything* was possible.

'You want it?' Becky said, gently digging her nails into his hand.

Stevie glanced at her and grinned. Becky was a devil in bed, he seemed to remember. She was insatiable and she did things he'd never heard of. 'Here?' he asked. The place was deserted and he was already as hard as iron.

Becky grinned. 'Not sex, you dummy!' she said, snaking her hand around his hip and squeezing his dick ... just a little too hard. 'This place!'

'Sorry, you lost me,' Stevie said, still feeling her hard fingernails on his dick, even after they'd gone. 'Do I want this place? How do you mean?'

'It's yours,' Becky said. 'If you want it.'

'This mountain?'

Becky nodded. 'As far as you can see. The whole of Los Angeles and all it contains. From the border with Mexico, right up to San Francisco, it can be all yours. All of California can be yours. You can own it all. And you can have power over it and its people. You can *use* them as you like.'

'I can?' Stevie grinned. 'That sounds good.'

'Every man, woman and child will answer to no one but you,' Becky said. 'Every animal. Every rat, every cat, every dog – all yours.'

'Oh,' Stevie said. 'Dogs! Like Dookie. Where *is* Dookie? He was supposed to cross over with us, wasn't he?' He frowned, distantly remembering being in the field with Becky, JK and his dog. And hadn't JK shot someone?

'All yours,' Becky said smoothly. 'And all you have to do is make me a promise.'

'Where's Dookie?' Stevie asked.

'He's safe at home,' Becky said, and Stevie recalled a light, sunny apartment down by the sea. He'd woken there this morning, with Becky draped across him and the dog sleeping on the foot of a huge bed.

'We can live like that for ever,' Becky said.

Stevie frowned. 'Why are you only wearing a shirt and your knickers?' he asked. 'I can kind of remember your trousers catching fire. Is that what happened?'

Becky smiled. 'Don't worry about it,' she said. 'Are you ready to own California?'

Stevie grinned back at her. 'Yep,' he said.

'Then say, "I pledge thee my eternal soul in return for the ownership granted me." Go on.'

'How long do I get to live?' Stevie asked.

'Eternally, if that's what you'd like,' Becky said.

Stevie sighed. 'Becky, the breeze just blew the flaps of your shirt apart and I saw the front of your knickers.'

'Just say the words, Stevie,' Becky implored. 'Hurry! There's not much time!'

'And I was wondering how long you'd had that huge dick that sticks out of the top of the waistband,' Stevie continued.

Becky flickered and vanished.

The devil stood in her place. It looked displeased. 'Make up your mind,' it said.

Stevie shrugged. 'Sorry. It isn't enough.'

'What more do you desire?'

'I desire to keep my soul for myself,' Stevie said.

'Then you die,' the devil said. 'And I'll have your soul. It's lawfully mine. It was promised.'

'Then you'd better kill me before I work out a way of keeping you locked up for eternity,' Stevie said. 'Go ahead and do it now, if you can!'

The devil clapped his hands.

Los Angeles vanished.

It was replaced with a huge lake of fire.

And Stevie was falling.

It was starting to get light when Katie Kane regained consciousness in Andy's workroom. Her head was splitting and she felt sick. The words *Break your heart, break your heart* were repeating in her mind as if they were running on a tape loop. But Katie's heart was broken already.

'I had a good run for my money, though,' she whispered, trying, and failing, to sit up. It felt as if her skull had been nailed to the floor. She moved her wrist in front of her face, trying to see the hands on her watch. It was just starting to turn from black to grey outside, so it could be anything between four and five thirty, she supposed. It was still too dark to read the hands of her watch.

It's too late now, anyway, she told herself. *Too much time has passed between knowing what I had to do and now. Whatever I could have done to make amends will be too late. Or whatever* I will *do as soon as I can get out of here. I'll still do it, just in case. I can't promise it'll do any good, Johnny and Becky and Stevie, but I'll do it anyway. But if it isn't too late for you, it's too late for me and the others from the Jane's Gang. We've been running a long time. Now time has caught us up.*

She tried to sit up, but her head hurt too badly.

Where are the others? Where's David and Jacqui, for Christ's sake? They should have been back by now. And Derek. Maybe he's out there doing his bit. I hope so.

Katie relaxed and lay back. The pain in her head eased a little. After a while, she lifted her hand and checked the lapel of her jacket. The long thin needle she'd found in her bedroom this afternoon was still there.

All I need to do now is get where I'm going and do what I have to do, she thought. *And I will. Just as soon as the pain stops, I will.*

In Frimley Park Hospital, twenty-five miles away from where Katie had just woken up and a few more from where Derek Sharp's walkabout was starting to ring the alarm in the nursing station, David Kane's eyes opened. All he could see was a white blur against a white blurred background.

He felt as if someone had tried to saw off his head with a breadknife. Then he began to remember. And as he remembered, the white thing that stood before him started to resolve.

It was Jacqui, whole and undamaged, naked as the day she was born. She reached out a hand to him and smiled.

We have to go now, she said. Her lips didn't move, but her voice was as clear as crystal inside David's mind. And the words soothed away the pain in his throat.

I'm cold, David said. He felt his lips flicker. He and his friends had spent years trying to become telepathic, and all it took was a little relaxation to achieve it.

You'll warm a little, Jacqui said. *Just as soon as you get up, David. Now come on, sweetheart, we have to go!*

Where are we going? David asked, shivering. He wasn't just cold now, he was frightened.

Jacqui shook her head. *I don't know, darling, but we'll go together. I think it'll be all right. I think we're going to be fine. Just get up. It'll be warmer when you do.*

And David found he *could* get up. He *slipped* into a sitting position, feeling weightless. Jacqui came closer and took his hand. Her own was warm and solid. Comforting. She pulled him gently.

David experienced a slight jerk and then slid forward, as if he were being tugged from quicksand that had finally decided to set him free. He landed lightly on his feet. He, too, was naked. Behind him, an alarm went off on a piece of machinery. He glanced back at the bed and experienced a slight shock when he saw his body lying there. It looked like a lump of Plasticene, roughly shaped in his likeness. Someone had mangled its throat then stitched it together again. David felt glad to be away from the thing.

I'm dead! he said, turning back to Jacqui. It was quite an uplifting experience.

Jacqui smiled. *Yeah, me too. Sorry about that. I killed you and then killed myself. That man Raymond made me do it.*

A crash team burst into the room and gathered around David's body.

Come on, Jacqui said, taking his hand. *Let's get out of here before they start jolting power through you. It hurts when they do that. They've just done it to me.*

Where are we going, Jacq?

Jacqui turned to him and pecked him on the cheek. *I've no idea. We'll just have to go and see, won't we?*

'What is it you desire?' the devil asked Becky. 'What has value to you?'

Becky didn't know where it'd taken her, except that the place was the most beautiful she'd ever seen. They stood on the balcony of a fairytale palace that must have been carved from fire and ice. Endless green lawns spread out around them as far as Becky could see; stands of trees provided shade, gazebos were dotted about here and there. Arches of roses in bloom stood over some of the paths that ran through the lawns. Exotic flowers grew in profusion.

It looked like heaven.

And Becky had just turned it down.

'I desire my freedom,' she said. 'That has value.'

'You may have it,' the devil said. 'All you have to do is take back your challenge.'

'And pledge you my soul, too, I suppose,' Becky replied.

'Your soul is mine,' the devil said.

'You're starting to sound like a cracked record, playing the same groove over and over again,' Becky said. 'It's not yours and you know it. If it was yours you wouldn't tempt me, you'd just take it from me.'

Stevie appeared on the nearest strip of lawn. He was naked and looking around in confusion.

'If there's nothing you want for yourself, perhaps you'll do a deal for a loved one,' the devil said. It pointed a finger towards Stevie. A huge knight in armour appeared close to him, hefted a glittering broadsword and marched towards him. Stevie turned and ran.

'Illusion,' Becky said, but that didn't stop her gasping when Stevie lost his footing and fell. As he scrambled to his feet the knight reached him and hit him in the back of the neck with the hilt of the sword. Stevie fell down again. The knight kicked him hard in the ribs. Becky heard Stevie scream.

'Three broken ribs,' the devil said, 'one of which has punctured his lung. This is not illusion. Only you can save him. Take it back!'

'I will not take it back,' Becky said.

Down on the lawn, the knight turned Stevie over with his foot. Bright blood foamed at Stevie's mouth as he tried to roll himself into a ball. The knight kicked him until he lay still, his arms outstretched and blood running from the corner of his mouth.

'He's in agony,' the devil said. 'Will you save him?'

'Just pack it up,' Becky said. 'I'm tired of it.'

'It's reality, my princess. And here's the deal. Either you take back your invocation or you watch your darling Stevie cut to pieces. And I'll make sure he doesn't die while it's happening. Now, I want to know your answer. Either say, "I take it back," or "Stevie is yours."'

'No,' Becky said.

The knight tottered back a step. He looked up at the balcony, saluted, then swung the broadsword in a low horizontal arc, just above Stevie. Becky heard the sound of meat slicing, saw a chunk of flesh and a gout of blood take to the air before she had time to look away. Stevie squealed, high and loud, spraying blood, and sat up, clutching himself. Becky could see the dent in his ribcage.

'Kill him, if you like,' Becky said, keeping her voice low and even. *It's an illusion, that's all*, she told herself.

'Ah, suddenly I understand,' the devil said. 'Suddenly I can see what makes your heart hammer with passion.'

Suddenly the castle and the grounds were gone and Becky was on the flat place on the mountain top where Prometheus was chained down waiting for the eagle to come and peck out his liver. Except that it wasn't Prometheus, it was Stevie, and it wasn't an eagle who was going to tear out his liver but Becky.

Becky, who was naked, sheened with sweat and full of Stevie's hard cock as she tore at the livid scar across his midriff. Becky, riding him as bursts of tingling pleasure ricocheted around her body, as she felt the scar tissue give beneath her burrowing, tearing nails, as she tore back the lips of his wound and thrust her hands deep into him. She found the thing that would take her to the highest point yet and tore it out of him, her screams mingling with his own.

And then she was back in the devil's room, on her knees, fucking empty air, while her hands clutched at nothing and the fiercest orgasm of her life ripped through her body.

The devil was laughing and Stevie was screaming at it to stop whatever it was doing to her.

'I didn't do it,' she heard the devil tell Stevie. 'You did.'

Becky was surprised to discover that nothing in the cavernous room had changed. She was still dressed in her shirt and pants, still drenched with sweat, and her neck was still sore. The devil still towered over her and it was still looking at Stevie.

'Now we know where Becky lives,' the devil said. 'We know the evil that burns in the depths of her unconscious. We know of her dark yearnings for bloodlust.' Its forked tongue snaked out and licked its lips. 'There is darkness inside every living thing and Becky's pleases me. I will take that darkness and fashion something magnificent from it.'

'It's only a story from a pornographic magazine!' Becky spat. 'That's not my innermost yearnings you've just made me live through, it's a piece of hack sex fiction.'

'Nevertheless, it spoke to you,' the devil said. 'It planted a seed in your mind which grew. And which I will tend.'

Becky scowled. But the fact was that the experience of having torn out Stevie's liver on the mountain top had been so real that she could still feel the slippery texture of his internal organs in her hands, still feel where his cock had been inside her. And she couldn't deny that it had felt good.

'I think it's time for the battle to begin,' the devil grated, glaring at Stevie. 'And, as Becky's champion, you are nominated to fight.'

Stevie nodded. Becky could see him shuddering with fear. He was outclassed and he knew it. 'I choose to fight for myself,' Becky said quietly.

'But you wear the maker's emblem.' The devil smiled. 'Remove it. And remove the swastikas.'

'Done.' Becky seethed, reaching for the earring.

'Don't!' Stevie said. 'Let me do it. He can't touch you while you're wearing that earring. I don't have any protection. I'll do it.' He turned back to face the devil. Tears flooded into Becky's eyes. Stevie looked so small as he put himself between her and the devil, so frightened and yet so determined. In that instant, Becky knew that she loved Stevie more than she'd ever loved anyone, including her mother; that she loved him more than she ever *would* love anyone else.

The devil grinned. 'Such bravery,' it growled. 'And such magnificent stupidity. Are you ready for battle, Stevie?'

Stevie gave a curt nod.

The devil's gaze shifted to Johnny. 'Did you honour your debt?' he asked.

Becky turned. Johnny was still staring at the universe shining through the floor.

'Yes,' Johnny said, without looking up.

'You have the amulet in your hands. Returned from the thief, Derek Sharp, father of my queen-to-be, and trickster.'

'Yes,' Johnny said.

'Then give it to me, now.'

'Don't!' Becky yelled. 'Johnny! For my sake don't give it to him!'

'That's cheating,' Stevie said angrily. 'We fight as we are. No extra weapons.'

The devil gazed down at him. 'I don't need weapons to dispose of vermin like you. The amulet is mine and I will have it back. Now.'

'You're gonna use it against me,' Stevie said. 'Or you wouldn't want it now.'

'Fool!' the devil said, and made a circle of its forefinger and thumb. It turned its hand palm up, shook it and flicked its finger at Stevie.

Becky saw a streak of white light and Stevie was in the air, falling to his back. A corkscrew of smoke followed his trajectory.

He hit the floor, his body convulsed and he made a heart-rending sound, something between a scream of agony and a cry for help.

'The amulet, Johnny,' the devil boomed. 'Give it to me. Quickly.'

Johnny didn't look up but shook his head.

'Johnny. Now!' the devil said.

'No,' Johnny replied, in a tiny voice. 'I want out.'

'It's too late,' the devil said. 'The deal has been struck. You had your thousand years of pleasure. Now you owe me your soul. You cannot refuse.'

'I just did,' Johnny said, looking up. His eyes were dark and angry.

'You are truly your mother's child,' the devil said. 'But you are mine too. Come to your father, your master.' It beckoned, and Johnny began to walk slowly towards it, the big silver gun in his right hand and the amulet dangling from his left. He looked to Becky as if he was resisting, but he was going, anyway.

Stevie had quietened now, but his body was still jerking spasmodically. Becky began to move towards him, expecting the devil to stop her. But the devil's eyes were fixed on Johnny.

The devil spoke again, this time in a soothing, melodic voice. 'I will set you free from your deal, Johnny Kane. You will be my emissary, my representative on earth. My wreaker of havoc. You may do as you please throughout eternity. If you hand me the amulet. Hand me the amulet and Becky's body is yours to use.'

'You want her,' Johnny said.

'We may both have her,' the devil said. 'I will have her for my queen and you may have her for a mistress. She will worship you, body and soul, just as she will worship me.'

'Stevie?' Becky whispered.

'Hurts,' Stevie gasped.

Becky glanced at the devil who was gazing into Johnny's eyes and talking to him softly. She quickly took out the earring, opened Stevie's mouth with her finger and placed it beneath his tongue. 'Keep it there,' she said, squeezing his hand. 'Don't spit it out.'

'All you have to do in return is shoot her,' the devil said. 'Shoot her now, Johnny. You have one bullet left in your gun. Use it. Give me the amulet and shoot Becky.'

'She'll be dead,' Johnny said.

'She'll be dead, but her soul will be mine,' the devil told Johnny. 'And once I own her, I can reincarnate her whenever I desire. She'll be able to accompany you during your life on earth while she's here with me. It'll be an ecstatic life for you, Johnny.'

'It's a deal,' Johnny said. 'But I keep the amulet until I've shot her.'

'Give it to me now,' the devil said, its voice rising.

'You can't take it unless I give it to you, can you?' Johnny said, sounding puzzled. 'Why's that?'

'Kill the girl,' the devil hissed, 'or I'll wink your soul out of existence.'

Johnny shrugged and turned towards Becky, who got up.

He was smiling as he came over. Half-way to her, he raised the gun.

Becky saw his finger tighten on the trigger and tensed. 'Don't!' she said.

'I'm sorry, Beck,' Johnny said. 'I have to do this. I love you, you see.' He stood before her, his back to the devil, and placed the long cool barrel of the revolver against her forehead. He squeezed the trigger a little and whispered, 'Old Yah-hoo is full of shit. He lied to me again.'

'KILL HER!' the devil boomed.

'He can't take the amulet from me. I have to give it to him. While I'm holding it, I don't belong to him.'

'HURRY, JOHNNY!'

'And I have a sneaking suspicion that he wants you shot so you can't get hold of it,' Johnny said. 'I always knew you were something special, Becky. Well, I guess it's time to say goodbye. Whatever happens, Becky, remember this: I loved you.'

'JOHNNY! KILL HER!' the devil roared.

Johnny winked at her, rolled his eyes, nodded back towards the devil, grinned and held out the amulet for her to take. Then he pulled the barrel of the gun away from her forehead, opened his mouth, put in the barrel and yanked the trigger.

'TRICKSTER!' the devil screamed.

It was light now but still early morning. Duke lay on his belly, his head between his paws, while he gazed up at the power lines in front of him. They had been crackling and sparking and glowing blue ever since Stevie and Becky and Johnny had gone to the *other place*, but Duke had been patient. It hadn't been his time.

But his time was close now. He could sense this in the changes he could feel coming from the *other place* and from the nearness of Old Andy. Old Andy had been distant at first, but Duke was aware that he was coming back. It was a confusing and frightening sensation, but Duke was used to those now. Badness was around. Bigger badness than he had ever experienced before.

Even though he'd been scared by the bang-iron Bad-Johnny

had hurt his ears with, Duke hadn't run far. He'd come back here and been patient and waited for Old Andy in spite of knowing that his master and pack-leader needed him. Good Stevie and Good Becky, for both of whom he would gladly have fought to the death, were being overpowered by the badness in the *other place*, but he sensed that Old Andy didn't know how to get there and needed to know. So he had waited.

And now Old Andy was close; so close that Duke would soon be able to smell him over the stench the dead woman and the dead gobbling had left behind as they'd vanished. Over the stench of the cat that he kept picking up off the breeze.

Duke caught that feline odour again. He recognized the smell. It was the stench of Leonard, the ginger man-cat that lived in his street. He had an old score to settle with Leonard: the cat had opened up his nose more than once. But Leonard's scent had changed, and it was worrying. Duke had seen Leonard in the *other place* and the cat had been larger. It had stalked up and down against the way home and Stevie and Johnny had decided to avoid it. Which meant that Leonard was dangerous. Duke's nose and all his other senses had confirmed this.

And Leonard was stalking now. And his scent was drifting across from the road where Stevie and Old Andy and Gone-Jacqui and Duke himself lived. And Andy was heading that way, quickly now.

Duke snorted and stood up. His hurt leg was stiff, but he shook himself loose, glanced around the field, sniffed the air and trotted to the path where he paused, sensing the danger emanating from Leonard. Old Andy needed to get to the *other place* and Duke thought the man-cat was there to stop him.

Old Andy was going to need help.

When he stepped from the taxi that had rushed him from Heathrow, Andy felt very old indeed. And very tired. He'd been to Dallas and back without stopping – the return flight had left forty minutes after he'd arrived – and he'd been travelling for twenty-two and a half hours. During that time, his life had turned to shit. He'd seen several innocent people killed, he'd lost his wife and, perhaps, his son, too.

He didn't know where he had to go or what he had to do, now that he was back in his own street – or even whether he was too late to do anything at all. All he had to go on was the fragmented recurring dream he'd had each time he'd dozed off on the return trip. In it, he was handing something to Becky, who was dressed in a torn shirt and a pair of white cotton knickers. Andy had dreamed the same thing over and over again, but had never seen what that thing was.

He decided to go indoors, equip himself with a weapon and hope to hell that Stevie and Jacqui and Duke weren't all in there dead. And if Stevie had survived, that he was OK. And if he was gone, that he had left a message of some kind.

Some sort of fucking hero you turned out to be, he told himself. *Getting on a plane to America when you should have been home settling all this shit. What are you gonna do now? You don't have a clue, do you? How can you blaze in and save the day if you don't even know who's alive and who's dead, or even where they are?*

He turned to the front gate, opened it and stopped dead in his tracks.

Between him and the front door was the biggest domestic cat he'd ever seen. It looked like Leonard, whom the Amis family from number nine had lost a week ago. But instead of looking thin and bedraggled, as missing cats did when they turned up, Leonard looked as if he'd been away on a body-building course. He wasn't just more muscular, he was at least four times his original size.

And Leonard was angry. The moment his yellow eyes met Andy's his back arched, he hissed and swiped the air in front of him. His claws were now almost as long as Andy's fingers, but black and curved and tipped with sharp-looking points. Andy's heart-rate jacked up and fresh energy hit him when his blood-stream flooded with adrenaline.

'OK, Pussy, if that's how you feel about it, I won't come in,' Andy said. He walked backwards until he was outside the gate again.

Andy knew that the cat was going to leap and as it tensed, then pounced, he slammed the wrought-iron gate shut.

It bent where Leonard hit it. The cat bounced off, skittered across the ground trying to find its feet and turned, hissing then yowling and finishing with a low, lion-like growl.

Then Leonard leapt again.

Andy ducked, but the cat landed on his head and shoulders, knocking him to the ground as it sank in its claws.

Andy writhed and squirmed as the animal clawed at the back of his head. He was bleeding, but the thickness of his hair had saved him from major damage. He got to his knees, but the cat clung on, its huge, sharp teeth trying to get a purchase on the nape of his neck. Andy elbowed at the maddened animal but it wouldn't let go.

I'm going to die, kneeling in the middle of an empty street, Andy thought. He reached over his head and buried his fingers in the cat's fur. The animal slashed a paw across the back of his wrist. Andy whipped back his hand, spraying his face with blood.

As Leonard finally bit into Andy's neck, he was hit by something hard and howling, something that knocked his breath from him and sent him flying back to the tarmac. Leonard's claws were gone from Andy's back, the teeth out of his neck. And a battle was taking place beside him.

Dookie!

In the fifteen seconds that followed, Andy understood why Duke had been classified as dangerous. He wasn't as quick as the cat and he didn't have claws to scratch with, but that big white grin flashed and bit faster than the eye could follow it. Duke looked mad.

Finally Leonard ran off down the road, clawed his way up the chain-link gates of the abandoned garage and vanished.

Beside Andy, Duke shook. Blood flew from the scratches in his nose and skull. His hindquarters were bleeding too, but he grinned up at Andy, wagged his tail and gave a playful yap. Then he trotted down the road, paused and looked back over his shoulder.

Andy frowned at him, then something caught his eye. Over on the other side of the ring-road, way up by the railway embankment, something blue was flickering.

'Over there?' Andy asked the dog, pointing.

Duke yapped again and began to trot down the road.

Andy followed.

Katie Kane woke again. She didn't know how long she'd been out this time, but her arm was dead. She used her other hand to straighten it and massaged it gently.

A few minutes later, she got to her feet. Her heart had to be broken and it had to be done now, before it was too late. She'd already wasted too much time lying here unconscious. Her head pounded and she felt dizzy and ill. But that didn't matter. In twenty minutes or so, nothing would ever matter again. Inside half an hour, if she could just stay on her feet and walk to where she had to walk, everything would be cool with a capital K.

According to her watch it was a quarter to nine. Katie didn't know what day it was and didn't care. *It's Kool Day again*, she told herself, as she opened the front door and went out into the fresh air. *That's all that matters. Just get the job done and you can relax. For as long as you like. Probably.* Katie found herself smiling. It seemed that she had been waiting for this for a long time.

The streets were busy with traffic, but Katie didn't notice the cars or the people. She had places to be, things to do, and she knew deep down inside her that she wouldn't be disturbed in her task. It was Kool Day, again, after all.

The walk to the alley took less than ten minutes. As usual when she was there, it was free of people. She approached the mouth-shaped hole in the path without any feeling of foreboding, fear or regret. Across the years, Jane's words rang in her ears: *It's not over yet. Live your life. When it's time, break your heart and seal what you've been keeping open.*

'Oh, I'll do that,' Katie said, standing before the hole and taking off her jacket. 'It'll give me great pleasure. I just hope I'm not too late.'

It was more difficult than she'd anticipated to extract the needle from her lapel – when she'd inserted it she'd left the eye protruding, but in all the fuss and bother back at Andy's it had gone right down inside. She worked frantically at the material, then decided she'd be better off pushing the needle down and getting the point to come out through the lapel than trying to extract it backwards. She could barely believe she hadn't thought of it before. It seemed as if something was trying to slow her down.

'Well, fuck you, whoever you are,' Katie said, as the needle's point began to show. She took it in her nails and dragged it out from the lapel. It glinted in the watery light.

Katie put it between her teeth and began to unbutton her shirt. She'd take off *everything*. It'd give them something to talk about when they eventually found her. *If they find me*, she thought. 'I'm going out with a bang,' she told herself. 'Not with a whimper.'

A few seconds later, she was naked in the cool morning air. She knelt beside the mouth-shaped hole, straightened up and felt between her ribs to where her heartbeat was strongest.

I hope to Christ I hit the right spot, she thought, *or I'm gonna look pretty dumb this afternoon when they ask me what happened.* She grinned. She felt better than she could ever remember feeling. She doubted she'd felt this good before all this shit had begun to happen. It didn't matter either way, now. What mattered was sealing the thing she'd been keeping open.

'Fuck it!' she cursed, remembering that she hadn't brought the thimble with her. *I'll have to do without it*, she thought. *After all, it isn't as if I'll be wanting to do much with my hands afterwards, is it?*

She took the needle in her left hand, laid the point in the hollow of her ribs in the spot she had chosen and wondered if she should, perhaps, offer up a prayer.

'I'm sorry I did what I did,' she said, looking up at the sky where her mother had once told her God lived. 'I'm sorrier that I didn't know what the fuck I was doing when I did it, too. I hope this will make amends. And if you're not big enough to accept my apology, then . . . FUCK YOU!'

Holding the needle between thumb and forefinger, she pushed. It broke her skin and went in a little way before her finger and thumb slipped down its length. The sensation wasn't so much of pain as of a numbing pressure that spread out across her breastbone.

Katie let go of the needle. It was deep enough to stay where it was. Blood was beginning to gather beneath the wound and a tiny red speck was growing at the puncture. Smiling, Katie made a fist and placed her thumbnail against the eye of the needle. Then, keeping her elbow steady, just below the height of her shoulder, she swung out her fist in front of her and, using all her strength, hammered it back. The eye broke her nail and sank through the soft flesh beneath it until it hit bone. The needle's point was driven an inch into her chest.

Hissing with pain, Katie twisted her thumb free and repeated the process. This time, the needle pierced her thumb and skewered it to the knuckle of the forefinger that lay behind it.

Break my heart! Katie thought, and used all her power to swing her right hand against the left fist pinned to her chest.

She felt the needle enter her heart. For a moment it seemed as if someone had exploded a small bomb inside her chest. Somewhere below her, something was trembling. Somewhere out there on the other side of this bank of pain, there was a smell of exotic plants and bonfire smoke. Katie felt herself sink down on her haunches as purple and black shapes swarmed and burst across the inside of her tightly closed eyes, matching the rise and rise of her agony.

The ground lurched.

Katie opened her eyes in time to see the mouth-shaped hole close and the crack behind it fade.

It was the last thing she saw.

Andy Warner was a man who had taken enough drugs to become used to dealing with sudden sensory shocks. The crossing to May Street didn't faze him one tiny bit. He experienced no dizziness or disorientation, just stepped out of one version of the world into another.

What *did* knock his brain for six was the discovery of which version of the world he'd walked into. It was May Street, almost exactly as he'd last seen it.

'*Fuck my old boots!*' he marvelled. The place even smelt like it used to. Then he noticed that Duke hadn't taken the reality-shift as well as he had. The dog was flat on the ground on his belly, struggling to get up.

Andy squatted beside him and hefted the dog to his feet.

Duke tested his legs with a few staggering steps, then steadied. He turned and yapped at Andy and began to trot down the street.

And I know exactly where we're going, too, Andy thought, as he ran along trying to keep pace with the dog. *We're going straight back to it. All this time we thought we'd got away with it and here it was. Waiting for us to return.*

So why was a monster cat put between me and this?

Andy didn't know the answer, but he was going to find out.

Number fifty-two was just up ahead.

Stevie was on his knees, the devil earring under his tongue and his hand deep inside the carrier bag as Johnny fell backwards, the top and back of his head gone, his brain and skull still flying through the air. He saw Becky grab at the amulet as it fell from Johnny's fingers and miss it by a millimetre. The tin diamond hit the floor and slid away. Just in front of it, the transparent floor liquefied and a black gobbling climbed out. The floor solidified and the gobbling stood there baring its teeth and hissing a warning at Becky.

'Battle!' the devil roared, flicking out the fingers of both hands. Stevie pulled one of the mirrors out of the bag and held it up. The thin stream of fire that jetted from the devil's hands hit the mirror and Stevie felt the heat wash over him. Beside him, Becky leapt into the air as the rope of flame hit the floor at her feet and cruised down the room.

The mirror in Stevie's hands felt hot and heavy. The fire hadn't bounced off the reflective surface but it hadn't hit him either. It must have gone inside the mirror. He shook it towards the devil.

The stream of fire shot from it, twice the size it had been when the devil had flung it. Crackling hungrily, it arced across the room and hit the devil in its chest. It vanished and was replaced by a nine-foot-tall column of roaring flames.

'Becky! Take the mirror!' Stevie yelled.

The gobbling was advancing on her, its teeth now five sizes too large and snapping the air. Backing away, she glanced from it to Stevie. He threw the mirror. She caught it, dropped to her knees and held it up as the gobbling charged at her.

'Bad move,' the voice of the devil said, from the column of fire, as the gobbling vanished into the mirror. 'It's a magnifying mirror and when my minion reappears it'll be much larger and it'll *still* be my minion. You'll have to break the mirror to prevent its escape. Oh, and Becky, my princess, your father is dead.'

'Liar!' Becky spat.

'Look in the mirror,' the devil said. 'See for yourself.'

'Don't!' Stevie warned, groping in the bag for the other mirror.

'Your mother's dead, too, Stevie.' The devil chuckled. 'And Katie. And David. Only you, Becky and your father remain. And I will have the three of you.'

Becky dropped the mirror she was holding. It shattered, sparkled and vanished.

'That's better,' the devil said, stepping out of the column of fire, which died to a tiny blue flame and sputtered out. Smoke wafted from its mouth and nostrils as it spoke. 'I hate mirrors because they stop me doing things like . . . *this*!' it said, and made a pass with a clawed hand. A small black thing whipped from his hand and hit Becky's midriff.

Becky squealed and dropped to her knees, clutching her stomach.

'I believe she gave the maker's trinket to you, Stevie.' The devil grinned. 'Pity it's a yang symbol, fit only for women.'

'But I still have this mirror,' Stevie said, holding it up.

The devil grinned smokily. 'Hmm,' it said. 'So you do. But how quick are you with it?' The devil held up its left hand, clawed fingers spread wide. Lightning danced from finger to finger and four bolts flashed.

Stevie was quick, but he captured only two in the mirror. One melted most of the rubber on the right side of his left boot, the other tore through the leg of his jeans, burning a gouge in his left knee. The pain was tremendous. As he fell, Stevie shook the mirror, but the magnified bolts of power went wide.

Becky whimpered, heaved and vomited.

Holding his leg and gritting his teeth against a scream, Stevie saw the lumpy dark mass that Becky was throwing up. Each time she gasped in a fresh breath, she vomited again. Then the first of the mass of dark lumps took to the air.

Oh, Christ, Stevie thought, *she's vomiting bees!*

The devil had launched a storm of hailstones at him. The chunks of ice battered into him, numbing his face and hands and blinding him. When the storm ended the mirror was face down on the floor, about ten feet behind him.

'Wasn't much of a battle, was it?' the devil said, holding up its left hand and working its fingers at something that wasn't quite formed. 'What other weapons do you have in your bag of tricks?'

Becky vomited again and heaved in air with a sound like an ancient pair of bellows.

The first bee that came towards Stevie was so bloated it could barely fly. He batted it away with his free hand and his watch flew from his wrist, skidding across the floor.

The devil blew plumes of smoke from its nostrils. Stevie could see the thing in his hand now: it was a piece of molten lava.

Stevie got up on all fours, moaning with pain, and dragged himself towards the mirror, hoping it wasn't broken. Just as he reached out for it, the smouldering rock whizzed past his ear and hit the back of the mirror. He heard it crack and groaned, the devil earring rattling against his teeth.

'It's all over for you, Stevie,' the devil said, from behind him. 'Get up, pick up the amulet and give it to me. I'll make your death an easy one. And your eternity enjoyable.'

'Get it yourself,' Stevie said.

'Do you think I wouldn't have done so already if I could?' the devil said angrily. 'It was gifted to Becky's father by Raymond. It must be gifted back to me. Now do as I say or I will crush you.'

'You'd better come and do it then,' Stevie said, as Becky puked up a fresh wave of bees. The carrier bag lay on the floor in front of him and he crawled towards it, wondering what good a spray-pump bottle of bleach could do him.

A gobbling was guarding the threshold of the house. Andy stopped dead in his tracks and froze when he saw the thing, but Dookie evidently felt the same way about this kind of monstrosity as he did about Leonard the killer cat. He charged past Andy, teeth first and howling.

The fight was fierce, but didn't last long.

A pride of angry lions would have had their work cut out if the Dukester had gone after them like that, Andy thought after he'd got over the tremendous amount of blood that had burst from the thing.

Duke trotted back to him, wagging his tail and grinning a red smile. It gave Andy a little hope. The dog went into the house and cautiously down the hall, nose to the bare boards. Andy followed him, his heart in his mouth.

With each step he took the hall vanished and Andy was

somewhere else. He stepped into the back of David's BMW and watched his wife cut David's throat, then her own; he stepped from there to the hospital where he saw the last movements Derek would ever make as he climbed out of bed. Then he was in the hospital room with Jacqui as her monitors flat-lined; then in David's room as his did the same. Then he watched Katie sacrifice herself to close the mouth in the path.

And then he was walking through the door of the room at the back of number fifty-two May Street.

What happened next happened so quickly that it was over in seconds, but so slowly that Andy had time to absorb every detail.

The inside of the room looked much as it had the last time he had been in there, but it was a great deal bigger and the floor appeared to be outer space. Andy's eyes lit on Becky – who was doubled over, puking bees – then on Stevie, who was pulling something from a Safeway carrier bag, then on the devil, the smouldering being to whom Andy had promised the soul of his firstborn.

Then he saw the amulet on the floor and knew what his recurring dream had been trying to tell him.

All of this happened in the split second during which Duke began to howl as if he'd turned into a demon himself. As Andy started towards the amulet, the dog bounded across the room and launched himself at the devil.

And latched on.

The devil roared.

Andy's next steps were slow-motion dream-steps. He was moving as fast as he could, but he knew that he wasn't going to be fast enough.

To his left, Becky looked up at him questioningly, her eyes imploring him. Her body convulsed and bees swarmed from her mouth.

Stevie was on his feet now, and stumbling towards the devil, a spray-bottle of bleach in his hands as if it were a Walther PPK.

The devil was clutching Duke's writhing body, and the dog's big white teeth were flashing madly, his head dipping and yanking at the devil's face, his paws scrabbling for purchase.

And the devil was bellowing.

Andy batted his way through swarming bees and launched himself into the air. He hit the glassy floor and slid towards the amulet.

The moment his fingers touched it, all hell broke loose.

*

Stevie saw Duke enter the room and launch himself at the devil. It was the dumbest, most heroic thing he'd ever seen. But Duke was going to die trying to save his master.

Stevie clutched the bleach and went towards the devil, his pain forgotten. 'Leave my dog alone!'

From the corner of his eye, he saw Andy dive towards the amulet, but his mind was fixed on following his dog's example. If he was going to die, he was going to *hurt* the devil before he did.

As the devil wrested Duke away from his face and flung him across the room, something happened. The light in the room grew brighter and a horde of red gobblings winked into being. To Stevie's right, Johnny's dead body began to get up and to his left a tangle of snakes appeared.

Ahead of him the devil was holding out its arms like Christ crucified. Fire danced around him, outlining its body and head. Its dark eyes lit golden, its thick tail twitched and swished, and its erection grew until it reached up to its sternum.

It's hurt! Stevie thought, refusing to allow himself to think of Duke, who was now dead or dying somewhere behind him. The skin of the devil's face hung in tatters. Its lower lip was torn almost to its chin and thick dark blood spouted from its neck.

Stevie pumped the trigger of the spray bottle as the first gobbling approached him. It exploded as soon as the bleach touched it, as did the next rank. Stevie spun around and squirted the bottle at the ones behind him, catching a glimpse of his dad, the amulet swinging on its chain in his left hand as he punched away the creatures approaching him.

Stevie turned back and advanced on the devil, clearing his way with the bleach while he groped in his pocket for the knife Johnny had given him.

'GET AWAY FROM ME!' the devil shrieked, still standing with its hands out.

Stevie took two paces closer, the earring in his mouth burning now, and pumped the trigger of the spray bottle. The hit was good: the first stream of bleach hit the wound in the devil's neck and began to eat into the flesh. He squeezed again, hitting the devil's mouth this time. 'Die, you bastard!' he yelled, and the earring popped out of his mouth, bounced at the devil's feet and vanished in a puff of smoke.

The devil brought its hands together hard. The clap shook like thunder through Stevie's ribcage.

'STOP!' the devil boomed.

And suddenly the room was silent but for Stevie's breathing, the sound of the blood pouring from the devil's throat and dripping to the floor and a pitiful whine from Duke.

Stevie glanced round. Everything was frozen in mid-movement. Andy was holding the chain of the amulet over Becky's head, about to place it around her neck. Becky was bent forward, a stream of bees locked between her lips and the floor. Johnny's body was heading towards them. Duke was at the far end of the room, still moving. He looked as if he was trying to get up but Stevie doubted that he would ever get up again.

'Your last chance,' the devil said. 'Fetch me the amulet and you all go free. Refuse and I kill you and the dog here and now. You no longer have any protection from me, Stevie.'

'Get fucked!' Stevie said, and pumped the trigger of the bleach bottle. The spray hit the devil's lower lip, which smouldered.

'It stings a little.' The devil grinned. 'But you can't kill an immortal.'

'Why didn't you freeze Dookie?' Stevie asked.

'Dogs are not my domain,' the devil replied, kneading the air with its left hand. Something round and silvery began to appear. 'This one will be your end.'

Duke howled.

'The animal understands.' The devil smiled. 'I thought he might.'

Stevie glanced at the silvery ball of magic in the devil's hand and wondered. It didn't seem to be solidifying. 'Are you stretching yourself a little?' he asked.

The devil said, 'I have almost infinite power. Second only to that of the maker. And the maker never stops time. It's . . . complex.'

Stevie nodded. 'A drain on the resources, is it?' he asked. He clutched the knife and, as the spell solidified in the devil's hand, he threw it. Hard.

Duke moaned.

The blade hit the head of the devil's phallus, penetrated it and pinned it to its stomach. The devil staggered backwards, screaming, the glowing sphere bouncing in its hand.

And there was Duke pushing at Stevie's right knee, demanding his attention. Something was dangling from his mouth.

My watch, Stevie thought in astonishment. *He's badly hurt and he's brought my watch.* And then he realized why and snatched it from the dog's mouth. Duke limped away as Stevie held up the watch. The back was polished to a shine. You could see your face in it. Just like a mirror.

Stevie was ready when the devil flung the shining ball of light.

It sizzled through the air, hit the back of the watch and vanished. The weight of the watch increased so suddenly that Stevie almost dropped it. Holding it tightly, he shook out the spell. It was no longer a perfect sphere, but it went back to meet its maker.

And time began again.

The spell hit the devil, who roared and fell to its knees, clutching at its head. Then it began to get up again, still howling.

It wasn't enough, Stevie thought. *It didn't give us the break.*

But it *was* enough. During the time it took the devil to recover, Andy dropped the amulet around Becky's neck. And the amulet burst into life.

Becky wasn't sure what had gone on around her since the devil had thrown the black thing at her. She'd dropped to her knees and begun to puke uncontrollably. She'd felt her strength fading and was sure she was going to die.

Then there was a flicker, during which everything stood still, and Andy was in front of her, grinning like a maniac as he draped her dad's junk-shop amulet around her neck.

The cheap tin charm lit up and shone with a blinding golden light. She could feel her body charging up with its power and she floated to her feet.

Becky found her mouth pregnant with words that needed to be said and she began to speak them. Although they were in a language she didn't know, she understood them. The first sentence translated as 'Get thee gone!'

And in a radius of ten feet around her, every gobbling, demon, snake and bee winked out of existence. Johnny was coming towards her, walking clumsily. She pointed a finger at him, said 'Rest!' and Johnny fell back.

The devil staggered forward. Fire danced around it, and blood, spittle and the juices from its erection fell to the floor at its feet and spattered away like droplets of water on a hotplate. It was howling and cursing her in that strange language, alternately trying to banish her and pleading with her, offering her everything her mind could imagine and more.

Becky walked forward, and as she moved, the floor cleared of gobblings and demons and the air of flying insects. Andy ran towards her and she took his hand, drawing him to her safety.

The devil made a circle from its forefinger and thumb and flicked a strike of lightning at her. Becky held up a hand and absorbed it. It tingled up her arm and lit a smile on her face.

'Be still,' she said, but the devil cursed and squealed, roared and spat fire, smoke and sparks at her. Stevie was away from him now, moving fast. Becky went towards him, but Stevie veered off and continued down the room, squirting the bleach at the mass of gobblings that had backed Duke into a corner. The dog was hurt – Becky could feel his pain – but he was still fighting and besting each thing that dared bare its teeth at him. Stevie would survive. Becky *knew* that. He'd done his part. And now she would do hers. Now she would sap the devil of the energy he had gained.

'Keep away from me, daughter of Jane!' the devil seethed, as she and Andy approached it.

Becky raised both her hands, palms outward, facing the devil. Her skin began to itch, to feel warm then hot as her magnetism leached the devil's power. And the closer she came to it, the greater her draw on its power became. The devil began to shrink.

'Release those whose souls you have stolen today,' Becky said, tasting the power of the foreign words in her mouth. 'Let them be!'

The devil spat a gobbet of flame at her feet, but Becky could feel its grip loosen, feel those souls wriggle from its clutches.

'Now be quiet, devil,' Becky said. 'Be still and rest. Sleep a thousand years.'

And the devil turned away from her, crept back to its throne, sat down and vanished.

A moment later, the amulet winked out and Becky discovered that she, Andy and Stevie, now carrying Duke in his arms, were once more in a stinking bare room in a derelict house.

For a while they stared at one another. Then Andy said, 'Well, that went a bit better than we anticipated, didn't it?'

Chapter Twenty

1972

The first sign that things hadn't gone quite as well as Andy had thought came when they were half-way back down the street towards the shop where they intended to take the fast track back to the field and the power lines.

An old woman came out of her house about fifty yards ahead of them. Not only did they see her, but she saw them and didn't like what she saw. Stevie was surprised that she could see them, but not at her reaction – after all, three injured people hobbling down the street covered in blood from head to foot wasn't a sight you saw every day. The woman let out a small scream, clapped her hand to her mouth, then turned and hurried back indoors. As they walked past her house, Stevie caught a glimpse of her staring out from behind her net curtains, her hand still over her mouth and a shocked expression on her face.

'She can see us, Dad,' Stevie said. His voice sounded odd in his ears, rasping and hissing. At some point the noise level during what had happened had injured his ears. He hoped it was only temporary.

'We'll be gone in a minute and she'll never see us again,' Andy said.

Stevie buttoned his lip and hoped his dad was right. All he wanted right now was to be away from May Street. But his dad was wrong about them being away from here in a minute.

The power source had gone. The gate had closed.

The plate-glass window of Leet's Store was merely a plate-glass window. Stevie looked for the barrier that had sealed off May Street from the Brook Street crossroads. That was gone, too.

'We could check down the other end at the playground,' Stevie said, 'but I think we'd be wasting our time.'

Becky nodded. 'Katie closed the gate,' she said. 'I knew that when the amulet began to work. I just didn't know what it meant. The hole in the alleyway linked nineteen seventy-two to our present. And Katie closed it.'

Andy sighed. 'A bit too quickly,' he said.

'What are we going to do?' Stevie said. In his arms Duke gave a sigh, which summed it all up, as far as Stevie was concerned.

Becky took Stevie's hand. 'There's nothing to go back for anyway,' she said. 'Your mum's dead. My dad's dead. Johnny's entire family has gone.'

'But we *can't* be stuck in 'seventy-two!' Stevie moaned.

'We're lucky to be alive at all,' Becky said. 'Count your blessings.'

'We'll be arrested in ten minutes, looking like this,' Stevie said. 'Then what happens?'

Andy chuckled.

'What?' Stevie said.

'I've just thought of something so weird I can barely believe it,' he said. 'It's 'seventy-two, which means I'm here *twice*. And I'll tell you another thing, too. Something else I just remembered.'

'What?' Stevie asked.

'We're gonna be OK,' Andy said. 'We're going to live in nineteen seventy-two and we're gonna be just fine. It's a good era, Stevie. You'll love it. And just think of the advantages you're gonna have. We know what happens between now and the when that we came from. It's gonna be fine here. Well, not here, exactly, but where we're going.'

Stevie shook his head. 'I can't keep up,' he said. 'What did you remember, anyway?'

'Come on!' Andy said, still grinning, and set off back down the street.

Duke began to struggle so Stevie set him down. The dog needed a vet – there were slashes in his head that would have to be stitched and Stevie thought one of his back legs might be broken – but he could walk, although he held the hurt leg off the ground.

Becky took Stevie's hand and kissed him on the lips. 'It's going to work out,' she said. 'We're together, that's all that matters to me. We can survive in this time. It doesn't matter. It'll be an adventure. A fresh start.'

Stevie hugged Becky and found a smile for her. In spite of his battle fatigue, his pain, his fuzzy hearing and his sluggish mind, he began to see possibilities. This wasn't what he'd hoped for, but it might turn out OK after all.

Andy stopped outside the house where Stevie and Johnny had met the younger version of Derek on his acid trip. 'Here we are,' he said, and pointed at the door.

'We can't go inside,' Stevie said.

'Why not?' Becky asked.

'It's your dad's old house. He might be in there,' Stevie said.

'I don't mind,' Becky said. 'I'd like to see him alive again, just to kinda—'

'He won't know who you are,' Stevie said. 'Dad, we can't go in!'

Andy smiled. 'Oh yes we can,' he replied. 'The door isn't locked. That's another of the things I've remembered. In 'seventy-two, when things were getting hairy for us . . .' He tailed off. 'We dealt drugs, you know that, don't you? Even if you didn't, you do now. I'm not going to keep a single secret for the rest of my life,' he said. 'I've seen what happens when you do. I'll fill in all the missing parts for you later. Anyway, after Raymond, things went wrong. We got busted and most of us spent time in jail. But before that we had a couple of scares. One was when Raymond was chasing us around – we thought he'd tell the cops. Another came later. Someone knocked us over and in our infinite paranoia, we thought it was the CID. This is truly phenomenal, kids!'

'What do you mean?' Stevie said.

'Someone hit us. Right where it hurts. And now I know who it was and why they did it.'

'You've lost me,' Stevie said, shaking his head.

'Someone broke into Derek's house,' Andy said, grinning. 'Derek went to London for the weekend and left the door ajar. It's stiff – doesn't shut properly unless you slam it. And while he was away someone burgled his house. We thought it was the drugs squad looking for acid, but it wasn't.'

Stevie shrugged.

'It's *us*, dummy!' Andy said. 'Derek's house was broken into on *this* day on *this* month in 'seventy-two. I remember it well because of the panic afterwards. But it wasn't the police in there, it was us. Me, you and Becky. Derek worried about it for ages, because, get this, the only stuff missing was a hacksaw and a few items of clothing. The bath plug-hole was blocked with dog hairs. He couldn't work out why. And neither could the rest of us. But I know now! I know, because it's *me* doing the breaking and entering. It's all working out, Stevie, we're gonna be OK.'

An hour and a half later, Becky and Stevie, now dressed in clothes that they'd stolen from their parents, and Duke, who'd shed a lot of hair in Derek's bath, followed Andy into a lock-up unit in a run-down trading estate on the other side of town. Andy had sawn off the padlock with a hacksaw he'd found in Derek's house. It had taken a long time and he had drawn some odd looks from passers-by. He didn't seem to care. He just grinned at Stevie and Becky and said, 'You're forgetting. I know the outcome here already. We don't get caught. We get away.'

The lock-up was little more than a glorified garage. It had a cement floor, breeze-block walls, lights, a tea and coffee machine, a door marked WC and fluorescent light fittings on the grubby ceiling. The place was filled, almost to bursting, with packing crates and used furniture.

'What *is* this place?' Stevie asked, recognizing his father's signature in the untidiness of the place.

'It's our cover,' Andy said. 'Or it was when I was younger. For the drugs thing. We own a company that owns a company that buys and sells furniture. It's untraceable. I know that because the cops never did find it. There's acid stashed here right now. Lots of it. But we haven't come for that. We've come for something else.' He sat down on a grubby PVC sofa. 'It's so weird,' he said. 'Jacq's dead. And yet she's still alive. I don't know whether I should laugh or cry about that. We had good times together, Stevie. In spite of everything. And what's even weirder is that we're all going to have to go away from here, knowing our loved ones are here and still living. We're going to have to go away without seeing them. If we stay, we'll screw things up big time.'

'The doppelganger effect?' Becky asked.

Andy nodded. 'That *and* the time-paradox stuff,' he said.

'What's the doppelganger effect?' Stevie asked. He didn't have any tears to cry for his mother or Johnny or the others that had died. Perhaps he would later, when the shock had worn off, but none of it seemed real right now.

'There's a school of thought that reckons everyone on earth has an identical copy somewhere,' Becky said. 'A double. It also reckons – although I don't know how or why – that if the doubles should meet, the balance of the universe is upset and the two cancel themselves out. They vanish with an explosion and in a shower of quarks or something. It reeks of bullshit but I wouldn't want to test it.'

'Me neither,' Andy said.

'So what do we do?' Stevie asked.

Andy took his wallet out and opened it and showed it to Stevie. 'Look,' he said. 'No money.'

'You've got credit cards there,' Stevie said.

Andy nodded. 'I have but their start dates are getting on for twenty-five years ahead of where we are now. I don't think anyone would accept them, do you? I could try using them, but if someone noticed – and they might – I'd end up jailed for fraud.

I'm gonna have to ditch these. Cut them up and lose them. Which brings me to one of the other two things I remembered.'

'There's money hidden in here,' Becky said, nodding.

Andy grinned. 'We lost sixty thousand pounds on the same day as Derek's break-in. Dope money we'd stashed away safely. In here. For a time we thought it was an inside job – that one of us had taken it – but we were all wealthy and none of us needed to steal it. Isn't that ironic? It *is* an inside job! One of us *does* need to steal it. I've got twenty grand in the bank, Stevie, but it's in the bank in our time, not in 'seventy-two. So we're gonna hit on the money in here. We're going to take half of it for us and leave the other sixty for the young Andy and company.' He got up and picked his way through the jumbled assortment of furniture, then disappeared from view behind an oak wardrobe.

Becky took Stevie's hand and squeezed it.

Duke huffed and began to lick his back leg.

'Here we are!' Andy said, picking his way back through the obstacles. He was waving a thick wad of banknotes. 'This'll give us a start.' He leapt over the back of the PVC sofa and sat down on it, grinning, while he fished in his jacket pocket with his free hand. He pulled out his packet of Silk Cut 100s, flipped open the top, took out a cigarette, plugged it into his mouth and lit it. As he exhaled, his face fell.

'What's wrong?' Stevie asked.

'I've only got two fags left,' he said, peering into the pack. 'And I can't get any more of these. They don't make them yet. Fuck it.' He took the last two cigarettes from his pack and gave one to Stevie, the other to Becky. 'Should be cigars at a time like this, a new beginning,' he said, 'but these will have to do. Let's celebrate our new start. Our victory.' He lit his lighter again.

Stevie sucked hard on his cigarette. The smoke made him dizzy. 'But we didn't have a victory,' he said. 'Not really. We didn't stop what's going to happen, or it wouldn't have happened to us.'

Becky shrugged. 'We don't know what we've achieved, as far as what's *going* to happen,' she said. 'We don't know how time works. But we've locked the devil away again and that's what counts. What'll happen to the Stevie and the Becky and the Johnny that aren't yet born, we'll never know. But we did what we needed to do. And we survived. That's a victory. It's what we're going to do next that bothers me. We shouldn't even be here in this town at this time.'

'Which brings me to the third and final exciting thing I've remembered,' Andy said, exhaling plumes of smoke from his nostrils. 'Earlier this year, the young Andy, the nineteen seventy-two version who has so much money he doesn't know what to do with it, bought a house in Venice Beach, Los Angeles. Right on the water front. He had secret plans to move there and live happily ever after. But then he found his wife didn't want to go and he got an agency to rent it out for him. And, according to the agency, a middle-aged Englishman with two teenage children rented it. A few months later, the Englishman, whose name I've forgotten, made a substantial offer on the house and the young Andy sold it to him. And do you know who that middle-aged Englishman is going to turn out to be?' He smiled. 'Who thinks it'd be a good idea to go and live in LA?'

Stevie felt an odd kind of relief settling over him. He smiled and raised his hand. Becky winked at him and raised hers too.

Andy nodded, stood and high-fived both their hands. 'And things will work out,' he said. 'If I'm going to buy an expensive beach house in Venice in a few months, things certainly are going to work out. But for now we have stuff to do. The dog wants fixing up, first. I have contacts who can do us passports and other documents that'll give us all new identities. We'll catch the train to London, hole up in a hotel and fix things. Are we going for it? Stevie?'

Stevie nodded, a feeling of excitement growing in him.

'Becky?' Andy asked.

Becky grinned and kissed his cheek. 'Of course,' she said.

'Dookie?' Stevie asked.

The dog huffed and batted his tail twice.

'Come on, then,' Andy said, getting up. 'Let's fade out of existence over here and fade back in somewhere where the weather's warm.'